The Bastard Gods

The Chronicle of Fu Xi Book III

Brian L. Braden

To the readers who waited patiently, my sincerest gratitude.
To Helen, thank you for the t-shirts.

Table of Contents

ACKNOWLEDGMENTS

Edited by Keri Karandrakis

Prologue: The Black Dragon.

"In a new dawn's light, I counted forty marks scratched into the mast by my beloved Atamoda. Seventy-four survivors wandered the decks. We knelt powerless before the mighty sea. The tempest stripped us of everything, and left us drifting on a salty sea upon two waterlogged wedding barges, our new arun-ki, without food or water. Yet, even through grief and hunger and despair, the sun brought hope. Below Atamoda's forty marks, our new Isp made the forty-first cut.

"The Scythian's blade sliced deep.

"In answer to our prayers, the seas remained calm. Ghalen found a few crooked hardwood sticks drifting near the barge. By the forty-third day, Levidi had carved them into useable spears. On the forty-seventh day, the Nameless God sent many fish from the deep, the likes we had never seen before. Strong beasts, yet not too strong for a Lo spear, no matter how crooked. When our thirst became almost unbearable, the rains returned. This time, they were gentle and mercifully short. Most delightful of all were the sea dogs that arrived on Day fifty-six from seemingly nowhere. Even after we slew several for their meat, bladders, and hides, the creatures still appeared from time to time, showing almost no fear and frolicking around the barges.

"We were babes floating upon our mother Psatina's womb, waiting to be reborn. The sea provided all we needed. The Lo rejoiced and resumed life. Outwardly I rejoiced with them, but the slowly sinking barge reminded me otherwise. Inwardly, I could not see the calm sea and abundant food. I could not feel the sun or hear the laughter. I only saw the endless, empty expanse that mirrored my loss. Day forty-one had never been cut into my heart. My soul waited for day forty to end, for the tempest to cease.

"I waited for salvation." - Conversations with the Uros.

- The Chronicle of Fu Xi

***

A serpent's shadow slithered across an empty world as the sun fled before it. He flew westward, darting from dark place to dark place, surveying the destruction wrought by his Enemy. The time for accounting had come, to take stock of his victories and plan his next move in this eternal war.

The Enemy's vengeful hand violently transformed this world's landscape in a matter of days. The Deluge had carved new valleys and canyons, laid waste to entire forests, leveled mountains on one continent, and lifted fresh peaks on another.

Now, in the dawn of a new age, the Deluge quickly retreated, leaving death's bloated stink across the land. In this continent's deep interior, shaggy beasts beyond count rotted on open tundras, or were buried under a sea of mud to eventually freeze into permafrost. Entire villages and nomadic tribes were entombed along with them. The Ice Men had all but been wiped from existence.

The Black Dragon sped above the rapidly receding flood waters choked with mud and shattered timber. Below him, the sea surrendered to muddy flats, muddy flats gave way to dry ground, and dry ground rose to highlands. The highlands arched into what was once a mighty mountain range straddling the continent. Now, it was a ragged archipelago.

Wild rivers raged through what were once pastoral valleys. Higher and higher, the Black Dragon soared up the eastern slopes until he could see the land beyond. There, glacial peaks poked above valley shadows.

By the Enemy's decree, this land had survived the Cataclysm.

The Black Dragon settled lightly onto a peak in a swirling cloud of sparkling snow dust. Smoky leather wings curled inward and collapsed into velvet robes. High black boots sank a few inches into the snow. A flowing mane of white hair fluttered in the wind, as pale eyes opened to survey the sterile world below.

The Deluge did not spare the world's high places, he thought.

The flood covered the mountains not in water, but ice. Creatures that fled up the slopes found themselves quickly buried under tons of snow. Old glaciers crumbled under new ice, and the avalanches scraped the mountainsides clean of life. The barren western mountains and eastern plains were of no importance — the Black Dragon knew few Tall Men dwelt in the high places or vast continental interiors. The Tall Men, the Enemy's beloved race, lived along the world's bountiful seas and oceans.

In an afternoon, all the coastlines had been redrawn. Tsunamis a thousand feet high wiped away fishing villages and mighty cities. Islands, and even continents, slipped beneath the waves as the polar glaciers crumbled, and oceans rose hundreds of feet. These doomed peoples were now lost to history, all by the hand of their vengeful Creator in a futile attempt to thwart the Black Dragon.

But not all the Tall Men were lost.

He turned his attention south, along the archipelago's spine where the southern ocean beat a hasty retreat toward its old boundaries. Atop one of those peaks camped the demigod Leviathan with his army. By the Black Dragon's doing, the bastard son of the Nephilim Poseidon had been spared. Leviathan would soon resume his march north, and bring with him a special captive.

He turned and peered across the sunset, where the western sea still pounded against the mountain cliffs, but only for a short time longer. Already the tides were beginning to turn, and soon the Great Sea would slink back into its basin. There, the Lo flotilla barely stayed afloat. The Scythian bitch still possessed Nuwa's Offering Blade, a weapon he must reclaim at all costs.

The Lo chieftain, however, still possessed the orichalcum staff given to him by Nuwa. The staff possessed great power, and stood between him and the dagger. He had to separate the Scythian from the staff's presence. Nuwa could thwart his plans, just as she had during the storm when he tried to take the knife and sink the Lo flotilla.

There was still the matter of the Ark, rapidly drifting away to the southwest. That problem required patience, and would naturally resolve itself once victory was gained over the Enemy's plans here. In the eternal war, this battle must come first.

Behind him, night's deepening shadows claimed the east. The Black Dragon sensed Nuwa's son drawing near, but he had effectively neutralized Fu Xi, despite Nuwa's success in saving her son's life. Without the Red Sword, Fu Xi lay naked before Leviathan's power. Without the Red Sword, Fu Xi would be also defenseless against the Guardian.

The Guardian...

The Black Dragon looked north, where the mountains gave way to a high valley largely untouched by the Deluge. The saddle-shaped valley stretched a dozen miles east to west. Like a natural citadel, isolated peaks towered over the valley's northern flank. Glaciers sheathed three of the citadel's sides, while an impenetrable wall of glacier-topped rock protected its southern flank. A waterfall tumbled down those cliffs into a small river that wound its way across the plain until it came to the valley's center. There, the Deluge had cut a maze of deep canyons where a wild river still thundered. From this distant vantage, he could just see the rim of lush vegetation peaking over the citadel's southern wall. In that most ancient place, the pieces would finally converge. Here, the Black Dragon's victory over the Enemy would be sealed, and Creation would fall into his hands.

A golden ray glinted in the west, and sparkled across the mountains like a shooting star. The Black Dragon grinned. "Dance if you wish, Nuwa, but neither you nor your Master have any power there. That is my domain. In that Place of Perfect Sorrows, Fu Xi and the Lo will perish."

The Black Dragon stretched out his arms and fell backwards into darkness, and became one with the night.

Part 1: Dominion of the Black Dragon.

The Lo called the afterlife Heli-dar. It existed far out to sea, beyond the horizon and deep in Sethagasi's womb. The sea goddess, always jealous of her realm, only permitted the righteous passage into Heli-dar. There, they dwelt in a place called the Lower Lands, a paradise much like life, but without pain or sorrow.

But woe to the wicked. Sethagasi reserved a terrible place for them. In the Upper Land, the moans of the damned floated on the wind and the sea could be heard but never seen.

-    The Chronicle of Fu Xi

1. Cage of Bones.

Time is a cage for god and mortal alike. Live long enough, and you find yourself walking with ghosts. Live too long, and others will soon treat you like a ghost. Behind the bars of his own cage, Aizarg often spoke to me of everyday life in his village on the Great Sea before the Cataclysm. His thoughts often turned to his son, Kol-ok.

"We strolled the narrow beach one morning at dawn, looking for clams. Kol-ok was little, and he would always carry a stick like a spear. One morning the fog was so thick the reeds were barely visible along the shore. Kol-ok would vanish ahead of me until I could only hear his little feet splashing in the water, before he would reappear with a handful of clams, always asking, 'Are these good ones, father?'"

Aizarg smiled tenderly as he relived the moment. "Eventually, as I expected, he ran out a little too far and finally realized he couldn't see me. He cried out in the fog, trying to sound brave, but I could hear his fear. 'Stay where you are,' I said. Of course, a few moments later, I found him.

"'What would you have done had I not answered?' I asked.

"'Shout louder,' Kol-ok replied." The memory made the old Uros chuckle. "I tried so hard not to laugh when he said that.

"'When will you be a man?' I asked him.

"'When I return from my Marsh Journey.' Kol-ok replied, proudly.

"'By rights, that is true. Yet, there will be a day when you become a man here.' I touched Kol-ok's chest. 'Sometimes that happens during the Marsh Journey, sometimes before, and sometimes after.'

"'How will I know when it happens to me?'
"'It's the day you shout for me, and I will not be there.'"

- The Chronicle of Fu Xi

***

At least two nights had passed since Kol-ok awoke with an aching gash on the side of his head, crammed into a cage too small to fully stand up and far too narrow to lie down. He remembered their landfall, meeting the old man on the shore, and then searing pain. He had not seen his mother since, and feared for her safety.

The cage hung from an iron chain secured to a wooden crosspiece, attached to a post driven deep into the ground. The chain and hook squeaked loudly if he so much as breathed deeply, or the slightest breeze rocked the cage. He'd become accustomed to the almost constant, high-pitched squeals.

As he slouched on the cage's rounded bottom, Kol-ok's legs uncomfortably pressed against his chest. The ever-present fog magnified Kol-ok's terror, making him feel disembodied as if he were alone in the universe. Dawn and dusk were the worst, when shadow and light turned every swirl into a human shape. At first, he wanted to believe it was only his imagination, but then the wisps transformed into demons.

Dozens had materialized from the fog and danced savagely around his cage the first day. Almost naked, their reddish skin provided the only color in a washed-out world. They leapt about, cackling, poking out their tongues, and taunted him with beast-like shrieks. A few wore rusty metal plates over their chests. Sometimes, they pounded against the bars with fearsome swords and clubs. A few jabbed him with sticks until he cried. Kol-ok had begun to scream, and they delighted in it and jabbed him more. He screamed for his father to come save him. He screamed for his mother to shake him awake and make the nightmare end. When Kol-ok thought he could take no more, a deep voice rumbled from the fog, and the demons ceased their revelry. One by one, they returned to the mist, occasionally stealing a glance over their shoulder as if to say, *We'll finish this another time.*

That first night was unbearable. The starless night was unimaginably deep, and Kol-ok feared it would last forever. With only his loincloth as protection, the cold iron cut into his flesh. His bruised body ached. The sound of rushing water in the distance teased him, but could not drown out the disembodied moans and screams floating in the darkness. A few times, Kol-ok imagined he saw the firelight trying to burn through the inky mist.

When the moans and screams were at their worst, Kol-ok began to wonder if he was dead, and this was Heli-dar's Upper Land. He thought of the red demons and the unseen voice that commanded them. What had he done to deserve being condemned to eternal punishment? Was it as Father had said, the world had become so wicked the Nameless God doomed all, even children, to damnation?

Deep in his heart, Kol-ok knew what he had done was wrong. Kol-ok remembered that night he caught Alaya stealing food, and how he had not told his father. To do so would have condemned Alaya to death under his father's own decree. He remembered how Alaya had begged him on her knees, and the fear and desperation in her voice. He never said a word, and wrestled with conflicting feelings for days afterward. Then, when confronted by Kus-ge the night of the wedding, he lied and took the blame to save Alaya.

For deceiving his father, Kol-ok had been condemned to hell.

He spent the fitful first night weeping and shivering, fearful the red demons would return. They did not, but morning did with the same gray light presiding over the world. To his surprise, a gourd hung by a leather string from the cage's bottom. He looked about, but saw no one. He pulled it up and found it heavy with cool, fresh water. Kol-ok quickly guzzled most of it, and then relieved himself through the bars. That's when he saw the black demon staring at him.

Kol-ok covered himself and shrank from the visage. The demon stepped around the cage just out of arm's reach, studying Kol-ok. Sandals crunching on the ground, his gait betrayed a slight limp. He wore a plain, sleeveless tunic of heavy, tan cloth, cut just above the knees, and carried no weapons on his narrow waist belt. A wide, tight metal band encircled his neck. The black-skinned apparition halted and stared at Kol-ok for what seemed an eternity.

He held a small carp by the tail in his right hand. The sight of the fish made Kol-ok's stomach growl loudly. The demon offered it and spoke in Lo, "Eat." The familiar word rolled thick and clumsily off the demon's tongue. The torment he had suffered by the red demons' hands remained fresh in Kol-ok's mind, and he fought the temptation to take the food.

The demon took a step closer and softly repeated, "Eat." His voice carried tenderness. Some of Kol-ok's fear ebbed as he studied the demon. With skin dark like midnight, a receding hairline and gray-streaked beard, he displayed age and worry's ravages. His eyes betrayed no malice, Kol-ok thought, but then again, demons were tricksters. This could not be a man, for men like this did not exist. Did they?

Kol-ok's hunger took over. He snatched the fish through the bars and slunk back as far from the demon as possible. He gave the fish a sniff. It smelled perhaps a day old, but by this point he didn't care if it was rotten. While the demon watched, Kol-ok used the square edges of the cage's bars to scrape off the scales. He pulled off its lower jaw and, with his finger, ripped the guts from the carp's soft underbelly before gorging himself. Kol-ok occasionally spit out fish bones as the demon began to speak in soft, measured words, as if Kol-ok understood him.

Kol-ok wouldn't call his tone kind, but it wasn't cruel. The demon stepped a few paces closer, whispering like a confidant. Mesmerized by the monologue, Kol-ok paused eating. Then he noticed a terrible scar on the demon's arm, as if a great gouge of flesh had been carved from his right triceps and then seared. The scar formed a crude design, like a cross between a snake and a fish. The wound looked only recently healed. The black demon caught his eye and glanced down at the scar. In that moment, Kol-ok knew this was not a demon, but only a man, and one who had suffered terribly.

Kol-ok pitied him, and did the only thing he could think to do: He smiled.

The man returned the smile with a slight nod, turned and walked away. A few moments later he faded into the fog, his footfalls swallowed by the dull roar of unseen waters.

Kol-ok returned his attention to the fish until he had eaten it all, and then finished off the water in the gourd. Hunger and thirst sated, Kol-ok adjusted himself as best he could in the cage and tried to make some sense of his situation. He thought about the black man, and wondered if perhaps he was a fellow condemned soul in the afterlife.

Maybe I am not dead, Kol-ok thought. *If so, where is this place, and where is my mother?* Maybe he could learn to communicate with the stranger, and learn where his mother was.

A sharp clang rang out above the roaring waters, startling him. Several more followed in quick succession. Kol-ok had heard this sound before in Shore Camp — it was the sound of a smithy working his forge. Perched on the bottom bars like a bird, he craned his head in the sound's direction, but saw only fog.

He could only judge time by the brightness or dimness of the fog, but the black man did not return, nor did the red demons. Kol-ok spent the rest of the day alone with his fears and hopes, with only the sound of rushing waters and the steady ringing of metal-on-metal to keep him company. Kol-ok wrapped his arms around his shoulders and began to shiver again as darkness fell.

Sleep eventually overtook him. Kol-ok dreamt of the black man, the red demons, and iron being twisted into tortured shapes.

2. Blue Fire in The Mirror, Part 1.

"Two brands, not one, scarred the arms of slaves born in Poseidon's Empire. Searing iron bearing the symbol of one of the eleven Sons of Poseidon greeted slaves as they entered this world. Then, when a woman's blood began to flow, and before a man could take a wife, the slave would be reacquainted with the brand. A freeman warrior representing their patron god would burn a full-sized brand over the tiny, faded baby's mark.

Over the slave's screams, the warrior would chant these words: "The road to power is paved with suffering." - The Last Scholar

- The Chronicle of Fu Xi

***

Kol-ok woke with a startle as a piercing shriek sliced through the darkness. It exploded with instantaneous agony, and then perished as quickly as it had erupted. It could have been any woman, but Kol-ok's heart told him it was Atamoda. He perched one foot resting on another on the cage's bottom and shook the bars. "Mother!" he shouted. The heavy cage swung back and forth, and, a moment later, his foot slipped through the bars, tearing some skin off his ankle. He slouched down, sobbing and calling his mother's name.

The deep clang of iron-on-iron resumed in the distance. Kol-ok huddled, whimpering like a child as dawn's light turned the featureless darkness into featureless gray. Then the metallic pounding ceased.

Something stirred at the mists' edge. At first, Kol-ok thought the black man might have returned. He prayed it wasn't the red demons. A figure seemed to swirl in and out of sight, as if about to congeal into human form only to fade once again. Kol-ok gripped the bars and pressed his face against the cold metal. He squinted into the mists and strained to listen, but only heard the ever-present rushing waters.

Several forms materialized from the fog at once. Kol-ok recoiled as several red demons stepped forward to encircle his cage. They stared with devilish smiles. Soon, perhaps a hundred ruddy faces leered at him like wolves about to feast. Then they parted, and eight men shuffled through the gap, struggling to carry an enormous stone basin slung between two thick beams. With vacant eyes, they looked like living skeletons.

The men's emaciated state shocked Kol-ok. Their ribs and pelvic bones protruded so far out he wondered if they might actually be dead. Naked except for a thick metal collar that hung slack over their bony shoulders, they shuffled to the cage, and then with great effort, lowered the massive stone bowl to the ground. A wave of heat hit Kol-ok from the shimmering mound of hot coals filling the stone brazier. The sight of the burning coals further stoked his dread as the living skeletons shambled from whence they came.

The black man he had seen the day before stepped through the line of demons, and stood beside the brazier. To Kol-ok's surprise, the old man he had seen the day he and Atamoda had made landfall appeared. He limped slightly until he stood beside the black man. The old man's grizzled beard only grew on the left side of his face. The faded scars of once horrific burns covered the right side from below his eye to where his neck disappeared under his goatskin cloak. Like the skeletal men, he wore an iron collar around his neck.

The black man wore a leather apron and carried a wide, leather bag slung over his shoulder. He dropped the bag next to the brazier, where it struck the ground with a muffled clink. The silent circle surrounded his cage as if waiting for something. The demons continued to leer at him as if he were a morsel. The black man and his companion, however, considered Kol-ok with sadness, and that is what terrified him the most. A judgement had been handed down, one all here except Kol-ok were aware of. Two more skeletal slaves stepped forward, this time carrying a thick log on their shoulders. They dropped it with a thud beside the brazier and vanished behind the crowd.

Kol-ok closed his eyes and prayed to the Nameless God all of this would go away. He prayed for his father, and for Ghalen and Levidi and Okta to come to his rescue. Maybe they had already made landfall, and were watching now, ready to rush in and save him. The child in him entertained such hopes, but the emerging man knew these were just fantasies. He couldn't shrink away. He couldn't run. Kol-ok swallowed, but had no spit. Shaking so hard he had to grip the bars to steady himself, Kol-ok opened his eyes just in time to see a giant step forward.

With skin darker than the black man's, as dark as a starless midnight, the giant towered at least two heads over all the others. He only wore a loincloth and high-laced sandals interlaced with golden cord. His wide chest and knotted muscles radiated power. A chiseled jaw and serious brow hung below a smooth, bald head, framing bright eyes burning with purpose.

The giant strode to the cage and halted. He bent low and peered at Kol-ok. The boy recoiled, which seemed to briefly amuse the great devil. Otherwise, he could not read the giant's impassive expression. Kol-ok had become a tiny bird, and the cats were gathered around, ready to stick their claws between the bars and rip him apart.

After a few long moments, the giant turned toward the black man and gave the slightest of nods. Before Kol-ok could register what was happening, half a dozen red demons descended upon the cage. Metal clanked, and Kol-ok tumbled to the damp ground. Strong hands dragged him toward the brazier. The red demons gripped Kol-ok's shoulders like vices, forcing him to his knees. A foot pressed so hard into his back Kol-ok thought his ribs would split. They forced his head backwards by the hair until he stared up at the giant lording over him.

A woman sobbed softly beside the giant, naked except for a thin, golden thong covering her intimate parts. Her head was lowered; long, black hair covered her face. Serpent-like gold and silver jewelry encircled her upper arms. A fresh and angry brand in a serpent shape seared her right arm. A delicate, unadorned silver collar clung tightly around her neck, attached to a braided leash held by the giant.

Atamoda pulled back her hair and looked upon her son. Then the giant spoke.

***

"Prepare this new slave for service," Leviathan commanded Amiran. A shout went up from the Olmecs at the impending branding. Amiran knelt beside the saddle bag, which now served other purposes. They'd eaten the horses months ago, and their bones littered this mountaintop-turned-island. He withdrew an iron hammer, a pair of thongs, a small hand-bellow, and a metal plug about half the size of his pinky. Amiran carefully rested these along the brazier's thick stone edge.

He looked up at Zelko. "Bring me water." Without a word, the old man departed.

Amiran placed the metal plug carefully in the thong's grip and, with a tin wire, tightly bound the thong's handle so the plug would not slip. The coals sizzled and erupted in sparks as Amiran plunged it deep into the fire. The thongs were forged from a specialized iron, its carbon content giving it a higher heat resistance. He needed the iron plug almost white hot, as hot as he dared without it running like liquid.

Quexil approached, hand resting on the obsidian dagger tucked into his loincloth. "Be careful, Twice-Burned. It would be unfortunate should you blemish the prince's prize." Amiran ignored Quexil's taunts and focused on the task. Zelko reappeared with a large water skin.

Next, Amiran shoved the bellows' snout deep into the coal pile and began to engorge the fire with as much oxygen as he could. With each huff from the bellows, the coal pile pulsated like a living creature. The pain in Amiran's right arm flared in unison with the fire. With much of his right triceps missing, Amiran had to lean on the bellow with his weight to achieve the required pressure. The scholar studied the coals with each air blast until the fire's color told him the time had come.

He turned and nodded to the Olmecs holding the captive, and they forced the boy's head forward over the log. From somewhere, a thick iron collar appeared. Amiran raised an eyebrow, as he had not seen what type of collar Leviathan had chosen for the new slave. Amiran had expected a common, hingeless bronze or iron collar. These were bent around the neck, and then sealed with an iron rivet, to stay on the slave's neck until death. Upon the slave's death, the corpse was beheaded, and the collar slipped off to be recycled for another slave.

Instead, an Olmec warrior encircled the boy's neck with a polished, hinged collar. Amiran did not make this collar, and didn't know any had been brought in the expedition's stores. Hinged collars were only reserved for slaves who might show promise as merchants, scholars, or perhaps dragon butchers. The mystery surrounding Leviathan's unusual treatment of this boy thickened.

Amiran withdrew the thongs and examined the glowing rivet. He nodded again, and Quexil forced the boy's neck harder against the log, to the point the boy's face began to turn red. Thongs in one hand, hammer in the other, Amiran quickly and expertly placed the rivet over the small ridges and its aligned holes where the collar closed. With two small hammer taps, Amiran expertly affixed the collar without a spark or hot metal touching the boy's flesh.

"Zelko," he said. The old man stepped forward and poured water over the boy's neck and head. The metal rivet hissed and then grew dark and cold, sealing the boy into the collar.

The woman sobbed and slipped to her knees.

The Olmecs released the boy, but stood closely behind lest he run.

Run where? Amiran thought. Forty-three days ago, the flood had transformed the mountain peak into a small island, trapping Leviathan's expedition as the world ended around them.

Tears ran down the boy's face as he tugged at the collar. Enough room remained for a man's neck to eventually snugly fit inside the ring, but not enough to allow him to pull it over his head. Whimpers turned to shouts of rage as he yanked and pulled and struggled against the metal. This elicited hearty laughter from the Olmecs. The boy tried to stand, but the warriors pushed him down to more howls of delight.

Leviathan remained expressionless, his gaze firmly fixed on the boy. Amiran suspected the demigod wanted the same answers he did, which would explain some of their special treatment. Two facts surrounding the castaways intrigued Amiran — their well-constructed reed boat and that both were relatively healthy and well-fed. While the boat showed signs of rot and water-logging, the boy and the woman had no provisions. He doubted they would have survived the flood in that small vessel; therefore, there must be substantial land nearby untouched by the flood. Leviathan saw that possibility as a potential source of fresh provisions and slaves. Amiran saw it as an opportunity to escape.

Amiran stumbled as sharp pain erupted across his cheek. "What are you waiting for?" Quexil shouted. "Your prince is waiting!"

Amiran nodded. "Yes, my lord." He knelt by the bag once again and removed a well-worn branding iron. This one had marked hundreds, perhaps thousands of slaves with Leviathan's mark, including the woman at Leviathan's feet. This brand, however, was not the one Leviathan had commanded Amiran to use. He set it aside and removed the second branding iron from the bag and inserted it just beneath the coals.

At Leviathan's command, Amiran had fashioned this new brand throughout the previous night, following the prince's unusually detailed instructions. This symbol had never been used before by any prince in the kingdom, nor by King Atlas or Poseidon himself. The brand's purpose, and the prince's intentions, remained a mystery.

Amiran removed the brightly glowing brand and examined it. "It must cool for a moment, my lord," Amiran said. Too hot, and the skin would melt and blur the image; too cool and the scar would eventually fade.

Leviathan nodded while the woman continued to quietly sob at his feet.

The sight of the iron stopped the boy's struggling. *It's obvious he is her son*, Amiran thought. *He has her eyes*. It wasn't difficult to understand why the prince had taken the raven-haired beauty as his pet. Her full curves and deep, intelligent eyes gave her a beauty that would have brought an excellent price in the Kingdom's markets. While she would suffer under the prince's affections, she would not suffer as horribly as if she had been cast to the Olmecs. Leviathan had also commanded Amiran to teach her the tongue of Atlas.

In the two days since she had been captured, Amiran (with the help of the old goatherd Zelko) had gleaned key structural components of the woman's language. It wasn't the differences that struck him, but the similarities to Zelko's speech, and even Attican, that gave Amiran hope the lands of the Gray-Eyed Queen may be near.

Atamoda. She had also divulged her son's name — *Kolok*.

Amiran had yet to share this knowledge with Leviathan. The scholar had to learn more, and to bring the woman into his confidence, before he could begin to feed the demigod select truths and strategic lies.

The iron cooled to a bright red. "It is ready."

"Get it over with," Leviathan said.

Amiran stepped forward. The boy's eyes grew wide with understanding, and he bucked against his captors like a colt.

Quexil pulled the boy's head back even farther until a gasp of pain escaped the boy's lips. Two other Olmecs stretched out the captive's right arm and rolled it forward until his triceps faced upward, ready for the iron's kiss.

The woman darted forward with such speed it even seemed to surprise the Leviathan. Dragging her leash, she leapt on top of her son, desperately trying to shield him from Amiran. One of the young Olmec warriors snatched her by the hair and roughly cast her to the ground. Laughing, he leaned over to strike her. A moment later, the Olmec lay dead on the ground, head snapped completely backwards. Leviathan calmly stepped over his twitching body as Atamoda crawled to resume her place shielding her son. Kol-ok wept and buried his face into her bosom as she rocked her child back and forth.

Atamoda looked up at Leviathan, repeating the same word through her tears.

"Tell me what she is saying," Leviathan commanded.

The iron in Amiran's hands cooled and faded. He placed it back into the brazier. He couldn't be sure, but the intent was clear. "*Mercy*, my lord. She begs for mercy on behalf of her son."

Leviathan knelt and tenderly cupped Atamoda's chin in his enormous palm. Her pleas died away under the power of his divine will. The demigod gracefully picked Atamoda up and cradled her in his arms, tenderly as if she were a child. He turned and carried her away. "Finish your work," he commanded over his shoulder.

The stunned Olmecs looked from their dead compatriot to their captain. Quexil's eyes shifted nervously from his men to the receding figure of his god. Amiran knew the power equation inside the camp had just changed. This woman's presence, and that of her son, had fundamentally shifted the order of the universe.

"You heard him!" Quexil spat. "Finish it."

The Olmecs snatched Kol-ok and forced him once again into the branding position.

Amiran again removed the iron and examined it. The metal's color announced its temperature was perfect for the deed at hand. Kol-ok gritted his teeth and glared at Amiran in the manner of an angry man, not a frightened boy.

"Hold him tightly," he told the Olmecs. "The design is complex. If he flinches, it will blur." Kol-ok grunted as the warriors leaned on him even harder. For a moment, Amiran thought the design might be too big for the boy's arm, but as the hot iron drew closer, it looked like a good fit.

Hot metal met flesh, and the familiar scream of a free soul becoming a slave echoed across the mountain top. Long ago, Amiran had grown used to burnt human flesh's stink, but never bondage's birthing cries.

The Olmecs released Kol-ok, who slumped unconscious over the log.

Amiran pulled the iron straight back and examined his work. "Water."

Zelko poured the rest of the water over the burn. The old man grunted and shrugged. "Looks good," he said with his strange, thick accent and considered his own brand, received over a month ago. "Why so different than ours?"

"I don't know."

Amiran considered the boy's new scar just below his shoulder — a dragon with wings outstretched as if just taking flight, with its slightly curved tail falling beneath.

∗∗∗

Tears blurred Atamoda's vision as Kol-ok's screams died away behind them. The giant sat her down in the tent's center on the rug covered with elaborate hunting scenes. He reclined on his bed, and quietly considered her. She fought the overpowering urge to run. Better judgement reminded her of the two warriors posted just outside the entrance.

He pointed to a small table near a large, ornate chair and made an eating motion. There she saw a silver tray stacked with salted meat, roasted fish and some type of unfamiliar yellow fruit. Beside the tray sat a jewel-encrusted metal goblet.

Atamoda's stomach growled fiercely. He must have heard it, because he smiled broadly. She stood and warily approached the table, never taking her eyes off him. She picked up a piece of the still-warm fish and sniffed it. It had been prepared in an unfamiliar manner, sprinkled with strange spices. Atamoda touched it with her tongue; salty with a mildly sharp tang, like some kind of sweet fruit. She could bear it no more, and took a large bite. After spitting out a few bones, she devoured it and began on the meat. It reminded her of the wild game jerky Lo men prepared for long fishing expeditions. Atamoda dipped her finger in the liquid and tasted it. Ula had once offered her wine that Ood-i had brought back from the trading camps. That wine had tasted sour and made her gag. This drink possessed a succulent sweetness almost too rich for her simple palate. In only a few minutes, Atamoda had cleared the tray and drained the cup.

Feeling a little lightheaded, Atamoda wiped her mouth with her hand and backed away, thankful for a full belly, but now expecting the worst. She had no doubts this would end with her rape, but she needed time to think and to form a plan.

He motioned with an open palm to the entire tent, as if inviting her to explore. The spacious tent, made from a tan, heavy cloth, stretched twenty paces long by fifteen paces wide. Three thick wooden columns lined each side and supported a wedge-shaped crosspiece lifting the roof. High on each column, an iron mount held a lamp. The lamps filled the tent with a dim, but steady light. A chest-high bronze brazier occupied the tent's center, full of brightly burning coals. It sat upon an iron stand with widely spaced legs.

The giant reclined on a raised platform fashioned from a reddish wood, polished so smooth it looked wet. Soft, colorful cloth bags, luxurious furs, and thick blankets were heaped upon a surface that seemed to mold to the giant's contours. The high-backed chair, made of wood black as midnight and also polished to a high sheen, sat at the foot of the platform facing the large central area. A golden, coiled serpent with fins like a fish, identical to Atamoda's throbbing brand, adorned the chair's back. Atamoda had heard tales the men brought back from trading camp of devices among the a-g'an called beds and chairs, made just for sleeping and sitting. Before seeing these with her own eyes, she'd thought the very idea absurd. Why would people make such things when one can simply sit on the floor or sleep on a mat?

The wine began to work its magic, and her fear dulled. Atamoda cautiously wandered about, touching this and that. He watched her the way an adult may watch a toddler taking their first few steps. That was when she discovered the mirror.

The giant sat up slightly and seemed to take exceptional delight in how the mirror fascinated her. At first, she tried to look behind it, to see where this strange 'other room' may be. It only took another few moments for Atamoda to realize her own reflection stared back at her. Not a dim or rippled reflection like when looking into calm water, but an absolutely perfect image. Atamoda touched it, expecting it to ripple. Instead, her fingers smudged the surface. Atamoda tugged at her hair (and was shocked to see a few strands of gray), stuck out her tongue, and turned to look at her hips. *Do I really look that way?* she thought. Atamoda wondered if she stared deep enough into her own eyes, she might catch a glimpse of her own soul. He fell back onto the bed in deep, jovial laughter.

Suddenly self-conscious, Atamoda met the giant's eyes through the mirror. Knowing how she must look, his laughter infected her. The moment quickly passed when she remembered Kol-ok's suffering, and how casually this extraordinary being snapped his own warrior's neck. He seemed to read her mind, and his mirth evaporated.

Through the mirror, the patesi-le dared to stare into a god's eyes, searching for his soul.

There, she saw blue fire.

Part 2: Cataclysm's End: Decrees of the Goddess Nuwa.

Sometimes, when an acolyte plunged the Offering Blade into Nuwa's old shell, it penetrated all the way to the Altar Rock. The orichalcum cut into the granite as easily as it sliced through flesh. I knew every nick, every blemish on the granite's otherwise polished surface, and associated each with an acolyte's face and name before she joined with Nuwa.

Yet, there were times when I returned from journeys to find new, mysterious marks in the Altar Rock. These were deep, driven by a hand far stronger than a child's.

- The Chronicle of Fu Xi

3. Mountain of Bones.

"Father, when will I grow up to be as big as you?"
"Many years after I am dust."
"Will I die, too?"
"Your mother doesn't seem to think so."
"How will I know I am a man?"
"When you know there is no one you can depend on except yourself."
"When did you become a man, Father?"
"The day my father died. I stopped being a man the day she brought me here."

He placed his trembling, liver-spotted hands on my hand. His touch felt like ice. "Time denied you a proper father. For that, I am sorry." He coughed until he spit up some blood. Then pulled the blanket over his shoulders and rolled with his back to me. "Begone now, son of Nuwa, and let me die in peace."

Mother always told me my father had a gentle spirit. I can attest only to his bitterness.

- The Chronicle of Fu Xi.

***

Fu Xi relentlessly pursued the flood as if he intended to make it answer for its crimes.

The ocean retreated west before him like a fleeing horde, leaving a barren land of mud and sand in its wake. Vast stretches of stinking slime, deep and treacherous, acted like skirmishers left in a retreating army's wake, slowing Fu Xi's progress and preventing him from following too closely. Sometimes, he would be forced to camp for days on end while the way ahead dried enough for him and his horse to pick their way through.

Those were the worst times, when the wind would die and clouds of black flies descended upon them. Heise's eyes always bulged in terror as the insects coated him like a living blanket, intent on draining every ounce of blood from the horse. Fu Xi caked his steed's flanks with layer upon layer of mud in an effort to keep the flies from driving the horse mad. Often, it wasn't enough, and he would be forced to cover the beast's head and lead him through the bogs. In those times, Fu Xi would lean close and whisper reassuring melodies to the steed in an effort to keep Heise from bolting. The flies didn't bite the demigod, and seemed content only making Fu Xi's life miserable. When the flies were nowhere to be seen, an oppressive hush fell over the world.

Flies or silence, Fu Xi didn't know what was worse.

Today, the ground felt relatively firm under his feet, and the northern breeze blew just enough to keep the insects at bay. The landscape's original character had been plundered, rendering it flat, smooth and empty. Not a stump or log remained, only mud and sand crafted in smooth, flowing patterns that gave testimony to passing water. Since leaving the sheltered place he'd come to call the Tranquil Valley all those months ago, Fu Xi hadn't spotted so much as a bird. If it hadn't been for the flies, he would have thought the world dead.

The flood had taken something from the land, raped it. The world seemed dazed, withdrawn into itself in mournful silence. Fu Xi felt like an interloper, intruding on private grief.

Yet, in the land he discovered a kindred spirit. Fu Xi mourned, too, and in this endless, empty place his spirit sought healing. What would be waiting for him beyond the horizon? Would he find the Man with White Hair, and perhaps even the brother he never knew? Would these quests, given to him by the Goddess Nuwa, finally fill his soul and bring peace to Fu Xi the Wanderer?

Fu Xi squinted and looked up, watching his breath float into an ice-blue sky. Though he had lost track of time, the lengthening days told Fu Xi winter would soon give way to spring. He hoped to eventually spot green shoots emerging from the mud. The wild grain he'd harvested and packed into the saddlebags in the Tranquil Valley was almost gone. If he didn't find grass soon, Heise would starve.

In a few miles, the sun had begun to sink into Fu Xi's eyes, and the land ceased its gentle southwest downslope. Here, he came to hard clay banks along a muddy stream. Barely a stone's throw across, it trickled from the north. Usually, he would ride across without a second thought. In the flood's aftermath, he dared not cross without seeing the bottom. The earth's flesh hadn't finished resettling onto its bones, and the river bottom might suddenly drop off into a sucking quagmire.

He dismounted and carefully led Heise across. Ice water invaded his kamik boots as he gingery probed the soft, spongy bottom. He never sunk past his knees and, in a few minutes, he had led Heise to the other side.

Fu Xi sat down on as close to a dry patch as he could find and peeled off his boots. Long ago, Fu Xi had taught the Tall Men along the glaciers how to make kamik boots from oxen or reindeer hide. He made these from much thinner deerskin he had acquired in the Tranquil Valley. Fu Xi felt pleased with its suppleness, but felt certain the boots weren't sturdy enough to last more than a season in this harsh environment. He didn't know if, or when, he would find deer again.

He ran the boot material through his finger and thumb, scraping off the glue-like mud. He shook his hand and let it spatter against the ground. Once he felt satisfied he'd emptied out all the water and cleaned off most of the mud, he put them back on, and stood up. The boots still squished.

Heise casually wandered a few yards away, head down as if foraging. He patted Heise's neck and scanned the countryside. To the west, a small protrusion barely poked above the barren horizon; a knoll just beyond a nearby rise, or a mountain peak a hundred miles away, there was no way of telling in this featureless landscape.

"That's the first significant terrain we've seen for weeks." He considered the stream running south, and the knoll to the west. "What do you think, friend? Perhaps the Man with White Hair is waiting just over that rise. Chase the water, or seek the high ground? Maybe we'll find the Gray-Eyed Queen. Or will we stumble across my half-brother?" Once again, doubt crept across Fu Xi's heart. "A god should have more patience." Fu Xi patted Heise's neck. "I bet you're tired of staring at me all day."

The horse flicked his tail noncommittally and kept his own counsel.

"Be that way. I don't care. Sometimes, you aren't much for company."

Solitude never bothered Fu Xi. He'd spent much of his long life wandering the wilds alone. Now, he craved the sound of a human voice. He needed to know someone, something, other than him and his horse had survived.

Fu Xi double-checked the saddlebags and their dwindling wild grain and dried meat supply, as well as the orichalcum armor given to him by Leviathan in Wu. After his first encounter with deep mud, he'd taken it off, knowing it would be a liability should he become entrapped. He rechecked the knots securing his lance to the saddle. An empty scabbard hung on the saddle's other side. The loss of the Traitor's Blade still stung.

Leviathan waited for Fu Xi out there somewhere. Without an orichalcum weapon, Fu Xi stood little chance of defeating the Son of Poseidon.

"Come on, Heise. Plenty of daylight remains. We have a long way to go."

The horse didn't lift his head at Fu Xi's nudge.

Fu Xi nudged harder, and gave the reins a tug. "Let's go."

The horse took a step and halted, head still low.

He peered down and saw several tender green shoots, perhaps only an inch high, sprouting here and there. Heise plucked one after another with his lips.

Fu Xi grunted and stroked the horse's neck. "Well, if that isn't a pleasant surprise."

He mounted the horse and followed the stream, and blush of green, south. It wasn't long before the stream turned west toward the hill. The scraggly grass followed it along the north bank, and thickened until it formed a thin green carpet. Fu Xi suspected the stream existed before the flood. As the waters receded, the waterway likely resettled close to its original channel. The stream and grass meandered, but steadily led Fu Xi west toward the distant hill. As he drew closer, Fu Xi realized it was not that far away, and judging by the rolling terrain slowly coming into view beyond, it was possibly the beginning of foothills.

Heise padded along at a leisurely pace, occasionally grazing on the ever-thickening grass.

"I suspect the stream will make a hard turn south by the time we arrive at the hill. We'll camp there, and you can fill your belly on all the grass you want."

As sunset neared, Fu Xi thought the shadows along the hillside looked unnaturally deep, even with the sun sinking behind the foothills. Heise began to prance nervously. It only took Fu Xi a moment to associate the unnatural darkness with the roaring hum rising in his ears. Swarms of flies billowed and ebbed as far as he could see, from the northern to southern horizons, along the foothills. They blocked the sun like satanic thunderheads, rising and collapsing again and again.

The stream sharply resumed its southern trek. Here, the floodwaters must have encountered the foothills, and a battle of titanic forces had raged between immovable rock and unstoppable water. The floodwaters had stripped away layer upon layer of clay until only denuded bedrock remained. The Deluge had fashioned an altar of sorts, a place to deposit its bloody sacrifice. Shattered timber piles, perhaps a thousand feet high, from countless distant forests rested against the cliffs. From the bristling pyre, rotting carcasses of elk, mammoth, and every creature imaginable protruded from the splintered jumble.

In the far distance, snow-covered peaks poked above the foothills. Fu Xi could barely make out deep green mountain pastures. The Deluge had stopped here. These mountains had halted its westward march, and turned the flood south.

But at what price?

Fu Xi crossed back over the stream's eastern side. The flies, seemingly satisfied feasting on the dead, did not follow him. He dismounted, and, numbed by the sheer magnitude of the horror, the God of Names knelt in the grass as if in worship. Heise pranced nervously behind him, ignoring the lush green carpet under his hooves. Even from a hundred yards and in fading daylight, the human limbs poking from death's wall compelled Fu Xi's attention.

As darkness finally fell, the flies grew silent.

Thousands of men, women, and children had been swept by the Deluge from hunting camps, villages, and cities without warning. They were likely races he'd never encountered, and spoke tongues he'd never have a chance to learn. Some were now entombed in this wall of death, judged guilty by the Emperor of Heaven and summarily executed.

The damned deserved to be mourned, he thought. Fu Xi looked to the sky and whispered, "Was their sin so great?"

The bones embedded in the piles seemed to glow in the twilight, standing out against the timber and animal hides. A phrase bubbled up in his mind, from something his mother, the Goddess Nuwa, had quietly hummed in his childhood. It was a poem, perhaps a song, from when the world was young.

Below the Mountain of Bones, a god's rage faced.

Heise's warm nose nuzzled him from behind. Fu Xi reached up and embraced his horse. "Fill your belly. Tomorrow we must find a way to cross this wall of death."

4. Night Visitors.

My time with my father passed like a dream one struggles to recollect when they awaken. By the time I took my first steps, he had grown too old to play. As I learned to ask questions, he had become too weary to answer them. The day he died, I appeared to be no more than a young boy, but with a mind already questioning the price of my immortality.

"Leave your father alone, Fu Xi," Mother would say. "Let him rest." Nuwa's shell, the one that birthed me, had also withered under time's onslaught. Most days, I left the mausoleum of Nuwa's Temple and descended the Silver Stairs into the village. I craved the bustle, laughter, and life that thrived at Tortoise Mountain's feet. Mother never objected. The people always welcomed Nuwa's divine offspring as one of their own. The village men became my fathers, and the women my nursemaids. In Nushen, I had playmates. Time passed me by like a snail, while they lived and died like the leaves falling in the autumn. When the day came when my mother summoned me to Tortoise Mountain to bury my father, I had already mourned the passing of many fathers, mothers, brothers, and sisters.

- The Chronicle of Fu Xi.

***

Across the decks, talking and laughing had long settled to light snores. Aizarg heard none of it, nor did he feel the wind. He held his li-ge amulet in one hand, his staff in another. The li-ge once gave him comfort, and the staff had provided protection. Neither of them now kept at bay the glowing yellow eyes preceding the demon to the surface. Just as it did every night since the stars returned, the unwanted visitor rose from the depths. "Why do you eat, Uros?" it hissed like water dripping on a campfire. "It only prolongs your misery."

"Be gone," Aizarg gruffly whispered and looked away from the silhouette. He glanced around to see if anyone heard him, but just like all the other nights, no one stirred. Ezra slept to his right beside Spako, and Su-gár curled up with little Bat-or on his left.

"Come to us and finally know peace." It extended a claw from the water. The sea's rippling surface froze around the bony digits. "I will take you to Atamoda and Kol-ok. The time has come for you to lay your burdens down. Let others carry them now."

"Go away." Aizarg's voice cracked as he recoiled from the raft's edge. Just as he did the previous nights, Aizarg raised his staff and hoped to feel the red metal begin to warm. "I said be gone!"

The demon did not sink back into the depths before the staff's power. He shook the rod again. "I said be gone!"

"Every night your desolation beckons me, like a crow to the dead, and every night you seek to banish me." The demon seemed to laugh. "Make up your mind, foolish man."

Aizarg covered his ears. "Go away!"

"Go away? Like you sent me away?" a new voice asked. Aizarg looked up and saw Alad standing before him. Tears welled in the young man's eyes, just as they had the day he proclaimed his innocence when Aizarg sentenced him to banishment. Alad's feet hovered a few inches above the water. Aizarg covered his face with his arm. "You are a deceiver!"

"You put me in a boat to die, yet you let Kus-ge and Ba-lok live even after their treachery?"

Aizarg bowed his head.

"Your wife and boy rot in the abyss while you lounge in the sun and fill your belly. You are despicable."

Aizarg weakly raised the staff. "I banish you," he sobbed.

"You have no power." Alad's image melted into the darkness.

"Uros?" Su-gár's voice interrupted the spell, and the stars returned to Aizarg's vision. She stood beside him at the raft's edge. Looking up at her, Aizarg thought for a moment he was looking at Ula's ghost. Su-gár's wild, dark mane resembled her late mother's hair, but her pale complexion and upturned nose were her father's gifts. Somehow, the odd features present in Su-gár's parents combined in such a way to grace her with extraordinary beauty.

"May I join your solitude?" she asked in typical Lo fashion.

"Please." Aizarg patted the deck beside him.

She settled down cross-legged and they both gazed across the sea in comfortable silence. The heavens above and the sea below perfectly mirrored one another. They watched the great river of stars cut the sky in two before plunging into the sea. Occasionally, a small shooting star flashed across the sky and vanished. Somewhere in the silence, Su-gár's hand found his, and she rested her head on his shoulder. Aizarg's apprehension began to ebb.

Finally, Su-gár whispered, "When I was young, I remember how much you would smile."

When you were young? Aizarg thought, amused.

"I never saw you without a smile. When our sco-lo-ti smiled, I felt safe, even when mother and father's fighting frightened me. That's what scared me at the Council of Boats. You weren't smiling, and I knew something must be terribly wrong."

Aizarg searched for something to say, but words escaped him. Perhaps a reply wasn't necessary, because Su-gár kept talking. *Maybe all I should do is listen*, he thought.

"When you and the quest party returned and Father wasn't with you, I wanted to jump into the water and let the demons have me." Su-gár hesitated, as if searching carefully for her next words. "I miss Mother and Father every day. I miss Atamoda and Kol-ok, too." Her hand tightened slightly, and Aizarg suddenly became keenly aware of Su-gár's body pressing warmly against his. "I want to see you smile again. I want to smile, too. We can find joy again…together." A power in her voice drew his eyes away from the sea and into hers.

Aizarg had suspected Su-gár's feelings for him for some time, even before the Cataclysm. In the world before, he took them for the innocent longings of a woman-child. Those feelings would pass as she matured and found true love among the young Lo men. Now her feelings for him had been tempered by the proximity of death, where life and love are at their most powerful. Tonight, Su-gár confronted Aizarg with a woman's power, a power which could lay his soul bare. Aizarg paused and searched his own thoughts, confronted his own heart's desires, and silently prayed to the Nameless God for strength and the right words.

"Your father and mother rarely smiled," Aizarg finally said. "They looked upon one another as a chain of bondage, not as a blessing. It was incumbent upon the village sco-lo-ti and patesi-le not to let such marriages form, but through circumstance with Ula and Ood-i, it did form. The village worked diligently to ensure your family became harmonious, but in that we failed. Atamoda used to say very little about your mother and father blended in harmony, except you. You, and only you, brought joy to their lives. You made them smile.

"You bring joy to my heart, too," Aizarg's voice cracked as he gripped the li-ge amulet. "But that part in my spirit and body you seek to reawaken cannot stir."

Tears slowly rolled down her cheeks. Her skin left his, and cool air invaded the gulf between them. Without a word,

Su-gár departed, and the Uros found himself alone once again.

This time, the demons did not return.

5. Okta, The Master of Boats.

Nuwa pronounced early in my life that I shall never marry, though I could take as many lovers as I desired. Once I grew into my eternal manhood, with a man's desires, I broached the question repeatedly throughout the years. Each time, Nuwa gently brushed it aside. It was not until ages later that she came close to anything that approached a satisfying answer.

"I see your children and their children. They will be giants among men. Your father's gentleness would be diluted in their bloodline, but your power will not. Nushen is not enough for such men. The world is not enough for such men."

Yet, in the millennia from my birth to the Cataclysm, I loved many women. To all my knowledge, not one had produced a child, let alone a 'giant among men.'

All sins are born of lies — it does not matter if they are uttered by mortal or god. All sins will be judged by the Emperor of Heaven — it matters not if they were committed by mortal or god. Nuwa's sins will forever remain hidden from me, but not the terrible price she paid for redemption.

- The Chronicle of Fu Xi.

***

The Lo desperately clung to a rotting corpse of wood and rope. The two massive wedding barges were depleted by months at sea, from storms, and now leaching by the endless salty ocean. Two barges, secured to one another end-to-end, were all that remained of the flotilla the Lo called the Arun-ki, the Village. It floundered only a few inches above tame waters. In some places, waves lazily lapped over the deck.

Under heaven's milky spray of stars, the Lo slept huddled along the Arun-ki's center, distributed as best they could to keep the barges balanced. Too much weight on one side would send the vessels tilting dangerously, and might break the weakened bonds holding the Lo's world together.

In the darkness, Okta squatted near the Supply Barge's edge and poked a log with his forefinger. Hardwood that should have been as firm as stone slightly gave. Even in the starlight, a sheen of moisture exuded around his finger. He probed a divot with his fingernail, and wooden chunks crumbled like overcooked meat falling off a bone. Okta gravely inspected the heavy rope cables binding the barge's logs together. All the pitch that had once sealed the cables had washed away, leaving the reed fibers naked to the sea. The frayed end of one rope trailed limply in the current. Okta found the other end near his foot and tried to retie the knot. The slimy cords disintegrated under the effort. He gave the rope a quick snap, and it broke effortlessly.

"Bah!" He tossed the rope overboard. It floated for a moment before a dark shape rushed up from beneath the surface and snatched it. The creature's fin cut the water like a blade. The giant fish lingered for a few moments near the surface. Then it rolled upside down, giving Okta a good look at jagged teeth lining its crescent-shaped jaws. It thrashed once, expelling the rope from its mouth, and then slipped below the surface. These monsters patiently circled the Arun-ki, waiting for the inevitable day when the rafts finally slipped below the waves. Okta feared this new enemy far more than the water demons, for these creatures could not be turned by a patesi-le's chant. Okta had studied the beasts since the first fin broke the surface weeks ago. He'd watched them devour other big fish with only one bite and knew it would only be a matter of time before these wolf fish turned the water red with Lo blood.

"Unless…" Okta whispered to himself as he lifted his gaze to the Milky Way. "Time is growing short." He did not know what he feared most, the day when the rafts finally sank and the wolf fish swarmed them, or the day they made landfall.

Okta deeply inhaled the salty air and then forcefully exhaled, trying to cleanse his worries and lose himself in his daily rituals. Those rituals began the same every morning, watching the sun rise alone. Here, he found a few moments of beautiful solitude, something his Lo heart craved, and something in short supply on the crowded barges. Soon, the Lo would begin to wake. For now, at the edge of the Lo's world, Okta used this precious moment to rekindle the fragile hope locked away deep in his heart.

He dared not speak this hope to anyone, for fear even uttering it would somehow bring ruin to any chance of it coming true. Of all the Lo clans, his people, the Carp, were the best fisherman, the best sailors, and the best raft builders. If the Crane and Minnow Clans had been spared, why would the Nameless God not spare the Carp? These thoughts ate at Okta, driving him to haunt the barge's edges searching the horizon for telltale signs of his people.

This fleeting moment's solitude, and his unshakable belief the Carp where out there adrift and alive, would have to be enough to see the Master of Boats through another day. Okta closed his eyes and rolled his neck, listening to each vertebra crack. Again, he inhaled deeply, but this time caught a faint, unfamiliar scent. Okta opened his eyes. He smelled flowers, but not like any that grew along the Great Sea. And then, a moment later, the fragrance vanished.

**

Nuwa's spirit swirled around Okta in the cool pre-dawn, studying him. He swayed in perfect rhythm with the glassy waves, unaware a goddess lingered on the night just beyond where his breath ended. This mortal had fascinated her from the beginning of the Lo's journey. She didn't need to read his thoughts to understand his secrets, his unquenchable hope.

He knows what Aizarg does not, she thought. She admired him, for without this man the Lo would be dead. Aizarg may be leading them to their future, but it was Okta that kept them alive in the present. The Lo have always looked down at the sea for answers. Okta, perhaps the greatest seaman his people had ever sired, had begun to look up. Night after night, he had begun to suspect the truth. He noticed the way the stars seemed to slightly shift each evening, and observed the way the puffy afternoon clouds raced by on calm afternoons. Okta knew it was not the clouds racing by, but the sea. He felt the great pull beneath his feet as the retreating tide carried the barges along like a fleck of grass. *He is a man fully of this world*, Nuwa thought. She felt his attachment to the sea, the way he sensed every undulating ripple beneath the timbers.

Nuwa tried to imagine how delightful the cool sea would feel on her toes, or perhaps how sensuous Okta's warm skin might feel beneath her fingers. *He is the kind of man I would have taken as a lover*, she thought. The very thought filled Nuwa with bitter longing for all that was, and never would be again. Memories of flesh tormented her until she did not know if she were a goddess, or a ghost. If Okta would have been born in Nushen, Nuwa would have recognized his greatness early. In the afterglow of the Offering Festival, she would have chosen him to be her new husband, just as she had for millennia. She had led countless young men up the Silver Stairs to her temple atop Tortoise Mountain. There, she would have kept him, loved him, until they both grew old. Eventually, he would have died, and she would have cremated him upon the same rock where she had laid all her husbands. The funeral pyre smoke signaled the village below the goddess had grown old, and ready to take a new mortal shell, and a new husband.

It should have been these generations of men, born in Nushen and raised in its sheltered righteousness, who ventured forth to teach those still in darkness. Instead, Nuwa sent her only son, a god, to do a mortal's work. In the end, her selfishness nearly destroyed both.

Across the world, other gods, driven by desires far darker than Nuwa's, sent men to do their bidding. Because of her sin, and those of her fellow Nephilim, mankind remained too long in darkness, and under the Black Dragon's dominion.

As the eastern horizon lightened, Nuwa felt herself drawn to other souls that had begun to stir across the Arun-ki.

6. Dawn.

Only a few months separated my father's death from Mother's next Offering Ceremony. These were the days before the convent's founding, and the establishment of the order of Elder Mothers who selected acolytes as candidates for Nuwa's next shell. In these most ancient days, the goddess would directly approach the candidate's family, and ask the father's blessing to take his virgin daughter as a new shell. Nushen was only a small settlement at the mountain's foot; there was not yet an Offering Festival. Offering Ceremonies occurred when the goddess decreed, and were not restricted to the spring planting season.

In the Inner Temple, in the Place of Perfect Sorrows, I watched Nuwa take a new shell. I did not understand the deep magic that brought Nuwa new life. My physical connection to my parents' flesh had finally been severed in fire and mist. Those I had inherited my eyes, nose, hair, and all my mannerisms from had turned to dust. Ah, but my heart I inherited from Nushen!

That night, clothed in a new mortal shell, Mother returned to the Inner Temple's tomb-like silence. I descended the Silver Stairs into the village to drink once again at the wellspring of love.

I remember every name, every smile, every tear. Those memories sustain me. They are my sanity's bedrock throughout eternity's long night.

- The Chronicle of Fu Xi.

***

In the pre-dawn twilight, Nuwa wandered unseen among the sleeping forms, much as she had done for centuries in

Nushen. Near the Supply Barge's upwind side, she came upon the intertwined lovers, slightly apart from the others on the deck. Despite the slight chill, somewhere in the night the wife had worked her way from beneath her husband's arm and the sea lion fur. Holding her man's hand, and with thighs barely touching, she exposed as much of her skin as possible to the cool air, and water seeping between the logs. Her swollen, arched belly reflected starlight.

Nuwa smiled inwardly, feeling a special bond for Alaya. Nuwa remembered how warm she would get at night as Fu Xi grew restlessly in her womb like a little fire. Fu Xi had made his mother toss and turn, unable to get comfortable. Nuwa couldn't understand why she, a goddess, couldn't will the baby inside to be at peace, nor will herself to sleep.

Nuwa extended her hand a hair's breadth above the skin stretched tightly over Alaya's belly. She sensed the unborn baby within turn her head. A thousand regrets, sharp and poisonous, welled up and stabbed the goddess's heart. Levidi grunted in his sleep, rolled over, and wrapped his arm over Alaya's midriff as if to protect the child.

From behind her, Nuwa sensed another restless soul striding across the deck toward the Supply Barge's stern, the place the Lo called Downstream. Drawn by Ezra's simmering rage, the spirit followed.

***

Ghalen rose from beside Sana as Ezra approached. "Where are you going?"

"To relieve myself," Ezra replied. It suddenly occurred to Ghalen that Ezra's eyes were level with his, with wide shoulders to match. The rich diet of fish and sea-dog meat had filled out Ezra's frame. Okta's adopted son had finally crossed fully over to manhood, and all vestiges of boyhood had vanished. He liked the Hur boy the first time he met him on the edge of the Black River, in what seemed an age ago. In the months since, he'd grown to trust Ezra as much as any Lo-born. While Ezra looked like a Lo-born, even down to his budding beard, in many ways he still carried himself like an a-g'an, a land dweller.

Ghalen crossed his arms and nodded to the port side. "You can relieve yourself over there."

Bluff called, Ezra looked about, exacerbated. "C'mon Ghalen, I need to talk to Virag."

Ghalen gave Ezra a sideways look. "Why?"

"It's important."

"You know the Uros's decree as well as I do. The traitors are to be isolated from the rest of the people until landfall, and then they will be exiled."

"Please, Ghalen. It will only be for a few moments."

"Do you intend him harm? I want him dead as much as you, but I will not defy the Uros."

Ezra straightened and met Ghalen's eye; his voice took a more formal tone. "Sco-lo-ti of the Turtle Clan, I mean Virag no harm. I only need a few words with the slaver. Nothing more."

Aizarg had dissolved the clans and the power of the chieftains, the sco-lo-ti, in a bid to further unify the Lo people, but Ghalen took Ezra's formal tone as a sign of respect and earnest. Ezra's mysterious intentions intrigued Ghalen, but instinct bade him not to press for more answers.

Ghalen stepped aside. "Don't linger long. And no trouble."

"No trouble. Promise." In the starlight, Ghalen saw relief sweep over Ezra's face as he slipped past and hopped the divide between the Wedding Barge and the Supply Barge. He stepped gingerly over the sleeping mounds of the Minnow Clan towards the stern.

An unexpected fragrance, faint and barely perceptible, drifted in Ezra's wake. A flower, perhaps, though what kind he had no idea. It evaporated before Ghalen could sniff the air a third time to be sure it existed at all.

Sana snapped upright. "She's here!" Her sleep-glazed eyes darted about as if searching for a stalking predator. She gripped the hilt of her strange red knife tightly, the one given to her by the old Minnow Clan hag who had thrown herself into the sea.

He knelt beside her. "Sana?" She didn't answer. In that moment, she bore an uncanny resemblance to her grandmother, Setenay. Her bewildered expression reminded Ghalen of the day they wandered through the numbing ice mist on their journey to Hur-ar. On that day, the dead had walked among them, and a terrifying power had seized Setenay and Sarah. That's how Sana looked now, as if possessed and peering across the invisible chasm between worlds. Ghalen looked about, frightened that the fog, or perhaps something worse, might emerge from the sea.

Ghalen saw no fog, and no spirits; only the clear night, crescent moon, and brilliant field of stars.

He caressed her shoulder. "Wake up."

Sana's expression sharpened, and then came to rest upon him. She released the dagger. "Why did you wake me?"

"You were talking in your sleep."

Sana closed her eyes, as if trying to remember. "What did I say?"

"I couldn't quite make it out." Ghalen lay down beside her, adjusting his body to avoid the wetness creeping up though the timbers.

As if nothing had happened, Sana laid her head on his chest and soon fell back to sleep.

***

Thin, silver-tinged clouds sliced the crescent moon. Nuwa felt her spirit cool and turn dark. She stared at Sana and the red-bladed dagger nestled in her waist cord. Almost two generations had been born, lived, and died since she surrendered that blade to a young Lo maiden on the windblown steppe. To the goddess's perspective, only a moment had passed.

Now, either grace or chance had delivered the cursed knife into the possession of this beautiful barbarian. Nuwa forced herself to believe divine fate bestowed Sana this dagger. If Nuwa believed it had fallen to Sana by mere chance, then the goddess would see to it the Scythian never saw another sunrise. In all the epochs Nuwa had dwelt on the earth, she'd rarely felt such primal hatred for a mortal like she felt for this woman. Nuwa turned and drifted away as the moon burned through once again.

7. Ghosts of Hur-ar.

Nuwa and I stood beside the funeral pyre. The flames transformed her latest husband's body into embers that floated into the night and danced among the stars. Her husband had died in his sleep. Mother's shell was once called Hua, and youth's flower had fallen from her body many years ago. It would not be long before Nushen would be celebrating another Offering Festival.

Since I had first cremated my own father several generations earlier, the duty of preparing the body, lighting the pyre, and burying the ashes always fell to me. As an obedient son, I carried out my responsibility even though I barely knew this man.

We did not speak as his body turned to ash. We never did. This time, I broke the silence. I could no longer contain the question that had burned in my mind since my father's funeral.

"Mother, why have you had no more children?"

Nuwa kept her silence, and turned away. She returned to the Inner Temple. I waited there until dawn, until the pyre had completely cooled. I buried my mother's husband, and returned to the Inner Temple.

The Goddess Nuwa had many secrets. As her obedient son, I never asked the question again.

- The Chronicle of Fu Xi.

***

Along the very edge of the Supply Barge, Virag and Kus-ge shared another night in exile. A few paces separated the two from Ba-lok and the rest of the Minnow Clan huddled together in the barge's middle, but the clear line of demarcation was enough to signify they were outcasts among outcasts.

As he had every night since the return of the sun, Virag sat cross-legged several paces from the edge, staring out over the dark sea, enjoying a few moments of solitary peace before sunrise. He did not mind his rejection by the Minnow Clan — he welcomed it. The night belonged to him, a sanctuary to scheme and contemplate survival should they ever make landfall. At dawn, he would curl up and slip his head beneath his fox-fur cloak's tattered remains. Warmed by the sun, he would proceed to ignore everyone around him and fall into a fitful sleep.

This end of the barge rode lower in the water, lopsided by all the weight of the Minnow exiles who stood against the Uros in the failed uprising. Water lapped over the edge and licked his feet. He would slide backward, but that would put him in closer proximity to people. Virag hated people, now more than ever.

Especially the woman curled up just beyond arm's reach. She curled up like a cat, concealing the cords that bound her wrist to the deck. So dangerous had Kus-ge become in her madness that Okta chanced sparing precious rope in order to bind her each night.

Virag recalled that first dawn following the tempest that had wreaked havoc with the barges and claimed the lives of Aizarg's wife and eldest child. They awoke to find the barges surrounded by thick fog, and thousands of dead bodies floating upon the still waters. Perhaps that is what had hurled Kus-ge into madness. She had screamed hysterically until Sana, with a well-placed punch, had knocked her unconscious. What followed next, Virag still had difficulty putting in context. The bodies had parted before what Virag could only describe at a mountain of black wood. He had seen the Black Fortress of the Narim countless times lording high above Hur-ar, a distant dark rectangle peeking behind the mighty wall far above the city. To see it drift by, against wind and current, only a few feet away, almost made Virag question everything he knew. The dead, perhaps all the world's peoples wiped out in the Deluge, had parted before the Black Fortress and vanished in the first dawn they had seen in forty days.

The Lo called it the New Sun, and believed the old sun had died and been reborn following the flood. The few hours between the rising of the New Sun and Kus-ge reawakening were the most enjoyable hours Virag had encountered since coming aboard these infernal rafts. The peace did not last.

First came Aizarg's pronouncement, harsh and swift, against Ba-lok and the Minnow Clan. They were to be banished to the Supply Barge, and stripped of anything that could be used as a weapon, to include personal knives. It was only at Okta's counsel that the Uros did not have the Supply Barge cut away. Okta insisted the two barges were more stable if they remained attached. Upon landfall, Ba-lok, Virag, and Kus-ge would be banished forever. Aizarg would extend forgiveness to any Minnow who chose to remain with the Crane, but no such forgiveness would be extended to the three instigators. Mournful wails rose among the Minnow at Aizarg's pronouncement. Virag didn't care. As soon as they made landfall, he would likely strike out on his own.

Ba-lok became sullen, his unearned braggadocios finally snuffed out. This meant the Minnow, the larger of the two clans, crowded onto one barge, forcing Virag all the way to the downstream edge and ending any illusion of privacy.

The next blow to his peace came when Kus-ge awoke. It was the way she wailed that made Virag uneasy, like a marsh panther in the dead of the night. She leapt up and sprinted in a blind panic across the deck, knocking down any who stood in her way. "You're doomed!" she screamed. "He will devour you!" Ba-lok and the rest of the Lo attempted to corral her, but she leapt into the sea. It took seven men to drag her back to the barges. It was then the Uros ordered her bound. Over the course of the days, her fear transformed into maniacal laughter and vicious taunts at any who drew to close.

That was how Virag and Kus-ge ended up in shared misery.

"Go away," Virag growled over his shoulder at softly intruding footsteps.

The footfalls halted a few paces behind him. Virag felt the familiar heat of hostile eyes boring into his back. There was once a time when he dealt with such situations flanked by burly Sammujad mercenaries. Now he would have to use his wits.

"I can't sit anywhere on this stinking barge without my ass getting soaked. I wish the damn thing would make up its mind and sink and get it over with," Virag remarked without turning, waiting for a response, or lack of one. He sorely missed his knife, which Aizarg's dog Ghalen had taken from him. "If the Uros was wise, he would lighten the barge by tossing over the weak and sick."

"If anyone should be tossed overboard, it would be you."

He turned and considered Ezra coldly. "Are you just going to stand there and stare at me? If you've come to kill me, hurry up and get it over with. Otherwise, get the hell out of here and leave me alone."

Ezra sat cross-legged between the slaver and the barge's edge and glared. Virag had been waiting for this moment for a long time, surprised it had taken so long to arrive. He had expected the moment to take the form of a knife in his back or across his throat. During their voyage, the boy had co-opted Virag's giant, Spako, but surprisingly made no attempt on Virag's life.

"You're blocking my view. Say your peace and go away."

Ezra finally said, "Do you know who I am?"

Virag chuckled quietly and met his glare. "I knew the moment I learned you were her brother."

"And you said nothing."

Virag raised an eyebrow. "Was I supposed to? If this is some kind of game, please let me know what the rules are so that I might have a chance to win."

"Every day since we've been at sea, I've contemplated killing you for what you did to Sarah."

"Then why didn't you, *boy*?" Virag emphasized the last word, hoping to draw Ezra into foolish rage. Virag spread his arms, as if defenseless. "Spako gave you his allegiance — you could have crushed me at any time."

"The night of the storm, I almost did. Only my loyalty to the Uros stayed my blade."

"*Tsk, tsk*." Virag shook his head. "Don't tell me Aizarg and his foolish mercy has infected a Prince of Hur-ar?" Virag looked Ezra up and down, assessing his foe with a new perspective. "Or better yet, a sewer thief. I grew rich bargaining at the Black Dragon's feet. We understand each other, eh, Prince? Why do you suffer these fools? You should have joined us the night of the tempest, not fought against us."

To Virag's irritation, Ezra didn't take the bait. "Yes, I was once the son of Prince Azubehl, but he is entombed beneath the waves with the rest of Hur-ar. I was also Blade, Prince of the Untouchables; but the sewer gangs are dead, too. Who I truly am is Ezra of the Carp Clan, son of Okta. And I didn't come here tonight to kill you."

"Then why did you come here?"

"To thank you for saving my sister."

Virag stared incredulously at Ezra, not sure how to react. "Your gratitude"—Virag shook his head in mild disbelief—"is misplaced."

"I am not naïve. I know what you truly are, but my sister possessed a forgiving spirit. It is for her sake I forgive, not mine. If you had not bought her, she would have ended up slaughtered on the altar of the Black Dragon. She would have never met the Uros, nor returned to Hur-ar where I saw her one last time." He paused. "And I would not be here."

Virag looked about, trying to hide his discomfort. He didn't understand gratitude given selflessly, as he saw no gain in it. "Are you going to tell me you owe me some kind of life debt?"

Ezra grinned. "It's already paid in full several times over. I first paid it when I held a knife to Shellbaz's back as you bid on Sarah. You only walked out of Hur-ar because of me."

Virag grunted with mild surprise. "So that explains it."

"I paid it again when I didn't kill you during the uprising."

"You think highly of yourself, boy."

Ezra dropped his voice, his expression as hard as iron. "These people don't truly know my past, but you do, Virag."

The masks were off, the pretending over. Virag knew he faced a foe every bit as dangerous as Bal-eeb or Tuma, worse even. This one thought he was good.

"You're the one who killed Slug and took over the Hur-ar underworld."

"Then you know what I am capable of."

"Yes, yes!" Virag shook the back of his hand at Ezra impatiently as if trying to whisk him away. "We are a long way from Hur-ar's sewers and palaces. Save your theatrics. I do not scare easily."

"No theatrics, only truth." Ezra paused as if taking Virag's measure afresh. "Ghalen was right, we should have left you in that tree with the rest of your men the day we found you. You should have drowned like the rat you are. But the Uros is a good man. Good men don't understand people like you, slaver."

Virag raised an eyebrow. "And you do?"

"These are my people now, my family. If and when we make landfall, I never want to see your face again. If I do, I will kill you. No mercy, no bargaining." Ezra stood in one fluid motion. He exhaled sharply, as if shrugging off a burden. "The Uros says we all serve a purpose, only known to the gods, or perhaps only to the Nameless God. Even you, Virag. I, for one, will be glad when you serve your purpose elsewhere."

As Ezra walked away, Virag called after him, "As will I."

Virag recalled those events leading to this moment, and the common tie between himself and this former High Prince of Hur-ar. This young man had been forced to flee when Bal-eeb the Usurper had overthrown his father, the doddering Prince Azubehl. Ezra's mother and his sister had been enslaved but, somehow, Ezra had caught wind of the plot and escaped. Virag's role in the conspiracy was simple: Bal-eeb guaranteed Virag would win Sarah at auction in order to quickly whisk her away from the city to the vast steppe. Ezra's death and Sarah's public degradation would put fear into rival royal houses, eliminate the old prince's bloodline, and secure Bal-eeb an ally on the steppe.

Fate had other plans. Ezra lived. Sarah, Bal-eeb, and Hur-ar died beneath the flood. The world ended, and Virag went on.

Like he always did.

"Making more enemies, eh, slaver?" came a woman's purr. Virag glanced left to see Kus-ge's smoky eyes peering at him from the darkness. He wondered how much she had overheard. *Probably everything*, he thought.

Virag shrugged. "What's another enemy?"

Kus-ge laughed and rolled over with her back to him.

For a moment, Virag caught an odd smell. He wrinkled his nose and looked around. He knew the scent, though he could not immediately place it, and his gut told him it had no business here.

"Jasmine," he mumbled.

And then it was gone.

The sun will be up soon, he thought as he readjusted his ass to find a new dry spot. Virag lay down and pulled his cloak over his face. "You should watch your back too, boy," he whispered.

8. The Horizon.

I knew something would be different about that day when I awoke well before dawn and found Nuwa standing over me. She wore the shell of a voluptuous young woman named Syning. Mother's selection of Syning two summers ago had made me uncomfortable, as the young acolyte had often drawn my eye.

"Roll up your sleeping mat and place it against the wall," she whispered. "It will be waiting for you when you return."

"Where are we going?" I asked, rubbing my eyes. Chen, her new husband, still slept a few feet away with his back to us. I liked Chen, even before Mother took him as a husband. Physically, I was a boy entering puberty, and I bonded with Chen as if he were my older brother. We spent a great deal of time together, which seemed to irritate my mother.

"Come and eat," Nuwa said. "Your questions will be answered soon."

In silence, I ate a simple breakfast of rice porridge and honey, while my mother watched. She ate nothing; her face was drawn and pale, as if she were ill. She avoided looking at my food, as if the sight revolted her. Sickness could not corrupt any shell Nuwa inhabited, and I could only deduce something tormented her spirit.

By sunrise, Mother and I stood on the Honey Lotus Bridge facing the dark forest beyond Nushen. Behind us, the village had yet to stir.

- The Chronicle of Fu Xi.

***

Ezra stepped beside Okta.

"Where have you been, my son?"

"Downstream, helping Ghalen keep an eye on the exiles."

Okta issued a snort. "I doubt they need much watching."

"Keeping them alive may have been a mistake."

"In these matters, Aizarg knows best."

"Does he?" Ezra snapped.

Okta never turned his gaze from the sea. Ezra had the same fire in his spirit as all young men, the fire of absolute self-confidence. "He is the Uros."

"I mean no disrespect, Father. It's just—" Ezra stuttered.

"You think he is too merciful."

"I think he underestimated the threat the traitors posed, and still pose."

"He knows."

Ezra pivoted and faced Okta, arms extended in bewilderment. "Then why do they live? Why would a king shelter enemies within his own kingdom?"

"Aizarg is not a king. He is Uros."

"What is the difference?"

"A king rules. An Uros is a leader among equals. His power is borrowed, not bestowed. He has no mandate to mete out death without first weighing the consequences. He will not be Uros forever, and those traitors spilled no blood."

For several long moments, father and son stood in silence as the sky began to lighten, and the stars began to surrender to the coming dawn. "Listen to the sea. Do you hear it?" Okta said without turning his gaze from the east.

"I hear lapping waves." Even though Okta had taught his adopted son much about the sea, the young man still had much to learn.

"This salty sea is strange, but it has begun to speak to me just as our beloved Great Sea once did. It carries us swiftly southeast."

"All I see is water. Unending water. And wolf fish." Ezra nodded to the left, where Okta spied a fin cutting the surface a few yards away.

"Where there are wolf fish, there are other fish. That means full bellies."

Ezra nodded. "The fish are plentiful now, as are the sea dogs. They should be showing up once the sun is high."

Okta nodded appreciatively at Ezra's statement. *He is learning.* "True." He glanced at his adopted son, heart swelling with pride.

"Why do the sea dogs keep coming back every day, even though they know there is a chance either we or the wolf fish will hunt them?" Ezra asked.

"Because fish gather beneath our rafts," Okta replied. "Little fish are drawn to anything that floats. They take shelter in the barges' shade and nibble at the slime collecting on the logs. They draw the bigger fish, which lurk just below. Below them, even bigger fish, and so on. I suspect the column of fish drifting beneath us has attracted both sea dogs and wolf fish. Our rafts have become hunting grounds."

"Hunting grounds." Ezra's voice dropped to a whisper as a large sea wolf slipped by. "We have plenty to eat, but every day the wolf fish grow in numbers, and our rafts sink a little more."

In the days that followed the sun's return, the Nameless God had provided much. Soon after the rains ended, the Lo were able to find salvage wood to fashion crude spears and scaffolds to replace those that had been destroyed in the great storm. In a matter of days, decks that had once been wiped clean by the tempest now bristled with makeshift scaffolding.

And then came the sea dogs.

Strange, playful creatures that had flippers like a fish, yet were covered with fur and barked like dogs, arrived the third dawn after the rains. A small pack of about twenty surrounded the barges, driving schools ahead of them. The fish were so thick the Lo merely had to pluck them out of the sea.

Even Aizarg could only shake his head in disbelief.

The fish filled the Lo's bellies, but with their new spears they were able to hunt any sea dogs that strayed too close. Without their braziers, the Lo could not cook. However, once they had constructed enough scaffolds, it became easy to dry the meat in the almost ever-present sunshine.

Even though they were often hunted, the sea dogs seemed at ease around the children, almost taking joy from their laughter. When the children dove into the sea, the sea dogs would dart playfully between their legs, and roll on their bellies and bark. Then, one such day, a sea dog lurched without warning out of the water in a bloody geyser. The children screamed and fled the water. The sea turned red as dark fins surrounded the raft.

After that, a lookout was always posted whenever anyone went into the water.

"Aizarg's Nameless God has brought us this far," Okta said. "He will not abandon us to the wolf fish now. It is landfall I fear most."

Ezra turned to consider Okta.

"You cannot feel it," Okta explained, "but the water below runs swiftly. Something every fisherman knows is swift currents often signal shallowing water. It reminds me of the Black River we sailed down when the flood had just begun."

"I remember." Ezra nodded.

"Now we have no sail, or poles."

Golden light glowed along the horizon. Voices began to stir behind them. The Lo were waking to a new day.

Okta continued in a low whisper, "It is no secret the barges are rotting from the inside, too. The ropes holding them together are starting to give way. If we strike anything, *anything*, the Arun-ki will disintegrate." Okta leaned in. "Ghalen, Levidi, and I have already discussed what must be done. Land or no land, we must be ready to abandon the rafts."

"We won't last long in the water."

Okta shook his head slowly. "That's why when land finds us, we will have to act quickly."

"An odd choice of words, Father."

"Land will find us, not the other way around. It will sneak up on us like a lion in the night and pounce. We must be prepared to meet it, or die."

"What must we do?"

"When the time comes, we will have to keep the barges balanced as best we can. Right now, they are joined end-to-end. If I had any rope, I would separate them and rejoin them side-to-side."

"To make it easier to shuffle people from one side to another?"

"Exactly, but that is no longer an option. When the time comes, we may be forced to divide the people and sever the bindings connecting the Supply Barge and Wedding Barge."

Ezra opened his mouth to speak when a tinkling splash caught their attention. Okta frowned and leaned backwards to peer behind Ezra. There stood little Bat-or, rubbing his sleeping eyes and peeing into the sea.

When Bat-or finished, Ezra knelt beside him and ruffled his unruly mop of hair. "What are you doing up so early, little man?"

"I smelt pretty flowers. Have we found land?" Ezra looked up at Okta, astonished. Okta shared the same thought. These words were the first Bat-or had uttered since his mother and brother were lost in the tempest.

"Bat-or! What are you doing?" Okta turned to see Su-gár quickly approaching, eyes puffy with sleep, hand smoothing her wild hair. "You know you shouldn't go to the edge without me," she scolded.

"I had to pee. I'm hungry." Bat-or looked about with an odd grimace. "Where are the flowers?"

Su-gár stopped and put a hand to her mouth, obviously just as astonished to hear the boy speak. Since Atamoda's death, she had become the boy's surrogate mother. She had also become Aizarg's caretaker.

Okta looked on as Su-gár knelt beside Bat-or and wrapped him in a warm hug.

"Su-gár," Ba-tor said sweetly. "I'm hungry."

"I'll find some fish," she said.

"Yes, that is a good idea." Okta winked at Bat-or. Aizarg kept his youngest son close at all times, which usually meant Su-gár, too. Normally, it would be good for a man to eventually take another wife after his first had passed on. But these were not normal times. Keeping his people alive hadn't afforded Aizarg an opportunity to mourn his oldest son and wife. Su-gár's affections for the Uros were no secret among the Lo, but Aizarg remained distant.

And then there was the matter of Ezra's feelings for Su-gár. Okta easily recognized the look in Ezra's eyes whenever Su-gár was near.

Su-gár picked up Bat-or and placed him on her hip. She smiled warmly at Ezra and Okta. "Would you like to eat with us upwind? The barge floats better up there — it's less wet."

"That sounds wonderful." Ezra rubbed his belly. "I am starting to get hungry."

"The sun is almost up," Okta said as he caught another hint of the strange, floral scent.

***

A swollen, orange sun peeked above the horizon as Nuwa drew close to the child in the young woman's arms. The boy rested his head on the woman's shoulder and stared at Nuwa as if he could see her. She reached out and tenderly brushed the boy's unruly hair from his eyes. To these mortals, it would seem as nothing more than the morning breeze.

The boy could never comprehend the titanic weight the Emperor of Heaven had bestowed this sliver of time, nor the small part he would play in it. "Look to the sea. Look to the dawn, little one, and tell them! Tell them what you see and change the world."

Bat-or's gaze focused on her for only a moment before he turned to face the rising sun.

***

Okta slapped Ezra on the back with a wide smile. "Let's go get something to eat, eh? I suspect we're going to have a busy day. Ghalen says those wolf fish look like they have tough hides. Maybe we can round up a few men and spear one. Perhaps we can make leather out of their skin to re-lash the decks."

Su-gár shivered. "Aren't they awfully big to try to haul on the deck? They might bite someone!"

Ezra drew his knife and deftly spun the tip on his finger. "If we can get one close, I can gut it."

"Or it will gut you!" Su-gár playfully bumped her hip against Ezra.

"Let me down!" Bat-or began to struggle. He slid from Su-gár's grip and dashed to the edge. "Look!" Bat-or shouted and pointed to the cresting sun.

A black speck on the horizon caught Okta's attention. His heart leapt as he finally recognized what danced atop the wave in front of dawn's backdrop. He clasped Ezra's shoulder. "Summon the Uros."

"What is it?" Ezra peered into the sunrise, trying to see what his father did.

"A raft," Okta said.

9. The Raft.

I remember the backpack's weight, and how odd the short sword felt by my side, or how the spear seemed too big for my grip. I also recall how my mother would not look at me.

"All you need to begin your journey is in the backpack."
"Why are you sending me away?"
"To fulfill your destiny."

- The Chronicle of Fu Xi.

***

"I said get away!" Okta shouted at the throng crowding around to get a look. "By Oetesy's beard, we must rebalance the barge or we'll sink!" Even the Minnow came to get a peek. Several lashings had given way under the strain.

With Ghalen's, Ezra's, and Levidi's help, they pushed, shoved, and cajoled the Lo away from the edge. Slowly, the barge flattened. Water sloshed around their ankles as it raced to rejoin the sea. Soon, the Wedding Barge settled back to its balanced state.

Okta returned his attention to the raft lashed alongside the Supply Barge. Elation and worry fought for control as he inspected the craft he had given up for lost in the storm weeks earlier. He looked over his shoulder at Aizarg.

The Uros quietly inspected the small raft. Sana followed a few steps behind. He caressed the sail twisted around the crooked mast. He bent down and tugged the crude straps holding the gnarled deck logs together.

Levidi, Ghalen, and Ezra soon joined them. Other than Aizarg and Ezra, the men did what came naturally to the Lo; they busied themselves straightening the rigging, cleaning the deck and inspecting the bindings.

"Once she ripped free, she must have been so light she bobbed high on the waves," Okta remarked. "She rode the same currents we did, just out of sight. It's the only explanation."

Aizarg frowned. Lines cut deeply around the corners of his eyes, giving his face an aged look that had begun to match his bright white hair. Instead of giving hope, the raft's arrival only seemed to add to the Uros's burdens. Where once he carried the red metal staff, he now leaned on it for support.

Okta stomped the firm deck — it was dry without a hint of water-logging. "She's small, but sound. We can put six, maybe seven people on her. It will take some of the weight off the barges. This might buy us a few more days."

Aizarg finally spoke. "Okta, this raft shouldn't be here."

Okta shrugged. "She's intact because she was well made."

Aizarg knelt and tugged at the thin, flat straps holding the crooked logs together. "Do you remember how we made these?"

Ghalen knelt beside him and tugged the firmly secured bindings. "We cut those from our deerskin clothes."

Levidi lifted the sail's corner, one unlike any crafted by the Lo. He caressed the wool, too thick and soft to be practical for everyday use. "Setenay made this from the garments you brought back from the Narim."

Ghalen twisted a thin deerskin cord tied to the sail and smirked. "I know where the sail's straps came from."

Unamused, Sana flashed him an irritated glance and returned her attention to the Uros.

Aizarg reached down and jostled the loose deck logs. Aizarg jiggled them easily, watching them rub against one another. Crudely cut from driftwood and still bark-covered, they lacked any pitch coating. "Master of Boats, tell me, how long did it take to make this raft?"

"The time it took you and Sarah to return from Hur-ar," Okta said, feeling the defensiveness in his voice.

"A day and a night, hastily constructed to save us from the Black River." Aizarg stood and wiggled the mast. It shook like a child's tooth about to free itself from the socket.

"All of us that stand upon this raft now are the same that stood upon it then," Sana whispered.

"Except Ba-lok," Ezra added.

They looked upon one another in contemplation before Aizarg continued, "The storm that took Atamoda and Kol-ok stripped away this raft, along with all our outlying boats and rafts. It wiped the decks clean of everything except the Arun-ki's main mast. Okta, you saw wreckage floating a few days later just as we all did." Aizarg plucked one of the taut deck straps. "These deerskin rags should be completely rotted, if just from the sun. The logs are firm, but they should be waterlogged. Some of the bark is still green."

"What are you saying?" Okta asked.

Aizarg ignored him and turned to Sana. "What do you have to say, Isp?"

Okta noted how quickly Aizarg had fallen into Sana's counsel, how he had begun to trust her much as he had trusted Setenay.

She shook her head. "I don't understand it."

"Then what does your heart tell you?" Aizarg asked.

"Anyone with eyes can see it should have been ripped apart," she continued, perhaps unsure under the stare of so many sea men. "It has been spared and returned to us. Maybe by chance. Maybe by fate. If this is by the hand of fate, then there is purpose, and perhaps powerful magic at work."

Aizarg let his gaze settle from man to man. "So be it. We honor fate. No one sleeps on this vessel except Okta and Ezra. No one may set foot on it except those who rode it down the Black River. Whatever magic the Nameless God placed upon this raft was meant for only a few." He turned to Okta. "Master of Boats, make it seaworthy again."

10. Redemption.

My breath quickened, and my heart pounded with overwhelming excitement. The trail before me led deep into the forest, which I had been forbidden from exploring up to this point.

Nuwa looked down at me. "Travel the length and breadth of the land bearing the gift of speech to the Tall Men. Seek them out, wherever they may be, and bring them from darkness to light. If they cannot speak, teach them. If they already possess speech, learn their tongue. Name all that is unnamed. Shun evil, and seek good. Remember all you see and hear, and bring this knowledge back to me when you return. This is your quest, my obedient son."

I swallowed hard. "I will do my best, Mother. Where shall I go?"

"Tortoise Mountain is Heaven's Middle Kingdom, the center of the earthly realm. All that lies east is Cin, the Right Wall of Heaven. All that lies west is Zuŏ, the Left Wall of Heaven. Cin is yours to explore; Zuŏ is forbidden."

"East it is." I took a deep breath. "When shall I return, Mother?"

"One day, you will see an unmistakable sign in the heavens beckoning you home. Do not return a day earlier."

It is not easy to put into words what I felt that morning. I will simply say, I felt alive. I had only taken a few steps when Nuwa called out from behind.

"Remember, you are my son, a god in your own right. You carry the blessing of the Emperor of Heaven himself. When you exhaust your provisions, you will learn to find more. Your blood is poison to beasts — they will shun you. No blade of stone, bronze, or iron can kill you. But beware the dragon, my obedient son. Always beware the dragon."

That morning I departed on my first quest, the Journey of Tongues. I would not hear my mother's voice again for forty years.

- The Chronicle of Fu Xi.

***

"You can close your legs, now." Ro-xandra replaced Alaya's loincloth over her vagina. Ro-xandra wiped her hands on her tattered skirt. "How has your breathing been in the past few days?"

Alaya shrugged. "Easier, I think."

"The baby kicks like a caught fish. Your shield is thinning. It won't be long now. You could go into labor anytime." The Minnow hag spoke the good news without joy.

Alaya half-sobbed, half-laughed.

Sana knelt beside Alaya's head under the lean-to made of stitched sea dog skins. She patted Alaya's hand reassuringly. "That's wonderful!"

"When the time comes, we will slip into the water along the edge." Ro-xandra eyed Sana coolly. "In my experience as a midwife, giving birth in deep water is not too difficult, but it should be the younger women assisting."

Sana leaned closer, not sure if she heard the midwife correctly. "Water?" Sana considered the wolf fish circling the rafts and thought it highly likely Alaya would be giving birth right here in this lean-to.

"You wouldn't know, now would you?" Ro-xandra scoffed. "All Lo women give birth in water. Only filthy a-g'an are birthed on land."

The wolf fish might have other plans, Sana thought, and for a moment contemplated cutting Ro-xandra's throat. Every word issuing forth from the midwife's lips carried an unspoken accusation aimed wholly at Sana. *You are the patesi-le. You are the Isp. You should be doing this, not I.*

"Summon me when your birth pains begin." Ro-xandra backed out on her hands and knees, leaving Sana and Alaya in the lean-to.

Sana fought the violent urges she felt against Ro-xandra and the Minnow.

Alaya adjusted her tunic and loincloth and rolled over away from Sana. Levidi and Ghalen had built this lean-to specifically to accommodate Alaya and the impending birth. It barely fit four kneeling women, but would be adequate to keep Alaya out of the elements and comfortable as her labor drew near. Levidi had stuffed rolled sea-dog furs in between the logs and covered it all with more skins to create insulation against the clammy deck, and provide a level floor.

Sana caressed Alaya's shoulder. "Rejoice! You heard what she said. Your child is healthy and will soon be here."

Alaya moaned, and cried louder.

Sana only felt more helpless in this new role as tribal holy woman. She had never given birth, let alone slept with a man. How could she console this woman? She had witnessed several births, but never midwifed. Those children were born in smoky yurts, to stoic Scythian women who were judged by how little they cried out in birth. The Scythian in her wanted to slap Alaya, to tell her to toughen up and be thankful. She felt her grandmother's spirit patiently instructing Sana to comfort Alaya.

"It's all my fault," Alaya whispered. "I've cursed this child." It spilled out quickly in between muffled sobs. In whispers, Alaya confided to Sana how out of fear for her unborn child, she had stolen food in the weeks preceding the mighty storm. She recalled the night Kol-ok had caught her stealing fish from the communal stockpile, and how she pleaded with him not to turn her in.

Alaya buried her face in the furs. "He lied for me, and I said nothing."

Alaya's tale left Sana stunned. "Why? You already had an extra portion each day."

"I can't lose this baby!" Alaya grasped Sana's arm. "I couldn't bear seeing Levidi in pain. He wants a son more than anything. Some nights I could not feel the baby kicking, only hunger gnawing my belly." She caressed her stomach. "I was so frightened."

Scythian babies were wrapped in death blankets as often as swaddling blankets. Death was a casual companion, especially for children and women. Yet, Sana had never experienced the magic of a life in her womb. She felt totally inadequate, a girl playing the role of a woman, playing the role of patesi-le.

The lean-to suddenly felt confining, smothering. She needed to escape. Sana clumsily patted Alaya's arm and muttered, "Everything will be fine." Sana pulled away from Alaya's grip and backed out of the lean-to. She stood facing the breeze, closed her eyes and tried to imagine herself once again on the steppe. She wanted to seize her favorite mare's mane and gallop to the endless horizon, away from this place and the crushing weight thrust upon her.

But the illusion would not hold. The wind carried too much moisture and the sickening scent of salt and rotting wood. Sana opened her eyes, and reality reasserted itself. The deck possessed a permanent, sickening lean. Huddled groups looked to her with desperation, not as an enemy, but as their holy woman, their healer. Sana desperately wanted them to stop staring. She felt herself drowning, as surely as if she had fallen overboard.

The worst part was Sana had begun to truly know these people. She felt herself drawn, no, *dragged*, into their lives. Each face had a name now, and a story. All of them, like her, had suffered terrible loss. She could no longer ignore them or their suffering. So much of their lives had become interwoven in hers.

What was left of her Scythian garb had vanished months ago, replaced by a new loincloth and tunic of sea dog skin, all of Lo cut. Alaya even taught her the Lo double-stitching pattern, and Sana adopted it, hoping to blend in as much as possible. Without thinking, she had begun to use Lo words for everything. She felt herself being reluctantly transformed, and a part of her deeply resented it.

She grieved terribly for her people, the Scythians, yet she had no one to confide in, even Ghalen. These people viewed the steppe horsemen as bloodthirsty savages. Her people had viewed the Lo as weak cowards. In her heart, Sana knew both were wrong, but now such thoughts had no place in this new age. More than anything, Sana wanted to talk to her father.

Sana loved her mother, but she adored her father. The world knew and feared him as the great chieftain Sawseruquo, uniter of the southern Scythian clans and scourge of Hur-ar. Sana knew him as an adoring and stern father who taught her every bit as well as he taught her brother, Tuma. The loss of her father haunted Sana's dreams more than anything else.

On the other side of the barge, laughter caught her attention. Levidi and Ghalen stood along the barge's high edge, leaning on their spears with relaxed shoulders in casual conversation.

Ghalen is always happy, Sana thought. *He belongs here. How can he understand the conflict in my heart?* Sana knew Ghalen tried. Anytime he saw her staring off and growing distant, he would ask her if everything was all right and try to get her to laugh.

He is still trying to teach me to swim, Sana thought with a faint smile.

Levidi said something, and both men burst out laughing. They enjoyed each other's camaraderie and friendship. Sana knew Ghalen would never be alone as long as he had Levidi and his people.

Sana, on the other hand, grew more isolated as the days passed. Without Atamoda, she had no guide, no teacher.

Ghalen said he understood her decision to delay the marriage, but part of her wanted him not to understand. She needed him to get angry and make demands. Ghalen only

71

smiled at her in that same, infuriating way, *that Lo way*, and told her he would wait. As badly as she needed to be with him, she could not begin a new life with Ghalen adrift. Sana would not marry until she had solid ground beneath her feet, and hope for a new life it would bring. The thought of being adrift with a child like Alaya, with only Ro-xandra as a midwife, terrified her. More than that, it was on the cusp of their marriage ceremony that the storm took Atamoda from them.

She needed to talk to someone. She needed her own patesi-le. Instead, she only met desperate eyes and the occasional hard stare from one of the Minnow Clan. And then she caught Okta staring at her.

With somber purpose, Okta approached. "Come."

Without a word, she followed. Stepping onto his raft filled Sana with the same unease she had felt that morning. It had taken Okta no time to put the disheveled, rickety little craft in order. Ropes without a hint of rot sat neatly coiled and ready. Without even a noticeable tear, the wool sail had been folded and secured neatly to the mast, waiting to be unfurled. It looked much as it had when she first stepped aboard along the Black River.

Okta casually paced about for a few moments, tugging on a piece of rigging here and there, briefly inspecting the sail, before turning his attention to Sana. "A life at sea is a series of daily habits. Everything must be inspected, and re-inspected. A good fisherman must know his vessel."

"I am not a fisherman."

"No, you are not. Nor will you ever truly be Lo."

His words landed hard, though she felt no malice behind them, only the truth's heaviness. He took a few steps closer to Sana and lowered his voice. "Nor is Ezra.

"Every day I see your confusion. You drift the decks, trying to feel useful, pretending to be an Isp. Sana, I think I understand you. I know what it feels like to be thrust out of your element by fate. I felt the same way as I walked dry land. And soon we may feel dry land under our feet again. Our roles will reverse."

Sana felt her defenses soften, and her shoulders relax.

"Do you know why I built this raft?" he continued.

"To save our lives."

He smiled, tugged on a strap securing the bound sail to the mast. That strap used to be part of Sana's chercheska, her traditional Scythian deerskin tunic. Memories of when Ghalen had forcibly cut it from her back should have filled Sana with rage, but instead she felt gratitude these men could fashion her garments into a vessel of salvation.

"Yes…and no." He paused and considered the horizon. "You would like my wife, Sana." The way he smiled warmed her heart, and made her ache for her father. "She has your temperament."

"Why are you telling me this?"

"Because I like you, too. And our people need you."

"Your people need a real patesi-le."

"Our people need something more than a patesi-le, or an Isp. They need you. As for this raft, it saved our lives that day along the Black River." Okta touched his chest. "It is also the path of my redemption.

"For a man of my clan to touch try land is considered an unclean act. Among the Carp, only women can touch land, and then only during their blood time. Before I left for the quest, my wife, my patesi-le, instructed I must build a raft has penance before I could return to the sea."

The words came out before Sana could consider them. "Then your redemption is incomplete."

Okta glanced around the raft. "I was wondering if perhaps you might have some insight what exactly my redemption is."

Sana shrugged. "I was hoping maybe you could help me find mine."

Okta chuckled softly. "If we can't help each other, maybe we could help someone else."

"Aizarg."

"Aizarg." Okta nodded. "I am concerned how quickly he is deteriorating. We are fed, the sea is calm, and the days grow long. He sits and wallows in his grief, keeping Bat-or close and rarely walking among his people. Su-gár's constant doting isn't helping."

"Su-gár loves him."

"She thinks she loves him, but Ezra truly loves her."

"Is this about your son?"

"This is about everyone snapping out of this spell before it's too late."

"What do you suggest?"

"You have to embrace your duty as Isp and set things to rights."

Sana's insecurity and defensiveness reasserted itself. "I have no idea what to do! I don't know how to midwife. Atamoda taught me very little before she died. No one trusts me. They see me as a Scythian, not the Isp."

"They see you as strong."

"They see a lie."

Okta raised his voice. "Then lie!"

Nearby, a few heads turned.

It wasn't anger she heard in Okta's voice, but desperation. He lowered his voice and stepped closer. "I know the truth. The people know the truth. They know when we finally feel dirt beneath our feet, you will find your place. You will find your strength, just like Ezra will."

Okta reached for a coil and began fretting over it, unrolling and re-rolling the line. Almost imperceptibly, his hands shook. No matter how he struggled to mask it, Sana felt his fear, and it terrified her.

He glanced up. "Sana, you are a rope that isn't rotting, a log that is still firm and floats high. If it floats and keeps your head above water, then hold on to it for dear life, even if it's only a lie."

11. It's Just A Fish.

*Under the cold light of a waxing crescent moon, I slipped into Nushen.
My long Journey of Tongues had ended. Paper lanterns hung from the
Honey Lotus Bridge in preparation for the upcoming Autumn Festival.
Nothing had really changed in Nushen except the faces and gossip. I
would have to relearn both, and the thought filled me with joy and
emptiness.*

*I wandered through the sleeping village until I found myself in the
Stone Garden along the forest's edge. The family burial plots had
grown, testifying to time's true passage.*

*A limestone slab bearing each family's symbol marked the plots.
Individual graves were only marked with unique patterns formed from
small stones and pebbles. It was the family matriarch's responsibility to
occasionally graze their goats on the plot, and remember each ancestor's
symbol and name. This knowledge was passed down from mother to
daughter.*

*During the Night of the Forgotten, the Autumn Festival's full
moon, the matriarchs set about cleaning their family plots. The Goddess
Nuwa would walk among them, pointing out hidden graves long
overgrown and helping the old women remember their ancestors.*

*I walked among the plots, and guessed who might be buried in the
newer ones. Mother, cloaked in Syning's old body, stepped from the
shadows. "Welcome home, my obedient son."*

- The Chronicle of Fu Xi.

***

The two men stood side-by-side at the barge's edge, in comfortable contemplation as if pondering something so casual as an afternoon swim. Arms crossed, Levidi rested all his weight on one leg like a crane, scratching the back of his calf with his toe. Ghalen leaned lazily on his crooked spear and scratched his nose. They talked softly as the enormous fin sliced slowly back and forth in the gentle waves several yards away.

"They're not serious, are they?" Ezra whispered to Sana. "It's almost a third the length of the barge."

"Yes," she replied flatly. Sana had witnessed this scene many times before among the Scythians. Ghalen and Levidi talked the way men do before the hunt, battle, or maybe just about to do something stupid. These were murmurs of strategy, scheming, and mischief.

Men and boys crowded behind Sana and Ezra, careful not to get close enough to the edge to unbalance the barge and incur Okta's wrath.

"It's too far." Levidi kept his voice level, but Sana detected excitement simmering at the size of the monster cruising just below the surface.

"I wonder how it tastes," Ghalen pondered.

"I bet it's wondering the same thing," Sana said just loud enough to ensure being heard.

Ghalen ignored her.

"Its hide looks tough," Levidi pondered.

Ghalen raised his eyebrow. "That it does. A spear may not penetrate."

"Perhaps its hide is thick enough to repair our deck bindings." Okta stepped alongside Sana, followed by Alaya.

"Don't encourage them!" Sana gave Okta a not-so-gentle shove.

Okta shrugged. "It's just a fish."

"Men are all the same. Not a shred of sense." Sana remembered how a much smaller wolf fish had snapped a sea dog in two with just one bite. This one looked like it could swallow a man whole. She looked around for Aizarg, and spotted him on the opposite end of the barge, facing away.

He will be of no help, she thought.

The wolf fish slowly cruised alongside the barge. Levidi, Ghalen, and the gallery followed.

"We're going to have to jab it hard to puncture the skin," Levidi said.

Ghalen shook his head. "It's too far for a jab. I'll have to throw."

Levidi pursed his lips and looked as if calculating the distance. "You'll just lose the spear."

"That twig isn't going to penetrate that thing's skin." Losing patience, Sana followed a few paces behind. The rest of the Crane lingered behind Sana, murmuring excitedly.

The sun lorded high above, and the dappling reflections made it difficult for Sana to see. The big gray fin, three hands high, sliced back and forth as if daring the men to attack.

Ezra leaned toward Sana and spoke in a low tone. "Even if they do spear it, how are they going to get it on the barge?"

"I have no idea."

After a few more minutes of discussion, they agreed to let Ghalen throw the spear.

"Remember, that is my spear," Levidi reminded.

"'I'll keep that in mind." Ghalen screwed up his face in concentration and brushed back his thick blond hair. Then, he cocked his arm.

Sana knew Ghalen's skill with a spear was legendary among the Lo. If any man had a chance of slaying the beast, it was him. The wooden tip hit dead square behind the wolf fish's head, and bounced off. It landed with a weak splash before drifting away.

Levidi shrugged. "Tough fish."

Ghalen nodded. "It will take metal to punch through that hide."

They looked at one another, and, as if reading each other's thoughts, grinned.

"I know that look." Alaya grabbed Sana's arm. "He's about to do something stupid!"

Ghalen and Levidi simultaneously drew their daggers from their loin-cloth straps.

"They're not…" Sana looked on in disbelief.

"They are!" Ezra smiled broadly and snatched the knife from his loincloth.

"One of us takes the top, the other the bottom," Ghalen said.

"Fair enough. Stay clear of its tail." Levidi gave each of his legs a brief shake to limber up.

"Good point."

"Jaws, too."

"Another good point."

"Levidi! Stop this foolishness," Alaya screamed.

"It's okay, my songbird," Levidi said, not looking back. "Me and Ghalen know what we're doing."

"Ghalen?" Sana asked incredulously.

"It's just a fish." Ghalen winked.

"A fish as big as a wooly rhino with a lion's teeth!"

Ghalen and Levidi nodded at one another and, knives drawn, leapt on top of the beast.

A cheer erupted from the Lo.

Ezra scrambled to join them, but Sana snatched him back by the arm. "No. You swim worse than I do."

Knife between his teeth, Levidi dove deep. Ghalen grabbed the beast's dorsal fin and plunged his blade just ahead of the fin.

Water and blood exploded across the barge as the beast rolled and thrashed. Sana finally saw the monster's true size. Bigger than a lion's, its teeth stood in jagged rows. If either man lost his grip, the creature would spin about and shred them. Just as bad, its crescent-shaped tail would smash them. The beast's eyes were like obsidian stones, lifeless and cold.

Every roll revealed Levidi clinging on top to the pectoral fin; each stab created a brief red bloom on its underbelly. Ghalen held on to a dorsal fin and sliced bloody ribbons down the beast's back.

Okta looked on, though to Sana he didn't seem concerned. "Ezra, go fetch one of the two good coils of rope from my raft."

Ezra slowly backed away, as if unable to take his eyes off the battle.

"Go, son. We're going to need that rope soon."

The beast suddenly snapped its body into a "U" shape, shrugging Ghalen off its back. Before Sana could register what was happening, the fish snapped the other way, slapping Ghalen with its tail so violently he sailed out of the water and onto the deck, bowling over several men lined up along the edge. His knife skittered along the deck and stopped at Sana's feet.

Okta clenched his knife between his teeth and dove in, followed by most of the Lo men. Soon, they covered the wolf fish like ants, knives piercing and slashing.

Ghalen lay unmoving. An abrasive rash covered his chest, weeping blood in some places. Sana dropped to her knees and shook him. "Ghalen!" She pushed on his chest, trying to rouse him.

Alaya knelt beside her. "He's not breathing!"

Ghalen reached up and grabbed Sana by the back of the neck, pulling her down and kissing her. Still kissing, Ghalen rolled over on top of her. Sana resisted, but Ghalen pressed her arms over her head and inserted his hips between her legs. His tongue, and the tang of salt and blood, filled her mouth and ignited Sana's Scythian passion.

He pressed harder and she pressed back, and let a moan escape.

Alaya scooted back and giggled.

"Sana?" Ghalen whispered tenderly.

"Yes?" Sana panted and fought the urge to push her pelvis harder against his.

"Where's my knife?"

She looked at him oddly, wondering if she heard him correctly.

He glanced left and his face lit up. "There it is!" He snatched it off the deck, scrambled up and leapt back into the water to rejoin the melee.

Sana exhaled and covered her face with her hands. "I hope it bites his head off."

Alaya giggled again.

12. Gathering of Butchers.

Mother and I walked arm in arm through the Stone Garden. She walked with great pain, and I suspected spring would bring an Offering Festival. Despite her discomfort, we began what would become a tradition upon my return from each quest. In my own private Night of the Forgotten, the Goddess Nuwa showed me the new graves and explained how each had passed.

Their faces drifted through my mind as if I had only seen them yesterday. I wept fresh tears with each name she uttered.

"Let that part of you die, my son, or one day the grief will overwhelm you," Nuwa advised. Her pronouncement's iciness took me aback. "Why do you look at me like that?" Mother's voice carried an unfamiliar edge.

"It is just that I cannot let that part of myself die, no matter how deeply it hurts."

"A few more thousand years of watching them perish may change your mind."

"Do you let yourself grieve for your husbands?"

"A goddess's grief is not your concern." Her eyes glowed in the darkness like a cat.

"I meant no disrespect."

She turned, and we strolled in silence for a few more moments while I collected my thoughts.

"You once told me that a god never forgets."

"Yes. And do you forget?"

"No."

"What is your point?"

"If I remember them, and I live forever, then they will live forever. I will remember those I encountered on my journey, and they, too, will live forever. The grief is a burden, but it is also my redemption."

Mother stared at me, as if seeing me for the first time. "Come, let us climb the Silver Stairs. I will make you breakfast, and you can tell me about your journey."

As we departed, Mother and I passed by the small, unkept mounds along the tree line. These were reserved for stillborn children and babies that died before being given a name.

"There are so many," I whispered.

Mother's pace quickened.

- The Chronicle of Fu Xi.

***

An oily sheen covered the water's surface. Under a dying sun, the beast's blood turned the water black. The carcass lashed alongside the barge had begun to stink. Alaya tenderly rested her head against Levidi's shoulder as they watched the women begin to butcher the wolf fish. "Do anything like that again and I'll kill you," she whispered.

Covered in bruises and abrasions, Levidi merrily hugged her. "You shouldn't worry so much."

"Men with expectant wives shouldn't take foolish chances," Sana said coldly.

Alaya grabbed Levidi's chin and gave him a peck on the cheek. "I forgive you, my brave fisherman."

The women who gathered around the carcass appeared overwhelmed at first by its size. They hesitated. "It's still just a fish," Ro-xandra barked with practical sternness and quickly organized them into two small teams. The first group, led by Ro-xandra, cut away at the tough hide while the second group sliced into the exposed flesh. In between the two groups, Spako grasped Okta's rope, which secured the wolf fish's midsection.

"I've never seen bones like these," Doinna, the talkative and frumpy Minnow girl, remarked as she sliced off a section of rib meat. "They are so soft and springy."

Sana noticed how Doinna always seemed to find an excuse to be around Spako, and wherever Spako went, Bat-or tagged along. That meant Su-gár wasn't far behind, which also meant Ezra would be lurking nearby.

Bat-or and the other children gawked and poked at the beast. Occasionally, Levidi had to shoo them off, only to have them slowly reassemble and begin the process anew.

"We'll have food for months if we can ever butcher that thing." Hands on her hips, Su-gár inspected the carcass. "How are we going to dry all that meat?"

"We need a lot more sticks." Sana looked across the decks.

"We don't have any more sticks." Ro-xandra scoffed.

"What about the rope we found on Okta's raft?" Doinna suggested. "We can string it between poles and hang the meat strips on that."

Okta issued a disapproving grunt.

As the shadows began to lengthen, Sana let her gaze wander from one huddled cluster of Lo to another, scattered across the decks for anything they could use to dry the meat. Her eyes briefly fell upon Alaya's birthing hut, but didn't want to consider dismantling that until the baby was born. She thought of the mast crosspiece on Okta's raft, but that would only hold a few pounds.

We will have to solve this dilemma soon, she thought, *or all this meat will be wasted*. She returned her attention to the carcass, where several men gathered around the creature's mouth. There, Ghalen sweated and huffed trying to cut teeth from the monster's jaws. As he freed a tooth, he passed it to the men. They ogled each serrated triangle in amazement, commenting at what good spear tips they would make.

Sana finally got her hands on one, and inspected it. Ezra appeared beside her, looking over her shoulder with intense curiosity. "I think it's too small to make a good spear tip," he said.

"Yes," she agreed.

Ghalen looked up from his work. "It's perfect for a light fishing spear."

"Or an arrowhead," Sana mused.

"Hmm." Ezra looked at the tooth thoughtfully. "It *would* make an excellent arrowhead."

Ghalen handed her another bloody tooth. "When we find land, you will have to teach us how to make bows and arrows."

"If we can find enough wood, and the right kind, I will," Sana said.

"We should consult the Uros as to what to do with these teeth," Levidi said.

Su-gár stepped back from the carcass and wiped her brow with a bloody hand, looking over her shoulder where Aizarg sat cross-legged, staring at the sea.

"I will ask the Uros regarding the disposition of the teeth," Okta said as he observed the women slowly carving the carcass. "The teeth will not rot — it is the meat we need to worry about. Long strips, ladies. Long strips. Keep as much of that hide intact as you can."

"Easy for you to say." Ro-xandra scoffed, plunging her stone knife into the hide with both hands. "It's like Scythian iron."

Okta handed her his metal knife. "Then here is some Lo iron, old mother."

To Sana's shock, the old hag almost smiled as she took the blade. "Thank you, sco-lo-ti."

"There are no more sco-lo-ti," Okta corrected. "The Uros has declared us one people."

"If you say so." Whatever softness Ro-xandra may have betrayed evaporated. She began to quickly peel away layers of the wolf fish's hide. Soon, gore and strips of flesh lined the barge's side.

Sana leaned out and ran her hand over the beast's gray flesh. If she stroked one way, the skin felt smooth. If she ran her fingers the other way, its roughness threatened to draw blood. This thing existed in a place beyond Sana's experience. Even in death, the creature's muscles felt taut and powerful and dangerous. Sana could never have imagined men, even Scythians, slaying a beast so large, so dangerous, so alien. Yet, the humble Lo did so.

The monster's eyes kept drawing her back. Tilted on its side, only one soulless orb stared up at the sky. *It looks no different in death than in life*, she thought.

"Heavy," Spako huffed. Sana noticed the deck had begun to tilt toward the carcass. Spako struggled to hold the creature against the barge.

"Hmm." Okta looked over the creature. "Relax your grip slightly, Spako."

Spako gladly obliged, and the carcass sank halfway underwater.

"It's not floating." Okta sounded confused.

"Why should it?" Sana asked.

"Most dead fish will float initially. This one doesn't. We may not be able to harvest it much longer."

She turned her attention to Ghalen, just an arm's reach away, as he leaned farther out over the water, merrily prying out one tooth after another. If he leaned out any farther, he'd fall in. She could tell Ghalen was considering slipping into the mire for better access to the creature's jaws. The bloody water around him ebbed with a sluggish thickness. Sana looked west and saw they floated in the center of a widening blood tide stretching toward the bloated sunset.

She caught sight of the first fin's silhouette as it turned broadside to the sun. It stood apart from the glistening sea. Sana spied another, and then another. Soon, dozens, perhaps more, smaller wolf fish began to converge on the Arun-ki.

Sana glanced at Ghalen and saw the water beneath him darken. She snatched him back just as rows of jagged teeth erupted from the water and snapped where Ghalen had just perched. They fell together on the deck, her arms wrapped around his shoulders. Ghalen squeezed Sana's hand in gratitude and quickly took in the scene.

"They are everywhere," he gasped. The fins seemed to materialize from nowhere. The water writhed and foamed in a frenzy as torpedo shapes darted about almost randomly. They attacked the carcass, thrashing and tearing away huge chunks. The women retreated from the carcass as Spako began to struggle to hold the rope. He inched toward the water as his feet slipped on the bloody deck.

"They're on this side, too!" someone shouted from the barge's opposite side.

Okta took his knife from Ro-xandra and, with a clean slice, cut the rope. Spako fell backwards with a thud. The carcass slid away and slowly sank, besieged on all flanks by a writhing mass of wolf fish.

An unexpected cold breeze stirred the deck, as a woman's voice purred from behind Sana. "We have slain a powerful sea god's pet." Sana turned to face Kus-ge. As if in a trance, Kus-ge's eyes rolled back. Her next words were dark and bloody as the sea. "He will take his vengeance."

"White water!" someone shouted.

The decks lurched upward. Amid screams, the world erupted into violence, and the Arun-ki entered its death throes.

13. Into the Chasm.

My sleeping mat had been unrolled and waited for me. Chen's sleeping mat was tightly bound and against the wall. His freshly deceased body waited on a funeral pyre outside.

In Nuwa's Inner Temple, we sat at the small table drinking tea. Mother questioned me about my Journey of Tongues.

Nuwa looked tired under the lantern light. Yet, her questions came quickly and lasted well into the day. I spoke at great length about peoples and lands I had encountered over the past forty years. She took great delight when I spoke in the many languages I had discovered. I continued my tale into the late afternoon. We shared a simple meal of lamb soup and bread as afternoon surrendered to evening.

She lit a candle and placed it between us on the table. "What did you truly learn on your journey?"

I pondered her question for several moments. "I carry home to you three great lessons, Mother. The one I learned first is that the world beyond Nushen is immense, far larger than I could have imagined."

Nuwa's eyes sparkled in that way that betrayed her divine nature, and hinted at the many secrets she kept locked behind them. "Creation is far greater than you can even imagine, Fu Xi. What is your second lesson?"

"The people in the world beyond live in great darkness. Yet, no matter how savage and ignorant, they are really no different that the

mortals that dwell in Nushen. They only need someone to point the way."

Mother stared at her tea and nodded slightly. "And your final lesson?"

I, too, stared down at my tea and the leaves floating at the bottom. "The farther away I journeyed, the more I realized Nushen is my home. Its people will always be my beloved family."

I caught Mother staring at me. The divine light behind her tear-brimmed eyes had ebbed, and I found myself looking at a stranger. She stood, leaned over the table, and took my head into her hands. She lightly kissed my forehead. This was the only time, before or since, my mother had ever kissed me.

"Fu Xi, you shall always be our beloved son," Syning's tender voice echoed with 10,000 whispers. She left the table and walked toward the Outer Temple.

"Come," Nuwa said coldly without turning around. "Night is coming. Help me bury my husband."

- The Chronicle of Fu Xi.

***

To Sana, it felt as if an invisible hand lifted and then threw her forward onto the deck. Terrified wails rose from the jumbled bodies scattered across the barge. Sana found herself near the upwind edge with several others. Before she could collect her wits, the barges lurched and began to spin.

Where only moments ago the sea rested tranquilly under an early-evening sky, it now undulated like a coiling serpent. The seas mounded up in rolling hills, like those of the steppe grasslands. Where once Sana looked across endless blue and green, now she saw angry gray water, foaming at the edges like the spittle of a mad beast. Water sloshed over the pitching deck, soaking her, and spurted between the deck logs like geysers. Beneath Sana, the deck flexed and strained against its bindings, expanding and then squeezing together violently, threatening to crush any foot or hand unlucky enough to slip through.

Blinded by salt water, Sana fought for breath and clung to the slippery bindings for life. Heads bobbed in the water several yards away, some treading water, a few already swimming toward the barge. The first one she recognized was Doinna, and then Ro-xandra. Doinna had begun to swim back, while the old woman struggled against the current.

Doinna quickly crossed the distance and reached for Sana's hand. Straining out as far as she dared, Sana could not reach her. Still lying on her stomach, Sana looked back to see Spako next to her, arms covering his head. He still had the cut rope tied to his waist. "Spako!" she screamed, but the terrified giant would not look up. "Spako!" She kicked him. Spako rubbed the top of his head and gave her a hurt look.

"Hold my feet!" she shouted above the roaring water. His brow dimmed for a moment in confusion before he spotted Doinna struggling at the barge's edge. His enormous hands encircled Sana's ankle. She stretched farther out, midsection hanging over the edge. She clasped Doinna's wrist and quickly pulled her onto the deck. Doinna grabbed the rope around Spako's waist and held on. He encircled her with his meaty arm as they huddled together.

Where is Ghalen? Sana thought, knowing he had been standing beside her before they had been knocked down. Then she saw him about twenty yards beyond Ro-xandra, confidently swimming toward the old woman. What happened next occurred so fast Sana barely had time to register the horror. As Ghalen reached for Ro-xandra, the old woman suddenly seemed to spring halfway from the water, and then lurched sideways in a crimson spray. Ro-xandra met Sana's gaze for a moment before her eyes rolled into the back of her head and she vanished beneath the surface.

Shocked, Ghalen could only tread water as another fin broke the surface several dozen yards behind him. "Swim!"

Sana screamed. Ghalen's powerful strokes seemed to only gain him inches against the powerful current.

The deck shuddered again. The log under Sana shifted violently, and several bindings snapped. Then, Aizarg appeared beside her.

"Spako, untie the rope from your waist," Aizarg commanded. The giant complied, and Aizarg quickly wrapped one end around his wrist and cast the rest toward Ghalen. The frayed end came up several yards short. Ghalen swam harder. Sana's terror became almost unbearable as every few seconds Ghalen disappeared behind the waves. She dared not look away, lest it be the last time she ever saw him. The rope floated limply and began to curl and twist, keeping it just beyond Ghalen's reach. Behind him, several fins drew closer.

Sana saw exhaustion creep over Ghalen's face. "Swim harder!" she shouted.

Something flashed to Sana's right. Alaya screamed as Levidi dove into the water and paddled toward Ghalen. He wrapped the rope several times around one wrist and stretched out with the other hand. What happened next occurred so fast Sana had neither the wits to scream or laugh. She only watched in stunned amazement as events unfolded.

A wolf fish erupted from the water and lunged toward Levidi. Without so much as loosening his grip on the rope, he punched it on the nose. The creature jerked away and darted below the surface.

Sana turned her attention back to Ghalen, but he had vanished. Levidi dove under, and Sana could only watch helplessly as the rope tightened and submerged. Long moments passed. Aizarg leaned forward, peering into the deep. The fins swarmed where Levidi and Ghalen had been only moments ago.

"Aizarg?" Sana's voice cracked.

He ignored her, still intent on the water as another jolt shook the barge. Sana thought she saw the rope vibrate slightly. With a grunt, Aizarg pulled hard. Spako grabbed the line and helped. Levidi broke the surface with an arm wrapped around Ghalen's waist. To Sana's relief, Ghalen's eyes were open, but he looked exhausted. Just as they dragged them onto the deck, the barge shuddered again and pitched hard to one side. Water sloshed over them, and, for a moment, Sana feared the barge wouldn't right itself. Then came a sickening ripping sound, like the skin of a slain animal being torn from its carcass.

Aizarg looked toward the Supply Barge. "The barges are separating. Everyone to the center!"

Sana supported Ghalen. He nodded dismissively. "I'm okay. Help the children."

Someone screamed. They all turned to see the Supply Barge floating by, tattered ropes trailing behind.

"Throw them the rope!" Levidi began to gather the remains of the rope.

"No, they are too far," Aizarg said. "Everyone to the center, now!"

Perhaps half the Lo remained on the Supply Barge, which rapidly drifted away. Sana caught Kus-ge's eyes across the widening gulf, and, for a moment, they shared a common terror.

Aizarg cupped his hands and shouted to Ba-lok on the Supply Barge, "Get everyone to the center! Keep the barge balanced!" Ba-lok nodded and, with a few other men, began to organize the people on his barge.

Despite the bucking deck, the Lo on the Wedding Barge managed to congregate in the center. With all the weight centralized, the vessel stabilized despite the seas becoming rougher. They huddled together around the mast, with Aizarg's staff lodged tightly in its hole. The children nestled in the center, surrounded by the women tightly clinging to them. With the exception of Spako, who gripped the mast with his eyes tightly shut, the men formed the outer ring, grasping one another's forearms to create a living corral to prevent any within from being washed overboard. Sana found herself with the men, grasping Ezra's arm to her right and Ghalen's to the left.

Only two men remained outside the congregation. Using Okta's rope to secure himself to the deck, Aizarg stood along the leading edge, acting as a lookout at what perils lay ahead. Okta remained with his tiny raft, fighting desperately to keep the two vessels joined together.

The barge entered a gauntlet. Exposed boulders and jagged stone pillars flew by, providing Sana some understanding of just how fast they were traveling. Sometimes the barge tilted up high upon the rapids, and Sana felt rocks tear across the vessel's sides and bottom. Then, it would drop almost vertically into dark chasms of rushing water before beginning the cycle all over again.

"Father!" Ezra tried to crawl toward Okta, but the waves dragged him toward the edge. Sana and Ghalen both pulled him back to the center.

Okta pointed in the current's direction. The first land they had spotted since the beginning of the Deluge had ambushed them.

Sana had never seen mountains so high, or so foreboding, and could not understand how they got so close without anyone spotting it. Seeing dry ground did not fill Sana with the hope she had been expecting. The lifeless gray wall thrust straight out of the sea, an impenetrable barrier stretching as far as the eye could see. Sana could not see where the mountains met the water, but she became increasingly aware of roaring like wind, only deeper and louder.

The current seemed to pick up speed, hurling them toward the cliffs. Once again, the Lo were powerless. This time, Sana doubted they would survive. Had the Nameless God finally forsaken the Lo?

Sana struggled to stand as the barge shot atop another crest. From this vantage point, she finally saw the mountains' base. A deadly current trapped the barge, dragging it into a narrow defile between two peaks. The sea poured down into it like a drain. Waves broke against the steep cliffs flanking the sunless chasm. An army of deadly rocks guarded the way, and shredded the sea into violent foam. Sana lifted her head, vainly trying spot the Supply Barge.

With a wet, grinding sound, the barge slammed into several sharp rocks jutting above the water like fangs. It bounced off and began rotating with an ever-increasing speed. Inside the huddle, the children began to scream. Between the spinning, powerful waves and slippery logs, Sana felt herself sliding toward the edge.

"Okta's gone!" she heard Aizarg shout. Okta and his tiny raft were nowhere to be seen. Only splintered wood and tattered bindings remained along that entire side. Several other logs began to loosen and separate.

The Wedding Barge began to disintegrate. A log, jutting out about twenty feet, snagged on a boulder and violently halted the barge's rotation. Everyone, including Aizarg, slammed flat against the deck. The log snapped, and the barge slowly started spinning again, only in the opposite direction. Sana screamed as a gap in the logs opened under her right thigh and then slammed together, trapping her leg in a crushing embrace. As they crested another rapid, the deck expanded again, and the log released its grip and she slipped free.

Sana stared down the defile's jaws. The next plunge would drag them into the gorge. Her stomach lurched as the barge tilted downward and plunged into darkness. A blade-like outcropping sliced the current in two, and blocked the gorge's entrance.

"Brace!" Aizarg shouted.

Sana wanted to shut out the horror, but the Scythian would meet her doom with eyes wide-open. She looked at Ghalen, and reached for him. Before he took her hand, the barge crashed head-on into the outcropping. It cleaved the vessel in two, and she tumbled into the water.

14. Virag's Game.

We watched Chen's body burn until the early hours. Shortly before daybreak, we returned to Nuwa's temple, passing under the Threshold Dragon's watchful gaze.

"Tell me of the omen that called you home," Mother said before we entered the temple.

I stopped and considered the dragon carved into the colonnade. "Far to the south, I came to a warm sea and could go no farther. It was a place that never grew cold, and the shore was white as snow. I lived among a tribe of fishermen called the Kin for several years. They were small and beautiful, like children. They lived naked and in harmony with nature, and shunned violence. They taught me as much as I taught them.

"It was as close as I had come to paradise. If I had not witnessed death among the Kin, I could have mistaken it for the Place of Perfect Happiness from your stories. My time there passed as if a dream."

Mother nodded appreciatively. "And what woke you from your dream?"

I looked to the stars. "One day, a strange song filled the air shortly before sunset. Deep and haunting, a more mournful sound I have never heard. I did not know if it was human or animal, only that it conjured immense feelings of loss and sadness. The villagers fled into the jungle, while I searched for the source. It came from everywhere, and nowhere. I searched until dawn, when the song ceased without warning."

"What did you see when the song ended?" Mother's voice turned grave.

"Far over the sea, there came a great flash of light in the sky. A blazing blue star slowly fell from the heavens, and extinguished before it touched the horizon. I've never witnessed such an event, and knew this must be the sign you had warned me of. I gathered my few belongings and began my return journey to Tortoise Mountain."

- The Chronicle of Fu Xi.

***

The moment the current tore the two barges apart, the Supply Barge had drifted south into calmer waters while the Wedding Barge plunged east into violent currents and quickly out of sight. To Virag, it was as if a hand separated the barges, sending one to certain doom and another to a second chance.

The Minnow Clan's subjugation at the hand of Aizarg and the Crane Clan had ended. A newfound energy and optimism spurred them to action. Ba-lok gathered his men and issued orders. They moved their fresh water, dried fish, sea dog meat, furs, and skins to the barge's center should they encounter more rough water. Freed from Aizarg's shadow, and Kus-ge's brow-beating, Ba-lok exuded newfound confidence. Would it last? Virag doubted it.

The excitement built further when the Minnow realized they were drifting toward the land. To Virag, the mountains looked like a terrible serpent's scaly back jutting from the water. The closer they drifted, the less hospitable it appeared. Virag didn't care; he merely wanted to plant his feet on dry land again. He gathered his meager possessions, a worn blanket and a few furs given to him by Ro-xandra, and settled onto the barge's edge to watch the approaching coast.

As the sun set, Kus-ge appeared beside Virag and stared in silence at land's ever-growing visage until nightfall hid the mountains from view. The Minnow huddled together for warmth and listened to the familiar sounds of sea meeting shore. They waited for dawn to reveal their fate. Virag didn't want to hold any hope for safe landing. *Hope is the appetizer before Despair's main course, the elixir of fools*, he thought. Virag had always survived by accepting reality as Fate deemed to serve it.

Ba-lok kept men ever watchful along the barge's corners, but in the darkest night, land surprised them with a light bump. Dawn revealed gray mists dancing in the mountain's shadow. The vessel had become lodged between two enormous boulders guarding a steep, rocky shelf. Gentle waves lapped against a ledge that was barely wide enough for the barge. It terminated about a hundred paces away from a cliff rising into the clouds. Virag didn't see any way to penetrate inland.

A dead end, he thought. Virag would never admit to himself any twinge of disappointment.

"It's a wasteland," Ba-lok remarked. The Minnow Clan timidly lined up along the barge's edge, as if wondering if the land was real and their long voyage might actually have come to an end.

Wasting no time, Virag snatched his possessions, shoved the hesitant aside, and leapt onto the shore.

"Virag," Ba-lok called out, but Virag ignored him.

The ground felt all wrong, and yet so right. The unyielding rock didn't move, but Virag swore it felt as if it were rocking under his feet. It seemed as if the mountains were floating, too, imperceptibly bobbing, and any thought they were rooted to the earth's bones only a cruel illusion. Virag grabbed one of the boulders to steady himself against the creeping nausea, thinking it would be cruel irony if the mountains truly were floating and the gods had left no dry ground anywhere. *This is real earth*, he thought, *and there are no gods*. Fighting back the queasiness with a few deep breaths, Virag soon felt better.

"We should wait until we know it is safe," Ba-lok called to him.

"You wait." Virag squatted against the cliff as far as he could from the water, and unwrapped a piece of dried fish.

Ba-lok stepped tentatively onto shore and knelt. He picked up a few pebbles and seemed to weigh them in his hand, as if wondering if all of this was real. One by one, the Minnow followed, stumbling clumsily off the barge and quietly milling about as if in a daze. A few women broke into sobs and collapsed to the ground. Virag didn't know if it was in gratitude for deliverance or in mourning for those who had died along the way. He didn't care, and only wished the landing was bigger so he could find a quiet place away from their infernal wailing. A family of three knelt and embraced, crying softly. Men hugged and slapped one another on the backs at their good fortune. Only the children seemed excited. A few giggling boys chased each other. They tried to climb the cliff before Virag shooed them away. Not to be discouraged, the children resigned themselves to scale the boulders on either side of the landing. Then, three Lo in particular caught Virag's attention.

Ten-ye', an older woman just past childbearing age, and her two teenage girls stepped off the barge last. These were Crane women who got trapped on the Supply Barge when the Arun-ki broke apart. It was their sense of isolation that caught Virag's attention, something he had keenly come to understand over the past many months. The three women settled a few feet away, huddling together against the cliff, and wiping away quiet tears. They had nothing other than their clothes.

Ten-ye' took out some sea dog jerky and an iron knife from her loincloth strap and cut two pieces for her daughters. "Let us give thanks to the Nameless God for this deliverance," she whispered to her daughters. "Let us also pray for the deliverance of the Uros and our people."

Virag grunted in amusement. Judging by what he saw yesterday, Aizarg and the rest of the Crane were likely dead. Then Virag's eyes fell on the knife Ten-ye' used to cut the meat.

That's a man's knife, he thought admiringly, *and a fine one, too*. She must have inherited it from her dead husband. Virag's knife, like those of all the Minnow, had been confiscated after the uprising. Without a good knife, they would not last long in the wilderness. *No one here except her has a knife*, he thought.

Ten-ye' caught Virag staring at her and quickly tucked the knife away.

She has nothing to worry about, Virag thought. *At least nothing more than any of them do*. Virag knew the ways of the Lo. The Minnow would simply bring Ten-ye' and her daughters into the fold as another member of the Clan. The Lo tradition of mercy and hospitality were legendary among the steppe peoples. Yet, he knew the Minnow were a different people now. Broken. Virag knew, with a degree of satisfaction, he played no small role in that transformation. *Still*, he thought, *there are only forty-two survivors here, and Aizarg's raft likely met its doom*. The daughters looked like good breeding stock, the kind of women he could have gotten a good price for in his past life. They would likely get taken by one of the bachelors, and begin the process of siring a new generation of Minnow should they survive.

In the meantime, Virag would think of a way to get that knife for his own.

Ba-lok looked about. "Kus-ge? Has anyone seen Kus-ge?"

Virag realized he hadn't seen Kus-ge since dawn. *Maybe she slipped into the water and drowned last night*, he thought hopefully.

Virag had watched the Lo, specifically the Minnow Clan, for months. He peered at them from beneath the canopy in his little boat tied alongside the Arun-ki as the endless rains fell day after day. He studied them from his bare corner of the Supply Barge during the exile following the failed uprising against Aizarg. In all this time, Virag had learned their names, their wants, and their weaknesses. Now, with solid earth at his back, Virag watched them again.

In all the months adrift, Virag hadn't dared himself the luxury of thinking of wine and women. Now that he had solid ground under his feet, he amused himself with thoughts about the Minnow women. As the women and girls passed by on the narrow shore, Virag assessed each one in a new light, with an eye toward the future.

A raven-haired young woman bent over the barge's edge, lifting a bulging waterskin onto the shore. *Kedkar is a good worker*, he thought, *and her figure has filled out on a diet of sea dogs' meat.* She would have fetched at least three silver crowns in Hur-ar. One by one, his attention drifted from woman to woman, girl to girl, and even the hags, assigning each a theoretical value should one day the opportunity to sell them present itself.

He made a game of it, switching from Hur-ar's gold standard to simple barter. *Ten bronze arrowheads for her…ten bear skins for that pair of sisters…*Virag found the game infinitely amusing. Once he had assessed the women's value, Virag turned his attention to the men.

An older man with fresh gray streaks lining his black beard, and deep crags around his eyes, leaned against the southern boulder. Virag recalled his name was Marebi, a widower and village blacksmith. Virag would not sell him. Such a skill was too valuable.

Two children, the girl Rev and her little brother Bazee, squatted next to Marebi as he picked through small stones and pebbles. *He's teaching them to look for flint*, Virag thought. It didn't take long before the children grew bored and ran off. Their parents had both survived. During the long voyage, particularly during the exile, these irritating brats always seemed to be underfoot. Virag also noticed these children didn't seem to be afraid of anything, particularly him.

Two copper for the boy and five silver for the girl, he thought. Bazee and his sister sprinted toward Virag and skidded to a halt near him. They looked up the cliff, as if considering climbing it.

"Come here." Virag crooked his finger at them, and tried not to sound too scary. They stared, but came no closer. Virag reached into his pouch and pulled out a chunk of dried sea dog meat. "You two look hungry." He waved it in front of them as one would tease a dog. "It may be a long time before we catch something to eat again, eh?"

Bazee licked his lips and reached out before Rev slapped his hand away. "You know Momma says don't talk to him!"

Virag grinned and tore the flesh in two. "It's yours, anytime you want it. And there is more."

"What do you want?" the girl asked suspiciously, looking over her shoulder to see if her parents were watching, but they were occupied offloading supplies.

Smart girl, he thought. "Just to talk. No one will talk to me, and I get lonely. We'll make a deal. You get hungry, you come see me. I ask questions, you answer them."

"What kind of questions?"

"Easy ones." He extended the morsels. "This one is free. Think about it. Next time, we chat." Before his sister could stop him, the boy snatched the meat and crammed it in his mouth. Reluctantly, she took the other piece before they darted off to try their luck scaling the boulders.

Satisfied, Virag put his hands behind his head and leaned back, relishing the cliff's firmness. He ignored the cold ground and the dampness seeping through the blanket. He was content for the moment. Virag felt his strength and confidence returning with every moment. He had survived. Fate had handed Virag a new chance, and he did not intend to squander it. They had reached a junction, and a new set of circumstances held rein.

Virag took a deep, cleansing breath, and considered the situation. Fate, it seemed, wasn't going to make it easy on him. The barge teetered steeply away from the shore, as the water inched lower by the minute. There appeared to be no exit from this narrow ledge. Virag began to suspect they were actually marooned high upon a mountainside. How high, he had no idea. If the retreating waters revealed terrain below as steep as that above, they could soon find themselves trapped.

The Minnow had no ropes to secure the barge to the rocks. Even if Ba-lok and his men had the strength to drag the barge farther onto the shore, there was no room to do so. It had begun to tilt backwards now so steeply that its bottom became visible. The swollen log's undersides were completely blackened with slimy rot, and were beginning to split like meat left too long on the fire. Every few minutes, a wet, popping noise announced a deck binding, strained beyond its limit, had surrendered. The stench of rotting wood permeated the air.

Even Virag knew the barge was dead. *Let it die*, he thought. *This barren ledge is a better place to die than the open sea.*

Hevas, Ba-lok's best friend and second in command, walked along the cliff's base, obviously trying to deduce a way out of their predicament. The squat, muscular man shot Virag a foul look as he walked by. *He's strong*, Virag thought, *and smart. He might be a useful henchman if I can convince him to follow me*. Virag had sensed Hevas's frustration with Ba-lok from the beginning. Like many of the Lo, Hevas possessed a twisted sense of loyalty that compelled him to follow men weaker than himself. It was said among the Sammujad that the wise man knows power is only for the strong.

The Sammujad are all dead, he thought grimly. *Well, all except me.*

The Minnow, namely Ba-lok and Kus-ge, had been allies of convenience against Aizarg and his lot. The time had come to reassess his alliances. Virag knew patience was in order. Watch. Wait. Plan. He must not act, or react, until necessary.

Around him, the Minnow appeared to be in a daze, which didn't surprise Virag. At sea, they knew how to survive. On this barren shore, they were helpless. By late morning, they had offloaded their belongings and supplies. After that, Ba-lok's decisiveness seemed to evaporate. By noon, paralysis gripped the Minnow Clan. Too afraid to attempt to push inland, and too terrified to chance the sea on the decrepit barge, most huddled in family groups.

To Virag, the answer to their predicament lay in plain sight — climb the cliffs, and look for a way off this narrow shelf. Seaweed and slime coated the rocks, making them too slippery, but the sun would take care of that in a day or two. Virag knew these Minnow had never seen mountains, but he knew the high country, having led several expeditions into the Adyghe Mountains to trade with the Aryan tribes.

Mountains are always hard lands, Virag thought, *and hard lands always breed hard men. If such hard men survived the apocalypse, they would likely be savage beyond reckoning. If Ba-lok and his men stick their noses too far into these mountains, they may not return.* Virag had no doubt the Minnow would hinder his chances to survive. He would leave them as soon as the opportunity presented itself.

A loud pop echoed across the shore and drew everyone's attention. With a jolt, the barge slid backward several feet before grinding to a halt. The Minnow exchanged worried looks. *It won't be long now*, Virag thought. He looked around and realized there was no place to relieve himself except in plain sight. "Just like being back on that infernal barge," he muttered. He stood and stretched.

The barge's impending threat to slide into the sea motivated the men to gather around Ba-lok, beseeching him as to what was to be done. Ba-lok looked unsure again, indecision etched into his face. *He's running out of time and he knows it*, Virag thought. *He is the son of a sco-lo-ti, still unable to live up to his father's great name. No longer does he live in Aizarg's shadow, nor does he have his grandmother whispering in his ear. He is a lost leader of a lost people. There are seeds of dissent here*, Virag thought. *Such cracks can be exploited.*

At sea, Virag was as helpless as a baby. On land, he was a fox. With this handful of men, and their meager resources, he could forge a new beginning. He need only remove Ba-lok from the situation.

And Kus-ge…

Virag looked about for her. She was nowhere to be seen, and no one, especially Ba-lok, seemed too concerned. Kus-ge's madness and near catatonic state had isolated her for weeks, making the Minnow patesi-le easy to ignore. Virag chuckled, thinking how Ba-lok in particular had made an art of ignoring his wife.

Virag strolled over to the ledge and looked down at the four-foot drop to the water. The current ran strong from north to south. If she fell in during the darkness, her body was long gone.

"I could have once fetched a fortune for the likes of her in Hur-ar," Virag whispered to himself. Her deep black mane, wild eyes, dark olive skin, and lithe figure had once even seduced the mighty Bal-eeb, Prince of Hur-ar. Kus-ge would still bring a good price, as long as the buyer didn't discover her madness before gold was exchanged.

Virag urinated over the edge, and then drifted closer to where the men held council. Two men had become de facto leaders of the divided Minnow, and argued their case to Ba-lok.

"Climbing the mountain is impossible." A wiry man called Zirev, Rev and Bazee's father, wrung his hands. "If we act now, it's not too late to push off and look for a better landing."

"We can't control the barge," Hevas snapped at Zirev as if he were a fool. "We were lucky to make this shore. If we encounter the same conditions the Wedding Barge did, we will soon meet the Crane's doom."

Zirev ignored him. "If we stay, we die trapped here like animals to starve!"

"We keep trying to scale the boulders on either side of the shore," Hevas countered. "There may be a way along the ridge."

"Bah! They are too high and too slick," Zirev said.

"They will dry."

The men devolved into shouting, despite Ba-lok's feeble attempts to restore order. Then, with a dull thud, Ba-lok dropped to the ground on all fours, shaking his head. Blood smeared his face. The men spun about, looking for the attacker.

Virag, too, looked for where the attack came from and noticed a furry lump lying on the ground in front of Ba-lok.

"Sco-lo-ti." Hevas knelt beside Ba-lok.

"I'm okay." Ba-lok slowly got to his feet and looked about. He wiped away the light smear of blood. "This isn't my blood."

Hevas knelt and picked up the mass of fur, revealing two scrawny rabbits, freshly gutted but not skinned, and bound together by a thin leather cord. Virag looked up and shielded his eyes from the sun. It only took a moment for him to recognize the silhouette lording high above them atop the cliff.

"Kus-ge?'" Ba-lok blurted.

"Hmm." Virag grinned. "Maybe she is still worth something."

A creaking rose behind them. The Minnow Clan turned in time to see the barge tilt and slide backwards with a wet, splintering sound. Before anyone could react, it fell into the water with a dull splash. In moments, the bindings burst, and the Supply Barge fragmented into individual logs, which drifted out of sight. Ba-lok and the rest of the Minnow Clan stared mutely at the lapping water where their barge once rested.

Virag returned his attention to Kus-ge.

"A hidden path lies beyond the southern boulder. It eventually leads up the cliff," Kus-ge shouted down to them.

"Perhaps we should gather some men and scout it," Ba-lok stuttered.

"It looks like she already has." Virag laughed and sat down again. He stretched out his legs, leaned back, and prepared to take a nap as the Minnow held their silly councils. For him, the path forward had become clear. The men talked, the women gathered driftwood and prepared camp, and Virag calculated the odds.

15. The Mountain's Shadow.

"You witnessed a female dragon's passing. From what you told me, it must have been an ancient one." Exhausted, Nuwa sat down on the stone bench beneath the Threshold Dragon. Her voice sounded weary. "When a doe dragon knows her time is near, she will take flight and climb high into the night sky upon what is called the Mother of Winds. There, she will sing her death song. In the first rays of daylight, her blood turns to fire and she will plummet to her death."

I sat next to my mother. "How do you know she was ancient?"

She shrugged. "The older the dragon, the longer her death song. You said this one lasted from dusk to dawn."

I contemplated what she had said. "Do you know what she sang about?"

"I do, my son, but humor your mother and tell me your thoughts. You heard her song, I did not."

"Loss," I said without hesitation.

The sun peeked over the forest beyond Nushen's tranquil valley. Nuwa, her shell's eyes pale and wrinkled, stared straight into the rising sun. "Sleep well tonight. When you feel rested, return to Nushen and visit the house of Nóngmín the farmer. Learn all you can from him. One year from today, you will set out on your next journey."

- The Chronicle of Fu Xi.

***

Wet sand squished up between Aizarg's toes as he struggled against land's alien solidness. He staggered forward with Bat-or's unconscious body slung over his shoulder. Rapids roared behind Aizarg, and his people's moans rose ahead of him. The Lo were strung along the shore amid the Wedding Barge's splintered remains. Every time Aizarg encountered a clump of dazed survivors, he met familiar, bewildered eyes. As Aizarg passed them, they stood and staggered after him. Some limped, but all were able to walk.

Levidi came running up the narrow sandbar, splashing through the shallow water, and embraced Aizarg. "Are you hurt?"

Aizarg shook his head.

"Bat-or?"

"He swallowed a lot of water, but I don't think he's hurt. Alaya?"

Levidi desperately glanced behind Aizarg. "I prayed she was with you!"

Aizarg shook his head grimly. "I have not seen her, but our people are strung far upstream and probably on the opposite shore as well." Aizarg looked back at the narrow gorge where the river spit them out into a wide estuary. Here, the waters slowed and flattened into shimmering ripples, as if exhausted from miles of unceasing violence. The river continued to spread out before being received by the open sea. Aizarg could see the bottom almost to the other shore. A sandbar choked with shattered timber blocked the estuary. This is where most of the raft's debris came to rest.

Several Lo staggered across the sandbar from the other shore. Aizarg saw Ghalen helping them. His stomach lurched when he spotted bodies splayed against the timber piles along the sandbar. "Ghalen!" Aizarg shouted, and pointed to the timber piles. Ghalen nodded and rushed to their aid.

Aizarg glanced around again as Bat-or groaned on his shoulder. "Have you seen Su-gár?"

Levidi pointed downstream. "She's helping the injured." Levidi's eyes widened. "Your staff?"

Aizarg considered his empty hand. "I can't worry about such things now. We must gather our people and care for the injured. That is all that matters. Go upstream, look for survivors, and bring them back here." He grasped Levidi's shoulder. "Don't worry, we'll find her." Aizarg pushed down his own fears to give his friend whatever strength and hope he could summon, but knew his words did little to calm Levidi's worry.

Levidi rushed upstream while Aizarg limped downstream. Bat-or moaned again and began to cry. Aizarg cradled his son in his arms and hugged him. "Everything will be all right."

Most of the Lo congregated just beyond the sandbar on the estuary's northern shore. Here, a wide promontory jutted into the sea. Su-gár rushed across the sand. Upon seeing her, Bat-or began to wail and held his arms out for her. Sobbing, Su-gár took Bat-or and embraced Aizarg's neck. "I thought I'd lost you!"

Aizarg nodded, fighting back the emotions threatening to paralyze him. He couldn't afford to surrender to them now.

"I can't find Ezra," she said.

"We'll find him. I need to you care for Bat-or. We must gather our people here on this beach and account for everyone. Find out who is hurt."

Ghalen led a line of survivors into their midst. Around them, people collapsed onto the sand. Some wailed and asked if anyone had seen their loved ones, while others embraced family.

Ghalen, only covered with a few scrapes, desperately looked about. "Sana isn't here. Did you see what happened to her?"

Aizarg shook his head. "I saw her fall in when we split in two. After that, I don't know. Levidi is looking upstream."

"I think she washed down the other channel." Ghalen looked lost. "I taught her to swim. She's strong."

"She *is* strong." He clasped Ghalen's shoulder. "Let's care for everyone here, then we'll begin to look for her."

Aizarg's gaze fell upon his people gathering on the beach. He searched their faces, struggling to place who was missing. Judging by their numbers, it appeared most had survived.

"What do we do, Uros?" a voice rose from the huddled assembly.

"Where do we go?" cried another.

Aizarg clasped his hand as if to raise his staff, only to remember it was gone. Doubt overwhelmed him. Aizarg felt as if he were missing a limb.

His people were on their feet, pressing in with beseeching eyes and outstretched arms. They shouted for deliverance. "What shall we eat?"…"Night is coming! Where shall we sleep?"…"We have no blankets!"

Aizarg felt like he was drowning again, sinking below his people's overwhelming needs. He searched for his voice, but could not find it. His chest felt hollow, bereft of willpower.

A man's solitary cry rose up from beyond the outstretched hands.

"Ezra!" Su-gár cried and dashed toward where the river met the sea. Aizarg and the rest followed.

The mountains' shadows fell far out to sea, blocking the sun and wind. The sandy estuary widened into a rocky, jagged shoreline which fell steeply toward the water. The waves didn't break against the rocky shore, but instead flowed swiftly parallel to the coast.

Covered with bloody scrapes and bruises, Ezra perched on the slick, algae-coated rocks and stared out to sea. "Father!" he shouted through cupped hands.

Aizarg and the rest gathered behind him. Far beyond the shadows, the waning day's orange light brightly lit a small raft bobbing on choppy waters. Aizarg could just make out Okta hoisting the makeshift sail.

"He's going to have a difficult time tacking against the wind and tide," Ghalen remarked.

"Father!" Ezra shouted again, waving his arms high over his head. "We're over here!"

"I can't believe he let himself get swept over the sandbar," Ghalen said. "I'd have thought he'd be able to ground it."

Bat-or made a dash to the water as if to play, but Aizarg pulled him back. "No, stay away from the water." The current looked wickedly strong. Aizarg could see the tide visibly retreat. Before their eyes, the estuary began to transform into small, stair-step waterfalls. A dizzying sense of scale assaulted Aizarg, as he realized where they stood was likely a mountainside before the flood.

Okta's sail rose and instantly billowed.

"Okta!" Ghalen joined Ezra in shouting.

"Why isn't he tacking the sail?" one of the men remarked. "It's going to take him forever to get back to shore."

"The wind and current are going to put him several miles south," Ghalen said. "I'll form a group of men, and we'll follow him along the coast."

"I'll go with you," Ezra said.

Suddenly, Levidi pushed through the crowd, looking out at the shrinking raft. "Is she with him?" he panted. "Is Alaya on the raft with him?"

"No, he is alone," Ghalen replied. "Once we recover Okta, we will form a search party for the missing."

As they talked, Okta quickly and efficiently moved about the raft, adjusting the rigging. The sail remained fully into the wind, and the raft rode upon the outgoing waves, gliding swiftly to the southeast toward the darkening horizon.

Ezra turned to Aizarg. "Why is it taking him so long to turn back?"

A terrible realization crept over Aizarg. Ghalen met Aizarg's eyes with a puzzled expression, and then an unspoken understanding passed between them. Levidi hung his head low and put a gentle arm over Ezra's shoulder, followed by Ghalen. Puzzled, Ezra looked around at those surrounding him.

Su-gár began to quietly sob.

Ezra's confusion deepened. "Uros, why isn't Okta turning around?"

"Because he can't," Aizarg whispered.

Ezra looked back at the raft. "Of course he can. He just has to turn south and tack to the shore. You said it yourself, Ghalen."

"He's leaving," Aizarg whispered. "Okta has served his penance, and can no longer touch land again. When Okta swore his spear at the Gathering of Boats, he sacrificed himself for his people, corrupting his soul to walk upon land in order to save the Lo Nation. He succeeded. Redeemed, he sails to find his people."

Aizarg wanted to believe the Carp Clan were alive and afloat somewhere out there.

Ezra angrily shrugged off the comforting hands and lunged for the water. "Father!" he screamed, "Come back!" Ezra splashed into the surf amongst the sharp rocks and instantly lost his footing, falling head-first and almost striking a stone. With considerable effort, Ghalen and Levidi pulled him from the water.

"Leave me alone." Ezra shoved them away and wiped tears with the heels of his hands. The people watched in silence, helpless as Ezra paced back and forth along the rocky drop.

Aizarg saw the pain and grief raging inside the young man, struggling to break free.

"He goes in search of his people," Ghalen said, desperately trying to comfort Ezra.

"Am I not his son?" Ezra shouted back. "Am I not good enough to be among the Carp?" He looked at Aizarg like a wounded animal. The Uros searched for the right words to ease his pain, to make Ezra understand, but couldn't find them.

Su-gár slipped unnoticed to Ezra's side and took his hand. He tried to pull away, but she refused to let go. "I am afraid, Ezra." Once again, Ezra tried to pull away, though only half-heartedly. Su-gár held on. "I am afraid," she repeated and gestured to the people. "We are all afraid. You told us stories of the steppe, and the giant mountains and all the adventures you and your sister had there. Your stories filled me with wonder, but now that I see mountains with my own eyes I am afraid."

Still staring out to sea, Ezra grew still.

"Okta told me once you are like your sister." Su-gár caressed his chest. "You are brave in ways we cannot be. You do not fear the mountains, like Okta does not fear the sea. Okta knew this, and that is why he did not take you."

Large, silent tears rolled down Ezra's cheeks. She lifted his chin. "With you, I will not fear the mountain."

Ezra buried his head in her shoulder and wept without shame. Su-gár embraced him, and they cried as one. Bat-or left Aizarg's side and hugged Ezra's leg. Levidi and Ghalen returned their comforting hands to Ezra's shoulders, and this time he did not shrug them off. The rest of the Lo closed in and surrounded Ezra, hands stretching forward in shared comfort and grief.

Aizarg stood apart and turned to the sea. Far in the distance, in the last glimmer of the dying day, Okta looked back and raised a hand in farewell. Aizarg raised his hand and uttered a silent prayer to the Nameless God. He thought about the day along the Black River when they set sail on that raft. Aizarg remembered what he said to Okta when they first beheld the flooded marshes.

"Do not fear this strange new sea, Sco-lo-ti of the Carp Clan," the Uros called out in a voice high and strong against the wind and sea. "Do not lose faith. The Nameless God did not bring you this far to abandon you now. Your people are out there, waiting for you. Wherever they are, that is your home." Aizarg lowered his hand and whispered, "The sea has washed his soul clean. Okta is, and will forever be, a man of the Lo."

As darkness crept over the waters, the last surviving raft of the Lo flotilla vanished over the horizon. The Uros turned his back on the sea, and led his people deeper into the mountain's shadow.

16. Mystery, Part 1.

Nuwa sent me on several quests bringing agriculture to Cin. I spent a decade in the north teaching tribes how to plant millet and wheat, and then another decade in the south teaching those peoples how to grow rice.

When I returned home, my adolescent body had fully matured. I appeared as a man in his early twenties. Though my mind and heart were ancient, I was plagued with a young man's desires.

Mother had taught the villagers the fundamental arts of civilization, both the masculine and feminine, long before my birth. Those skills were passed from generation to generation, even modified and improved over the centuries. I learned those arts not from Nuwa, but from the villagers themselves.

I had many teachers in Nushen, but no one to explain the mysteries of women.

Then, one summer afternoon, Nuwa sent me to the house of Xigong the Weaver to prepare for my next journey.

- The Chronicle of Fu Xi.

***

The scent of roasting meat woke Sana's nose, which woke her belly, which woke her mind. She opened her eyes to a roaring campfire surrounded by darkness. Sana found herself on a blanket. A spit with small meat strips, perhaps fish, hung over the fire; the strips were beginning to turn brown. Comfort and confusion battled for dominance. Dull pain wracked her limbs, confirming this wasn't the afterlife. She

113

reached beyond the blanket and pushed her fingers into smooth, well-rounded pebbles until she touched the damp sand beneath. She heard rushing waters nearby, and knew this camp wasn't far from the rapids. The land's solidness felt odd, and she imagined she could feel the deck's ghostly movements beneath her. She clenched a handful of earth and held it to her nose, inhaling its muskiness.

"Thank you," she whispered to the Nameless God. Sana wanted to cry great sobs of joy and sadness at her deliverance. Instead, she stretched like a cat, rolled on her side, and let the fire's luxurious warmth wash over her.

This side of the blanket was hot, so Sana slid over it and let the heat soak deep into her aching muscles. Sana laid her head on her arm and stared into the flames. She enjoyed the reality that no deck logs poked her back, and sea water didn't soak her bottom. Despite her hunger, she didn't want to move, ever.

No one shared the campfire. A part of her cried for answers, to call out for the others, to hear the story of who pulled her from the rapids and how they arrived here, wherever here was. The other part felt safe and cared for, and satisfied to wait. Sana could tell by the smell and the way the thin fillets browned over the spit that they would soon be ready.

The campfire summoned the Scythian's childhood memories. Sana closed her eyes and remembered how her body sometimes ached after a long day riding, and how she would curl up by the fire just like now. This felt like home. She could almost smell the horses.

Sana sniffed the air. She *could* smell horses. "Ghalen," she called out, just above a whisper. She caressed the blanket. *Wool.* The Lo did not use wool.

Footsteps approached. A horse whinnied.

Sana bolted upright and reached for her daggers. Gone.

Across the fire, a man emerged from the darkness and considered her. He held her red metal dagger.

***

Fu Xi considered the beauty crouching across the fire, as if ready to spring at him. He balanced the heavy blade sideways in his open palm in a non-threatening manner. He didn't want to spook her more than she was. She reacted like a trapped animal.

Fu Xi raised the blade and spoke in Atlantean, the language of Leviathan and Amiran, hoping he would get a reaction. "You and this dagger were the last thing I expected to find washed up along this shore." She made no appearance of comprehension. He switched tongues, this time speaking Attican, the language Amiran said was spoken by those who served the Gray-Eyed Queen. "I thought it best to confiscate your weapons until we get to know each other better." He held up the woman's four other small daggers wrapped in a leather strap that had begun to rot. The steel blades showed signs of corrosion, as if exposed to salt water without being properly oiled and cleaned.

Her eyes narrowed on the blades, but again, remained silent. He switched back to Cin. "Do you know how difficult it was to get those small, wet knots untied from around your thigh?" Fu Xi sat down with a huff on a log across the fire and tossed the four small daggers in front of her. "You can have those back. Don't worry, your honor is still intact." He tucked the red blade into his belt.

The barbarian woman frowned at the sight of her weapons so casually returned by a possible enemy. Fu Xi enjoyed her confusion. "It's not that I trust you, it's just you can't hurt me with those." He patted the red blade. "This one is different. I'm going to keep this."

Fu Xi had followed the retreating flood until he found himself trapped between sea and these mountains' east face. He had spent days looking for a pass west through the maze of peaks and flooded canyons. Eventually, he'd settled on this narrow, but passable canyon and followed the river upstream. Soon, the bank became more precarious, and the canyon steeper, forcing him into a tributary's side-canyon. He knew this river wasn't naturally this high or violent. The waters were brackish, hinting at a salt sea somewhere on the other side of this mountain range. Then, before sunset, the bank opened onto a wide, tranquil stretch of river. The canyon widened. Hundreds of crows gathered along a sandbar strewn with broken timber, feeding on dead fish washed up in the eddies. These were the first birds Fu Xi had seen since leaving the Tranquil Valley. It's also where he had found the unconscious woman draped across a log. Crows had surrounded her, waiting to feast.

Fu Xi removed the stick from the spit and popped a fillet in his mouth, gingerly chewing the piping-hot meat. Dead fish carpeted an eddy along the opposite shore. Some were mountain trout, while others were brightly colored saltwater fish. Hardy carp and salmon swam slowly in a circle, trapped in a calm backwater on this side of the channel. Fu Xi was thankful the woman remained unconscious all afternoon, and didn't see his antics trying to scoop fish out with his hands.

The dark-haired woman remained in a defensive crouch, but didn't bolt. He held out the stick with its remaining fillets. "Eat. If I wanted to kill you, you'd be dead."

The woman snatched a piece, scooted away, and crouched at the shadows' edge. She never took her eyes off Fu Xi as she devoured the fish. He shrugged. "Have it your way. It's warmer over here." Fu Xi looked up and sniffed the air. "The water is warm, but the air is cool. Mist will choke these canyons before dawn." He could already see a few fog tendrils hovering above the firelight and mixing with the smoke. Fu Xi returned his attention to his meal. "There is snow covering the peaks to the north and south. The Emperor of Heaven is returning nature's cycles to their rightful places. I think spring is coming, but the snows may not be over. It's best we hurry west and find where these warm waters"—he pointed the stick at her—"and you, come from. Hopefully, the Deluge retreats there, too." Fu Xi grabbed another piece and placed the stick back on the spit.

He chewed slowly, considering the young woman as he occasionally spat small bones into the fire.

She looks like a woman who has seen much of life, he thought, *but with a body of a girl just coming into her own.* She caught his stare and defensively pulled her knees closer to her chest.

She knows what I'm thinking, he thought, amused.

The woman stared at the remaining fish on the spit. Fu Xi motioned invitingly. "Go ahead." She snatched all but one strip. He laughed. "You are a good guest. I've had my fill. You can take that one, too." He pointed at the remaining strip. She plucked it and quickly gobbled it up.

"You're healthy. You've obviously been eating. I also doubt you swam down this gorge. That log you were draped over looked to have once been part of a raft. That means you were not alone." Fu Xi leaned back and stretched his legs toward the fire. "Where are your friends, I wonder?"

She finished the fish and licked her fingers. The girl tied the thong sheathing her blades to her upper thigh. Then, she curled up on the blanket, all the time never taking her eyes off him. They remained that way for much of the night. Fu Xi stared into the fire and remembered. She stared at him, her thoughts a mystery. Occasionally, he fed driftwood to the fire. The crackle mixed with the ever-present echo of thundering waters.

"If you are not going to sleep, perhaps we can talk. Or maybe I'll talk and you listen. There will come a day we will understand each other, and I will not be able to speak so freely, so I better enjoy this opportunity." He chuckled again, but his mirth didn't seem to infect her.

"I can't blame you for being suspicious. I wouldn't let my guard down either, no matter how my host tried to allay my concerns." He poked the embers with a thick stick. "It's been a long time since I've talked to anyone except a horse, and he isn't much for company." Fu Xi chewed on that thought for a moment. Heise was tied to a log just beyond the firelight. "Have you ever seen a horse?" He remembered how villagers along his journey from Wu reacted in terror to his horses. "Somehow, I think you'll handle it. You'll have to, or walk. I don't have time to teach you to ride, especially Heise. He's temperamental." Fu Xi paused to reconsider. "Arrogant is more accurate. He needs a strong hand."

Hearing his name, Heise gently whinnied from the darkness. The woman bolted upright and peered toward the sound.

Fu Xi grinned. "You can see him at first light." He poked the fire again. "Huise would have been a better mount for you. You should have seen her. She was strong and gentle." Sadness washed over him as he remembered escaping the Roof of the World, the enormous mountains that marked Cin's western border. The journey killed her, but not before she carried him to safety. "She saved me from a horrible fate, you know. I would have been crushed and buried under a mountain of ice, perhaps for thousands of years, unable to die."

Fu Xi caught her staring at him quizzically. She didn't appear as tense, but he could tell the woman would never fully let her guard down. She stretched out and placed her head on her arm. Her eyes softened under the fire's spell as a curl of luxurious hair fell across her cheek. The flickering light danced across her curves. Fu Xi guarded himself against letting his gaze linger too long.

"Mind you, I am no stranger to solitude. I have spent years without seeing another soul. In the end, I always knew there would eventually be someone to share my tales, even if it was my mother. This time, I didn't know if that would hold true.

"When Mother said I would find no men on my journey, I didn't think about finding a woman." He waved his hand dismissively. "Oh, I don't count the donkey men. I'm not sure they were human, or even real. So much of that time seems like a dream." Fu Xi watched the firelight dance across her skin. Her body shimmered through the smoke and heat. "You seem like a dream."

Fu Xi realized he let his gaze linger too long. She slowly drew her legs closer to her chest, and slid a hand close to the daggers' hilts.

She's tough, Fu Xi thought.

"Amiran told me only the Atticans and Atlanteans possessed steel, and yet you do not appear to speak either tongue. Your physical features also remind me of Amiran's young apprentices, Ercole and Elda. You possess four blades of some of the finest steel I've ever seen, and one blade of orichalcum. I will discover your name in the morning, and you mine. That is how we shall begin our journey into each other's secrets. Until then, I shall call you Mystery."

Driftwood was plentiful, so Fu Xi kept the fire roaring. Always one to enjoy long silences, now he had an urge to talk. Mystery didn't seem to have any inclination to sleep, and kept Fu Xi under her gaze the way a tiger might wait for an opportunity to pounce.

Fu Xi slid off the log, and used it as a backrest. He considered the flames. "I taught fire craft to the Tall Men on many of my early journeys. The ice covered most of the land back then. Tall Men were so rare in those days, with darker skin to match the deep forests where they dwelt." He glanced up to the sky where the Milky Way cut across the canyon high above.

"It took me many centuries before Nuwa said she could finally smell the smoke of a thousand campfires across the Four Winds. Men feared fire. Fire was the servant of dragons, and dragons despised mankind, especially the Tall Men."

Fu Xi shook his head at the darkness, as if it still held a threat. "Bull dragons used to live in high country like this. If one caught wind of you stumbling into its territory, Nuwa herself couldn't save you." He threw a stick on the fire. Embers erupted and climbed into the night. "Even a god must retreat before dragon fire." Fu Xi considered her. "I don't suppose you've ever seen a dragon?" She made no response other than slightly lifting one eyebrow.

He reluctantly pulled his attention away from her and back to the fire. "Yes, funny thing, fire. It's warm and beautiful until it burns you."

Under Mystery's smoky gaze, Fu Xi spoke well into the night. It felt more like a confession. He spoke of ages forever vanished. He did not care if she understood, only that she listened. The words tumbled out and flowed into the night. He told Mystery about his beloved Nushen, one moment laughing at tales of joyous homecomings, and growing somber when remembering the Stone Garden. Fu Xi wanted someone else to remember those he once loved, their faces, hopes, and passions. The god spoke openly of Nuwa's Three Realms, divulging secrets never revealed to a mortal. Somewhere in the telling, Mystery closed her eyes.

Fu Xi watched her sleep and spent the remainder of the night studying the red blade. This knife, and how the barbarian woman came to possess it, deeply perplexed the demigod. In many aspects, it was almost identical to Nuwa's Offering Blade. The golden spirit dragon twisted a third of the way down the crimson blade, just like Nuwa's Offering Blade. Unlike Nuwa's instrument of renewal, this dagger had a slightly longer blade that tapered to a narrow point. Nuwa's Offering Blade had a broader, leaf-like tip. In all the epochs on Tortoise Mountain, he'd never known Nuwa to possess more than one Offering Blade.

He wouldn't know Mystery's secrets until he could talk to her. That process would begin in the morning.

The firelight reflected off the red blade, bathing Mystery in bloody light. Soon, the neglected fire subsided to embers, ready to be rekindled with the new day.

17. Sea of Lies, Shard of Truth.

The widow received me with great respect. With rosy cheeks and twinkling eyes, Xigong possessed a warm, welcoming spirit. Her back strap and loom bar hung on the wall. Baskets filled with hemp flax were piled in the corner. We spent that first afternoon becoming reacquainted over tea and custard tarts. When I departed on my last journey, she was a young bride. Now she had become a plump, jovial widow. She told me about her marriage, her late husband, and how she lamented that she had no son to carry on his name. She caught me up on the comings and goings among the village families and the juiciest gossip since my departure.

Finally, as the shadows grew long and the tarts were gone, she leaned closer. "It is not for me to question the Son of the Goddess Nuwa, beloved be her name, but it is said in Nushen 'men till, women weave.' I am curious — why do you want to learn a woman's craft, Lord Fu Xi?"

"Lady Xigong, as the goddess once taught men to hunt you will teach me to weave. I will then teach women across Cin's far distant corners. Every bolt of cloth spun until the end of time will trace its patterns back to you. You, Xigong, shall be known as the Mother of Weavers."

She fanned herself, flush with excitement. "Mother of Weavers? Oh, my! When do you want to start?"

Distant thunder rumbled, and I didn't hear the interloper slip into the hut behind me. Dressed in common rough-hewn trousers and shirt,

121

she dumped a basket overflowing with sumac between us and took off her dǒulì hat. "Mother, there isn't enough here to dye Chuanli's trousers. I will go back for more later, but rain is coming."

Lady Xigong rose excitedly. "Shinglay, we have a visitor."

Maybe it was the way Shinglay's luxurious hair tumbled about her shoulders. Perhaps it was the tiny dirt smudge beside her upturned nose, or the innocent way she cocked her head when she didn't recognize me. I still don't know how it happened, but in that moment the centuries fell away, and I was truly a young man.

- The Chronicle of Fu Xi.

***

The mountaintop made a perfect prison, but within its confines, Atamoda had almost complete freedom. Her gold bracelets and bejeweled necklaces jingled with each step. Her flowing golden garments were as light as cobwebs and shimmered like the sun on the sea. Atamoda's Lo sensibilities still found them restricting. Her sandals, with their delicate golden cords, would disintegrate should she try to run, but proved effective at protecting her feet from the bone shards littering the encampment. Atamoda didn't want to look at the bones, because they reminded her what the Olmecs did to the weak.

Every time Atamoda stepped from the luxurious tent, she knew Kol-ok's fate hung upon Leviathan's whim, and she must do all in her power to protect her son. Atamoda knew the opulence Leviathan showered upon her proved just as effective a cage as the one her son had occupied for these many months.

Atamoda pulled her cloak tight against the wind as she skirted the tents reserved for the Olmec warrior elite. The mountain resembled a table, with a relatively flat top about a quarter-mile wide and falling sharply away on three sides. The southern slope, while steep, could be traversed by means of a narrow trail leading to the gorge below.

Leviathan and most of his warriors were down there now, directing the slaves and scouting the way ahead for the planned departure. Below the gorge, the muddy southern sea pounded the mountainside, but unlike the distant western sea, it had ceased its retreat.

Twice-Burned once told Atamoda that eventually the army would enter the gorge and resume the march north, which had been interrupted by the Cataclysm. That day now loomed close at hand. Atamoda glanced over her shoulder at the sinking sun warning her Leviathan and the Olmecs would be returning. She needed to hurry.

The icy wind gusted around Atamoda, and she clutched the felt bag against her chest. Snow still dusted the shadows. Twice-Burned promised spring would soon arrive, and the air would warm as they descended the mountain. She prayed to the Nameless God he was right. Atamoda made her way south, past where the army bivouacked. She entered the commons, where the warriors practiced their deadly arts every morning. Kol-ok's cage hung in the field's center like a trophy.

The cage's iron hook twisted in the wind, creating a constant shrill. The sound followed Atamoda everywhere, reminding her that Kol-ok hung in a cage like an animal. No one, not even the wise slave Twice-Burned, knew Leviathan's intentions for Kol-ok. Under threat of death, Leviathan specifically forbade Atamoda from speaking to her son. These secret excursions were her only opportunity to catch a glimpse of him. Most times, the large bear skin covering his cage prevented Atamoda from seeing Kol-ok. She had to console herself he was safe, and not starving in the slave pens.

If Kol-ok had been thrown into that hell pit, he would likely be dead already. Twice-Burned once told Atamoda hundreds of slaves had made it to the mountaintop before the flood struck. Now, perhaps only seventy remained. The healthiest, mostly men, shambled down the mountain every day to clear rocks and debris from the gorge. The weakest remained behind in the pens, awaiting their turn to die.

The familiar stench of filth and death assaulted Atamoda as she drew near to the pens. Unable to stand under the low ceiling, they squatted or lay in the mud, though few could stand even if they wanted. Atamoda peered into the shadows, where half-rotted animal skins partially blocked the pen's windward side. Thankfully, she didn't see any new dead bodies. Wide eyes in skeletal faces stared silently like living ghosts. Atamoda could have never have imagined humans could go on living with so little flesh on their bones. She didn't want to look at them, but dared not avert her eyes. She felt them sucking hope from her spirit faster than she could offer it.

Atamoda's mind drifted to her people. Were they still alive? Did they have enough to eat? She pushed those thoughts aside, and took one more look around to make sure she wasn't followed. Satisfied, Atamoda reached into the linen bag and withdrew scraps from the god's own table. These usually fell into the Olmecs' hands or Leviathan's body slaves. Atamoda stole as much as she dared. She quickly broke the horse jerky and heavy cheese into small pieces.

Starvation had made all these survivors into old men and women. The man with the strange slanted eyes and up-turned nose was no exception. Atamoda called him Pug. The strongest of the near-dead, Pug always met her at the bars. Today, Pug's hands trembled more than usual as he took the morsels and broke them into even smaller crumbs. As Atamoda tucked the empty bag under her cloak, Pug did what he usually did — made sure everyone else had at least one bite and left nothing for himself.

"You have to keep your strength up," she softly scolded him. She knew Pug didn't understand her words, but felt certain he understood her intent.

From a fold in her dress, she removed a small strip of salted pork no longer than her finger. She pointed at her own open mouth.

Pug gestured at the rest of the survivors.

"No, Pug. You must keep your strength up, too."

After a moment of token resistance, Pug relented and opened his mouth. She placed the morsel on his tongue. Atamoda watched Pug slowly chew as another wind blast rocked her. Would spring ever arrive? As the days lengthened, even the god's personal larder grew thin.

Pug reached out and took her hand. His flesh felt like stone. He placed the back of her hand to his forehead and then released it. Pug touched his fingers to his lips, and then his heart.

Pug's eyes grew wide, and he shrank away from the bars.

Atamoda felt hot breath on her neck and spun about.

"I would kill you now if I could." Quexil caged Atamoda between his outstretched arms and the wooden bars, viciously baring needle-like teeth inches from her face. Exotic, spotted furs heaped over his shoulders made him look like a beast.

"Gods take pretty things like you all the time." His breath stank worse than the slave pens. He fingered her bracelets and leered as if preparing to devour her. "Gods always give pretty things to their pretty things. You are no different. One night, you will no longer please him. He will toss you to me like the scraps you feed these pigs." He pressed closer, sniffing her neck. Atamoda felt his member stiffing against her thigh, and knew she faced real danger. "I will take you. You will no longer be a pretty thing." He snapped his teeth at her. "You will be *scraps*."

Atamoda forced herself to look directly at him. "I am patesi-le, a powerful witch. I have fought demons and sailed through the Realm of the Dead unscathed. You do not frighten me."

"Your body says differently," he sneered.

He did terrify her, as much as the water demons or the floating dead, or the Cataclysm. Quexil terrified Atamoda because she knew shards of truth drifted upon his sea of lies. Yet, Atamoda had her own shards, and her own lies. She leaned closer and whispered seductively into Quexil's ear. "With only a word, I can make your penis shrivel and your teeth fall out. Tell me, what will your wolves do to a wounded leader?" She felt his excitement shrivel away.

Quexil slammed Atamoda against the bars hard enough to make her wince.

"Great Lord Quexil," a voice called from behind. "Prince Leviathan commands your presence in the gorge. He bids you bring ten men and a jar of oil." The man known as Twice-Burned knelt, head bowed. Behind him knelt the old goatherd, Zelko.

"Get it yourself, dog," Quexil spat.

"He asked for you, Mighty One. However, I would be honored to do the Lord of the Ocean's bidding while you linger here with his woman."

Quexil spun about and delivered a vicious kick to Twice-Burned's gut, sending him toppling into the mud. The Olmec stomped Twice-Burned's ribs and stomach before storming off, leaving the slave curled into a ball and gasping for air.

Atamoda squatted beside him. "Why do you provoke him like that?"

Cradling his stomach, Amiran wheezed and tried to smile. "Your Atlantean is getting better."

18. The Olive Girl.

We spent the summer mornings with her mother, where I learned the loom's secrets. By afternoon, Shinglay and I would work the fields collecting hemp for flax. It was then we would slip away into the forest to the river.

The Encircling River surrounded Tortoise Mountain. It flowed beneath the Honey Lotus Bridge and into the forest, marking the village's boundaries. Bright wildflowers and deep greens made the grotto a magical garden. On summer evenings, Nushen's young lovers made their way down the steep banks to rendezvous along the shore. For generations, secret confessions and acts of love bloomed beyond the elders' sight. Young men would beckon their lovers to join them beneath the waterfall, where the river ran swift and shallow, with a traditional love song.

"I live upstream, you live downstream
From night to night of you I dream.
Unlike the stream you are not in view,
Though both we drink from River Blue
Though both we drink from River Blluue!"

I never sang that song to Shinglay; it was not her way. She was a listener possessing a quiet, contemplative spirit.

We spent our afternoons farther downstream, where the waters ran deep and silent. We would sit on the blanket we had woven together until the shadows grew long. The plain, undyed blanket was the first textile I had ever made. I will not say it was perfect, but it was ours.

- The Chronicle of Fu Xi.

***

When Kol-ok was only a little boy, a Sammujad trader had visited shore camp. He only remembered two things about the trader — he stank like a dead beast, and had a beautiful, bright yellow bird in a cage. Kol-ok remembered pitying the little creature as it fluttered about, and how he wanted to fling open the little door and set it free.

Now he wondered if someone would free him.

The bearskin tarp blocked most of the wind and Kol-ok's view. Furs stuffed into the cage's bottom and around his shoulders provided enough warmth to prevent freezing to death. When the wind swung the cage back and forth at mid-day, it often rocked him to sleep. Mostly, his life consisted of trying to keep the circulation in his legs.

As the days blurred together, he grew used to the surrounding sounds and camp routines. A war drum and warriors' feet pounding on dirt woke him every dawn. Rain or shine, they gathered on the camp commons surrounding him. They always lifted the flap, as if demanding he watch. The warriors wore only loincloths during the morning ritual, even in the bitterest cold. They lined up several rows deep, swaying as one to the drum; slowly at first, then picking up speed with the beat. In unison, they fiercely shouted war cries that echoed off the peaks and challenged the roaring waters. They pounded their chests, slapped their thighs, stomped and clapped in perfect timing with their leader, the terrible one with long limbs. His eyes bulged with fury, and his tongue protruded like a living corpse.

Afterwards, the red men heaped wolf skins on their shoulders for warmth. Sometimes, they wore fantastic metal clothes that looked as if they could turn away the sharpest blade. They spent the remainder of their mornings in battle drills with spears, clubs, bolos, and swords.

Kol-ok had never imagined such fierceness. *Not even the Scythians could withstand an onslaught from warriors such as these*, he thought. He felt shame in his admiration, but a part of him wanted to dance with the warriors, and be fearless like them.

After the morning training, the red men dispersed. It was during this time they briefly released Kol-ok under a guard's watchful eye. For a short time, he could wander freely about the open square formed by the surrounding lean-tos. The warriors no longer taunted him as they did before the branding. Kol-ok relieved himself, stretched, and often stole glances toward the god's tent, trying to catch glimpse of his mother. He tried not to look at the slave pens, where vacant eyes stared from behind wooden bars.

Kol-ok knew both he and his mother were being treated far better than the other slaves. It wasn't difficult to understand the god's intentions with his mother, and that filled Kol-ok with rage. Kol-ok's purpose, however, remained a mystery.

All too soon, the guard would lock him back in the cage and drape the bear skin over the top, sealing Kol-ok from the rest of the world for another day. Soon, he would hear whips crack and unintelligible threats as the warriors herded the slaves down the mountainside. Not long after, the camp grew quiet again, and would remain so until almost sunset.

This afternoon came and went. The air inside the cage warmed just enough to lull Kol-ok into fits of sleep. Eventually, dimming light and gnawing hunger told Kol-ok afternoon had passed.

"Hello, Songbird," Elda exclaimed with her usual smile. She tucked back the skins and let cool air invade his cage. She spread out a thick woolen blanket and knelt. "More fish," she said.

Kol-ok slowly and clumsily formed the complicated Atlantean words. "I…like…fish."

She giggled and popped a dried nugget into his mouth. "*Fissshhh,*" she admonished. Her next words spilled out so quickly Kol-ok didn't understand. "Please…slow."

She handed him another chunk and reclined on her knees. "I...said...you will never learn to speak properly."

He chewed slowly, savoring the smoky taste and her company. "I try."

"I know." She touched her lips. "Eat."

"Eat," he repeated.

She watched him in silence. Then Elda looked to the side, beyond where Kol-ok could see. A worried shadow crossed her face, and she made as if to stand, but then sat back down and returned her attention to Kol-ok.

She smiled and shook her head, as if dismissing Kol-ok's unspoken concern. "Eat."

Elda and the sun emerged from the fog not long after they branded him. In that moment of greatest despair, he found hope. Elda's olive skin seemed too perfect, and her delicate hands without so much as a callus. In all things, she moved with precision and grace. He felt absolutely clumsy by comparison. When it was warm, she wore a simple linen dress that fell just below her knees. When it was cool, she wore a long, woolen dress with a cape to match. All her garments were either pure white or light gray. Elda held great standing in camp. The red men never looked at her with ill intent, and always parted when she passed.

When Elda first came to him, Kol-ok wasn't sure if she was real, or perhaps his imagination. These thoughts evaporated when Kol-ok first glimpsed her brand and delicate collar. Whenever Elda smiled at him in that sad way of hers, it revealed an all too human heart, and made Kol-ok ache for her even more.

So many things set her apart, like the delicate spear with three points burned on her arm. No other slave he'd seen bore that brand. All other slaves, except him, bore the serpent's mark. Both he and Elda had unique brands, and were treated significantly better than the other captives. It made Kol-ok wonder what unique gift he might unknowingly possess that warranted his special treatment.

There was so much he wanted to ask Elda, but his lack of skill with her language presented a frustrating barrier. In those rare moments he stumbled on the right words, Elda offered few answers.

"Amiran says spring is coming, but many cold days remain." Elda reached into a black cloth bag and withdrew several white and gray clothing items. "Therefore, the Great Lord Leviathan has permitted you warmer clothing."

"Thank...you," he stuttered and briefly examined the garments. The long, gray shirt felt thick and soft. She watched him intently as he put it on. Kol-ok beamed at her. "Warm!"

Elda returned the smile, but he could not help but notice her sadness. Kol-ok pointed to her heart. "Sad...why?"

Elda put on a happier face. "Your mother is well. She says she loves you and to be strong."

Kol-ok closed his eyes and forced back the tears. He could only nod for a few moments. "Tell...I love, too."

Elda nodded in return. Kol-ok could see she fought back tears as well. His heart sank not only for his mother, but knowing this likely marked the end of Elda's visit. She would neatly fold her blanket, close the flap, and return to the ornate tent beside the grand tent.

Elda touched his chin and raised his head. Elda had never touched him before. Kol-ok's heart soared. Her sadness was replaced with an impish grin. "I want to show you something..." He didn't understand her last word, but it sounded good.

"Watch!" With closed eyes, she lifted her face and took a deep breath. "*Elda*," she exhaled slowly, then snatched the air in front of her lips. Elda closed her other hand over the fist and peeked between her fingers as if she caught a firefly. She extended her hands through the bars. "Listen!"

Kol-ok leaned forward suspiciously. "Hear nothing."

"Then you are deaf." She stuck out her tongue mockingly. Kol-ok leaned back and patted his chest. "Make...fun me."

"You mean 'Making fun of me'," she corrected. "Be quiet and just watch."

Elda slowly uncovered her hand, and then extended her index finger as if pointing before lowering it to the ground. With her finger, she began to scratch squiggles in the moist earth. Some looked like flames or maybe wisps of mist floating over calm waters. Others looked like dust blowing in the wind.

She pointed to the squiggles on the right and then slowly moved her finger left over each mark. "Ehhl-duhh," she said slowly.

Confused, Kol-ok cocked his head sideways.

"You look like a puppy when you do that." She giggled.

Embarrassment jabbed him, and he felt a little dumb. Sometimes she made him feel that way, though Kol-ok knew she didn't mean it. He was just the son of a Lo fisherman, and Elda knew of things he could not possibly imagine.

"*Kohll-ok*," she said slowly, and repeated the snatching motion. This time she drew different squiggles in the dirt. Elda again pointed to the squiggles on the right and slowly moved her finger along the marks. "Kol-ok."

Elda looked up at him, searching his eyes for any trace of understanding. "This is how you make words immortal."

Was this some kind of magic, like his mother's patesi-le magic? Was she casting a spell? He wondered if this was something taboo, but quickly dismissed the thought. Elda would never do anything to hurt him.

He shook his head. "No understand."

"You will." Kindness and patience filled her voice. "I will teach you." That meant she would return, and it filled Kol-ok with unspeakable joy.

Elda stood and began to gather her blanket, shaking it off and neatly folding it as not to get any dirt on her clothing.

Despite Kol-ok's legs being asleep, he lurched up into a crouch so fast it made the cage swing and startled Elda. He seized the bars and pressed his face against them. Kol-ok spoke quickly in Lo, partly because he couldn't speak with any confidence in Atlantean, but mostly because he knew she wouldn't understand. His heart commanded him to confess, but wasn't ready for Elda to understand the truth burning inside.

"I love you!" he blurted. "I know you don't understand me, but I love you, Elda. I will love you forever. I don't know how, but I will break out of this cage and take you away from this place. The giant and the red men won't be able to stop me. We will find my people and I will make you my wife." He paused and gulped. "By the Nameless God, so help me, I swear this."

Elda considered him quizzically for what seemed like an eternity. Now she looked like the confused puppy. "That sounded important. Would you like to start over again in a proper tongue?"

Kol-ok slumped back against the bars, emotionally spent. He shook his head. "More lessons. Then I tell."

Elda shrugged. "Suit yourself. I will see you tomorrow. I'll try to have Amiran smuggle you some fish for breakfast, but don't count on it." She looked about, a worried expression clouding her face. "Lord Leviathan will be returning to camp soon. I must be back before he arrives." The mention of the giant's name robbed the exuberance he felt only moments ago.

Elda's smile quickly returned as she re-arranged the skins on the cage's exterior to block the wind. Today, unlike before, she left a small opening he could close himself.

"Until tomorrow, Kol-ok."

"Until tomorrow, Elda."

Elda turned to go, but hesitated. She knelt down as if it were an impulse, and scratched a few more squiggles before departing.

Kol-ok leaned forward and placed his head against the bars again, considering the new marks and trying to divine their meaning. There he remained until the deepening cold made his hands and nose numb. Reluctantly, he closed the flap and retreated into his iron cocoon to put on the clothes Elda had given him.

19. Once Burned, Twice Burned.

Shinglay and I lay together on our blanket. It was a late summer's day, when the wind didn't stir and the Encircling River ran low. As usual, Shinglay said very little other than inquiring about my many adventures.

She listened patiently, caressing my chest, and sometimes kissing my neck and cheek. Her mere touch ignited my passions, but I dared not surrender to them. To take her virginity would leave her stained in the village's eyes. I wanted Shinglay to find happiness. If she could not marry me, she deserved to find a mortal man she could love. Xigong should have grandchildren, and Nushen needed another generation of weavers. My love for Shinglay was selfish. My passion could destroy her life. No good could come of it. Yet, I could not tear myself away.

"When we are together, I sometimes forget you are a god and I am only a maiden. If Nuwa's will forbids you from marrying me, and honor forbids you from taking me, then why are you here?" she whispered.

I shrugged. Thunder rumbled closer.

"Answer me." She prodded my side, making me squirm.

"You are my quiet place."

She laid her head on my chest and seemed to contemplate what I had said. If I released the truth from my heart's cage, it would devour the both of us.

"You are my safe place," she replied.

A sudden breeze, cool with the promise of coming rain, stirred the leaves.

"Knowing these things, why do you keep coming here with me?" I regretted the words the moment I spoke them, afraid she would come to her senses and leave.

"When I am with you, and hear your stories, I see beyond my short life." Her finger traced over my heart. "It gives me peace knowing you will carry me in your heart for all eternity. In there, I will be forever cherished. When my ears hear you say, 'I love you,' my heart hears, 'Do not be afraid'," Shinglay said.

"When you say 'I love you,' my heart hears, 'You are not alone.'"

Shinglay kissed me deeply, and I uttered a thousand silent prayers to the Emperor of Heaven. I prayed for the moment to last forever. I prayed to become mortal, and take Shinglay as my wife. I prayed for many children, and to become the father I never truly had. I prayed to fully become one of Nushen, and not Tortoise Mountain.

Slow, fat raindrops dripped down through the forest canopy upon us as Shinglay straddled me. She opened her tunic and revealed herself.

"No," I whispered.

"It is my choice." She placed my hand on her breast.

Our passions took control. My mortal blood swept the god aside. I could not, I would not, be denied. I rolled over and threw Shinglay to the blanket, stripping off the rest of her clothes. Shinglay eagerly opened herself, pulling me down upon her.

Before the moment we would have become one, that sweet union neither of us had ever before experienced, the thunder transformed from gentle rumbles to sharp, powerful claps. A downpour assaulted us in hard, cold sheets. A blinding blue flash erupted overhead and the tree beside us exploded in burning splinters. I shielded Shinglay as another tree erupted under the onslaught.

Naked, we grabbed our possessions and fled the garden.

- The Chronicle of Fu Xi.

***

Zelko and Atamoda supported Amiran as they crossed the Olmec practice field. Their presence drew cold stares from warriors gathered around campfires. Atamoda stole a desperate glance toward Elda as she knelt before Kol-ok's cage. Elda had been tasked with feeding Kol-ok each evening just before sundown. Atamoda desperately wanted to linger and catch a glimpse of her son, but she knew that would be unwise.

Elda spotted them, and Atamoda saw concern darkening the girl's expression. Elda made a move to stand, but Atamoda smiled reassuringly and gave a little wave, as if to say 'He's okay.'

"Beak Face got you good this time, eh?" Zelko cackled, one good tooth flashing when he smiled. Amiran tried to laugh, but winced instead. Atamoda had seen Amiran take worse beatings at Quexil's hands, but now hunger had slowly eaten away his resilience.

They shuffled behind Elda's small tent on the compound's north side, where shadows shielded them from view. Behind them, a precipice dropped steeply into the gorge. A stiff mountain wind washed over them, sending fresh chills through Atamoda. Amiran collapsed, clutching his stomach and trying to catch his breath.

Atamoda knelt beside him. "Move your hands and let me see."

"He only knocked the wind out of me," Amiran sputtered.

"Yeah, but he knocked all of it out of you!" Zelko laughed and cocked his pointy, goat-hair cap forward.

Amiran shot him a dirty look, which made Zelko cackle even louder. It seemed to Atamoda that Zelko took pleasure in irritating the wise man. *They make a strange pair*, she thought.

"I said let me look at it!" she repeated forcefully and pushed his hands away.

They spoke in Lo, or at least a hybrid of Lo and Zelko's similar dialect. They never spoke Atamoda's language openly, only in private moments like this, and even then only in hushed tones. It had become their secret language.

Zelko, that odd little goatherd, was the first to encounter Atamoda and Kol-ok shortly after their landfall. Zelko had tried to warn them to get back in their boat and flee before it was too late. She didn't understand, and Atamoda and her son were captured shortly after they stepped onto the shore.

Zelko had been captured in the gorge by Leviathan's army the day the Cataclysm struck. He called his captivity "a temporary inconvenience" and his slave brand a "souvenir." A native of these mountains, Zelko dressed from head-to-toe in goat skin. Wispy gray hair poked from under his conical cap. His toothless grin made him look a bit mad, and he possessed an unusually springy step and keen eye for one who appeared so old. Zelko's otherwise jovial appearance and personality clashed with grotesque scars smearing his left profile. The scars earned Zelko the nickname "Once-Burned" by the Olmecs. Smooth, pink burn scars contrasted with deep wrinkles covering the rest of his face. The wounds rendered his left eye blind and milky. Being a healer, Atamoda wondered how someone, especially one so old, could survive such terrible wounds. She once asked him how it happened, but Zelko shrugged and vaguely mentioned a terrible fire.

The similarities between his language and the Lo tongue were striking, and enabled Amiran to quickly learn how to converse with Atamoda. Zelko told her he was born long ago in a small village far to the west, nestled against these mountains. As a child, Zelko remembered hearing tales of a great freshwater sea to the north, as well as a vast saltwater sea to the south, though he had seen neither. He left his village as a young man with only a few goats, a broken heart, and an oath never to marry.

Zelko's gods dictated a deep love for humanity, which flew in the face of everything Zelko knew about humanity. "Do not judge me harshly, patesi-le," he once told her. "I love people, I just hate being around them. I reckoned the best way not to offend the gods was to avoid people, especially women." Since then, he'd lived the hermit's life, preferring goats to people.

Atamoda opened what was left of Amiran's rotting tunic. She gently pressed on his stomach and ribs, searching for tell-tale signs of serious injury. He winced a few times as she pressed on his left ribs. His black skin, which struck Atamoda as so exotic when she first beheld him, had now taken on a grayish pallor and hung loosely from his bones.

They were among the camp's few "privileged" slaves. Being particularly useful to Leviathan, they were better fed than those in the pens. By better fed, this meant Amiran and Zelko weren't starving yet, but the regular beatings and poor diet slowly took their toll on the man Elda sometimes called "scholar." Atamoda never understood the full meaning of that word, but Elda said it loosely meant "wise man."

"Thank you for helping me, Amiran. But Quexil wasn't going to hurt me," Atamoda lied without looking up.

Amiran's breathing quickened when she pressed a bit harder on his abdomen. Atamoda searched the rest of his torso for serious wounds.

So much about Amiran, this place, and these strange people remained a mystery. Fresh scars covered most of his upper body, but Atamoda found only a few older scars anywhere else on his skin. The most terrifying scar of all mangled Amiran's upper right arm. Elda said Quexil had sadistically sliced off Amiran's old brand, a three-pronged spear like Elda's. Elda had explained she was the property of Poseidon, "The Father of Gods" to whom even Leviathan bowed. Amiran had once belonged to the same powerful entity, and Atamoda guessed he also received equally good treatment. Before Atamoda's arrival, something had changed, and Amiran had fallen from favor. Yet, Leviathan still needed him.

Leviathan's twisted snake symbol now seared Amiran's arm, most likely burned while Quexil's inflicted wound still bled. It had healed into a monstrous shape covering

Amiran's entire triceps all the way to the shoulder. This scar had earned him the name "Twice-Burned," which Leviathan and the Olmecs used with mockery. Elda explained it was a term for an untrustworthy slave, the lowest of the low in Atlantean society. The twice-burned were often public slaves, used only for the most demeaning tasks.

Amiran had branded Atamoda shortly after her capture. She feared and hated him at first, until Atamoda realized he, too, was a victim. In the months that followed, Atamoda had learned to respect and care for Amiran. She never called him Twice-Burned, and only uttered those words if absolutely necessary in the presence of the Olmecs or Leviathan himself.

Atamoda withdrew her hand and retied the leather cord securing his tunic. "You're lucky — nothing is broken. Next time, he may kill you."

Atamoda smelt a trace of smoke on the air. A moment later, the trace grew to a strong odor. Blue tendrils crept over the cliff's edge. "Smoke rises from below," she said, puzzled and looking to Amiran for answers.

"We are out of time," he replied. "The remaining debris blocking the way north is dry enough to be burned away."

She shuddered at his pronouncement's dreadful implications. "How long?"

"One day to burn. One day to cool. One day to clear. Then camp will be struck and the army marches north."

The Cataclysm had deposited shattered timber into the gorge, blocking their way off the mountain. Not long after her arrival, when the waters had receded enough, Leviathan's expedition set about clearing it. From dawn to dusk, slaves worked ceaselessly clearing the debris. Amiran usually directed the work.

As the waters receded, this once isolated island revealed itself to be a mountaintop, one of many in a range stretching northeast. To the south, the waters ebbed away, leaving only a river in its wake. According to Amiran, the army had arrived here on many ships only days before the Cataclysm.

He provided little detail, other than they were an expedition from the far side of the world. Their original plan had been to march north through the narrow canyon. They climbed this mountain to escape the Cataclysm, and survived off the expedition's vast provisions. Now, with supplies and food running desperately low, their way off this mountaintop prison finally opened.

When Atamoda asked him why the Atlanteans journeyed so far from their native land, he only replied, "Conquest." When she had pressed further, Amiran would not discuss it.

These people were like the Scythians, she thought, but on a scale far grander, and grimmer, than the steppe horsemen.

"The time has come to implement our plan," Amiran whispered.

"I can't." Atamoda raised her hands as if to ward off his words.

"You must."

"Please, patesi-le, listen to him," Zelko beseeched. "He has a good plan. You will be safe." Zelko always called her by her Lo title. She found it comforting. In the many months of her captivity, she'd come to care for these two. If it had not been for Amiran, Elda, and Zelko, she would have been helpless before Leviathan and his Olmecs. They gave her the knowledge to survive, and hope for Kol-ok. Now, Amiran asked Atamoda to abandon everything in a desperate gamble to stop Leviathan.

"I will not leave Kol-ok," she said with finality.

"Leviathan will not hurt him," he paused. "But if you stay, he will hurt you. The only hope for Kol-ok is the Gray-Eyed Queen. Only she has the power to confront Leviathan."

Though Amiran spoke sparingly of his journey here, Atamoda would not have believed any of his tales had she not been in an immortal's presence every night.

"How can you know for sure this goddess dwells just beyond Zelko's homeland?"

Amiran clasped her hands. "Zelko's homeland is only a week's journey west. The Sea of Azur is only two weeks beyond that. That is where we will find the Gray-Eyed Queen. Zelko and I have hidden enough food and supplies for the journey."

Atamoda wanted to share Amiran's hope. Maybe Aizarg and her people were out there, too. Then she remembered the enormous wave that had descended on the world, and wiped out all she had known. She remembered how it had lifted the Lo flotilla to the clouds, and how she had almost touched the sky before being cast back into the maelstrom. Atamoda recalled the unstoppable rain and the endless sea, and the great storm that signaled the beginning of the end for the Cataclysm.

"You don't know if this Gray-Eyed Queen and her people survived," Atamoda whispered.

He nodded in resignation. "You are correct. I only have to hope that if we survived, so did they."

"You ask me to risk much on just hope."

"That is all I have to offer." Amiran put his hands on her shoulders. "We will find the Gray-Eyed Queen. When she learns her brother is here, on her eastern flank, she will come with an army."

"You do not need me. I will stay and watch over my son."

"Elda will watch over him. He is beyond your help. Only the Gray-Eyed Queen has the power to save him, and she does not know we are at her kingdom's door. I cannot escape without your help. If you help me, you cannot stay."

"You would so casually leave Elda?" she said, and regretted it when she saw the pain her words inflicted.

"She means as much to me as Kol-ok means to you," Amiran said firmly. "This is the only way I can save her."

Atamoda struggled to find the right words and not let her frustration interfere. "Since we've been able to understand each other, you've spoken in riddles. You say I am intelligent and that you trust me, yet there is so much you

142

won't tell me. I can see it in your eyes, *scholar*." Her difficulty forming that Atlantean word only magnified her frustration. "You, Elda, even him!" She pointed accusingly to Zelko. "You keep things from me."

Amiran and Zelko exchanged grim looks. "Zelko, please leave us," Amiran said. "Get five pen slaves and take the oil jars Leviathan requested down the gorge. Tell him I am hurt and Atamoda is tending to my wounds. If he asks what happened, be truthful. Let Quexil deal with the consequences. Warn us before Leviathan returns."

Zelko shrugged. "If you say so."

The old man slipped out of sight, leaving Atamoda and Amiran alone. They knelt for a long moment with only the flapping tent to break the silence. Amiran stared at the stony ground in deep concentration before speaking. "You *are* strong and intelligent. If the Lo are anything like you, then they are an amazing people. Yes, I've told little about who we are, and where we come from, but I had my reasons."

"I still don't understand," Atamoda said, her frustration ebbing.

"Have faith I only conceal to protect. In time, you will know everything." He looked over her shoulder at the sinking sun. "Atamoda, in Leviathan's tent there is a large box. It's called an Expedition Chest, and its surface is marred by fire. It has clasps of the same red metal as Leviathan's sword."

Atamoda nodded. She'd looked upon that chest many times, marveling at the workmanship, and how the red metal reminded her of Aizarg's staff and Sana's dagger. "It's beside his bed. That's where he rests his sword."

"Before we break camp, you must steal what lies within it. I will tell you how to unlock it and disarm the traps."

"Traps?" She felt alarmed.

"Do not be afraid. I will instruct you."

"What is inside?"

"That is more difficult to explain." Amiran sighed. "He prizes the contents highly, and without it Leviathan cannot fulfill the destiny that drives him relentlessly north. By taking it, we buy Kol-ok and Elda time."

"What is it?" she beseeched.

"Listen closely, because we have little time before Leviathan returns." Amiran told her how the army found itself on this barren mountaintop far from Poseidon's Empire. She listened intently as Amiran recounted the tale with great skill. Occasionally, Atamoda asked a question, but mostly she listened. Revelations, both magnificent and horrifying, spilled one after another from the scholar's mouth. By the time Amiran had finished, the smoke rising from the gorge had grown into a thick column and descended upon the mountain. An orange, hellish light painted the smoke's underbelly as darkness crept across camp.

"Now do you understand?" he asked.

Numb, Atamoda could only nod.

"There are gods greater than Leviathan and the Gray-Eyed Queen, even greater than Poseidon. I fear Leviathan has struck a bargain with such a god. That bargain is why we survived the Cataclysm and why Leviathan is determined to press north at all costs." He took a deep breath. "And it's the reason why he needs Kol-ok."

Atamoda emerged from the spell to find Zelko looking down at them. "He is coming," he said.

Amiran stared at Atamoda, as if trying to gauge her reaction. She saw him differently now, and understood his immense courage. Somewhere, deep inside, an unfamiliar feeling budded in her heart like a dark flower. It found fertile soil and took root. For a moment, Atamoda found herself hating Amiran, more than Quexil and Kus-ge and Virag and Fate for destroying her life. She hated Amiran for speaking the truth, and laying a terrible choice at her feet.

"I need…time," she stammered. "You ask so much of me."

Amiran nodded. "I will find an excuse to return early from the gorge tomorrow. We will meet again then, and I will explain everything you must do."

She heard many footsteps echoing up from the gorge, getting louder.

"We must hurry," Zelko said.

Atamoda stood and brushed off her dress. Zelko helped Amiran stand.

Atamoda turned to Amiran. "What of this other god you spoke of, this Fu Xi?"

Amiran looked off to the darkening east. "If the Cataclysm spared him, he may be a powerful ally. Without the Gray-Eyed Queen, I fear he isn't strong enough to stop Leviathan alone."

20. Blue Fire In The Mirror, Part 2.

I stood in Nuwa's Second Realm, my clothes still dripping. Mother stood by the Eternal Tree in the center of the Place of Perfect Sorrows, her back to me. Even deep in her temple, I could hear the lighting and thunder attacking Tortoise Mountain. Mother lovingly caressed the Altar Rock. Behind her, at the conjunction of the four streams, the Eternal Tree's leaves had begun to turn brown, even though Nuwa's current shell had many years of life left. My backpack, bulging with supplies, sat on the marble floor beside her.

"Are you an obedient son?" She spoke without turning, her voice barely above a whisper.

"I am."

"You have learned enough from the Widow Xigong. You will leave immediately. Do not return until I can hear the loom's clack on all of Cin's four winds."

I summoned all my courage. "I wish to take Shinglay with me."

"You will do no such thing!" Nuwa snapped. Her anger charged the air and took me aback.

"Why?" I asked.

"You know my law. Nothing from Nushen may leave my valley."

"You permit me to leave."

"You are of Tortoise Mountain, not Nushen." Her words fell like a knife stroke.

"Then permit me to stay until Shinglay grows old and passes to the Emperor of Heaven. Then I will go on my quest."

"I've already permitted you to take any woman you want. You don't need her. Your quest begins now. I have spoken."

"I don't want to 'take' Shinglay. I want to love her!" I said defiantly.

Nuwa slowly turned. Blue flames danced in her eyes, and encircled her in snake-like tendrils. The golden dragon on her gown seemed to come alive, slithering across her body. "Shinglay is a dust mote, passing through a ray of sunshine. I am your mother, the Goddess Nuwa. I am eternal."

I do not know where I found the courage in the face of my mother's divinity. "It is not my purpose to disrespect you, honored mother." I held out my arms, pleading. "Surely you must understand how I feel. Without love, eternity is too much to bear."

"Love carries a terrible price. It is the tender curse. You should learn to bear eternity without it."

"Have you learned to live without it? What of me, mother? Is it love you feel for me, or something else? What of your husbands? Did you truly love them or did you just 'take them'?" I didn't conceal my scorn.

Golden light filled the temple, blinding me. I felt myself knocked to the floor, and I slid across the marble until I came to rest against a pillar.

"EVERYTHING I DID, I DID FOR LOVE!" Her voice resonated like a beast's roar.

I picked myself up. Diminished, mother sat crumpled on the floor beside the Altar Rock. Her aura of power had evaporated. In that moment, I pitied her.

"I'm taking Shinglay and leaving."

"Disobedience carries a terrible price, Fu Xi." Nuwa's voice carried a dark edge.

I turned and walked away, lying to myself that I was prepared for whatever may come.

"Do not turn your back on me!"

In my pride, I kept walking.

In her pride, Nuwa uttered her next words. "I banish you."

There was light, and then there was darkness. I awoke, alone on an unfamiliar shore as the sun rose over the sea.

- The Chronicle of Fu Xi.

***

Atamoda crossed into another world as she entered the warm, cavernous tent. She drew the flaps tightly behind her, closed her eyes, and took a deep breath. She wanted to shut Amiran's words outside, and never have to face the terrible decisions he laid at her feet. She opened her eyes to find Leviathan's two Erubian slave girls staring incredulously.

"Where have you been? Hurry!" the older of the two lisped. "He will be here soon." The woman-child's upper lip caved into her mouth, and only a few bottom teeth held up her lower lip.

In the large, open area between the throne and entrance, the body slaves busily prepared Leviathan's bath. To their right, a small standing-only ceramic basin, filled with steaming water, waited for Atamoda.

She had delayed too long with Amiran. Etiquette demanded Atamoda be bathed, dressed, and ready when the master arrived. The body slaves quickly helped Atamoda strip. She stepped lightly into the basin, wholeheartedly embracing this Atlantean custom. To her, a bath substituted for the Great Sea's cleansing waters. Soap and bath oils, however, took some getting used to. The luxurious hot water soaked into her feet. She never imagined slipping into hot water, like a piece of meat to be boiled, could feel this good. The two body slaves scrubbed Atamoda from head to foot, though there was no time to wash her hair. Reluctantly, she stepped from the basin, letting the heat radiating off the nearby brazier caress her. They hastily dried Atamoda with a towel made of a wondrous material called cotton, and then massaged scented oils into her skin.

Wrapped in the towel, Atamoda dashed to the tent's back corner, where Leviathan afforded her a small table and chair. She stepped lightly over the bare ground. The intricate rugs that usually filled the common area had been rolled up and placed in the corner to avoid getting wet. A dark wooden chest, inlaid with silver in geometric patterns, sat beside the table. Atamoda opened it and rustled through exotic garments, pulling out the one she thought might please him. She slipped behind a black wooden screen intricately carved with fantastical beasts and dressed.

This was also another Atlantean oddity that mystified her. The Lo had the minimum of modesty, often appearing naked to one another, especially when swimming. In the Lo mind, nakedness and sensuality were not the same. To the Atlanteans, nudity and sensuality were synonymous. Amiran explained that in Atlantean culture, suggestive clothing could be more sensual than no clothing. The wardrobe in the chest seemed to bear this out.

Atamoda selected a white gossamer slip so thin and light it might have been spun from a cloud. Next, she pulled out a delicate golden braid waist chain. Pearls strung down gold and silver chains attached along its length dangled just far enough to conceal her intimate areas.

While Atamoda dressed, the slave girls strained to carry the ceramic basin outside and dump it behind the tent. The large bronze tub was far too heavy for the women to lift, and common slaves were forbidden from entering the tent. Therefore, the Olmecs brought it in and out when Leviathan desired a bath. The Olmecs also portered water from the river running through the gorge. The women heated it in iron pots over a bonfire outside the tent.

The women ignored Atamoda as they resumed pouring large clay jars of steaming water into the tub. Atamoda knew they resented her, and she didn't blame them. These body slaves received a quarter of the rations she did. They lived in a lean-to near the Olmecs' concubine tent, and not in the slave pens. Once Atamoda had learned to speak passable Atlantean, she attempted on several occasions to make conversation. She'd even given them some of her rations, which they snatched but continued to rebuff her offers of friendship.

Atamoda knew they were slowly starving to death, and it shamed her. The women had stopped menstruating, and their hair and teeth had begun to fall out. They willingly gave their bodies to the Olmecs for scraps. Sometimes, they received an extra morsel, sometimes only torment. They worked tirelessly to keep Leviathan's palatial tent clean and orderly. To do anything less risked being thrown back into the slave pens.

Under no circumstances could Atamoda displease Leviathan, either. The consequences for her and Kol-ok were too terrible to imagine.

Elda and Amiran had labored to teach Atamoda not only how to speak the god's language, but also Atlantean customs. Atamoda quickly learned how to address the god and the Olmec freemen, as well as all the important courtesies.

"You must exercise the utmost caution when in his presence," Amiran once said when they were alone. "Never forget he is not like us. He is the ancient son of an immortal god. We are only dandelion fluff floating on a breeze. He cannot be killed by a common blade. His blood will turn to fire should it ever escape his veins.

"Know this. He has taken a special liking to you, and this is dangerous. It is not unusual for a god to take a mortal pet, especially exotic barbarian morsels. I suspect you're different. He has killed one of his own freemen to protect you. That is unheard of. Do everything he asks. Please him. Lull him into your confidence. Be patient and obedient. That is how you will survive."

"If it is so hopeless, why do you resist him?" Atamoda had asked bluntly.

Her frankness seemed to genuinely surprise Amiran. "What makes you think I resist him?"

"You speak to me in Lo only when you are afraid someone is listening, when you say dangerous things, like now."

Amiran's shock had transformed to a respectful acknowledgement. "You see much, patesi-le."

Atamoda found Amiran's use of her Lo title, and his perfect pronunciation, flattering. She pointed to his arm. "I sense how much he hates you. You frustrate him, and he can't just cast you aside. Leviathan needs you, doesn't he?"

Amiran had nodded. "Yes, at least for now. Scholars must be adept at mentally sparring with gods, otherwise we die young. You, however, should not try to outwit him, or think you can read his moods or thoughts. Leviathan is fathomless, like the ocean. His wrath is the lightning bolt from a clear summer sky."

"Then what hope do you have in opposing him?"

"My hope is that he continues to underestimate me. Mortals only have one weapon against the gods — turning their own arrogance against them."

The memory passed, and Atamoda glanced over the screen at the girls. Rotted cloth barely covered their flesh. Amiran told her that forced nakedness was often a way Atlanteans would demean slaves. Robbing someone's modesty also robbed their humanity.

Bathed and changed, Atamoda felt herself relax. She sat down and began sorting through the crystal vials lined up on the table. Glass, that beautiful ice that never melted, how she loved it! Each small vial contained clear fluid that exuded a unique and pleasant scent. Atamoda had become familiar with all of them, and knew by now which ones the god preferred. Tonight, she selected one that seemed to make him somewhat gregarious. Elda said it reminded her of Attica's floral breezes.

Jars filled with strange creams, powders, balms, and ointments littered the tabletop. Some had a mildly pleasant smell, but most were odorless. Elda called these makeup, to beautify the face.

"Don't worry about wearing them," Elda had told her. "In my experience, makeup is only for ugly or vain women. You are neither."

Ornate boxes of bedazzling jewelry were tucked away in the tent, but Atamoda rarely wore them. They reminded her too much of her simple li-ge amulet, the only adornment she had ever worn. She tried not to think about the li-ge; it only summoned memories of Kus-ge's learning visage as she cut the amulet from her neck. Yet, sometimes when Atamoda thought of Aizarg, she unconsciously reached up expecting to feel the familiar bone and leather amulet, but only encountered her cold slave collar.

"If this is an expedition of conquest, why did you bring all of these trinkets for women?" Atamoda had once asked Amiran.

"In case the god should find any beautiful trophies of conquest," Amiran had replied.

A large, dark bottle and empty goblet at the table's end beckoned Atamoda, though she tried to ignore them. The girls placed it on her table every morning, but unlike the food, they never attempted to steal any. If Leviathan smelled wine on their breath, or staining the lips, he would slay them on the spot. Wine was forbidden to slaves and Olmecs alike. Yet, Leviathan shared it freely with Atamoda.

Atamoda reached to uncork the bottle, but pulled back. She'd grown too fond of the liquid's magic. As her time in opulent captivity stretched on, the occasional glass became two or three. Whenever a bottle emptied, a new one would be waiting the next morning.

She desperately wanted a drink now.

I am a trophy of conquest.

"No," Atamoda whispered to herself, and instead picked up one of the exquisite hair brushes. Of all the treasures available for her use, the combs and brushes were her favorites. Elda told her the bristles were made from the spines of sea creatures, and the handles from the tusks of magnificent animals larger than a hundred men. Her Lo brushes, lost so long ago, were fashioned from wood and fishbones. Atamoda would leave everything in the tent behind without a second thought, but she so dearly wanted to keep the brushes and combs forever.

She caressed the wooden tabletop's glass-like finish. This space made her feel beautiful. None of these exotic, pretty things were hers, yet they made her feel safe. Here, in this opulent sanctuary high upon a desolate mountaintop, Atamoda felt cherished. She hadn't felt cherished since Aizarg left for the Valley of Beasts. She had come to love this little space, and that love brought tremendous guilt.

She brushed her long, dark hair, and stared into the greatest wonder in this chamber of wonders. Atamoda looked back at her own reflection. Her thin collar reflected the fire light and drew her eye.

Atamoda felt utterly torn. She knew goodness dwelt in Amiran's heart. He would die to protect Elda. Like Aizarg, he was a man of duty and honor. Amiran, like Aizarg, often denied his heart's own desires for what he thought would benefit others.

Atamoda knew how the scholar felt about her, even if he could not admit it to himself. She often caught his longing glances. This evening, it wasn't all pain that quickened his breath when she examined his wounds.

She glanced over at the heavy chest sitting across from Leviathan's bed. Atamoda couldn't reconcile Amiran's tale with the emotions battling for dominance in her heart.

Hur-ar and the fearsome Scythian horse lords were at the bottom of the sea, wiped away by the Nameless God. Leviathan had not only defied the Nameless God, he remained powerful and ready to conquer the world.

Atamoda found herself trapped between a mortal and a god locked in an unspoken war. The fate of both, as well as her son and Elda, depended on what she did next. She looked down at the nearly empty goblet in her hands, not remembering pouring it. The wine's warmth had already begun to spread through her belly.

Here, she felt safe. Here, she felt cherished.

Amiran's words echoed in her mind. *He has killed one of his own freemen to protect you. That is unheard of.*

Does he cherish me? she thought. *Or am I merely a trophy of conquest?*

Atamoda sighed and put down the goblet as a cold draft washed over her. Leviathan filled the tent's entrance, sword in hand, studying her through the mirror's reflection. Their eyes met, and once again Atamoda caught a fleeting glimpse of blue fire.

21. Chamber of Wonders and Shame.

I'd been farther from Nushen, and longer away before, but never without hope. Darkness deeper than anything I had experienced before or since possessed me. I shunned all human contact. Thoughts of Shinglay and my beloved home tormented me. I felt my humanity slipping away year by year as I merely existed beside the unchanging sea. The clothes rotted from my back, but I did not care. My beard covered my nakedness. I found myself becoming more animal than human, to the point of eating raw fish and living in a cave. To feel nothing became my only objective.

Thirty years into exile, hope and fear kindled anew when the old man stumbled into my hermit's cave. How he found me along the Sunrise Sea, or how he survived the trek across Cin's wilderness, I will never know. He collapsed in my arms and uttered one word, "Home."

He died before I could even ask him his name. He had no possessions, other than the rags he wore and the rolled up blanket on his back.

Shinglay's blanket.

Nuwa had never permitted one from Nushen beyond her protected valley. I do not know if the goddess sent him, or if he escaped to find me. I only knew I had been beckoned home.

After cleansing myself in the Sunrise Sea, I fashioned a loom, foraged wild hemp, and made myself new clothes for my long journey west.

A year later, I walked into Nushen on a bone-chilling winter's eve. I expected Nuwa to strike me down as I crossed the Honey Lotus Bridge, but the sky remained gray and silent. The Eternal River had turned to dust. The fields were blackened and the livestock gone. My beloved Nushen teetered on oblivion's edge. The starving and desperate people rushed me along the avenue, calling my name and begging for deliverance. I had seen many desolate peoples in my journeys, but never thought I'd witness my beloved Nushen suffering so.

A maelstrom swirled over Tortoise Mountain. I rushed up the Silver Stairs. Weeds and saplings choked the pathway, and vines covered the Threshold Dragon like a curtain.

Darkness reigned inside Nuwa's temple. The lanterns were long dry. Fashioning a crude torch from cloth scraps, I entered what felt like a tomb. Dust and filth blanketed the temple. Sludge and mold choked the four streams emanating from the raised fountain in the courtyard center. The Eternal Tree stood bare and lifeless at the courtyard's center. I found Nuwa curled up at the Altar Rock's base, just where I left her when she banished me those many years ago.

She hid her face from the light with hands gnarled with age and sickness. Iron-gray hair, matted and uncut, covered her soiled gown like spiderwebs.

"Mother," I whispered. "I have come home."

"Be gone!" her voice cracked weakly. "Do not look upon me."

I held the torch higher. Shinglay's face looked up in confusion.

- The Chronicle of Fu Xi.

***

Atamoda and the body slaves lay prostrate. The wind ruffled the tent. Atamoda heard the ever-present shrill of Kol-ok's cage rocking in the wind. The strong smell of wood smoke accompanied the god. She heard metal rattle, signaling he'd removed his scabbard. A heavy clink testified he had placed his sword on the heavy chest. The sound of chewing told Atamoda he'd found the meat and wine.

"Come," he commanded the body slaves as if speaking to dogs. They leapt up and rushed to his side. On cue, Atamoda rose and took her place behind the screen. During her training, both Amiran and Elda made it clear she was forbidden to observe the god bathe. The body slaves were permitted to see the god nude, much as pets can see their master naked.

"Concubines are different," Amiran had stated, though he seemed at a loss to explain why.

Atamoda understood why Leviathan did not want her to see him unclothed, even though his body was magnificent and perfect in every respect. That one aspect of the god's personality she understood completely, even if Amiran did not.

The scholar was a paradox. In many ways, he seemed wise beyond even Leviathan himself. In the ways of the heart, he was utterly ignorant.

Atamoda stole a glance at Leviathan as she slipped behind the screen. Soot streaked his chiseled iron arms. One slave had begun to loosen his golden sash while the other knelt to unlace his boots. They looked like children compared to him.

Leviathan caught Atamoda's eye as she slipped behind the screen.

Every night since her branding she'd been in Leviathan's company, yet even now Atamoda could not read his expressions. She believed every word Amiran and Elda had told her about this demigod, yet so much about Leviathan seemed like any other man.

He ate and slept. His touch was warm, and to Atamoda's surprise, often tender. Sometimes, late at night curled up at the foot of his throne, she often heard him lightly snore. The first time she heard him pass wind in his sleep, she had to stifle a giggle. Though Atamoda never witnessed Leviathan use it, a chamber pot rested under his bed, and the body slaves emptied it daily.

Atamoda remained behind the screen as light splashing and dripping filled the tent. She caught herself peeking through the small crack at the screen's hinge point. Leviathan leaned back in the tub, massive arms resting along the rim. Eyes closed, his broad chest was just visible. The slave women leaned over him, scrubbing his body with dispassionate efficiency. Washing complete, they held up two broad towels and waited for the god to stand. Self-conscious, Atamoda turned away.

A few moments later he called, "Come, Atamoda."

She stepped from behind the screen, hands clasped demurely. Clad in a pure white loincloth, the god stood on a rug as the women rubbed his body with oils that warmed the muscles and moisturized the skin. One woman stood on Atamoda's upside down basin to reach Leviathan's shoulders. Atamoda had no reference for the oil's scent, but it reminded her of sunshine pouring over the Great Sea on a hot summer day.

"Wine," he commanded.

Atamoda filled his goblet and placed it on the tray. Then she knelt beside his throne and dutifully waited. One slave placed golden slippers on Leviathan's feet, while the other, still standing on the basin, dressed him in an intricately-folded linen garb the Atlanteans called a toga. The toga was pure white, except for a thin golden stripe down the center.

Leviathan sat on the throne. The body slaves dipped water from the tub with large clay jars. Several Olmecs appeared and helped empty the vessel. In only a few minutes, enough water had been removed for two strong warriors to lift the tub and carry it from the tent. After removing the wet towels and soiled clothing, the body slaves returned and lay on their bellies before the throne.

"Great and Glorious Lord, how may we serve you next?" they asked in unison.

"Go."

The slaves slid backwards on their bellies from the tent.

"Feed me," Leviathan commanded.

"Yes, Great Lord," Atamoda replied. She started with an olive and placed it in his mouth, continuing with the various dried fruits, cheeses, and dried meat. He occasionally took a sip from the goblet. It continued this way, as it always did, in silence unless he chose to speak.

"Twice-Burned reports you were once a holy woman, is that correct?"

"Yes, Great Lord."

"What gods did you worship?"

She opened her mouth, but Leviathan cut her off. "Don't tell me…the sky?"

"Yes, Great Lord."

"The sea? The sun? The moon? Maybe all of them?"

Atamoda bowed her head, shamed by his flippant tone.

"Yes, Great Lord. Their names are…"

"I don't care what their names are. None of them are real. With barbarians it's always the same. Sun god, sky god, earth god, god of this, god of that. They never know what to do when presented with a real god." His stare burrowed through her. Atamoda lowered her eyes.

Leviathan took the tray from her hands and placed it on the chest.

"Tell me, holy woman, what sacrifices did your gods demand?"

"Food and small totems which carry our prayers."

"Petty sacrifices for petty gods." Leviathan took an olive, placed it in her mouth, and watched her chew.

"Your gods are false, no different from those worshipped by a thousand tribes on a thousand shores. One can recognize true gods by *how* they are worshipped. Would you like me to tell you, holy woman?"

She nodded obediently.

"A god is only as worthy as the sacrifice they demand. The only worthy sacrifice is blood. Some gods require the blood of animals." Leviathan laughed and swirled the wine in his goblet. "They work cheap! These are the gods of old witches and wives' tales."

Leviathan pinched a piece of dried horse meat and placed it on her tongue. She chewed the tough morsel while he continued to talk. "True gods, powerful gods, demand human sacrifice. If you want something from them, it will cost you. Have no doubt, these gods are real and powerful." He lifted his goblet to her lips. "Drink," he said softly and tipped the goblet higher and higher until she drained the cup. A thick trickle ran down her chin and between her breasts. Leviathan slowly ran his fingertip from her lips down her chin, following the crimson trail. He put his finger to his lips.

The wine's warm magic kindled her blood.

"I see many questions swirling in your eyes, holy woman. Tonight, if you so choose, you shall learn the greatest secret of all. This knowledge carries incredible power, but is heavy. Far heavier than any mortal can bear, even for the Caste of Scholars. Do you think yourself strong enough to bear the weight?"

She felt herself grow numb, and stepping across an unknown threshold.

"Perhaps something not so chewy this time." He placed an olive to her lips and smiled. "I will tell you a secret about the gods who demand human sacrifice. It is these gods who need mortals, not the other way around. A man can go through his entire day, hunting, farming, making love…it doesn't matter, and never think about the gods. Only when they are afraid do mortals call out for deliverance. When such times come, a man will sacrifice his own child to make the fear go away."

"There is no forgiveness without blood," Atamoda said absently, as if the voice wasn't hers.

His eyes narrowed. "Where did you hear this?"

"I don't know, perhaps a dream."

"The gods who feast on blood are obsessed with mortals, and torment them to no end." His hand fell to her side, and lightly caressed her hip. "These gods are not truly powerful. There are those more powerful still. Do you know what I speak of?"

Atamoda felt light; her blood burned at his slightest touch.

Leviathan placed the goblet on the tray. "Bring me your brush and sit before me."

She emerged from the trance, baffled at the god's behavior. He'd never spoken or treated her this way. She obeyed, and Leviathan proceeded to gently brush her hair. Each stroke sent her deeper and deeper into divine euphoria.

Leviathan spoke softly, his voice floating through the air and into her soul. "Truly powerful gods come to serve, not take. We are patient shepherds." Atamoda didn't understand, only wishing his hypnotizing voice would never stop. "In return we only demand loyalty…and *obedience*."

The brushing ceased. The trance broke. Atamoda opened her eyes. Leviathan towered above her, grasping the red sword.

"Are you loyal, holy woman? Are you grateful?" He placed the sword tip beneath her chin.

"I don't understand, Great Lord," she stammered.

"I bring you into my inner domain. I treat you with kindness and bestow privileges I do not give my best warriors. I've asked nothing in return, nor have I taken your body. Are these things I say not true?"

The warmth evaporated. Atamoda fought to keep her voice from breaking. "They are all true, Great Lord."

"Is it true you have stolen food from my own table and given it to the pen slaves?"

Atamoda swallowed hard. "Yes."

"Is it true you stole blankets from the storage tent, *blankets meant for my warriors*, and also gave them to the slaves?"

"It is true."

"Did you conspire with Twice-Burned to carry out these acts of betrayal?"

Atamoda sensed a trap and chose her next words carefully. "I asked for his help. He agreed. The fault is all mine."

"Why?" He stared at her, seemingly perplexed.

"Because they are human, and I am Lo."

"I can put you in the slave pens."

"If that is my fate."

"What are they to you that you would risk everything to help them?"

"A life without love and mercy is a fate worse than death."

"Mercy…" He gritted his teeth. "Damn that word."

"Mercy is the sacrifice my petty gods demand, Great Lord."

Leviathan roared. He spun about and cleaved the iron brazier stand in two. The burning coals spilled onto the wet ground where the tub had been sitting and sizzled. "I should throw you to my warriors. There is no word for mercy in their language."

Atamoda's heart almost stopped at the thought, but she summoned her courage. "What of my son? Will your wrath extend to him? He is innocent."

Leviathan laughed deeply, but without mirth. "His fate is already spoken for."

"Before you pronounce judgement on me, Great Lord, I beg you tell me my son's fate."

"Your son is fated for greatness you cannot begin to imagine." Somehow, that did not allay her fear.

Leviathan placed the sword under Atamoda's chin once again, compelling her to her feet. Atamoda stood defenseless before the god Amiran said ruled all the world's seas, commanded thousands of ships, and who slayed beasts who breathed fire.

"I will not abandon you to the slave pens. Nor will I hand you over to my Obsidian Guard. You understand I cannot have a slave willfully disobeying me?" His tone sounded almost apologetic.

She nodded quickly, fighting back the tears and knowing her end had come. Kol-ok would live on, though his fate was still a mystery. Perhaps, somewhere out there, Aizarg and her people still survived. Amiran would find a way to steal the chest's contents without her and escape.

The metal pressed against her flesh felt warm, as if generating its own heat. Fear and consequence evaporated and Atamoda, Patesi-le of the Crane Clan, dared look directly at the god. He would have to face her when he ended her life. Atamoda's story would end here, at the hands of the god she pitied. Leviathan would have to endure for all eternity in a hellish existence devoid of love.

In Leviathan's eyes, Atamoda saw determination and the ghost of blue fire.

He flicked his wrist. She heard a clink.

Heart pounding, Atamoda stared down at the collar cut cleanly in two laying at her feet. She rubbed her bare neck. Leviathan placed the red sword upon the throne and picked absently at the morsels on the tray.

"I don't understand."

"You're free, or is the broken collar not clear enough?" He bit into the olive, not looking at her. "Be proud, you've joined an elite group. I've only cut the bonds of four mortals before you."

"My son?" her voice cracked.

"Kol-ok is not mine to free."

"I won't leave him." Determination returned to her voice.

He shrugged. "Then you have a problem. I cannot have a freewoman wandering the camp, eating my rations. By Poseidon's decree, only warriors and sailors can be freemen. I doubt you'll make a good warrior, and I currently have no use for a sailor."

Atamoda felt dizzy. Her mind reeled. *He must be toying with me*, she thought, *but to what purpose?* Amiran's warning echoed in her mind, but Atamoda couldn't hide her heart like he could. "Why?" was all she could manage to say.

He looked up from the tray. "A god does not answer to a mortal, but these are exceptional times." The strange blue light in his eyes momentarily flared again. "And you are an exceptional woman."

He recharged the goblet. "Poseidon once loved a mortal. She bore him ten sons, my half-brothers. She took my father's sanity to the grave with her." Leviathan drank deeply and continued, "Not all at once, of course. A god cannot forget, and every day her memory tormented him, sapping a small measure of his mind. For thousands of years I watched him slip into madness. I vowed to never fall in love with a mortal." He brought the full weight of his stare upon Atamoda. "It is a vow I fully intend to keep.

"My father's kingdom is wiped away. In these new lands, I have been promised a new kingdom." He stared into the distance, as if seeing through the tent walls. "I will succeed where Poseidon failed."

Leviathan approached Atamoda, holding a slice of dried, yellow fruit. The scattered coals gave his immense silhouette a blood-red outline. The blue fire simmered in his eyes like stars in heaven's vault. Leviathan skimmed the fruit teasingly across her lips. Atamoda's vision swam and her knees trembled.

"Eat." Leviathan's voice was like a calm sea on the darkest night. Breathing heavy, Atamoda delicately nibbled the succulent fruit. He held the cup to her lips and she drained the goblet.

Leviathan touched her bare shoulder like a feather, and she drew in a sharp breath. His caress traced a path to her slave brand. The scar had been numb to this point. She often found herself idly touching the scar, curious if she would ever feel anything there again. Now, Leviathan's caress had reawakened the dead tissue.

All those nights lying at the foot of his bed like a pet, Atamoda wondered how she would react when Leviathan finally decided to take her. Would she fight? Would she scream and claw and kick with her dying measure? Now, the moment had finally come, and Atamoda closed her eyes and leaned her head back, paralyzed by overwhelming pleasure.

"You are not here by accident." His fingertip glided farther down. Her gown's delicate clasp surrendered, and cool air invaded her naked curves. Leviathan's light touch became firm and needful. He bent down, voice pouring gently into her ear like the lion's purr. "There is a place in this new land where the holy tree grows. You shall eat its fruit and live forever." His finger glided in a circle around her navel. "Your womb shall become a sacred place. You will be exalted as the Mother of Gods and Queen of the Earth. You will never die, Atamoda, nor shall you ever fear or be alone again."

A new fear grew inside Atamoda, a terror not unlike when she saw the giant wave looming over them at the Cataclysm's beginning. "What..." she panted, barely able to form the words. "What *price*?"

His warm breath filled her ear. "Tell me I am not alone."

Atamoda felt herself lifted, just like that mighty wave had once catapulted the Arun-ki above the clouds. That time, when she reached for the glorious sun, the barge was thrown back down into darkness and terror.

This time, lifted by a god's passion, Atamoda finally touched the sun.

22. Mystery, Part 2.

I left Mother at the Altar Rock, and found myself outside, staring at Nushen far below. Rage, grief, and madness battled for what was left of my soul.

Nuwa's shell was young when she banished me. By taking Shinglay's shell, Nuwa had betrayed all she had taught me. Knowing Shinglay had likely obediently sacrificed her body to the goddess made the act even more treacherous. Now the goddess was withering away, trapped inside Shinglay's dying body and slipping deeper into insanity.

If I did nothing, I would become my own mother's executioner. Shinglay would die, and Nuwa would forever lose her grip on this world. Nuwa would become and remain spirit, and her hold on Nushen would end.

My beloved Shinglay suffered. The only path to end that suffering was death. If I killed Shinglay, I killed Nuwa.

Would the Emperor of Heaven judge Nuwa for what she did to Shinglay? Would he judge me for my disobedience?

Desolate, I raised my hands to the sky, begging Heaven to show me the way.

The silver torch beside me flashed into flame. Then, one-by-one, the other torches flared to life, leading to the village below.

The path before me wasn't the one I desired, but the one I had to take. By nightfall, I had returned to the Threshold Dragon with Zheshung, a girl not yet twelve summers. With her mother's blessing, she had selflessly offered herself as Nuwa's next vessel.

- The Chronicle of Fu Xi.

***

Darkness lightened into a gray curtain as Fu Xi led the horse into the water.

The fog materialized every bit as thick as Fu Xi had expected, cloaking the canyon walls and dulling the rapids' roar. Judging by the wet rocks and mud along the shore, Fu Xi estimated the water level had dropped several feet overnight. He tasted the water, and noticed a significant decrease in salinity. He suspected the flood must have receded below this river's original elevation.

Firmly grasping Heise's reins, he led the stallion deeper into the pool until the water reached his waist. Fu Xi splashed Heise's flank, using his hands to groom the horse. As the caked mud melted away, Heise's black coat once again took on an elegant shine. Fu Xi carefully inspected the animal for any wounds or sores. The horse seemed to enter a trance, barely breathing under Fu Xi's rhythmic grooming. The act became cathartic for Fu Xi as well. Soon, he felt someone watching them.

Silhouetted against the mist like an apparition, she stood motionless on the shore. Fu Xi remained quiet and continued to bathe the horse. To his surprise, Mystery slipped into the pool. Alternating bands of silver and black undulated outward as her fingertips caressed the mirrored surface. Her wild mane caught the water, and trailed behind like a royal train. She drew closer, her silhouette slowly materializing into the stunning woman from the night before. A perfect quicksilver reflection preceded her, as if Mystery existed in this world and the next. He thought of the red dagger tucked into his belt. Could she be a demigod like him? Mystery never looked at Fu Xi, but stood so close he could feel her heat. Mystery held him in a spell, just as Heise held her in a spell.

Mystery raised a trembling hand to touch Heise's neck. At the last moment, she stopped, and acknowledged Fu Xi's presence like a guest who commits an offense and seeks her host's forgiveness.

He nodded at the horse.

Mystery rubbed Heise's neck and ran her fingers through his mane. She closed her eyes and rested her head against the horse's flank, listening to him breathe. Heise didn't seem in the least bit bothered by this stranger, and appeared to be enjoying her attention. She waded around Heise, washing and rubbing much as Fu Xi had, but finding dirt Fu Xi apparently had missed. Mystery expertly massaged the knots from the horse's shoulders and upper legs, something Fu Xi never considered doing.

It became obvious Mystery wasn't just familiar with horses — she knew their husbandry on a deep level. In this way, she conjured memories of Sunnah, Leviathan's horse master. Her olive skin and slender facial features didn't mark her as kin to Sunnah's people, but Mystery seemed connected with the horse on a spiritual level, very much as Sunnah had.

Mystery softly whispered to Heise. Fu Xi soaked in every syllable, ears keen for anything familiar. The guttural, halting rhythms seemed familiar even if the words were not.

Heise gently nuzzled her neck. Mystery laughed, and for an unguarded moment, shared a heartfelt smile with Fu Xi. The corners of her eyes began to mist, and he could see Mystery fighting to conceal her emotions.

Whatever horrors she has endured during the Cataclysm, he thought, *Mystery likely never thought she'd see a horse again*. The long-absent joy of human companionship threatened to overwhelm Fu Xi. He patted Heise. "Horse."

She nodded and also patted Heise. "Ippa."

Ippa. During those many days with Amiran in the Great Library of Wu, he'd observed the scholar instruct Elda and Ercole. While most lessons were conducted in Atlantean, Amiran occasionally instructed in their native Attican. The

Attican word for horse was *hippa*. Fu Xi felt certain Mystery's physical racial resemblance to the Attican twins was more than superficial. Her people, and language, must be distant cousins to the people locked in a war against Poseidon's Empire. That meant the Gray-Eyed Queen and her armies mustn't be far. Maybe the Man with White Hair, and even Fu Xi's long-lost half-brother, could be nearby, too.

If Mystery survived, then others likely survived, too.

That meant it wouldn't be long before he would be able to speak to her. It was only a matter of getting Mystery to relax and keep talking.

Fu Xi took Heise's reins, led him to shore, and tied him to a driftwood log. Mystery resumed her place by the smoldering fire, hugging herself tightly against the morning chill. She never took her eyes off Fu Xi as he saddled Heise.

"I think we're going to camp here a few more days. There isn't much dried meat left in the saddlebags. With your mouth to feed, we'll soon run out." He tossed the saddlebags over the horse and secured them. "There are plenty of fish here, at least for now, and abundant wood. We'll need to catch as many as possible and smoke the meat. That may take a few days. In the meantime, we'll scout the surrounding area, and I can see how well you ride."

She crouched by the fire, stirring the coals and tossing in a few small sticks. Fu Xi considered her tattered loincloth and barely concealed breasts. "You're going to need something warmer than that."

He turned and stared into the fog concealing the impenetrable cliffs. "I think the highlands may have been spared. Game might still be plentiful higher up. Maybe we can kill a deer or goat and fashion you new clothes…"

Then all became darkness.

***

Bright sunlight shone down between the canyon walls in milky shafts. Fu Xi sat up, collecting his thoughts and rubbing the prominent goose egg on the back of his head. The saddle, minus the saddlebags, rested on the ground in front of him. Hoof prints in the mud, widely spaced at full gallop, marked her downstream escape. He would have shaken his head in disbelief, but it hurt too much.

Skull throbbing like a hangover, Fu Xi slowly stood. Mystery's expertly delivered blow had been intended to incapacitate, not kill. *Such skills are taught,* he thought. *She's a warrior, or at least hails from a warrior tribe.*

Fu Xi felt for the red dagger. Gone. If she had used that blade on him…

Does she understand the blade's power? he wondered. He felt for his personal knife and was shocked to find it still tucked neatly in his belt.

Blue wisps danced over the campfire. The fish he had prepared for their breakfast had also vanished. The river had subsided several more feet since dawn.

"Hmm," he grunted. It didn't surprise him Mystery left the saddle. Amiran told Fu Xi the saddle was unique to the Atlanteans. Sunnah's people had ridden bareback.

A familiar bundle wrapped in a rabbit pelt rested on the saddle. Grinning widely, Fu Xi knelt down and picked it up. Folding a corner over, he found dried jerky inside. Mystery had left him a single ration.

She stole his horse. His head hurt. Fu Xi should have been angry, but felt lighthearted. He tucked the jerky in his tunic, scooped up the saddle by the clinch straps, and threw it over his shoulder. With a spring in every step, the God of Names followed the tracks.

She is obviously a good rider, and Heise is swift, he thought, *but the trail is rugged and treacherous. She will have to double back many times to find a way through the side canyons, just as I did. The ground is soft — she will leave a well-marked trail. She will have to rest and make a fire at night, especially given her scant clothing.*

Fu Xi had time and patience. He squinted up at the bright blue sky and let the sweet, clean air fill his lungs. "A walk will do me good. Who needs a horse, anyway? Especially one that betrays you for the first pretty face we stumble across." Fu Xi threw back his head with deep, cleansing laughter.

Then, he whistled and began to sing.

"I live upstream, you live downstream

From night to night of you I dream…"

23. Decisions.

I retrieved the Offering Blade from its cradle in the inner sanctuary. As Nuwa slipped away, so did Nushen.

Thirty years of dust and filth covered the Altar Rock. I laid my blanket over the place where a thousand blade strikes from the orichalcum blade had nicked and gouged the granite. I cradled Nuwa and placed her on the slab. She passed in and out of consciousness as I patiently explained to Zheshung where to stand, how to hold the blade, and what to expect. Eyes wide, she kept fearfully looking at Nuwa's filthy, emaciated form. The reality of her choice crushed down upon this brave child.

"Lord Fu Xi, what is wrong with her?"

"The goddess is lost inside Shinglay. You must help her find her way."

Nuwa moaned, and I heard Shinglay's suffering bubbling beneath the goddess's consciousness.

Zheshung stumbled backwards from the small steps beside the Altar Rock. The dagger clattered to the floor, and she began to cry. "I want to go home!"

"Hear me, Zheshung. Tortoise Mountain and Nushen are one. The goddess cannot dwell in Shinglay's shell any longer. Nushen, and your mother, suffer because the goddess suffers. If Nuwa passes into spirit, Nushen will perish. Only you can save our world."

172

Not in 10,000 years will I forget the child's terror, or her bravery. Shaking, she picked up the blade and resumed her place on the steps. Trembling, she held the crimson blade over Nuwa's body. The goddess grew still, as if sensing her suffering had come to an end.

I stood beside the Altar Rock. In the dingy light, I kept my gaze locked on Shinglay, remembering what she looked like in the summer sun. I needed to see her eyes, her spirit, one last time. I needed to say goodbye.

I heard the hilt thud against her chest, and the tip bite into granite. Nuwa inhaled, and her eyes flew open, and then the faint blue ember in her pupils faded.

Shinglay rolled her head toward me as sunlight exploded through the clouds, bathing the Altar Rock. I searched, but did not see even the briefest recognition, or even lucidity in my lover's eyes, before she passed to the Emperor of Heaven. I did not need to look at Zheshung to know Mother now dwelt inside her. Her small hand calmly removed the knife from Shinglay's chest. I wrapped Shinglay in our blanket, slumped to the floor against the Altar Rock, and held her close.

Grief washed over me, deeper and colder than the Great Flood that would one day submerge the world. For how long I remained against the Altar Rock, holding my lover tightly to my breast, I do not know. As with my passion for Shinglay those many years ago, my mortal blood swept the god aside. In answer to a prayer I did not know to pray, the Emperor of Heaven granted me merciful oblivion.

When my divine blood reasserted its lordship, so did my rational mind. I emerged from a waking dream to find the Place of Perfect Sorrows bright, clean, and fully restored to its former glory. Clear water flowed through the four canals from the fountain. Pink blossoms covered the Eternal Tree's lushness. The silver torches on the Seven Columns burned brightly.

The decay that once filled the Place of Perfect Sorrows had somehow infested me. My clothes had rotted away to tattered rags, and my beard and hair stretched between my legs. Mother stood over me, hand outstretched. Zheshung's shell was now that of an adult woman. "Welcome home from your long journey, my obedient son. Your mat is unrolled and waiting."

Weakness gripped my flesh. In my long bondage to grief, I had withered away to skin and bones. Mother supported me as I hobbled to the Inner Sanctuary. This is when I saw my blanket lying beneath the Eternal Tree, covered with peach blossoms. Neatly folded, Shinglay's dried blood dyed its fibers.

- The Chronicle of Fu Xi.

***

Atamoda pulled her feet under the thick blankets and curled into a ball. Frigid air nibbled her nose, forcing her deeper into the down-stuffed silk mattress. *This must be what the womb feels like to the unborn child*, she thought: warm, safe, protected. The bedclothes smelled like him. Leviathan's presence lingered here, like ozone after a lightning strike. Her body ached from last night's passion. Noises sharp and unyielding penetrated her citadel of pillows and soft furs. Heavy canvas flapped and rippled like a cracking whip in the gale. Rusty iron shrieked unceasingly against rusty iron as if being tortured. Atamoda burrowed deeper in the covers like a tick. Slowly, the cold and noise pursued her into the bed's depths until she could no longer ignore it. Wrapped tightly in the bedclothes, she sat up and looked across the empty tent. Ashes filled the brazier. In the darkness beyond the unstaked tent walls, men shouted over the wind.

They are breaking camp, she thought. *The time has finally come.*

Atamoda threw off the furs. Her breath misted as she relieved herself in the chamber pot and then rummaged through the chest for the warmest garments she could find. In a few minutes, she wore high gray leather boots and a long-sleeved black velvet dress. The clothes were snug, as they had been intended for Elda as she matured during the long voyage. Still shivering, Atamoda quickly combed her hair and then wrapped herself in a thick, wolfskin shoulder cloak that fell well past her knees.

In the chest were also warm clothes for a young man, very similar to Elda's. Those were untouched.

Atamoda drank the last of the wine directly from the bottle, grabbed a torch from the wall, and ventured out.

The wind stole Atamoda's breath and penetrated her clothing like needles. Her hands had already begun to grow numb. The gravel's crunch suddenly gave way to squeaky softness. Atamoda held the torch higher, and saw small snowdrifts. She glanced over to Kol-ok's cage. To her relief, more furs had been heaped over the cage, and the nearby bonfire blazed brightly.

The eastern sky began to brighten as several slaves shambled past under their Olmec taskmasters' watchful glare. Almost naked, they shivered uncontrollably. She feared what the freezing cold would be doing to those in the slave pens.

Atamoda's fears were realized when she found the pens empty except for several bodies huddled together, frozen in the mud and filth.

A hand touched her shoulder. Atamoda spun around to face a grim Zelko. "Come."

Numb in body and soul, she followed.

"Most of the supplies and slaves are already in the gorge," he said as they walked. "It's warmer there, out of the wind."

"Where is Leviathan?" she asked, trying to keep up with his quick strides.

He glanced over his shoulder at her clothes with a disdainful look. "Already in the gorge, supervising the caravan's assembly."

They passed more slaves bent under heavy supply bundles. Occasionally, a whip's crack pierced the darkness. They passed by Leviathan's tent again. Beside it, a work detail busily dismantled Elda's small tent.

"If you're going to help us, you better do it quick before they take down the god's tent."

They came to the camp's northern perimeter, and the Olmec shelters. Snow-covered, they were all abandoned. The warriors were on the move, never to return to this place.

A weak fire burned in front of one the lean-tos. Zelko halted and pointed inside, where a figure curled into ball among old branches and bones. "They left him for dead in the pens. I brought him here. He won't last long."

"Pug!" She fell to her knees and covered him with her wolfskin cloak. "I don't have anything to eat," she sobbed. Pug dully considered Atamoda as she watched his life drain away, as if he had been holding on only long enough to see her again.

Pug's arm shook violently as he took her hand and touched it to his forehead, but could not complete the greeting. Atamoda steadied his hand and touched it to her lips, and then her heart. Pug smiled, closed his eyes, and never opened them again.

Atamoda turned to tell Zelko, but the goatherd had vanished, replaced by a fully risen sun. Jagged shadows stretched across camp like claws. Ragged storms danced among the distant peaks, painting the mountains in alternating bands of gray clouds and golden sunlight.

"It's gone!" Atamoda gasped. A muddy plain stretched to the western horizon. The sea that had deposited Atamoda and her son here, the one she hoped might reunite them with her people again, had finally slipped away.

Atamoda sobbed, mourning not only for gentle Pug, but also her dying hope. She buried her hands in the snow and remembered how Aizarg once described seeing it as he climbed the Cliff Road on his quest to the Narim. The snow was too far away for Aizarg to touch, but he told her how he longed to put some in a bag and bring it home. Atamoda scooped up two fistfuls, and felt it slowly melt away.

A sudden gust howled around her, and clouds enveloped the mountaintop. The fire died away as the mist thickened. When it cleared, Amiran stood a few paces away, staring impassively. Behind him, Leviathan's tent flapped in the gale, occasionally revealing the scorched chest.

Amiran's account of the great odyssey to reach this place swirled through Atamoda's mind. The time had come to choose. Fate left her no option, and for that she hated Amiran.

Atamoda looked down on Pug's body.

Leviathan offered me immortality, to be safe and cherished. Forever.

The wind strengthened, and from across the encampment, the hinges on Kol-ok's cage screeched.

***

One needs only to live a little while to grasp that everything changes, even eternity. After my exile, and Shinglay's death, Nuwa changed. Her transformation manifested itself in a series of decrees that shaped Nushen's, and all of Cin's, future.

Nuwa decreed Offering Ceremonies would only be held in spring, and only when her current shell neared its natural end. She also decreed the establishment of the Order of Sacred Elder Mothers, and the convent under the willow tree. Charged with cultivating acolytes, willing virgins all, to serve as Mother's shells, the Elder Mothers ensured harmony existed between the goddess and the village.

Nuwa decreed her husbands were no longer prisoners of her affections, and could roam freely between Tortoise Mountain and Nushen. In the years following this edict, Mother took fewer husbands, and sometimes spent entire lifetimes alone. In those times, I stayed with her, and she did not seem so distant. She, too, spent more time among the people. In so doing, I think she found some measure of peace.

Eternally bound to one another, Nushen and Nuwa existed in balance. That balance was reflected in Mother's spirit, and I believe it was the first step on her path to redemption for her secret sins.

Joy filled my heart as Nushen flourished. I was the Silver Stairs, joining Heaven to earth. I accepted my role as Heaven had dictated. Nuwa decreed any unmarried woman choosing to share her body with me would not be spoiled for her wedding bed, though she could never become an acolyte. Yes, over the centuries, I found pleasure with some of Nushen's daughters, though not many. Too many reminded me of Shinglay. I satisfied my mortal blood's passions far beyond Tortoise Mountain on my many journeys, where the names and faces did not remind me of the hole in my heart.

Centuries before the Cataclysm, I found myself alone in a shaded grotto far from Nushen. I knelt beside deep, swift waters, holding the blanket Shinglay and I had woven together. Time had turned it brittle, and the once bright bloodstains had faded to dull brown. I touched the small hole where the Offering Blade had penetrated, and the material crumbled. It turned to dust and blew away on the cool breeze of an approaching storm.

I will keep my promise, my love. You live in my heart, safe and cherished.

Forever.

- The Chronicle of Fu Xi.

Part 3: Before the Cataclysm.

"As it was written by Master Vulcan in the Ancient of Ancients, the gods taught humanity the Four Great Gifts: fire, agriculture, animal domestication, and weaving. These were the primary colors which colored our path from darkness to light. The gods saw their handiwork, and were pleased.

With the Four Great Gifts, humankind, namely the Academy, brought forth civilization's rainbow of arts and sciences: the wheel, pottery, writing, metallurgy, mathematics, music, poetry, medicine, textiles, engineering, and astronomy. All of these disciplines sprung from mankind's intellect, not from Poseidon's Sons." - The Last Scholar

- The Chronicle of Fu Xi.

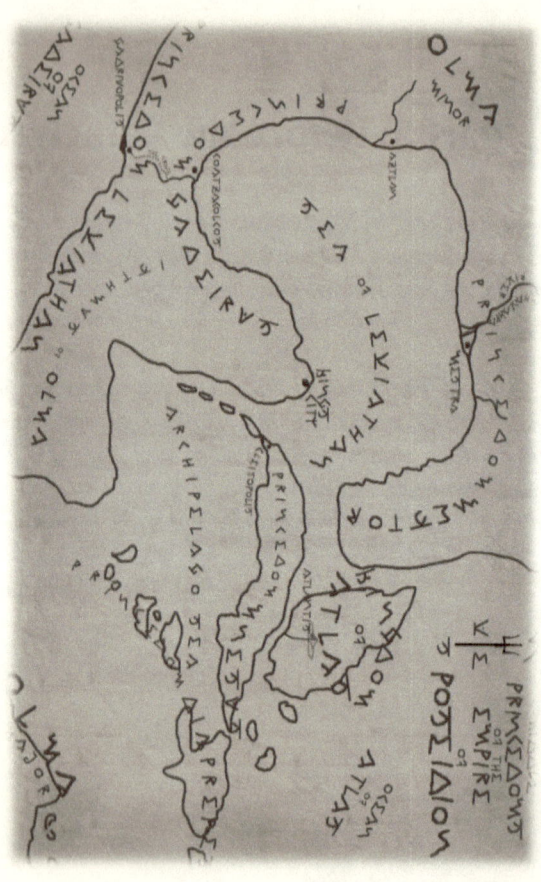

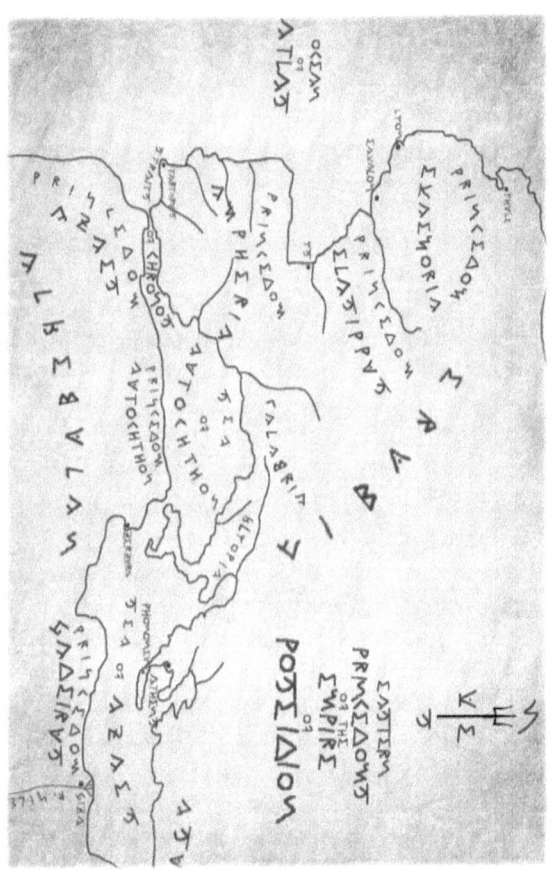

24. The Splendid Emptiness.

"Thou art immortal." - The First Lesson of Poseidon to his Children, from the Ancient of Ancients.

- The Chronicle of Fu Xi.

***

Ages ago, when the world was young...

Hunger drove him onward into the forbidden wilderness called the Bewitched Lands. The elders said it was the dominion of demons and witches. The dry season lasted longer than any in memory, forcing the hunter deeper into the swamps than anyone from his village had ventured before. Armed with a blowgun, he hoped to find monkeys and deer to feed his starving family. He slogged through mangrove swamps, listening for the tell-tale howl of monkeys in the canopy above.

At first, he thought the thatch hut on the small island might be a hunter's shelter. Blanketing vines gave the hut the appearance of a green cave. He called out, but no one answered. Stone knife in hand, he ducked through the narrow opening. After a moment, his eyes adjusted to the dimness and he caught his breath against the overpowering stench.

A single ray of light from the smoke hole illuminated a body casually resting against the center pole. Two hollow eye sockets bid the hunter to join her. She had shriveled to the point the skin wrapped tightly to her bones. A forest of mold sprang up from the floor, feasting on the ooze seeping from her corpse and weaving its way into the dead woman's long, gray hair.

Bright eyes blinked from the shadows, unearthly and piercing. He raised the blowgun, thinking it a monkey, but then lowered the weapon. A naked child, perhaps seven summers old, nestled against the corpse's side. With skin as black as the shadows, the emaciated girl suckled at death's breast. Bones and partially eaten animals covered the hut's floor. The hunter stumbled backwards as a dark blur lunged at him. Instinctively, he jabbed the knife at the attacker and felt it sink deep into flesh. A boy, almost identical to the girl, fell to the dirt, clutching his abdomen.

Pity replaced fear. These children must have stayed with their mother after her death. Now they were starving and wild, and he had unintentionally killed one of them.

A faint sound, like sizzling animal fat thrown onto a fire, grew louder as the boy's whimpers grew quieter. A scent like that following a lightning strike filled the hut. The hunter looked down to see the blood covering his knife bubble and turn to mist. The blood pooling in the dirt did the same. The boy faced him with clenched fists and bared teeth. The knife wound had vanished.

The hunter fled. For a day and a night and another day, he crashed recklessly through the underbrush until the swamps turned to jungle, and jungle turned to forest. He ran until he collapsed amongst his village's huts, clinging on death's precipice.

In the days that followed, word spread across the island-continent of the bewitched hut and the demon children. From the jungle tribes along the eastern rain forest, to the farmers in the central plains, to the coastal fishing villages, the tale of the dark-skinned children with blood that boiled finally reached the capital's canals and streets. Wagging tongues carried them into the Alabaster Pyramid itself. King Atlas, most powerful of Queen Cleito's ten immortal sons, entered his father's court. He whispered the incredible tale into Poseidon's ear.

"Bring them before me," the Emperor of the World commanded.

***

The boy fought them at every step, from the moment the giant men tore them from their hut to their arrival in this place of many people. Unlike the smaller men and women who cleaned and bathed them upon their arrival, his bites and scratches had no effect on these giants. Where the others would scream and bleed, the giant men laughed and swatted him down.

This must be what the insects and small animals I tormented in the jungle felt like, the boy thought. Insignificant. Helpless. Alone. *Insects can still sting*, he thought. *They can bite, too.*

Sister did not fight. She only looked on in silent awe at the wonders surrounding them. They both knew their lives had forever changed, though to what ends they could not begin to fathom.

Scrubbed clean and heads shaven, the children stood defiantly in a circle of ten giants who considered them with cold mirth. With full beards that fell across bare, muscled chests, they exuded vitality and power, much like the place the children found themselves.

The boy felt as if drowning in light. So much light poured into the grand chamber it hurt the boy's eyes and seeped through his eyelids. The overwhelming sounds and sensations left him numb. He could never have dreamed of anything so high or grand as the pyramid's vaulted ceiling. Thick sunbeams poured down from narrow window slits. The light struck four gilded mirrors, two on either side of the stone chair and each taller than a man. They reflected the sunlight back to the ceiling, where it diffused softly on red metal leaf upon the chamber. The floor, like immobilized water, reflected the light into the pyramid's dizzying heights.

Voices and laughter echoed from seemingly every direction. People strolled by outside arched doorways along each wall. Dressed in flowing clothes of every color, they glanced into the grand hall and whispered excitedly to one another before hurrying off. The overwhelming sensations filled the boy with panic and an urge to flee.

Lush trees, much like those found in the jungle, lined the hall's two sides like pillars. Colorful birds roosted in their branches. He found their songs eased some of his fear. The boy badly wanted to climb into their dark shade and join them. Beyond the encircling men, a small tree stood isolated in the court's center. Gnarled, bent, and not much taller than the boy, it grew from a raised fountain. Water gurgled over the fountain's low wall and cascaded in a glassy shimmer into an encircling moat, which split into four small channels. Level with the floor and narrow enough for even a child to step across, the streams extended in four directions. Two terminated on either side of the hall in shimmering pools beneath the pillar trees. One vanished outside the archway on the chamber's opposite side, and the one closest to where they stood disappeared into a culvert below the raised platform.

The giants parted, and another man stepped forward. He seemed frail in comparison to the giants. His gray-streaked beard stretched to his midriff, and lines etched his face. He wore white cloth around his waist like the bigger men, but one also draped over his shoulder. The material looked as if made from clouds. The boy had never seen his mother put cloth on her body, or theirs. He wanted to touch the material, to experience what it felt like.

This man didn't consider them with mocking hatred like the giants did, but seemed curious. He gestured the giants to step back. They bowed slightly and obeyed. The boy instinctively understood this man possessed authority over the seemingly more powerful beings. Why? They looked as if they could crush him.

The man with the lined face knelt intimately close. "Do you understand me?"

Sister nodded, and began to whimper as if sensing his power, too. The boy worked up the courage to caress the garment's hem. It felt soft and smooth and satisfying to the touch. The man's smile carried both reassurance and menace, as if to say *I will let you do that once. Just once.* A deep understanding awakened inside the boy. This man exuded power as great as all the light pouring into the grand chamber. He reminded the boy of the wind that shook the jungle's trees, felt but never seen. With this unseen power, he wielded control over the giants.

"Stop crying," he commanded Sister. "You live and your mother is dead. This is the way of things. Make peace with it." He stood and commanded one of the giants. "Bring them."

The giant seized their arms and followed the old man across the grand room and up the cascading staircase onto a marble platform overlooking the court. An imposing stone chair dominated the platform, unadorned except for the two stallions' heads forming the armrests. Several paces behind the throne, two wall pillars flanked an entrance leading to a dark inner chamber. The giant shoved each child against a pillar, bowed to the old man, and then backed away.

"Do not move from that place unless permitted. You have been chosen to guard my naos, the inner temple," the old one commanded. The children looked at one another quizzically. Then, the old one rejoined the giants. Together, the group strode away.

"H-how long must we stand here?" Sister timidly called out after him.

The old one turned around. "Until the days and nights melt together like candle wax." He gestured to the gathering crowd outside the archway. "Observe them wither and die, generation after generation, and learn who *you* truly are. Only then will you learn my first lesson. Serve me well, and I will bestow upon you a name worthy of a god."

With that, he turned and departed, leaving the children alone in the splendid emptiness.

25. Remember.

"All dragons were born at dawn. With her jaws, the mother dragon would gently extract her single egg from the warm compost heap, where it had incubated for a decade. She would deposit the crimson egg, the size of a full-grown ram, on a cold rock facing east. Waiting for sunrise, the egg cooled. Feeling death's oncoming chill seeping into its sanctuary, the fawn inside would awaken to a cruel choice: tear its way to the sun, or die. Forged in its mother's womb, the thin orichalcum eggshell proved stronger than steel. A dragon had to prove itself worthy, even before drawing its first breath." - The Last Scholar

- The Chronicle of Fu Xi.

***

Remember...the last word her mother spoke before vanishing into a long-ago sunrise. It reverberated in the young dragon's memory, as hopes and fears collided in her heart like waves crashing against the cliff below.

Instinct compelled her to step off the ledge and soar, as her mother had, though this time for different reasons. The musk tickling her snout beckoned her towards the false dawn, but trepidation held her claws firmly to the cool stone, lest the message carried on the wind might only be a cruel dream. The fact that she detected the bull dragon's scent on this sacred morning, the anniversary of her birth, wasn't lost on her. Perhaps the Mother Serpent sent an omen of good fortune.

The future, and whatever it held, must wait until she completed the Naming Ceremony. At dusk the previous evening, the Naming Ceremony began with the Serpent Mother's star hanging motionless in the north. Perched upon this lonely cliff, she traced the heavens with her eyes. Each star had a name, but only the Serpent Mother knew them all. She could only recite her lineage. From the Heart of the Dragon, the young doe worked her way from star to star, paying homage to the name of every female dragon in her lineage through the countless ages. With practiced timing, they rolled off her snout with perfect pacing, so she would speak her own name exactly at dawn's first ray, the moment of her birth.

As the eastern horizon lightened to a rosy pink, the doe finally came to her mother's star. Her mother instructed the ceremony should be a source of inner peace and joy, but until this morning it only brought an overwhelming sense of isolation. As the years went by, the dragon performed it only out of duty and in remembrance of her beloved mother.

Her mother had spoken for hours on end of the days when the wind was thick with the tang of other does. They sailed the heavens chasing bull dragons' coppery, blood-like musk, enticing them to mountain strongholds. Each scent carried a name and a unique message. Having spent her life utterly alone, the doe found such things unimaginable. Until now, she'd only known empty winds.

For the first fifty years of life, on the mountain cliff where she had hatched, the doe's mother had taught her the Naming Ceremony. Then, one spring, the tarsal glands on the young dragon's hind legs began to ooze, signaling sexual maturity. In that year, the elder dragon watched as her daughter completed the ceremony unassisted. When the young doe finally came to her own star, and uttered her own name, the matriarch spread her wings and took to the sky.

She never saw her mother again, nor detected her scent on the Four Winds. Until last night, she had never encountered the scent of another of her kind.

The young dragon fled the icy peaks and jungle lowlands of her homeland a year ago, driven east by men and their arrows. Seeking her kind, she crossed an enormous ocean, but only found this sea and more humans. Three days ago, exhausted and seeking shelter from a gale, she discovered this shallow cave overlooking a rocky coast. She rested and fasted, and prepared for the Naming Ritual. The storm blew by, and upon a crisp eastern breeze scrubbed clean by the gale, his message found her. She'd never encountered such a scent, but her ancient urges, so long dormant, told her exactly what it was. Far across the world, a powerful bull dragon called for a mate.

With a low, purring rumble, the dragon spoke her mother's name and then shifted her gaze to a star just cresting the eastern horizon. Sparkling blue and delicate, like frozen dew hanging from a blade of grass, it fled the blinding dawn close on its heels. In a few moments, the star would vanish in the new day and would only reappear on her birth anniversary, at the exact latitude of her birth cave. Why her mother picked that particular star for her daughter's name, one which only appeared briefly once a year, the dragon would never know.

In that moment, right before the sun swallowed her star, the dragon spoke her own name.

What will my name sound like spoken by another? she thought. *Spoken by a lover?*

Now, only one act remained to complete the Ceremony.

She cracked her jaws, letting a thin trickle of fiery liquid spatter onto bare rock. It pooled into a small glob of blue flame, heating the stone to a dull red. She dipped her foreclaw's tip into the fire until the warmth threatened to grow into pain. She withdrew the talon, briefly examined the white-hot tip, and then pressed it against the cave wall. The granite softened, and slightly gave way. With a few quick, graceful strokes, she completed the ritual.

Daybreak erupted across the glittering sea. The dragon answered its call by spreading her enormous, butterfly-like wings. Unfurled like sails, they dwarfed her snakelike body. Sunlight warmed them, and the warmth mixed with the traces of the bull's pheromone pulsing through her blood. Her body tingled with a sensuousness she'd never experienced. The light filtered through their delicate membranes and blood vessels, turning the cliff behind her into a kaleidoscope of blues and reds. As if sensing her joy, the gentle morning breeze lifted her effortlessly over the sparkling sea. The dragon left behind a lifetime's loneliness on the barren cliff and vanished into the sunrise.

The mark slowly cooled high above the crashing surf. It represented a single word, telling any of her kind who may one day take refuge in this cave her name and her star's name. This was the word her mother spoke long ago when she watched her baby rip open the orichalcum shell, and burst forth into this world in a blaze of blue fire.

"Remember."

26. Asleep in the Icy Womb.

"*In studying the Ancient of Ancients, Master Gremis learned it was Vulcan who smuggled the Goddess Athena from the Kingdom. All eleven of Poseidon's sons launched their fleets, scouring the empire in search of her. Her brother Leviathan pursued with the most zeal, never suspecting she hid on his own flagship. He became the unwitting agent of her escape.*

"*Athena, and the bastard child she saved from Poseidon's wrath, hid in the crates storing the expedition's dragon chains. The heavy chains made excellent ballast, and were stored always in the hold's lowest point among the bilge and rats. An expedition could last over years and never open those crates.*

"*On a moonless night along the Erubian coast, the goddess slipped overboard with the child she refused to murder.*

"*The irony isn't lost on history that dragon chains, perhaps the Empire's most horrible symbol of subjugation and death, became the catalyst for mankind's only hope for liberation.*" - The Last Scholar

- The Chronicle of Fu Xi.

***

Climb! her instincts screamed. *Climb above Heaven's endless white pillars, beyond man's eyes and the arrow's reach. Let the thin air be your sanctuary, where emerald and maroon scales can blaze gloriously against a robin's egg sky.*

The young dragon suppressed her survival instincts for another, equally powerful urge. She'd lost his scent, and desperately needed to reacquire it. Fortunately, only a light afternoon headwind challenged her as she soared above giant cedars blanketing a steep coastline.

Down she dove, skimming over a calm cove, picking up speed before catching an updraft and climbing over a rocky promontory. Seagulls and eagles parted, giving way to the sky's true regent. She swooped down the other side, cedars gently brushing her underbelly, before settling above a wide beach.

She turned her arrow-like head from side to side, taking short whiffs. Letting the air ricochet inside her enormous sinus cavities, a thousand times more sensitive than a wolf's, she sifted through messages meant for others, desperate to reacquire a trail gone cold.

Occasionally, she flapped her wings. Graceful and slender, her long neck and tail stretched equidistant from her midsection. The Creator had fashioned her to soar in the icy heights, beyond clouds' reach. There, the Mother of All Winds howled eastward, and could carry her hundreds of miles each day. Up there, eternal night tinged even the brightest day, and the sun burned cold. She would not climb until she detected his scent once again, even if it meant her life.

The Mother of All Winds carried his scent from hundreds, perhaps thousands of miles from the east and deposited it over the sea, where the onshore winds carried it to the coast. The rocky slopes might snag the delicate message like a twig snatched from the ocean tide. Here, she stood the best chance of reacquiring it. Thousands of powerful scents, wild and dark, filled the salty air, threatening to overwhelm the one she sought. These scents told tales of beasts living and dying and mating, but none of them concerned her.

Other scents, however, concerned her greatly.

Men's reek corrupted this land, just as it had in all the lands she'd passed along her journey. She even caught traces of their scent high above the ocean, and spotted their ships plying the waves far below. Like a plague, they spread across Creation's face. Their sweat's acid-like stink made her nauseous, but their blood's coppery odor struck her with terror. They hunted her kind to the edge of oblivion. Most disturbing of all is how readily they slaughtered one another. Why the Heavenly Father and his daughter, the Serpent Mother, would allow, let alone create such creatures brought the young dragon to the edge of disbelief.

A sharp tingle, like a bolt of pleasant electricity, shot through her body.

I smell him!

She flapped hard several times, climbing until she caught a fleeting trace again.

Instinct excitedly whispered to her, *His scent has ridden the eastern wind for many days; several sunrises have washed the strength from his spore. He is still far away, but you're getting closer. Climb now. Climb to the Mother of All Winds and sleep in her icy womb. She shall carry you to your lover. Climb!*

The long beach terminated in a tree-covered cliff jutting into the sea like a natural jetty. She knew the wind would be crashing against the escarpment's ridge like the water's waves crashing against its base. The dragon flapped hard, picking up speed in anticipation of riding those invisible currents skyward. She felt the tailwind slowly strengthen and lift her up the slope. The tailwind transformed to a strong headwind as she crested the ridge, catapulting her upward. That is when their stink washed over her.

A sheltered cove spread out before her. Half a dozen ships anchored to her left. To her right, tents and smoky fires covered the beach, beyond which high hills lined the south like a wall. Her only avenue of escape lay above.

Most humans feared dragons enough to stay clear. These, however, were the humans which dwelt along the world's coasts, the ones in the billowing ships that clad themselves in metal. These were a different breed of man, the ones her mother had warned her about.

She beat at the air as whistling arrows climbed to greet her. The dragon twisted and turned, struggling to climb even faster. Just as her mother once taught, she placed her shadow over her enemies, thereby cloaking herself in the sun. Her underbelly scales and wing membranes shimmered and transformed to match the sky's pale blue.

Rage filled the dragon's heart, rage at the wind and terrain for masking her enemy's scent until it was almost too late, and rage at herself for being too focused on his scent as to ignore all else.

Dive down upon the wooden ships and spray them with fire-bile, Instinct shouted. *Watch them burn and hear the men scream in agony!*

"Never give men battle," her mother's voice drowned out Instinct's battle lust. "They may look like monkeys, but they are truly ants. Kill ten, and twenty will spring from their blood. They will swarm you, biting with iron and wood until your fire-bile is expended and your scales are breached. Men can only drag you down to misery and death. Fly, beloved daughter, fly! For only in the heavens are you truly safe."

Soon, the shouting and whistling arrows grew silent. Adrenaline and Instinct faded, and the air cooled sharply. She looked down. The cove appeared as a crescent along a vast coast, the ships now pieces of flotsam. The men shrank to insignificance.

The dragon thanked the Serpent Mother for deliverance and extended her wings to their full width, inviting the wind's loving caress to carry her skyward to the Mother of All Winds.

The temperature dropped as the air grew thinner. Her blood began to cool, and her heart slowed. The dragon's scales tightened against the sheet of icy frost sealing them in place. Then, as the sky grew darker above, she felt the sudden, yet not unexpected lurch, as she joined the air river hurtling eastward. Her heart leapt for joy as she became one with the Mother of All Winds.

No longer afraid, she let her scales transform into glittering shades of azure and emerald.

The dragon became a star.

I can still smell him!

That meant the Mother of All Winds flowed directly over his territory, and would deliver her to his kingdom's heart.

Slightly dizzy from happiness and the lack of oxygen, a state of semi-hibernation slowly crept over the doe. Before closing her eyes, the dragon glanced once more at Creation surrounding her.

The sun's brilliance lacked warmth, its rays sharp and devoid of comfort. The sky above lay on her like a cold, black blanket. Only the blue world below held warmth's promise.

The doe knew the Serpent Mother often sent visions to dragons this close to Heaven, and she often wondered if other dragons shared hers.

The world below is curved and the universe above endless.

She closed her eyes and dreamt of fire.

27. Reconciliation at Blood Point.

"In all of Creation, only three powers can kill thee: The will of your Great Father Poseidon, dragon's fire, or a divine hand wielding orichalcum. Always honor thy Father Poseidon, slay all dragons, and greet thy siblings with affection and a red sword. Be obedient in this, and ye shall live forever." - The Second Lesson of the God Poseidon to his children, from the Ancient of Ancients.

- The Chronicle of Fu Xi.

***

Elda woke from a fitful sleep to the heavy thud of boots strolling across the deck.

She sat up, rubbed the sleep from her eyes, and looked about in the darkness for the sound's source. Elda saw no one. It wasn't uncommon for the captain to stroll the deck in the deepest night, but these didn't sound like the captain's high-heeled boots. Those made a distinct hollow rap, like death's door knock.

The Mistress of the *Orion* terrified Elda since the day they were brought aboard. Her black boots melted into equally dark woolen trousers and a long coat that seemed to swallow the light. With cropped-short pepper-gray hair and leathery skin, Elda felt certain the captain's perpetual scowl was incapable of supporting a smile, and her heart equally incapable of supporting compassion. No matter how bright the sun, the captain always seemed to drag a piece of midnight with her to the ship's deck.

The sounds of boots ceased. Elda didn't see the captain, or much of anything, across the deck. An oil lamp gently swaying from a spike on the mast barely penetrated the muggy fog. Elda welcomed warmth's return, even one as humid as this. She glanced down at her brother sleeping beside her. Despite the tepid air, Ercole had wrapped himself tightly in his white, woolen cloak.

Though she could not see them, Elda knew the crew and several paying passengers were sleeping across the deck, too. Except in bad weather, the crew and passengers slept above deck.

Nearby, sitting on a coil of thick rope and propped up against a barrel, Yenda snored like a donkey. Elda's eyes fell on the hatch leading to the hold. She could sleep with Yenda's snoring, but the misery that often floated out of that hellish pit filled her with waking nightmares.

Elda lay down beside her brother, mind racing with what tomorrow might bring. Earlier that day Elda had overheard Yenda and the crew talking about their imminent arrival in the City of Atlas. She welcomed the prospect of standing on solid ground again, but tomorrow filled Elda with dread at their unknown fate.

She couldn't get comfortable, and rolled onto her back. No stars tonight. That was the only thing Elda would remember with any fondness about their journey — the incredible stars. The stars made her think of home, and in night's long darkness those memories nourished Elda like mother's milk.

Yet, those sweet memories always carried Elda to the same bitter threshold, the day the Atlanteans arrived at her village.

It had all happened so quickly.

***

Clang, clang, clang…

Papa's hammer rang out the reassuring beat that started the day, just as it had every day of Elda's life. Their family cottage and smithy lay high on a ridge along the northern hills, which overlooked the plain and harbor beyond. Papa's hammer would echo off the hills and into the village below. *"Wake up, wake up!" the hammer tells the village every day!* the people would say about her Papa. She didn't know why, but this made Elda proud of her father, and proud to be his daughter. The villagers would trek up the hills every day to have Papa repair something of bronze, copper, or tin.

Clang, clang, clang…

On that warm spring morning, Ercole busily stacked charcoal next to the forge and stoked the fires. Her brother would soon take up a hammer alongside Papa, which made Elda happy because that might finally shut Ercole up for a few minutes and give her some peace. Elda busied herself with her morning chores, consisting of salvaging driftwood and brush from the hillsides, and feeding sticks into the clay oven behind their cottage.

Mama, wearing her favorite beautiful red and yellow dress, called a peplos, hummed softly as she kneaded dough on a flat rock. She'd mix the flour, spring water, and yeast on the stone until it was just right, and then would pound it flat. Elda would then slide the baking stone into the oven with a long, straight pole. Soon, baking bread's aroma filled the cottage compound.

Elda couldn't wait until morning chores were over so they could get busy sewing. Papa had traded enough of his bronze and iron work in the village market to acquire Mama a bolt of quality flaxen linen. Everyone knew Elda's mother made the most beautiful peplos in the village, and she had promised to make Elda a dress with the new material. They'd spent much of the early spring collecting the berries and roots necessary for the dyes, and Elda couldn't wait to wear it.

Elda realized Mama's humming had stopped. She looked around. Her mother wasn't there. The hammer had fallen silent, too.

Then came the scream.

Elda ran around the cottage to find her mother staring horrified at forest of black masts crowding the harbor. Smoke black and thick, like from Papa's furnace, roiled into the sharp blue sky from the village docks. Hundreds of flaming balls rained down onto the village from the black fleet.

Papa materialized beside Elda and Mama, spear and shield clasped in his hands. He commanded them to go inside and not come out until he returned. Ercole tried to grab one of the unfinished swords and follow, but Papa shooed him back. "Not this battle, Ercole."

No kiss for his wife or daughter, no 'I love you,' just Papa setting off in his stern, matter-of-fact way, as if he were going off to barter with the charcoal monger. He still had on his leather apron as he ran down the path to the village.

Elda never saw him again. By nightfall, she and Ercole would be ripped from their mother's arms, tied like pigs, and carried down the hill over the shoulders of enemy warriors as flames engulfed their cottage and her father's forge.

As they huddled among several other captured women and children on the beach, enemy warriors pointed at them and talked in excited, hushed voices. Others came to look at the twins, men with red skin and tattoos and fearsome clubs. In the firelight, Elda saw gold exchange hands, and the children were whisked away to waiting boats. That's when the Atlanteans had begun to treat the twins differently than the other captives.

Aboard a ship in the harbor, the man they would come to know as both bodyguard and disciplinarian, Yenda, handed them a bucket of fresh water and sponges and gestured they should wash off. Squat and powerful, Yenda wore filthy white linen trousers. Black tattoos depicting gruesome scenes covered his red skin. When he frowned, the geometric patterns on his face bunched together to make him even more fearsome. Afterwards, he handed the children clean, white linen loincloths and cloaks. Scowling, Yenda pointed to a place on the deck and motioned for the children to sit. Elda could hear sobs rising from the ship's hold, and wondered if their people were held captive below. Embracing one another and crying in the darkness, the children watched their village burn. By dawn, a fresh tide carried the ship west, away from the shore and the enemy fleet.

So began their long journey to the Kingdom of Atlantis.

The children's special treatment at their captors' hands perplexed Elda and her brother. During the voyage, the children were allowed to roam the deck, but usually confined themselves near the bow where the moans and screams rising from the hold were faintest. In fair weather, they slept on the deck. During storms and ice, they slept in a small storage compartment. The children ate the same porridge and strange, sour green fruit as the crew. They were even allowed to bathe, albeit in salt water.

During the voyage, Elda did her best to pick up what she could of the Atlantean language, which mostly consisted of Yenda's name, and basic words like "eat" and "drink."

As for those they knew were kept in the hold, the children were forbidden from even peering down the hatch, which stayed open in calm seas. Sometimes they would hear whips crack, followed by deafening screams, all of which was met by laughter from the sailors on the deck.

Elda remembered as they watched bright cliffs lining the Straits of Chronos pass off both sides of the ship. Her father had told them stories of this place, and how it marked the end of the Attican world, and the beginning of the ocean named for Atlas, King of the World. Elda recalled how the water turned from tranquil blues and greens to an ominous iron gray. Then the waves transformed into frigid mountains.

For weeks at a time, the winds howled and bit like a thousand vicious teeth. Icy spray soaked everything. The ship pitched so violently Elda felt certain they would die. Sometimes, she prayed for death. Ercole and Elda would huddle for days in a small compartment adjacent to the captain's quarters near the stern. In the darkness, the twins held each other as the sea thundered against the hull. Sometimes, water washed under the door. They vomited into a bucket until they had nothing left in their stomachs, and then they heaved some more. When they weren't sick, they cried. Sometimes the door would fly open and Yenda would stick his head in and laugh at their misery.

As they neared the heart of the Empire of Atlantis, the waves diminished. The salty spray warmed, and Elda and Ercole's fear of the ocean became a fear of the unknown.

***

Elda's eyes flew open again. The boots returned, stirring her from those terrible memories. She turned to see someone leaning against the rail, staring out into the inky blackness. The ruddy lamplight swung slowly across his visage. She recognized him. He had come aboard only a few nights earlier, when the ship had briefly stopped at an island port to take on water and supplies. He wore a plain, olive-drab tunic of Attican cut with a wide leather girdle, and a cape of the same material. She knew high quality cloth, and while plain, his was the finest. He kept to himself near the bow, hood always obscuring his face.

She watched as he turned something over and over in his hands, as if contemplating it. It might have been a dagger or maybe a small sword wrapped tightly in leather, but she couldn't be sure in the darkness. The man began to slowly unwrap the item, but stopped and cautiously looked about.

Elda feigned sleep, one eye cracked.

He turned around and resumed unwrapping the item. Her instincts were correct, it was a dagger, but unlike any Elda had ever seen before. Even from her vantage point, and with one eye closed, the exquisite golden hilt, shaped perhaps like a snake, glimmered in the feeble light. It wasn't the gold that made Elda almost gasp. The blade glittered like

202

liquid blood. The lamplight seemed to swim along the crimson metal as the stranger reverently turned the blade. It reminded her of the last gasp of sunlight on a clear autumn day as the stars began to shine. He cradled it in both hands for what seemed like an eternity before extending his arms over the railing.

Then he let go.

She never heard a splash, as if the sea and fog conspired to conceal the deed.

He stood motionless for several minutes and then said in Attican without turning, "Remember what you saw this night, girl. Speak of it to no one, not even your brother."

He turned away, his footfalls fading into the mist.

Perplexed, Elda rolled over and, as if under a spell, quickly fell into a dreamless sleep. She woke to a muggy dawn and the shrieks of the condemned.

***

"It's not over, is it?" Trembling, Ercole kept his eyes tightly shut. Elda draped one arm over her twin brother's shoulder and peered at the hatchway. Moans and shrieks rose from the hold as if it were a portal to the underworld.

"No," she whispered.

The boy buried his face in his hands as the children pressed themselves against the railing, shrinking as far away as possible from the horrors unfolding behind them. A moment later, the pig-faced sailor climbed out of the hold again, this time carrying the naked, limp body of a young woman over his shoulder like a sack. Like all the rest, he casually tossed her over the railing as if emptying a chamber pot.

Ercole flinched at the splash, but didn't dare look. Elda could not turn away. The woman, an Attican like them, briefly surfaced and opened her eyes before the sharks tore her apart.

"I want to go home," Ercole cried.

"I can see land. We will be there soon, and all of this will be over," she said. Under stiff sails, the merchant ship quickly cut through turquoise waters toward a lush coastline in the hazy distance.

"What if they throw us overboard, too?"

The thought had crossed Elda's mind, too, though she didn't dare voice it. Ercole was her twin, but in many ways she was eldest. "They won't. They are only throwing over the weak and sick."

The captain asked the pig-faced sailor something as she stared down with shadowed eyes from the forecastle. Elda had picked up some Atlantean, but not enough to understand them.

The sailor shielded his eyes from the sun as he looked up at the captain and shrugged. He replied in a nonchalant tone, as if they were discussing what to have for breakfast. The captain turned away, to which the sailor waved his hand, and placed the other on his back hip like an old woman returning to the kitchens.

"Why, Elda? Why?" Large teardrops began to roll down his cheeks. "Why are they killing them?"

"I don't know," she replied.

From behind, a man said in Attican, "They're culling the merchandise. Sick and dying slaves drive down the lot's price at auction." Hood still concealing his face, the stranger from the previous night casually leaned on the railing beside them. "Merchants factor this cost into the expedition's price." He pointed toward the coast. "That promontory over there is called Blood Point. This is where the slaver captains reconcile the books, so to say, before putting into port." He gestured to the blood-stained water. "That's why the sharks gather here."

Elda shook with rage. "That's horrible."

"Make peace with horror, young lady," he said. "You are about to be surrounded by it." He removed his hood, and Elda tried to hide her shock.

He laughed heartily at her reaction.

"What happened to your face?" Ercole asked in his typically blunt way.

He pointed to the blunted, blackened end of what might have once been his nose. "The Icelands took my nose." He wiggled his fingers, revealing ten shortened stumps. "And then some." He pointed to his eyepatch. "This was taken by a creature so hideous that if you saw it, it would give you nightmares to the day you died."

"We will have nightmares plenty without talking to you." She tried to pull her brother away, but Ercole resisted.

"Icelands?" Ercole asked. "What's that?"

The stranger put his hands on his hips and considered Ercole like a wayward pupil. "I guess an Attican boy wouldn't know much about the Northern Icelands, eh?"

"Do not talk to him," Elda cautioned. Despite his long, gray hair she could see his ears were also just stumps.

"What village do you hail from, boy?" he asked, ignoring Elda.

"Phononeus," Ercole said. "Me and my sister, that is."

Elda nudged her brother. "I said stop talking to him!"

Again, Ercole ignored her. The stranger had seemed to divert his fear.

The man considered them. "Phononeus fell in the spring." The stranger's expression softened. He had an old man's long gray hair and short pepper beard, but a young man's posture and vitality. Other than the deformities, his face showed little signs of aging. What few lines he had, Elda could tell they came from worry like Papa's had.

A spear tip lowered in front of the stranger's chest.

Elda turned to see Yenda. The stranger gave a slow, deep bow to the sailor and spoke in a reverential tone. Then he raised his sleeve, displaying a trident brand.

Yenda shouted and pressed the spear harder against the stranger's chest. Then he scowled at the children in that fearsome way that made Elda want to look away.

"Yenda!" the captain called from the aft deck, followed by unintelligible words.

Yenda reluctantly lowered the spear and shook his fist at the stranger. Muttering under his breath, he shuffled off.

Elda stared at the man. He held some kind of stature among these people. Maybe he could finally give them the answers they desperately sought.

The man turned and bowed slightly to the children. "I am Alec, Imperial Scholar, servant and slave to the Great God Poseidon. I am your escort to the Imperial Academy."

"Why didn't you tell us that when you came aboard?" Elda said, exasperated.

"I wanted to watch you, to see who you really were." Alec smiled. "I needed to know if you were truly worthy of the title 'Royal Butcher'."

"Butcher?" Ercole frowned. "I'm going to be a king's butcher? I'm supposed to be a blacksmith like my Papa."

Elda frowned, too. "Doesn't your king already have plenty of butchers?"

Alec smiled warmly, and for a moment he didn't look so ugly. In fact, Elda could imagine the missing flesh back on his face. He might have been very handsome once. "Not that kind of butcher." Alec knelt down in front of them. "Let me see your hands."

Ercole looked to his sister as if seeking permission. She hesitated and then nodded. They extended their hands. Alec's touch was gentle as he examined their hands the way Papa would examine a fine sword or spearpoint. "I see delicate hands and keen eyes." His good eye burrowed deep into Elda's soul, as if searching for something, before considering Ercole. "Young man, I can tell you had yet to pick up your father's hammer. What remains to be seen is if you two have stout hearts."

Alec stood once again. "You children are worth more to the captain than the entire hold full of slaves. If you pass your training with Grand Master Amiran, she will be paid a bonus equal to a hundred ships full of slaves."

Elda and Ercole looked at one another, jaws agape.

"It has been almost forty years since a set of twins completed the grueling training to become a Royal Butcher.

Both must successfully complete the training, or neither passes the test."

Elda looked around at this enormous ship, its crew, and haughty captain. Until the invasion fleet showed up at their front door, with its dozens of ships and thousands of warriors, Elda could not have imagined such incredible, or terrible wonders. Her father and the village men often spoke of the war with Atlantis, but it was something far away. Now that world was crushingly real.

"I don't understand," she asked. "What is it that makes us so valuable?"

He turned to the railing and leaned upon it, looking at the coastline. "Dragons."

"Dragons!" Ercole shouted excitedly.

"Dragons aren't real," Elda scoffed.

"Of course they are." Alec shrugged. "Well, they *were*." He glanced up and held his hand to the sky as if imagining it full of the mythic beasts. "They once reigned supreme, on every continent from the Icelands to the jungles to the deserts. Dragons once ruled the earth." He lowered his hand. "And it's been a generation since one has been seen."

"Papa told us stories about dragons. He said they were huge! And they breathed fire!" Ercole held up his fingers like claws and snarled.

Elda shot Ercole an irritated glance and returned her attention to Alec. "I'm not sure I'm keen to the whole idea. If they are gone, why exactly does Poseidon want us? He is a god, isn't he? We're just children."

"Will I get a sword?" Ercole interrupted.

Alec smiled at the boy and ruffled his hair. "I think you have answered the 'stout heart' question."

Elda rolled her eyes. "Will you shut up?"

Ercole pushed her away, the fear of being tossed overboard having melted away under the reality of his new status. "You shut up. I want to hunt dragons!"

"You said we must both pass the training, or neither of us pass," Elda continued. "What would become of us if we fail?"

Alec glanced back at the hold, and then met Elda's eyes. Fear caught in her throat. Ercole didn't seem to hear Alec's last comments and continued on exuberantly. "What is the Imperial Academy…" The boy stopped in mid-sentence and stared past Alec, wide eyed. His face grew pale. "Mama?"

Elda turned and saw the pig-faced sailor emerging from the hold with an emaciated woman dangling limply over his shoulder.

Confused at first, Elda didn't know what her brother meant. Then she saw the rags of yellow and blue.

"Mama!" Elda shouted and rushed forward.

The pig-faced sailor frowned in surprise at the two children rushing him. Suddenly, a meaty hand painfully clenched Elda's neck from behind and lifted her off the deck. Yenda howled with laughter as he held the children the way one might pluck up wayward puppies.

Elda kicked and clawed at him, but it only made him laugh louder. Pig-Face began to laugh, too, and the raucous spread to the crew.

"That's my mama!" Ercole shouted through tears.

Mama's once luxurious hair hung in limp, matted strings. Sores and scars from numerous whippings showed through her torn dress. Mama's ribs and shoulder bones protruded so sharply Elda didn't know how they didn't rip through her skin. Bruises covered her arms, and dried blood streaked her thighs.

Pig-Face carried her to the railing, laughing the whole time. He paused and placed a finger on his chin with a questioning look. He slid the woman off his shoulders and into his arms, and then held her out to the children like an offering.

Hope sprang in Elda's heart. Ignoring the pain, she reached out desperately for her mother. "Please, I beg you!"

The sailor suddenly spun around as if to hurl their mother overboard. Elda and Ercole screamed, but the sailor pulled back at the last second. Mama's head and limbs flailed about violently, but her sunken eyes never opened to the sun.

Alec stepped forward and looked up at the captain, speaking quickly. The captain seemed to consider his words and then nodded.

Alec approached Pig-Face, who seemed disappointed his fun had been interrupted. Alec gently touched the Attican woman's neck and then her wrist. He looked up at the captain and then stepped toward Yenda and the children. The crew watched expectantly. Alec spoke a few words, and Yenda released the children.

They rushed to Mama, but Alec stopped them. He held them tightly by the shoulders. "I offered to buy her in the name of the Imperial Academy. I have that authority…" He held Elda's gaze. "But only if she were still alive. I am deeply sorry."

Elda's heart dropped into the abyss. Ercole screamed as Alec held them tightly against his chest. "Don't look."

There was a splash, and the crew roared with laughter.

Elda heard herself repeating the word *why*. Ercole turned his head from Alec's chest to hers, and the twins embraced one another.

The terrible splash announcing her mother's end burned through Elda's grief and branded her spirit. They were now truly alone, and would always be alone. If they were to survive, Elda must ensure she and her brother remain together, and pass whatever trials lay before them. She could not fail, and could not let her brother fail. They were all each other had.

"Remember what you saw last night, Elda," Alec whispered in her ear. "One day, all of this will pass."

28. Leviathan's Pillar.

"A god must be patient." - The Third Lesson of the God Poseidon to his children, from the Ancient of Ancients.

- The Chronicle of Fu Xi.

***

"A god must be patient." Leviathan whispered it like a protective ward. He stared at the Alabaster Throne's high back, and Poseidon's court beyond it, just as he had done stretching back into time's endless corridor.

He slowly twisted the sword's tip into the floor, and felt the satisfying "pop" as the red blade gouged the marble. Each sharp crack reverberated in the tomb-like chamber. Stone chips clattered between his feet and across the grimy floor.

He leaned against the column that had come to be known as Leviathan's Pillar. His back found the well-worn hollow in the stone, formed over centuries. He raised his eyes to the pyramid's ceiling where sun rays probed meekly into dingy air, only to die in the chamber's dark belly. Dull torchlight and darkness reigned where once cleansing sunlight danced. Poseidon long ago decreed the four mirrors tilted down. The colorful birds returned to the sun and, one by one, the pillar trees died, were cut down and hauled away.

There was once a time when no shadows fell in Poseidon's Temple. In the brighter past, court's vibrant comings and goings accompanied Leviathan's waits. Artists, poets, musicians, scholars, merchants — freemen from the Empire's many castes — gathered around the courtyard's Fountain of Creation. They bowed before the Alabaster Throne to receive Poseidon's wisdom, and relay news from the Empire's far-flung reaches. Leviathan remembered their clucking tongues and inflated sense of importance. They arrogantly mingled with the Sons of Poseidon, as if equals.

Alongside his sister, Leviathan watched them wither and die as the years melted together like candle wax. *The mortals perished, but not before their lies and flesh corrupted my father like poison accumulating one drop at a time*, Leviathan thought.

Another sharp report, followed by a brief clatter, announced the floor had surrendered another marble chip.

Over the centuries, Poseidon's summons grew less frequent, but each visit to court became more uncomfortable. One year to the next, the columned halls grew darker. Courtesans slowly replaced artisans. Temple priests replaced scholars. Laughter gave way to cries of gluttonous ecstasy. Where once he dispensed enlightenment, now Poseidon swam in decadent mounds of flesh. Young men and women captured from across the Empire were marched in chains into the naos to serve the mad god's insatiable appetites.

Leviathan glanced across the dais at the other column. *Athena's Pillar.*

Another chip broke free between his feet.

The orgy's sounds often assailed Leviathan as he waited until his father granted him an audience. The column shielded the demigod from witnessing his father's unfettered indulgences transpiring in the inner sanctum. Each cry of ecstasy would drive the red blade's tip deeper into the marble.

As the years passed, Poseidon's summons for Leviathan and Athena, known across the Empire as the Bastard Gods, grew more infrequent, sometimes stretching hundreds of years between visits. With the exception of Atlas, the Sons of Cleito soon avoided the Alabaster Pyramid entirely.

Leviathan's spies reported Poseidon's growing taste for blood as much as pleasure. His father's slide into paranoid madness led to purges among the high castes. Aided by Leviathan's whispers, the god saw rebellion and treachery everywhere. During the First Purge, tortured screams replaced pleasure inside the Alabaster Pyramid. When the bloodshed finally abated, almost all the free castes had been abolished, replaced by the rule of collar and brand.

Atlantis had become a slave empire.

Leviathan found waiting for his father's audience during the Great Purges unaccompanied by the usual shame. In those days, Leviathan held hope his father might finally emerge from under the spell mortals had cast over him. It didn't take long for that hope to die.

Now, as Leviathan waited once again, his hope had been rekindled. Freshly erected wooden crucifixes lined the city's canals and streets, some with bodies already hanging on them. That's why the dead silence from the naos behind him perplexed Leviathan. Something had fundamentally changed in Atlantis, and within the Alabaster Pyramid.

A wizened acolyte scurried onto the platform and lay prostrate at Leviathan's feet. "This lowly slave begs the privilege of serving the Mighty Prince with food and libations, while he awaits the Glorious One."

"Go," Leviathan commanded and twisted the blade again. Marble flakes struck the slave's face, driving him backwards down the stairs.

"As you command." He slithered away into the gloom.

Poseidon's summons demanded immediate compliance, and even a demigod could not refuse. As always, the summons' purpose remained a mystery, but throughout history Poseidon only summoned the Bastard Gods for dark tasks requiring orichalcum steel.

Leviathan returned his attention to the ceiling, his mind drifting into antiquity when Father issued the bloody decree; the decree Leviathan obeyed, but Athena did not.

"The world is too small for so many gods," Poseidon had pronounced and tilted the last mirror to the floor. Eternal sunrise died inside the Alabaster Pyramid and darkness reigned. "No more bastards." On that day, an acolyte brought an unnamed babe, a child that could not die by mortal blade, and thrust it into Athena's arms.

In the years to follow, there would be others. Sometimes infants, but often toddlers. The task only fell to the Bastard Gods. Leviathan chose obedience. Athena chose rebellion.

From somewhere in the darkness, Leviathan heard a baby suddenly cry out. The sharp wail, as if it had been wounded, echoed inside the chamber.

Again, the time had come. He brought the sword close to his face and watched the torchlight's reflection ebb up and down the unblemished crimson edge. *That's all it takes*, he thought. *A flick, and then I can return to my ship and more important matters.*

A shadow crawled across Leviathan's peripheral vision like a black fly. He turned to see a pale man leaning casually with folded arms against Athena's Pillar. His featureless black clothes melted into the darkness, giving the illusion of a floating head and hands. He met Leviathan's gaze like an equal. Leviathan's rage swelled at this mortal's insolence in the presence of a god. He strode across the platform, determined to break the pale man like a rotted stick.

The pale man grinned and twisted behind the pillar.

Leviathan looked behind the pillar, but the stranger had vanished. Leviathan sprinted from the dais and scanned the court chamber, but the stranger was nowhere to be seen.

"Why does my son not wait in his appointed place?" a stranger's voice called from behind in the First Tongue. Leviathan had never heard this voice, but its underlying power rang all too familiar. He turned to face a young and powerfully built Erubian man, an Attican no less, clad in a thin robe.

Leviathan wanted to believe this wasn't Poseidon, Father of the Eleven Princes and Emperor of the World...*his* father. The power in his voice and the faint blue glow in his eyes betrayed the divine spirit lurking within.

He's taken another shell, another Attican, Leviathan thought in disgust, but concealed his feelings. Leviathan despised hearing the First Tongue on an Attican's lips. The demigod's disgust rapidly gave way to caution, unsure if madness or sanity lurked beneath his father's mask.

Poseidon's attention drifted about the chamber for a moment and then settled on Leviathan's weapon. "Sheath your sword. It is not required today." Poseidon turned away. "Come."

Before following, Leviathan glanced over his shoulder, looking vainly for the pale man and wondering if he really had heard a baby's cry.

The last time he'd seen his father, the god possessed a different body in a long chain of increasingly Erubian shells. Across Atlas's Ocean, the Kingdom and his half-brothers waged war against the white-skinned barbarians, and yet the godhead himself increasingly wore their skins.

Yet, irritation at his father's choice of mortal cloaks faded, replaced by curiosity as to the reason for his summons. If not to slaughter another unwanted progeny, then what would compel Poseidon to hold private council with his bastard son? They emerged into sunlight and soft breezes on a balcony overlooking the city. Several beautiful slave boys and girls, the god's body slaves, knelt around a steaming ceramic tub.

Leviathan glanced sideways at the shell holding his father's spirit. The sunlight revealed fresh blood streaks staining the white silk robe and coating his hands. Dark circles surrounded young eyes. What should have been supple skin hung sallow, a victim of too much darkness, too much drink, and too much pleasure. The god stared unblinking at the sun. Only a twitching eye interrupted his flaccid expression. Leviathan considered his father the way he studied a distant squall at sea. Would it turn black and violent, or only deposit a gentle shower before surrendering to blue sky?

Poseidon shed his robe and stepped into the tub. Like a bull covered in cowbirds, he stood impassively, arms outstretched, and let the children scrub every inch of his body.

Leviathan averted his eyes, and saw two ebony curial chairs beside a bronze table. Platters piled high with fresh bread and fruit covered the table.

"Sit. Eat," Poseidon commanded as the body slaves poured water over his head. "We have much to discuss." Never had Poseidon invited Leviathan to eat with him, let alone to sit in his presence. That was a privilege reserved for Atlas and his brothers.

Sober purpose dwelt in the god's voice. Leviathan felt certain the god currently commanded all his senses. Experience, however, taught him these bouts of sanity were always short-lived. The god's benevolence could pass at the slightest provocation. Poseidon's tantrums were famous, even among the common people. Anything, from a slave's wayward glance to an odd scent, could plummet the god into a rage. During these spells, storms often materialized over the Alabaster Pyramid like a black whirlpool and swept across the city. The next morning, bodies could often be seen floating in the canals.

The demigod knew he would have to tread carefully this morning. Leviathan, Regent of Oceans, feared nothing under the sun or the moon except the terrible power that dwelt within this Attican's body.

Testing the winds, Leviathan slid into the smaller chair and proceeded cautiously. "I doubt breakfast would warrant you sending a fast ship across the ocean to fetch me." He glanced around cautiously, half expecting to see Atlas and his ilk emerge from behind a curtain with red steel to slay their half-brother once and for all. Leviathan grinned inwardly at the thought. *But then who will do Father's dirty work?*

Poseidon steered clear of his sons' infighting, even when it erupted in open war. Any counsel he took, he took from Atlas, his favorite and the Empire's anointed king.

Leviathan picked up a peach and took a bite, juice dribbling down his chin. He peered across the sprawling capital and its five concentric, encircling canals.

Clad in a fresh toga, and wavy black hair slicked back, Poseidon settled into the chair beside him. An Alkebulan slave girl knelt before them, holding a golden tray with bread and dipping honey.

Poseidon's face came to life, eyes drilling into the slave. "That is not the tray I desire."

Her eyes widened fearfully. She bowed apologetically and slunk away, reappearing moments later bearing a silver platter piled with white powder and a small reed straw. Again, Leviathan struggled to hide his disgust as Poseidon inserted the straw in a nostril and, with great whiffs, inhaled the substance the Olmecs called the White God.

Refined from leaves grown in distant Olma Major, the magical powder gave warriors courage before battle. Too much, and it destroyed a man. Leviathan just watched his father inhale enough to kill ten warriors.

He will be taking a new shell soon, Leviathan thought, *as this one will soon melt under the power of the White God.*

Leviathan had witnessed more than one Renewal Ceremony. In days of old, only the sons of the Kingdom's finest families could compete for the honor of hosting Poseidon's spirit. In those days, Poseidon kept a shell until old age, when the body could no longer contain his powerful spirit. Games and festivals were held in the months leading to the summer solstice, when the god would receive his new shell inside the Alabaster Pyramid's inner sanctum, witnessed only by the High Priest. The god would embrace the kingdom's mortal son before laying atop the granite slab.

Instructed by the High Priest, the young man would deliver the death cut with the ancient Red Blade, an orichalcum dagger dating back to the dawn of time. The god's spirit would then inhabit the new shell, and Poseidon continued his reign as a living god for another lifetime. The celebrations continued until the autumn equinox, as the god toured his kingdom atop a golden chariot pulled by two pure white stallions, so all would know the face of their benevolent god.

Those glorious days had long passed.

In a constant stream of debauchery and hedonism, his father now consumed mortal shells in quick succession. Sometimes, he would not wait for the first strands of gray hair before the temple priests scoured the slave markets for another prime specimen. Under slavery and unending war's crushing yoke, the kingdom had forgotten the Renewal Ceremony. The festivals, games, and celebrations were no more. The kingdom's masses, perhaps not even Atlas, knew when Poseidon had taken a new form.

"You look uncomfortable," Poseidon said as he stared at the sun. "Do you find my present body displeasing?" His forefinger tapped erratically on the armrest.

"Your shells are not my concern. I am only curious as to why you honor me so with a summons." Leviathan picked up his goblet for another drink.

"Give me your sword."

Leviathan stopped in mid-sip. He felt Poseidon's heavy gaze briefly fall upon him, weighing him, judging him, dissecting him. The White God now danced beside blue fire. Leviathan knew the waters ahead just grew more treacherous.

Leviathan handed over his blade.

Poseidon examined the sword. He flicked the blade left and right. Then he considered Leviathan with a cold smile. "Did you know that only the fire-bile of doe dragons was used to make these swords? I made the ten swords for your brothers, but the Scholar Vulcan made the two for you and your sister."

Up to this very moment, Leviathan had assumed his father had forged all the red swords. The thought of a mere mortal having the skill to forge such a holy object somehow diminished it.

Father told me that to diminish me, too, Leviathan thought.

"What of your sister's sword?" Poseidon asked and handed the weapon back hilt-first.

"Still safe in my possession." Leviathan found himself breathing again.

"And what news of my wayward daughter?"

Leviathan took a long draw from the goblet, giving his response serious consideration before speaking. "Gadeirus could answer that question better than I. It is his fleet, not mine, the Gray-Eyed Queen is so fond of repeatedly sinking."

"Atlas tells me the Atticans have renamed their capital city in her honor. 'Athens' they now call it."

"Yes, I am aware. Her armies swell with escaped slaves from our Erubian colonies. But I'm sure I can add nothing to what the king has already told you."

"I desire to hear it from you."

Leviathan briefly considered this might be a trap, a way to pit him against Atlas. "I find it curious that our enemies have begun to adopt the toga, the garb of our own illustrious scholars."

"I've had my eye on them now for some time," Poseidon said dryly. "Tell me, what is your perspective on our fortunes during this war?"

"And if my perspective differs from Atlas?"

"I know what is truth, and I know what is deceit. Speak."

"My Obsidian Fleet dominates the king's ocean, that is truth. The Atticans haven't stuck their noses outside the Straits of Chronos since I sent their western fleet to the bottom three years ago. Our trade routes are safe, from

Atlantis all the way to Avalon. Atlas's Ocean is Leviathan's lake. When you put your faith in my ships and my admirals, I deliver victories." Leviathan downed the wine and signaled the slave to refill the goblet.

"Now tell me of matters east of the Straits of Chronos."

"What is there to tell? The Sea ofAzaes and Giza belong to Gadeirus. Atlas decreed the Eastern Fleet his. It is no affair of mine."

Poseidon grunted. "He has Atlas's confidence. Do not forget Gadeirus also builds a new city in my honor."

Don't let him goad you, Leviathan thought. "Perhaps if Gadeirus weren't so busy erecting statues along the Nile, *Athens*"—he said the word with venom—"would be ashes by now." Leviathan's grip tightened on the goblet. "Gadeirus may capture a small coastal village here and there, but when he faces the Gray-Eyed Queen directly, he loses."

"Gadeirus believes we can absorb the losses, and Attica cannot. We merely need to be patient."

Leviathan's temper flared, and he abandoned caution. "She can afford to be patient, too. At Atlas's command, 350 of my best warships lowered my serpent flag and raised Gadeirus's stallions. A year later, half rot at the bottom of theAzaes . East of the Straits, a quarter of our resupply ships have been captured or burned. The kingdom cannot absorb such losses forever.

"She strikes with impunity along the Erubian and Alkebulan coasts. Her fleet grows, ours shrinks. Mark my words, if Gadeirus's Eastern Fleet suffers one more defeat, Attica will be emboldened to send her ships down the Nile and strike Giza itself. If Giza falls, we will lose our grip on the Sea of Azaes and perhaps even the Sea of Autochthon as well. What, pray tell, Father, other than *my* Obsidian Fleet, will prevent your daughter from attacking Atlantis itself?"

"Atlas sat in that chair less than a week ago. His analysis of the strategic situation in the eastern empire was somewhat different than yours."

"Why doesn't that surprise me?"

Poseidon turned to Leviathan. "I summoned you this morning to strip you of the remaining Obsidian Fleet."

Leviathan hurled the goblet to the floor and leapt from his chair. The slaves flinched.

"Those are my ships! My ships, my admirals, have kept this kingdom safe!"

"This, I do not dispute," Poseidon said calmly.

"Atlas no longer has the courage to face me, is that it? Does he finally admit he fears my growing power?"

Poseidon's eyes narrowed and flared. "This is my will. As I once stripped Azaes of Giza and the sea that bears his name, I can strip you of your imperium. Forever."

Leviathan slid back into his chair, but would not look at his father.

"I have taken counsel with Atlas. He feels the situation in the eastern Azaes has changed. He believes your sister has committed too many resources to her fleet, and not enough to protecting Attica's northern land frontier. Gadeirus will divide the fleet, assigning half to Azaes to protect the coastal trade routes. Gadeirus will commit the other half to harass her fleet. He has adopted an attrition strategy to wear her down at sea, while your half-brothers Ampheres and Evaemon will come ashore in Calabria with an army of 10,000. They will march east along the Icelands, and arrive at Athens's walls before the first snow, just as our ships attack from the sea. We will crush your sister's city as it prepares for winter. I have instructed Atlas to slaughter all the Atticans, man, woman, and child. Upon the city's ruins I will rebuild the Mountain of Bones, and this time there will be no mercy."

"And what of my sister? Which of my dear brothers will be given the honor of administering orichalcum to her lovely throat?"

"She will be brought back in chains for me to deal with."

"And I am to sit idly by while my brothers claim all the glory and treasure with my fleet?"

"As of today, you are lord of the Western Fleet. The Oceanus Gadeirus is now yours."

"There is no war in the west. There is nothing in the west."

"Nevertheless, the west is yours."

Leviathan threw his head back and laughed. "Gadeirus finally grew tired of his big, empty, impoverished ocean, eh? You will have me twiddling my thumbs in Gadriuopolis, an exiled bastard, while the Sons of Cleito claim glory in the east."

"You're not going to Gadriuopolis. You shall move the western capital to Wu."

"Wu?" Leviathan grew intrigued. "Wu is too far to keep adequately supplied. The Western Fleet is decrepit, stripped to supply the war in the east. Gadeirus's Ocean is too wide. The islands stretching across its vast expanse have nothing to offer, other than waystations."

"I have assembled a new fleet for you, unknown to your brothers. It already lies in anchor in Wu."

"Why Wu? It is rich in timber and stone, but not enough to sustain the cost of even a modest fleet. Only Cin shows potential for empire, but you have long forbidden its exploration."

"The ancient decree is lifted. The once-forbidden lands are yours. Expand my western empire into Cin."

Leviathan paused and chose his next words carefully. "Is this a convenient ploy to get me out of the way, lest I interfere in the war against my sister?"

"I am splitting the Empire. All lands beyond the western coast of the Olmas are now yours. Atlas will rule the Eastern Empire, and you the Western Empire. He shall reign on the rising sun, you shall hold dominion over the setting sun. Your charter is clear, your imperium undiluted. Explore Cin, conquer its peoples, and bring them under my dominion. Do not delay; leave for Wu with the next tide."

Leviathan's mind reeled. "I am honored. But why the urgency?"

Poseidon turned to his bastard. "What I tell you now I've never shared before, even with Atlas. At the dawn of time, there were ten of us; ten gods to shepherd the races of men. In Cin you will encounter one of them, my sister."

Leviathan sat in stunned silence while Poseidon summoned the slave to bring the food tray again.

"I know you've heard the legends of other gods. You must have read the accounts recorded by Expedition Scholars over the generations."

Leviathan nodded. "Yes, but I long ago abandoned any interests in chasing the myths."

Poseidon nodded. "Now you know they are not myths." He took a bit of bread from the tray, dipped it in honey, and chewed slowly. "I reign above my children a thousand-thousandfold greater than you reign over men. There are mysteries of existence you will never comprehend. It takes great power for a being of spirit to exist in a world of flesh. My brothers and sisters were not as strong as I am. All but two abandoned their earthly shells and melted back into Creation's foam from whence we came. Their memory is lost to the minds of men. Only Gaia and I remain." His gaze pierced Leviathan. "Like me, she is powerful, and known by many other names."

"Why do you reveal these mysteries to me now and not my brothers?"

"Because you are stronger than they are…" The god paused. "And more ruthless. You must deal with my sister before you can conquer Cin. Do not confront her directly; you will lose. Her heart has always betrayed her, and the way to her heart is through her sons. Find and befriend one of them. Avoid the other at all costs until the time is right."

"How will I know the difference?"

"You will know," Poseidon said dryly. "Each son possesses something you need. One knows the way to Gaia's temple, deep in Cin's heart. She possesses her own Renewal Dagger, which she calls the Offering Blade." The god's eyes suddenly flamed to life. "You must bring her dagger back to me."

Leviathan shook his head in disbelief. "If she is like you, then she is powerful and will destroy me."

"You will find a way. Return with Gaia's orichalcum dagger with the utmost haste, and on that day both halves of the Empire will be yours. You shall supplant Atlas as King of the World."

Leviathan's pulse quickened. In that moment, he knew he would find a way. He knelt before his father. "Your will shall be done."

"You will take Amiran, Master of Scholars, with you."

"Why?"

"He has the knowledge and skills once possessed by his ancient predecessor, Vulcan. You will require those skills."

"And what knowledge is that?"

"The knowledge to bring back what Gaia's other son possesses." A cloud covered the sun, and cast the city in shadow. "Detailed instructions will be sent to your flagship in a sealed scroll. Only some of these instructions you will share with the scholar. When he has served his purpose, kill him. There is something else you must know. This knowledge I have also never shared with your brothers. Learn this, and use it when the time is right."

Leviathan listened raptly, his heart racing, as Poseidon imparted the stunning knowledge. Afterwards, Poseidon leaned back and squinted at the sky, as if he could see the sun through the thickening clouds beginning to rotate over their heads. "Damn the sun. It serves only to remind me of what I cannot forget."

Poseidon lowered his eyes from the sky to the slave girl kneeling at his feet, still holding the silver tray of bread and honey in her outstretched hands. A cold gust swept the balcony, and thunder rumbled from above.

He stroked the girl's cheek. "In the darkness, only our own light shines. In the darkness, nothing looks down upon us, judging us, reminding us we are not...*forgiven*."

He snatched her by the hair and stood, holding her writhing, kicking form off the floor. The other slaves fell prostrate, whimpering and covering their faces. The wind roared to a gale, overturning the table and chairs. Poseidon considered the screaming girl as if she were a curiosity.

"Rule, my son. Rule without reservation. Rule without regret. And above all, rule without mercy."

Poseidon strolled into the pyramid, dragging the slave behind.

Leviathan slipped out of the temple, eager to begin preparations for the coming journey. Behind him, screams rose from the inner sanctum.

29. The Delusional Peace.

"Be warned, a god never forgets." – The Fourth Lesson of the God Poseidon to his children, from the Ancient of Ancients.

- The Chronicle of Fu Xi.

***

Slavery's smell permeated Amiran's senses. Blood, sweat, and fear drifted across the Fifth Ring Canal and penetrated the cool garden in the city's heart. He tried to recall the scents from the shores he'd landed upon during his many expeditions, but the city's stench smothered them all. How had Amiran never noticed the city's oppressive humidity growing up in her slums? How could he have ever been accustomed to that thick, sour mix of sewage and garbage which often seeped into her most privileged quarters? It wasn't until his first expedition, when he filled his lungs with an uncorrupted sea breeze, that Amiran understood how poisoned Atlantis truly was.

With each breath, Amiran felt the city seeping into his pores, slowly killing him. Not counting a few short trips into the neighboring countryside, he hadn't left the city in almost ten years. Below his loose tunic, Amiran felt sweat trickle down the roll encircling his waist. Like a dog too long on the leash, he'd grown soft. He knew all the wine didn't help, but knowing and doing were distinctly different things. Master Olorun's wine numbed him to the reek that the fragrant garden could not repel. The wine, however, could not suppress the anger festering deep within Amiran as he watched the scene unfolding across the canal.

From his vantage high above on the Imperial Promenade, Amiran watched the ship slowly lumber along the canal's opposite shore. Heavily laden with war's spoils, the carrack's fat belly crawled through the oily water, pulled into the city's heart by a team of horses and teamsters along the shore. Just inside the well-worn horse tracks, slaves dug holes for crucifixes. Some of the grisly crosses already had victims. Across the canal, Amiran heard a crucified temple priest, still wearing his purple robes, begging for death. The City Guard had been instructed not to strip the prisoners, but leave them in their garb as a warning to the lower castes. The horses pulling the ship didn't care to look up at the bodies, and the teamsters didn't dare.

The ship passed beneath the East Dolphin Bridge. The graceful stone arch, high enough for even the tallest ship to pass beneath and wide enough for ten men to walk abreast, connected the Imperial Promenade to the greater city beyond. Above the ship, another execution squad crossed over the bridge. Another temple priest had been condemned.

A scholar led the procession, reading from a scroll listing the offender's supposed crimes. The guilty dragged his own cross, flanked by heavily armed warriors to protect him from being ripped apart by the mob until his sentence could properly be carried out. Behind them, entertainment slaves followed: musicians, street performers, and dozens of public whores all ready to service the mob. Farther behind, slaves pulled carts piled high with bread. All of this benevolence was courtesy of the Emperor Poseidon himself.

If the gods will do this to the privileged, Amiran thought, *what horrors will he visit upon you lowly commoners?* The common slaves didn't care. They wanted blood, entertainment, and to see the privileged slave castes suffer. Whispers spread through the city of treason and treachery inside the Alabaster Pyramid. Something had stirred Poseidon's wrath, and fears of a new purge set Atlantis's high castes on edge. The commoners poured into the Fifth Ring from as far away as the coasts to participate in the bloody festival.

The mob paid little attention as the ship passed under the arch toward the Fifth Canal wharves directly across the canal from where Amiran stood. Atop the ship's aft mast, the pennant bearing Prince Gadeirus's black stallions hung limp in the heavy air. As the ship neared the dock, sailors in filthy white trousers tossed mooring lines to waiting slaves. Merchants from the public slaving houses, easily identified by their ample girth and golden togas, lined the wharf, waiting eagerly for the vessel to disgorge her grim bounty.

"Merchants," Amiran snorted softly. Since the days of the Great Purge, all mortals, save warriors and sailors, were condemned to slavery. This included merchants. As with the caste of scholars, the gods permitted merchants freedom's illusion. Unlike the scholars, merchants fed on the misery of their fellow slaves.

Amiran leaned against the chest-high wall, which gently curved in both directions. It guarded the sheer drop off into the Fifth Canal, which separated Atlantis's gleaming heart from her outer slums. Amiran drank in the city's sweeping vistas, and her terraced avenues rising above the Fifth Canal. Here, ten palaces surrounded the Alabaster Pyramid, Poseidon's temple in the city's center. The Imperial Promenade, which lined the Fifth Canal's inner shore, encircled them all. Its bustling markets, cafes, and brothels catered to the two free classes and the four privileged slave castes. The highest slave caste, the scholars, dwelt in the Imperial Academy, a campus of columned limestone edifices on the Inner Ring's opposite side from Poseidon's temple.

This morning, the Promenade's beauty didn't command Amiran's attention. He couldn't tear his eyes from the events unfolding across the canal. Amiran wanted the wine to assert its delusional peace, but it only intensified his simmering unrest. Even the self-assured voices of youth chattering behind him could not draw his attention.

Their laughter was too loud and forced. Amiran knew they wanted to impress Master Olorun with their brilliance. Thankfully, a gathering of young poets usually meant abundant wine, which the Imperial Academy's Grand Master took as a legitimate reason to observe Olorun's morning lesson. Amiran emptied the cup in long swig and refilled it from the decanter resting atop the low wall.

The cracking whips carried across the canal, as the sailors beat the slaves stumbling down the gangplanks. In a few moments, Atlantis would swallow them. As he watched, Amiran whispered a forbidden poem from a forgotten scroll.

"Whore and mother, salvation from the wretched darkness deep,
Gather all your children low under maroon sun, bathed in terror.
Offer up bread and pluck their mortal souls, no divine tenderness cede.
Slave Empire, with hopeless loathing men fall under your whip and collar."

"Did you say something, Grand Master?" Olorun's deep, velvet voice stirred Amiran from his trance.

"I was only clearing my throat," he said over his shoulder.

"Perhaps the Grand Master would enlighten us with his perspective?" Olorun goaded him.

Amiran turned toward the bright and eager plebeian scholars sitting cross-legged beneath the hanging garden's dappled shade. All in their fourth and final year of formal education, the upperclassmen's white togas lacked a full-fledged scholar's purple stripe. On the spring equinox they would pass beneath the Arch of Olives, the Imperial Academy's hallowed threshold, and there, in the shadow of Poseidon's Temple, be branded with the Trident. For the rest of their lives, they would serve Poseidon and his immortal sons.

Amiran stepped under the vine-blanketed trestle and sat beside Olorun on a stone bench. "My apologies, Master of

Poets, my mind wandered to other matters. What were you discussing?"

Olorun glanced at Amiran's goblet like a disapproving wife, before clearing his throat. "Does man possess any inherent creative spark beyond what is bestowed by the gods?"

"I thought you were reciting poetry this morning. If I had known this was a philosophy lesson I would have stayed in bed."

The scholars laughed, clearly enjoying being in the Grand Master's presence.

"You are here, and drinking my wine, Grand Master, so you are stuck with the question." The statuesque, bronze-skinned poet, known as much for his striking physical grace as his brilliant mind, once again put his best friend under his steely gaze.

"Oh, all right!" Amiran huffed in mock protest. "It is your wine I suppose."

He paused and considered the question for a few long moments as he rolled the silver goblet between his palms. "What do your students think?"

A bright-eyed Erubian with hair like fire, and an attitude to match, spoke up. "All mortal gifts are bestowed by Poseidon himself, as it is written in the Third Act, Twelfth Verse of the Song of Atlas."

Expecting exactly that answer, Amiran's response fell like a well-rehearsed counterstroke. "Does that refer to physical or spiritual gifts?"

The student shrugged. "Both, I assume."

Amiran leaned forward slightly and let his gaze fall heavily on the Erubian. "And when do scholars assume anything?"

The redhead lowered his face and blushed.

Erubians make poor gamblers, he thought. *Their pale skin often betrays their thoughts.*

"All of you, think back to your initiation, when you stood before the Masters and recited the Song of Atlas."

Amiran pointed to a tan-skinned Alkebulan, whose ancestors likely hailed from the plains and deserts east of Giza. "What is the First Foundation Stone of Knowledge?"

"Recitation!" he spat out reflexively.

"Yes, recitation. It is the stone upon which all other scholarship rests, the mechanical ability to remember and recite facts without distortion." Amiran raised a finger. *"Without distortion."*

Amiran caught Olorun's eye. The poet winked and bowed slightly before stepping to the overlook wall to pour himself a fresh cup and cede the class to his friend.

Amiran continued, "Assumptions are only opportunities for distortion. Assumptions are hooks upon which butchers hang bloody lies. Let us examine what we know. In the First Verse, Poseidon stands upon the newly formed Earth and summons all the creatures to serve him. Which creature turned his back upon him?"

The students looked at one another, unsure why the Grand Master would ask such a simple question, and perhaps wondering what traps may be hidden in the answer.

"Man, of course," one answered meekly.

"And what did Poseidon do when man refused the immortal's summons?"

"He slaughtered man, woman, and child and fashioned their corpses into the Mountain of Bones as a warning to all other creatures," the redhead answered again.

"Why?"

"As punishment for mankind's arrogance, his pride."

Amiran took a sip and pursed his lips. "And yet, here we are." He nodded to the towering pyramid, clad in shimmering white stone. "Humanity thrives in the shadow of Poseidon's Temple, fashioned from stone, not bones."

He sensed the redheaded plebe's delight at the interchange. He had the Grand Master to himself, the other students too intimidated to be drawn into an exchange with Amiran.

"Because he fell in love with the mortal Cleito," the red head replied with uncertainty. "She begged for mercy on behalf of all mankind."

The upperclassmen looked at one another, puzzled. Amiran read their thoughts. Here they had a rare chance to discuss truly great ideas with the Grand Master himself, the exalted head of all the colleges. Yet here he sat reviewing the simplest, most fundamental of all concepts, the first verses of the Song of Atlas. They likely hadn't given the creation stories a single thought since initiation's terrible days, when the voluminous Song had to be recited with exact inflection, word for word, before the Council of Masters. One slip and they would be doomed to spend the rest of their lives as a common public slave.

"Why did Poseidon fall in love with Cleito?"

Silence.

"Anyone? Come on, you've never known a woman's love, but you've *thought* about it. Why would the God Poseidon fall in love with a mortal, especially at his rage's zenith?"

More silence and confused looks.

Amiran pointed again to the Erubian. "You, recite the first eight verses."

The young man stood, and with perfect tone, inflection, and cadence, obeyed the Grand Master's command.

"What beast stares back, this Graceless spirit?
Under blackest bough, mute soul lurks.
Dark purpose, slayer without claw or fang,
Mystery, oh mortal cloaked in godly form?

"Speak! Poseidon commands his pale reflection,
Wind and wolf, sea and sky obey the mighty call.
Yet Man turns away, offering no glorious tribute,
Slaughter or salvation, a god's cold choice.

"Upright creature judged Abomination, unworthy,

From sow's belly, the bloody suckling ripped.
'Drag the beast from Darkness to Light, Death!'
Beneath jackal and rat, slain for god's pleasure.

"Upon Alkebulan's bloody plain, Wrath or Madness?
Under Black Wing shadow, babes torn from breasts,
Judgment's Red Sword stacks the Mountain of Bones.
Vulture and hyena feast on fleshy mountains.

"Dawn's pale lament, scream fades to rattle,
Divine scorn spares lesser beasts, but not Man.
For vanity, the Sun strikes down the lowly dust,
Lest it conspire with the wind to hide His glory.

"Bloody dew settles, tears usher sunrise agony,
From jungle lair deep, one word seeps forth.
'Mercy,' the first words borne of mortal lips,
Wild beauty, ebon flame lights the crimson plain.

"The god's wrath turned, orichalcum blade mute,
On morn's milky blanket, tender syllables creep.
'Mercy,' she begs for the living and the dead.
Untouched by carnage, eyes bright and unafraid.

"Below the Mountain of Bones, a god's rage faced,
Forbidden innocence, sweetest incarnation.
Under a lonely sunrise, the god surrenders.
And forever forsakes His perfect reward."

Amiran let the words slowly sink in. The Erubian looked to Amiran, who nodded and motioned for him to sit. "I repeat my question. Why did Poseidon fall in love with Cleito and spare mankind?"

"Beauty," the scholar from Giza quickly replied.

Amiran waved his goblet toward the slave auction across the canal. "Beauty is cheap, a toy for sale every morning on the block."

"Cleito possessed great love," another offered.

"So do dogs, but I hear they make poor queens," Amiran scoffed. The class snickered.

"She was wise," the Gizan spoke up again.

"Ahh! Wisdom, the most beautiful jewel of all." Amiran took another sip, warming to the lesson. "Explain."

Leaning against the wall, Olorun laughed. "Poets and an engineer, sipping wine and discussing philosophy. We're in trouble now."

Amiran wagged his finger. "Don't distract me. It isn't my fault you turned your class over to me, and you're not getting them back!"

"Wisdom." Amiran tapped his lips, as if considering the word. "At the sounds of mankind's slaughter and suffering at the hand of the vengeful god, Cleito didn't run and hide. Naked and unafraid, she stepped from the jungle and confronted Poseidon, speaking the first word uttered by humankind…*mercy*." He let that word sink in, scanning their faces for understanding, before continuing, "Cleito possessed the power of speech. She understood the divine mandate of mercy, and possessed the inherent wisdom to appeal to a higher power's compassion…even in the face of slaughter. This is fact, no assumptions made.

"She came to the god a stranger, already filled with these powerful gifts. Poseidon spared mankind not to bestow these gifts, but *because* of them."

The students looked at the Grand Master in awe.

"Let me put it another way." Amiran joined Olorun at the wall and beckoned the students. "Come."

They crowded around as Amiran pointed to the forest of masts stretching up and down the canal along the wharf. "Your first expedition will soon be upon you. There is much of this world yet to explore. That is why scholars must have a certain mastery of all the sciences and humanities. I've taken part in twenty-three expeditions, and Master Olorun has sailed on…" He looked to his friend.

"Twelve."

Amiran continued, "We've seen humanity from every corner of the world, every shade of hide and heart. Regardless of differences and dispositions, some aspects are universal to all men. A smile, a grimace, a nod, a clenched fist; these gestures are both universal and inherent."

Olorun's smile vanished. The students looked uneasy as the Grand Master's words skated the edge of heresy.

"And language! With the exception of those shaggy, sub-human creatures which inhabit the northern wastes, all men possess the gift of speech."

"Who are we to know where mighty Poseidon may have spread his gifts beyond what is recorded in the Saga?" the Erubian spoke again.

Amiran shrugged and nodded, but he really wanted to scream, to tell these comfortable children, so smug in their own intellectual prowess, they knew nothing of the darkness that gripped the Alabaster Pyramid.

Amiran's good-natured smile vanished. He downed the goblet in one long gulp and wiped his mouth, leaving a red stain across his sleeve. "Then why, upon countless shores, is Poseidon's name unknown? Tell me, why do the aboriginal tribes from the Icelands to the deep jungles of Olma Major speak the names of *other* gods?"

"But, as it is written," the Erubian protested, "'All those marks of grace which separate man from beast are divinely given.'"

"I do not argue that, but once again you make an assumption."

"Amiran!" Olorun hissed under his breath. Amiran ignored him.

"Come here." He placed an arm over the redhead's shoulder and pointed to the line of slaves disembarking the carrack across the canal. "Do you have any memory of Erub?"

"I was born in a farming village beyond the First Ring, Grand Master. I have no memory of my mother's homeland, other than the stories she told."

"This is how your mother came to Atlantis, just as mine did. Look at their collars. Consider the welts left by the whip."

"Grand Master…" Olorun touched his sleeve, but Amiran shrugged him off.

Amiran felt the young scholar's discomfort. Only his reverence for his Grand Master kept him from squirming away. Amiran didn't care. He belched softly, the reek of sour wine and heresy on his lips. "When an expedition lands on a foreign shore, sometimes we are welcomed, and sometimes we are attacked. Answer me this, if all our talents are divinely inspired, why isn't submission to Poseidon equally inherent? Why do the tribes in the world's dark places fight so fiercely for their freedom? Shouldn't they flock to us, eagerly seeking Poseidon's benevolent yoke?"

"Uh…I…it is man's pride that incurs Poseidon's wrath." The Erubian glanced briefly to Master Olorun as if asking for help.

Olorun snatched Amiran's goblet. "Come, Amiran, the lesson is over."

Amiran leaned close to the man's freckled face, flushed and beginning to sweat. "Does pride come from the gods, too?" Amiran pointed to the ship as several naked, nearly starved children stumbled down the gangplank. "Their pride? Does not the word 'mercy' hold the same power when spoken by a child? What if something else stayed Poseidon's wrath? Perhaps the realization that he, in *his* pride, in *his* wrath, nearly destroyed something precious, something divinely created, but not by *his* hand. Perhaps pride is the only gift the gods ever truly gave us, the dark chain binding us to one another."

Behind them, a commotion penetrated the garden's sanctuary.

"Make way!" a voice comfortable giving commands barked from beyond the covered gardens. A snapping whip parted the crowds along the Promenade. Amiran saw two spears pointing upward coming their way. "Make way for the Imperial Courier."

The throngs separated, revealing a scholar not much older than the students, flanked by two fearsome Olmecs. Amiran's heart dropped, though he struggled not to show it. Only one of the Eleven Princes used Olmec warriors, the rest finding the savages too bloodthirsty to control.

The Purge has come for us, he thought. *Which cross out there is being made for me?*

The students parted, leaving Olorun and Amiran to face the messenger and his escorts. Amiran recognized Arouraios, a former pupil and irritating sycophant.

"Amiran, Grand Master of the Imperial Academy?" the former student said with unnecessary formality.

"Arouraios." Amiran nodded slightly.

The royal messenger uncapped an ivory scroll tube, removed and unrolled a thin parchment, without so much as waiting for Amiran to dismiss his class.

"Listen and obey, all present, to this decree by the God Poseidon, Author of Creation."

The Master Scholars and the students dropped to one knee and bowed. The words which would next be spoken represented the will of a living god. All within earshot along the Promenade also dropped to one knee, some even laying prostrate.

Eyes narrowed, Arouraios paused and looked about as if challenging anyone not to give him their rapt attention before he continued, "The God Poseidon hereby directs the faithful slave Amiran, Grand Master of His Majesty's Imperial Academy, to report to the Imperial Wharf before the next high tide. From there he will accompany and faithfully serve as Fleet Scholar the Eleventh Prince of the Kingdom, Monarch of the Seas, the Great and Mighty Lord Leviathan on his expedition to the edge of the world. He will remain in Prince Leviathan's service until the expedition returns in glorious triumph or until his death in obedient service, whichever shall come first.

"These are the words of the God Poseidon, father of King Atlas and the Eleven Princes, Master of sky, earth, and sea."

Without another word, Arouraios rolled up the scroll, and returned it to the case. Flanked by the two warriors, he wheeled about and departed without another word. After a few moments, the unnatural silence along the Promenade became an excited hum. The street's bustle began anew. The students turned and considered Amiran with a mix of shock and disbelief.

Olorun shook his head and whispered, "It's hard to believe that little Parrot used to be one of your best students."

"He made his choices, and now we must make a few of our own." Amiran turned his back to the class and spoke to Olorun in a low whisper. "Send word immediately to our friends the Owls. Tell them to assemble in the usual place and with haste."

A peal of unexpected thunder made all turn and look up at the swirling, dark clouds rapidly building above the Alabaster Pyramid.

30. The Rebellion of Owls.

"Gods spring from Poseidon's loins to wield power. That is thy purpose. The road to power is paved with mortal subjugation. That is their purpose." – The Fifth Lesson of the God Poseidon to his children, from the Ancient of Ancients.

- The Chronicle of Fu Xi.

***

The enlightened men embraced the darkness, wrapping it tightly about them like the linens swaddling the surrounding mummies. The rigid dead rested against the wall, seemingly begging for a drink. Amiran sympathized. Only cobwebs and rats' nests filled the empty wine nooks, and Amiran found that somewhat depressing, especially now that his head had begun to ache.

While not the deepest corridor in the limestone labyrinth below the Imperial Academy, it was perhaps the most remote; only a genius or a god could pick their way through the maze to reach it. Over the years, these four men had ample practice finding this lost wine cellar.

They gathered around the rough-hewn table. Fresh air and dappled sunlight's scent still clung to their bleach-white togas. The red and purple stripes embroidered down their outer hems declared them Master Scholars, leaders of their respective colleges. Amiran not only chaired the College of Engineering and Metallurgy, but an additional gold stripe signified his role as Grand Master of Colleges, High Scholar of the Imperial Academy, and First Slave to Poseidon.

A half-melted candle illuminated faces that considered Amiran with a mix of pity and trepidation. His mind raced with countless possibilities, none of them good. In fearful tones, the worried intellectuals questioned him.

"But why is he sending you?" Olorun pressed. "It's unheard of. You're too old and valuable to be a common Expedition Scholar."

"What will we do in your absence?" queried Kalisto, Master of Astrology, as he chewed his fingernails.

"Who will take your place, and what does this mean for the cause?" asked Theron, Master of Physicians.

Amiran raised his hands. "You know everything I do. We must limit ourselves to the facts at hand, and wait for our brothers to arrive."

Amiran looked around the table. *We are soft men*, Amiran thought. *A lifetime wearing the white toga has made us this way. Perhaps our lofty spirits ask too much from weak flesh.*

Sandaled feet approached beyond the chamber's archway. Two forms emerged from the blackness and solidified in the dingy candlelight, one tall and gangly, the other shorter and dressed in a plain traveling tunic and cloak.

Amiran sighed in relief. Master Gremis and Master Alec's arrival completed the conspiracy.

A thin face, deep-set eyes, and large nose gave Gremis the look of a wizened eagle. Spindly arms poked from a toga that hung on his frame like a collapsed sail wrapped around a mast. He jovially slapped Amiran on the back and placed a bulging kerchief on the table. Untying it revealed a generous chunk of cheese and red grapes. Gray eyes twinkled beneath wild eyebrows as the old man strolled around the room, shaking hands as if he had just stepped into a faculty meeting.

"Good afternoon, my fellow Owls! I apologize for our tardiness. I had to make certain arrangements first. I encountered young Master Alec on the way down and convinced him to assist me in 'liberating' a bit of sustenance from the kitchens as we passed by."

With a clunk, Alec placed a burlap sack on the table and promptly removed a dusty wine bottle and six ceramic goblets. The candlelight made Alec's frostbite scars even more ominous, especially since the youngest Master of Mathematics in the Imperial Academy's long history did not seem to share Gremis's enthusiasm.

"It's good to see you again, Alec," Amiran said to the man he hoped one day would replace him as Grand Master.

"It's good to be seen." Alec gave his former teacher a forced smile.

"I see the north still doesn't agree with you," Amiran acknowledged the new frostbite scars. "How long have you been back?"

Alec smiled and nodded at Amiran's belly. "And I see the city still agrees with you. I've been back for several weeks. My apologies for not stopping by to pay my respects sooner, but Master Gremis had me running errands."

Kalisto raised an eyebrow. "Food and wine at a time like this?"

"Especially at a time like this!" Gremis clapped his hands. Soon, wine filled the goblets, and Amiran found himself nibbling the cheese. Gremis seemed to have calmed them by his mere presence. Amiran might have worn the gold stripe, but Gremis led this conspiracy and, no matter how dire the circumstances, always provided steady leadership.

Gremis raised his cup and spoke the secret words that had united the Owls since the time of Grand Master Vulcan, "Never accept a collar around your mind, or a brand on your soul. Let freedom's spark simmer in your thoughts and heart until the moment is right to set the world on fire. Be the path that ushers in a world without the gods."

"Until all men are free!" they repeated and downed their cups.

Alec spoke up, "The news reached me moments after my ship docked. My source in court says the expedition's official charter is to reinforce the tiny colony at Wu, as well as explore Cin."

"Poseidon has forbidden Cin's exploration since its discovery centuries ago," Kalisto said.

"Apparently, that has changed," Olorun said dryly. "The Gray-Eyed Queen halts the Empire's march east, so the gods turn west."

"Poseidon's Paradox, the decree forbidding Cin's exploration…" Amiran leaned over the table, brow furrowed. "It has always been a mystery, one we've often debated. No other land has ever been forbidden for explorations. Something has changed."

Alec continued, "My friend says the truth is somewhat more intriguing. The king wants his troublesome half-brother out of the way."

The men glanced at one another, each privately contemplating the implications those words carried.

Kalisto finally uttered their unspoken fear. "Do they ever grow weary of spilling our blood for their petty quarrels?"

"Let's not jump to conclusions." Gremis held up his hand to Kalisto. "This may not mean a new civil war. Master Alec, what else does your source tell you?"

Alec took a deep swig and continued, "No, it's not war, at least not yet. The princes fear Leviathan's ambitions as much as the Gray-Eyed Queen's growing rebellion. Except where Leviathan's Obsidian Fleet gives battle, the war against Attica isn't going well."

Kalisto spat on the floor. "All that monster knows is war."

Alec continued, "Sabotaging the efforts of Atlas and his ilk is one thing, sabotaging Leviathan's war machine is something else entirely." The scholars nodded grimly.

"However, every battle that isn't clearly a win against Attica is seen by the masses as a victory for Athena. Our operatives have been successful in spreading that news throughout the kingdom. My source says Atlas is painfully aware of the discontent beyond the palace gates. He fears his half-brother will see this as weakness, and use his Obsidian Fleet to strike the Sons of Cleito. Atlas's nightmare is to find himself at war on two fronts, against Athena in the east and against Leviathan on the high seas."

"Leviathan and Athena despise one another," Theron said. "They will never join forces."

"They don't have to," Gremis interjected. "The Bastard Gods need only crush the Ten Sons of Cleito between them, before turning on one another."

Olorun placed his head in his hands. "The slaughter would be horrific."

Amiran contemplated what he had just heard. "There is no love lost between Cleito's sons and Metis's bastards, but Leviathan has never given an indication of rebellion. Of all the gods, he has pursued his sister's defeat with unmatched zeal. I don't need to remind you of the atrocities his Olmecs have wrought against the rebels.

"Atlas would rather have the monster and his Olmecs in Attica than far off Wu. No, not rebellion. If Leviathan departs to conquer Cin, it is likely Poseidon's choice. It only deepens the mystery, and it still doesn't explain why I am going."

"Dammit!" Kalisto shouted, voice cracking. "All this expedition nonsense can wait. By Vulcan's arse, Alec, is it done or not?" The little man crossed his arms tightly, still chomping on what was left of his fingernails.

They all stared at Alec. He scanned their expectant eyes. After what seemed like an eternal pause, he said, "It is done."

Kalisto's gaze dropped to the floor.

"Does Poseidon know it's gone?" Theron finally asked.

"Judging by the unusually high number of crosses sprouting up around the city, I would say 'yes,'" Alec said.

"You said it would be several years before he noticed!" Kalisto snapped at Gremis. "You said the dagger wasn't removed from its sacred vault until immediately before the Renewal Ceremony."

"Enough!" Amiran held up his hand. "We all agreed the risk was worth it. I will not have second guessing and incriminations."

Kalisto continued to glare at Gremis, who comfortably ignored him. "He obviously knows it's gone." Gremis shrugged. "But Poseidon doesn't know who took it or how. If he did, all of us would be hanging on crosses now, or worse."

"Innocent temple priests and court slaves are dying in our place," Olorun said.

Gremis nodded, his mirth drained. "True. A new Purge has begun, and we are responsible. We will have to bear that weight to our graves, or a cross. Yet, mankind has taken its first step on the path of liberation from ages of slavery. Thanks to you scholars, the Dagger of Renewal has been stolen and cast into the deepest ocean. It is lost forever. That wretched monster in the Alabaster Pyramid will die in his current body, and his offspring will fall upon one another in war. Without their father to keep them apart, they will finally put their red swords to good use and begin killing one another."

"Eventually, the Purge will spread to the Imperial Academy," Kalisto warned.

"Maybe," Alec said. "But for now, Poseidon still trusts us or he wouldn't be sending Amiran on this expedition."

"But it still is a mystery," Olorun said. "There are dozens of talented young scholars wandering the courtyards, just itching for such an adventure. Never has the king sent a Master, let alone a Grand Master, abroad as a simple fleet scholar."

"Do not be so quick to bemoan the role of the 'simple' fleet scholar, dear poet." Gremis raised a gnarled finger and waved it over the dim candle. "The ship's scholar is to knowledge as the footman is to a great army, victory's foundation." Gremis's eyes transfixed on the flame. "Poseidon and Leviathan be damned, I would trade places with you in heartbeat. The lust for discovery still courses strong through these old veins."

He looked up at the assembly. "Remember always, humility is the beginning of wisdom. Wisdom is the foundation for knowledge, and knowledge is the wellspring of enlightenment. Our beloved Academy was built on more than these cold stones." He motioned to the mummies. "The sacrifices of these 'simple' scholars brought the world to us. Our sacrifices will bring the world freedom!"

Olorun lowered his head. "Forgive my pride, Master Gremis."

Gremis smiled warmly. "If pride can so thoroughly infect the gods, what can we mere mortals do to protect ourselves from her lustful embrace? However, if we never forget we are *mortal*, humility will always be our shield."

Gremis put his hands behind his back and walked around the cavern's edge, a ghostly figure in steady candlelight. He brushed away cobwebs and lovingly caressed the damp rock and wine nooks. He impishly put his finger to his lips and let out a boyish giggle. "As a young plebe, my friends and I came here to get drunk! We sat among the dead, recited poetry, and drank ourselves blind." He chuckled. "It was the only place we could get rowdy and not get caught."

Amiran smiled. "You old bag of bones. If I recall, you slapped me with a seven-week detention after catching me wandering the catacombs when I was a plebe. You hypocrite."

"Hypocrite?" Gremis shrugged. "Not at all. I punished you for being careless enough to get caught."

They erupted into laughter, and the candle seemed to glow a little brighter.

Gremis continued, a shade more serious, "I've always found it intriguing what the Academy sees fit to store in these forgotten places."

Amiran welcomed the momentary distraction from his predicament. He didn't know what his mentor was about to say, but he'd be richer for the experience.

Gremis raised three bony fingers. "Three treasures once occupied these halls…" He lowered one finger at a time as he slowly uttered his list. "Wine, knowledge, and the dead."

Gremis returned, his hands behind his back, and continued to stroll around the men. "Sadly, only the dead remain. Perhaps that says something about us, eh? In ancient times, Poseidon, in memory of his mortal wife Cleito, founded the Academy. These catacombs *were* the Academy back then, not a tomb but open to the sun, a place of learning. Once we were King Atlas's beloved children, the princes our patient shepherds."

The old Master stepped closer to the candle light, the mirth gone. His shadowed eyes stared as if in a trance. He reached up above the nooks and caressed the limestone, where an owl's faint image had been crudely scratched. He recited Athena's last words to Master Vulcan before she slipped overboard and vanished into the Erubian night. "'*Be like the owl, beloved Vulcan. Watch quietly from the shadows with unblinking eyes. Shun those colorful, noisy parrots who will only betray you. Be patient and bide your time, for the day will come to strike wisely, strike swiftly, and strike silently.*'"

Gremis turned and faced the men. "That is why you are here, my fellow Owls. You know the story, but it bears repeating. Only this select fellowship knows how Athena saved Grand Master Vulcan from the Purges, and how Master Vulcan in turn helped her escape from Poseidon. Together, Vulcan and Athena crafted the Dragon's Egg and hid it deep within these catacombs.

"It was when my friends and I explored places far deeper than this chamber, that I stumbled upon the Dragon's Egg, hidden long ago during the first Purges. I kept it hidden, and spent the rest of my life trying to discover its secrets. Oh, on that glorious day when its lid finally opened…" Gremis closed his eyes and bowed his head, as if reliving that moment. "It was if I stood upon the shores of a new continent!"

The candle dimmed, as if the air was suddenly sucked out of the room. Gremis's voice became low and cold. "I learned the truth about the history Poseidon wanted buried forever. There was a time when men and gods were equals, and worshipped the true Creator, a power far greater than even Poseidon.

"You know the tale, my fellow Owls. You've peered into the Dragon's Egg and read the Ancient of Ancients and learned the First Tongue. This world became like wine to them, powerful… seductive…intoxicating. Grace and flesh cannot co-exist for any length of time without temptation, without corruption. The Sons of Poseidon have succumbed to both, and men will never be free while they walk the earth."

Gremis shook his head, and his eyes focused on Amiran. He smiled and said, "Pride, my dear friend, is the only realm where mortals hold advantage over the gods. Our mortality permits humility, as both a shield and perhaps an avenue to this great, unknown Creator. As long as we live under the heel of these gods, we will never come to know Him." Gremis opened his arms, as if the truth were obvious. "Brothers! Our souls are like the catacombs, dark, empty places sealed off from the Creator by slavery's darkness. Humility is like this candle. It provides only a glimpse of the Creator's light, enough to give us peace. Peace gives us clairvoyance to fill our empty souls with what we choose! Whether that is death, knowledge, or sweet wine, the choice is ours."

Gremis returned to the table. "We should not fret over our personal fates." Gremis paused, letting the dreadful implications of his words sink in among the conspirators. "If we dwell on that possibility"—he loudly tapped his finger against the wood and looked straight at Kalisto—"then we have chosen spiritual death. If that is the only truth we carry from this place today, we might as well crawl into the nearest sarcophagus and open our wrists."

"There is much talk of truth," a voice said from the shadows. "Ponder this, then. We have been fighting so long for mankind's liberation, I dare ask, is mankind worth it?"

They all turned to Olorun. He returned their shocked expression. "Forgive me, brothers. I ask only from a purely intellectual perspective."

"How dare you question this sacred fellowship!" Kalisto huffed.

Amiran held up his hand. "Everything should be questioned, especially our most cherished beliefs." He looked at his old friend. "Go on."

"Amiran, you remember the mob on the bridge today. Who in this city is worthy to claim leadership's mantle from the gods? The Temple Priest? The Parrots? Us? The mob? Who among us is ready to rule?" The poet held out his hands as if begging for an answer. "Shall we hand imperium over to the freemen? I dare say the freemen have been worse than the gods. Warriors and the sailors are instruments of atrocity, slavery, and genocide. Or do we just give power to our patron goddess, Athena, and hope she remains benevolent? Pray tell, brothers, who shall rule if not the gods?"

They stared at one another and the candle. Even Gremis seemed at loss for words.

"My point is intellectually valid. Judging by your faces, it is one we have not explored thoroughly." Olorun leaned against the wall and crossed his arms.

"It is a valid point, Master Poet, and yes, one we haven't fully addressed in this august circle," Amiran said. "Victory over the gods has been such a far-off possibility, thoughts of what comes after have been neglected. I for one do not believe we should look to the City of Atlas, or even the greater Empire for those that will lead the way."

"Explain." Gremis leaned against the table, obviously intrigued.

"Humanity within the Empire is tainted. We've all been on expeditions. We've seen tribes who rule themselves, that is before they were crushed under Poseidon's heel. Some have been benevolent; most have been savage. Humanity's salvation is on the frontier, waiting on an undiscovered coastline. They will be a free, virtuous people, humble and grounded in simple truths lost to those of us who dwell in the gods' shadows. Their morality will be founded in love, not power. What we are will be abhorrent to them, yet they will not judge us, only show us the path forward."

"Do you really believe that?" Olorun said.

"I must believe it," Amiran said, defiantly lifting his bearded chin. "Anyway, such musings are not pertinent to our present situation. Gremis is correct. We have won a tremendous victory. If our conspiracy were known, we would already be hanging from crosses along the Grand Canal."

"It's irrelevant what the gods know or don't know," Gremis said. "We must proceed with our plans as if we will live forever, while living each day as if it were our last."

Buoyed by Gremis's words, the conspirators seemed to relax, except Kalisto, who appeared just as agitated.

"What of Poseidon's order and its implications for the Grand Master?" Theron nodded to Amiran.

Gremis turned to Alec. "Tell the Grand Master what else you gleaned from your court confidant while I retrieve something from the outer catacombs."

"At this very hour Leviathan is in the Alabaster Pyramid taking counsel with Poseidon. Two deep-hulled ships, the *Orion* and *Leo*, are anchored at a coastal wharf, loading supplies for a three-month journey. Tonight, they will depart with Leviathan's new flagship *Draco* for the treacherous Straits of Gadeirus. If they survive transit through the gap, they will sail up the continent's west coast to Gadriuopolis. Amiran, you will depart for Coatzacolcos aboard a light caravel, a three-day voyage west. From there, you will travel via the King's Road across the Isthmus of Olma. A fleet has already been assembled in Gadriuopolis for the voyage across the Oceanus Gadeirus."

Amiran considered the news. "The *Draco* is the most feared warship in the fleet, and Prince Gadeirus's personal vessel. It's commanded by the legendary Captain Ploarchos."

Alec spoke. "Reflagged on Poseidon's order, not the king's."

"Are you sure, Alec?" Amiran said, astonished.

"I am sure of it. This is all Poseidon's doing, not Atlas's."

"We are presented with several mysteries this morning," Amiran remarked. "Rarely does the mad god give audience to his bastard son. It is rarer still when Poseidon meddles in his sons' affairs, let alone interjects himself in how Atlas administers the kingdom."

Alec continued, his voice lower, "My source tells me crates with strange chains have been loaded in the *Draco's* hold. Master Amiran, you will find what follows even more interesting." His scarred face looked otherworldly in the candlelight. "Before our connections in the Alabaster Pyramid could steal the dagger, we needed a foolproof way to quickly get it out of the city. This fell to me, as you all know. What you couldn't know was how I did it. I needed a cover story to book passage on a ship transiting deep water to dispose of the dagger. I couldn't draw attention to myself, so it had to be something believable. After a few well-placed bribes, I discovered that an expensive shipment of war booty was earmarked for the Imperial Academy. The laden scrolls bore Poseidon's seal." He held out his arms as if the rest was obvious. "I had my cover story. I convinced the merchant I was the Academy's official representative to meet the cargo at Bird Island, and sail with it until it reached Atlantis." Alec took a deep breath. "Disposing of the dagger was easy. No one ever suspected me. The interesting part was discovering what the cargo was."

Kalisto huffed, "Enough of the damn theatrics — what the hell was it?"

"Two Attican slave children, twins, wearing white loincloths. They're now enjoying a meal in the kitchens upstairs."

The table erupted in excited discussion. The knot suddenly released in Amiran's belly, and relief washed over him. He put his hands on the table, leaned over, and took a long, deep breath.

The candle flickered dangerously.

"You look relieved, Grand Master," Kalisto remarked.

"I am. Now I understand why I am going." Amiran exhaled, straightened, and adjusted his toga. "There are no plots within plots here. Leviathan thinks, perhaps correctly, dragons may still dwell in unexplored Cin. Since I am the kingdom's leading expert on dragon lore, and the last living Royal Butcher to harvest one of the great beasts, I am going. It's that simple."

"You will be taking more than Dragon Butchers with you, Grand Master," Gremis said. "You're taking the Dragon's Egg."

"No!" Amiran protested. "Losing it would be disastrous. Having it fall into Leviathan's hands would be worse."

"We both know he cannot open it, nor can he destroy it…providing you are still willing to die to protect it."

"Well, yes, but that's not the point. It is irreplaceable. I will not take it."

"Oh, you will," Gremis admonished. "Regardless of who is leading this expedition, or for what dark reason, it can still serve a noble purpose. If the fleet makes it to Wu, the Dragon's Egg will be safer in that obscure corner of the Empire than under Poseidon's nose. I fear this coming Purge will be far worse than the one of Vulcan's time. These catacombs may not be deep enough to protect us or the Dragon's Egg."

"That's a hefty gamble!" Amiran interrupted.

"Perhaps not," Alec said and looked at Gremis as if seeking permission. Gremis nodded.

Amiran looked suspiciously from Alec to Gremis. "What aren't you telling me?"

"As you know, before I took this mission on behalf of the Owls, I had recently returned from an Academy posting in the north. It's no secret in this fellowship, or in the Academy, the Icelands have become an area of study dear to me."

"I've read every one of you reports." Amiran nodded. "Your work has been invaluable."

"Grand Master, most of my work in the north has been for the Merchant Guild, assisting them with the Empire's copper mines, with some logging harvest and exploration along the glaciers. The situation in the north has changed dramatically." Alec removed a scroll from his tunic and spread it across the table. In exquisite detail, the map showed Olma Minor's known lands. A glacial wall lined the far north, with annotations where all the copper mines were located along the Icelands' edges. A series of mighty rivers drained the continent's eastern side. The rivers flowed from the Icelands and into the enormous Hahawakpa River basin, which in turn drained into the Sea of Leviathan.

"I'm sure most of you are familiar with reports of massive mudflows pouring into the Sea of Leviathan with greater frequency," Alec said.

Olorun nodded slowly. "Yes, sometimes they even stain the waters surrounding the kingdom."

"The Southern Current that drains the Sea of Leviathan is bringing the mud from the Hahawakpa River delta. The mud comes from the far north, where glaciers are breaking apart at an alarming rate. Unprecedented floods are sweeping across Olma Minor's northern frontier. Walls of water flatten forests and mountains. We've lost thousands of men and a dozen copper mines to these floods."

"So?" Kalisto said. "The northlands are a continent away. The Empire can get its copper from the Erubian or Asuian colonies, albeit at a higher price."

"Let him finish," Amiran said. "This isn't about copper, is it, Alec?"

He shook his head. "No, it isn't. During my last expedition, I climbed the glacial mountains at the top of the world. They are thousands of feet high. They hold another ocean on top, like a tub. I've explored some of this ocean with the natives, in small boats they call kayaks." Alec looked around the table. "The glacial ocean is vast, my brothers. The dam holding it back is failing.

"If it breaks all at once, a wall of water a mile high and thousands of miles across will descend down the Hahawakpa River basin and pour into the Sea of Leviathan. Once there, it can only funnel through one place before it pours into Atlas's Ocean." He pointed to the island of Atlantis on the map.

"What is your evidence it will burst all at once?" Theron scoffed. "I mean, isn't it already releasing pressure a little at a time? That, to me, seems like a more realistic scenario."

"It does sound a bit alarmist." Olorun rubbed his chin, still looking at the map.

"If not acted upon by an outside force, such as an earthquake, the glacial ocean may continue to vent slowly." Alec tapped the map. "But I don't think time is on our side. I've seen the glaciers first-hand, gentlemen. They are thinning and crumbling at an alarming rate."

"How long?" Amiran asked.

"Days. A century. A millennium." Alec rolled up the map. "If I survive the Purge, I'm going to solicit the Academy for funds to mount a dedicated expedition."

"I'm sure my replacement will be agreeable to such an expedition." Amiran looked about the room. "Provided my replacement comes from this room."

Kalisto looked up at the ceiling. "I'm sure the Parrots up there are already clucking about who will replace you as Grand Master."

Amiran knew Kalisto was right. As the years went by, more and more factions in the Imperial Academy thought political considerations more important than academic credentials. The conspiracy had dubbed such scholars "Parrots," sycophants who slavishly curried favor among the Eleven Princes. They pursued power over knowledge, more comfortable clucking in court than pursuing study and research. They seemed to find reasons to avoid expeditions, and looked down at those eager to travel to the Empire's wild frontiers. Parrots served power and not truth, and their ranks seemed to grow with every new Academy class.

"What makes you think the Dragon's Egg will be any safer in Wu?" Amiran asked Alec.

"We don't," Gremis interjected. "To send it east sends it into the center of the Ten Princes and war. It would attract attention, which could be traced back to us. To send it south into Olma Major risks it falling into the Olmecs' hands. It can sit in a quiet corner in Wu's library, while things back here settle down…or don't.

"We have hidden it in Prince Gadeirus's Expedition Chest, the one I carried for him on many journeys. It's completely logical you might need an extra chest in case you really do find dragons."

"Brilliant," Amiran agreed. An Expedition Chest contained all the valuable tools necessary to lure and harvest a dragon. It could only be opened by the Expedition Scholar, and would protect the Dragon's Egg from detection while not raising Leviathan's suspicion.

"Of course it's brilliant, I thought of it." Gremis laughed.

The men considered the map in silence for several long moments before Amiran spoke. "What if I fail?"

Gremis considered his former apprentice. "What if we all fail? We're likely to perish in this Purge, or the next, before the mad god finally dies. You will probably end up shipwrecked or drowned before you even reach Wu. You might be killed by savages or that ghastly Obsidian Guard, or even by Leviathan himself.

"If you succeed, the Academy's treasured knowledge survives, the gods perish, and a brighter chapter is written in mankind's history."

31. Where the Snake Hides.

"My master once taught me that should an expedition meet disaster, the scholar's navigation kit, above all else, must be saved. This is why so much care was spent engineering these chests. It was small enough to carry, but large enough for the essentials. It was waterproof and lined with white stone to protect it against fire. Its cipher was known only to the scholar. A scholar and his navigation kit were one. Contained within was his mind, heart, and soul." - The Last Scholar

- The Chronicle of Fu Xi.

***

Fond memories from Amiran's youth seemed to omit an expedition's common discomforts, which only magnified with age. It took him longer to get his sea legs, and the unexpected, albeit mild, nausea he experienced on the high seas surprised him. A stiff back and sore neck greeted him every morning as he struggled to rise from the ship's deck. The Sea of Leviathan's brutal humidity left Amiran soaking by late morning. He didn't miss relieving himself in a small pot on a dark, pitching deck. Though he found the ship's simple porridge and salted pork rations more agreeable to his digestion than the Academy's rich fare. Wisdom told Amiran he'd eventually grow re-accustomed to the austere life; it would only be a matter of time and will. Despite the discomforts, Amiran felt at peace. This was where he truly belonged.

Amiran gladly lost himself in the Expedition Scholar's age-old daily routines like a holy rite. His beloved navigation kit lay at the heart of these duties.

Every morning before dawn, Amiran prepared his navigation kit for the day ahead. This was the same kit he'd carried on every journey since his Temple Voyage. An Expedition Scholar took many chests and articles along to adequately serve his fleet captain, but the navigation kit was universal to all scholars. He ran his fingers lovingly over the relief inscription carved into the cypress lid. Coined by Grand Master Vulcan himself centuries earlier, it graced every scholar's navigation kit: "*All that is observed is worthy of measurement. All that is measured should be done so accurately. All that is measured shall be recorded.*" Amiran would then place his hands under the steel-lined lid and enter the combination on the three-button mechanical lock. Inside, three stacked wooden trays fit snugly on top of one another. Priceless articles were nestled into contour-matching, felt-lined cavities carved into each tray. The top tray only contained Vulcan's Box, an engineering masterpiece of delicately balanced gears and springs.

The Empire was united by two great forces: Poseidon's Will and the Imperial Academy's Web of Time. The heavy bronze chronometer called Vulcan's Box, sometimes called a time sextant, was the heart of expedition navigation and record keeping. Latitude could be judged by the stars, but longitude needed accurate time keeping. Every morning Amiran inspected the device, and used the silver key in the kit to wind it a specified number of turns. Every Vulcan's Box, whether on a ship or in a colony, was initially synchronized to the Master Box located in the Academy's Ivory Tower, and that date was etched on the box's bronze backplate. Through a series of regular dispatches, each chronometer was regularly updated from the master clock. These scattered, synchronized time pieces created the Web of Time, uniting humanity and the Empire, and forever changing the Academy's perspective on the universe.

The second tray contained the expedition maps, plotters, compass, and sextant. It also held two long, narrow glass vials. One, called a thermal column, was permanently sealed and contained a small amount of quicksilver. This was for reading temperature. The other, called a density column, was a simple glass tube, open at each end, accompanied by a ceramic cup with a mounting clip and a sealed iron jar full of quicksilver. All of these were carefully wrapped in fleece to prevent breakage.

The third tray contained the scholar's log. Waterproof ivory scroll cases contained enough clean papyrus to last a year. A tightly-sealed brass inkwell and bronze stylus fit snugly into custom slots. This is where older scholars, like Amiran, kept their magnifying glass.

Each day the Expedition Scholar recorded the voyage's progress in his log, all in strict accordance to ancient protocols. If and when an expedition returned to Atlantis, or even an established colony, the scholar's logs would be turned over to the library for certification, cataloging, and reproduction. Amiran's exhaustive annuals, accumulated since his Temple Voyage, were forever enshrined in the Imperial Academy.

Amiran would always leave his students with this thought: "If you return home with your expedition kit intact, you have ensured your immortality."

The short voyage to the Isthmus of Olma might have been a well-plied trade route, but to Amiran this place might have been the far-side of the world. Twice a day he carefully took sextant and time readings to confirm their position. He backed up these calculations via plotter and map by known landmarks along the archipelago passing slowly to their south. The fleet captain had plied this same route countless times, and knew the way without sextant or map. She indulged Amiran's redundant navigation as the four fat-bellied merchant ships plodded westward. It surprised Amiran when she asked him to inspect her sextant, compass, and charts to ensure they were updated against the Academy's latest information. He humbly obliged, although concerned she might take insult should he find her tools or skills lacking. Thankfully, he found the captain's charts and logs in superior order, and she seemed to take great pleasure in this.

Every time Amiran opened his expedition kit, he found Elda looking over his shoulder. The curious child asked questions, but he would only answer them if she spoke in Atlantean. He found her company agreeable, and enjoyed teaching her. The lessons accelerated her grasp of Atlantean, and seemed to put Elda's mind at ease. He'd come to discover when Elda wasn't afraid, neither was Ercole.

Elda and Ercole were brave, of that Amiran had no doubt. They'd witnessed their parents' murder, their village's destruction, and survived the arduous voyage across Atlas's Ocean. The children's resilience served them well as they adapted to their new lives as Royal Butchers. Perhaps it was the knowledge they were no longer in danger, or they could walk the decks without fear, but the children noticeably relaxed during the voyage. Perhaps it was that Amiran was there to answer their questions, and put their minds at ease.

Amiran spent much of the short voyage instructing the children on the Atlantean language and customs while they sat for hours in the billowing sail's gentle shade. As the tropical sun deepened Ercole and Elda's olive skin, they both rapidly gained a rudimentary understanding of the Empire's tongue. Elda embraced the lessons, but Ercole wasn't so enthusiastic. "What does this have to do with slaying dragons?" he asked impatiently in Attican.

"How do you slay a dragon?" Amiran responded in Atlantean.

Ercole scrunched up his face, struggling for the right Atlantean words. "Big spear. Maybe bow." He made as if pulling back a bow and letting the arrow fly, complete with an enthusiastic "whoosh" sound.

"Here"—Amiran grinned and pointed to his temple—"is where you slay a dragon." He leaned back. "We slay all monsters in the mind first, even the those we spawn ourselves." Amiran reconsidered his words. "Especially the ones we spawn ourselves."

"Why us…" Elda paused and searched her thoughts for the correct words. "…must kill dragons? I mean, you say few dragons…live, maybe none? Should not we let them live?"

Amiran smiled. "You're asking me if there are so few dragons left, why don't we just let them live?"

Elda nodded.

"Well, it's because the Great God Poseidon decreed long ago they should be wiped from existence," Amiran replied matter-of-factly, and then studied her response.

She crossed her arms and seemed to shrink. "It sounds…*seems*"—Amiran could see her frustration with the language—"not fair." She finally gave up and continued in Attican, speaking quickly and with passion, "If there are any dragons left, they aren't bothering anyone. We're searching them out to kill them, like the ships did when they came looking for me and my brother."

Amiran leaned close and spoke low in Attican, "I see justice burns in your heart, young lady. Let it smolder, but don't let it run wild. Not yet. Keep that flame hidden until the time is right. Be patient and bide your time, for the day will come to strike wisely, strike swiftly, and strike silently."

"When will I know the time is right?"

"When you know the spark can set the world on fire."

"Land ho!" the lookout's call interrupted from high above. Ercole jumped up and darted to the bow. Amiran and Elda followed.

A distant shore, low and flat, bisected a golden sunset and crimson sea.

"It's beautiful," Elda said.

"That is the Isthmus of Olma, the narrow strip that chains two great continents together. Ahead lies the Port of Coatzacolcos, *the Place of the Serpent*, named in Leviathan's honor." Amiran placed a hand on each child's shoulder. "This is the Empire's oft-forgotten backdoor. Do not let the beauty before us fool you. This is the land of the Olmecs, where Prince Leviathan recruits his fearesome Obsidian Guard, some of which you will soon meet. We must cross it before our adventure can truly begin. Tonight, we anchor and disembark at dawn."

***

The blazing sun above and the perfect white sand below conspired to blind Amiran. Sweat stung his eyes as he squinted at the anchored ships. A typical Atlantean port, the jetty built from native limestone, jutted half a mile into the turquoise sea, forming the breakwater's backbone. The artificial harbor's other sides, including the entrance, enclosed the giant rectangle before rejoining the beach. One could find identically designed ports along the shores of five continents. These massive, yet simple structures were the Empire's toe-holds on many shores. Their design and construction were primary skills taught to all scholars.

A long line of slaves portered supplies from the jetty to the beach. Burdened by chests, crates, and bags, they passed Amiran, huffing and stumbling in the soft sand. The procession snaked its way up the steep dunes. Most of these supplies would stay in Coatzacolcos, as part of this region's trade with Atlantis. The rest would be loaded into wagons bound for Gadriuopolis, a hundred miles south across the Olmec Isthmus. There, the Western Fleet awaited them.

Amiran briefly wondered about the *Draco's* progress. By his calculations, she and the small fleet were thousands of miles south, and had likely not rounded Olma Major's southern tip yet.

Elda and Ercole stood in Amiran's short shadow. Under the relentless noon sun, their linen tunics blurred into the

260

bleach-white sand. He would not let them out of his sight. He wasn't only responsible for their training, but their safety.

The sailors watched the slaves offload from the rigging and the decks. Being freemen, they took no part in the manual labor. Amiran caught sight of the last slave coming their way from the jetty, signaling offloading's conclusion. Amiran had counted every item, ensuring nothing was skimmed to line the captain's pockets, though he doubted this small fleet's captains would steal from this expedition. Most of the cargo bore Leviathan's personal seal, and Poseidon's as well.

Under two warriors' watchful eyes, the two Expedition Chests and his navigation kit were already loaded onto Amiran's personal wagon.

Amiran turned to the cabin slave, the captain's personal property, waiting patiently beside him. The small Erubian boy, woefully thin and perhaps only ten, patiently held a wooden tray, atop which rested the manifest, a stylus, and an inkwell. The angry red whelps on his bony shoulders stood in stark contrast to his pale skin.

Amiran signed the manifest and the child turned to leave. "Halt, boy," Amiran commanded and grabbed his arm. "You've forgotten something."

Fear flashed across the boy's face.

Amiran considered the slave's tattered rags. "How long have you served your captain?"

"Two summers." The northern Erubian wilderness flavored his accent. *He must be tougher, or smarter, than he looks to have survived such maltreatment so long*, Amiran thought.

"I bet you're good at stealing, and hiding things?" The boy didn't answer and lowered his eyes.

He's afraid I'm toying with him, he thought. Amiran reached into his knapsack and broke off a large hunk of cheese. "Here." He gave it to the boy. "I doubt even you could hide that in those rags, so you better eat it fast before you get back to the ship." The boy snatched the morsel and scurried down the dunes, stuffing his mouth the whole way.

That might keep him alive a little longer, he thought.

He turned to the two children beside him. These two Erubian slaves were as far removed from the life of a deck slave as possible. Yet, they still carried the title "slave," which in the Empire's eyes made them less than human. He saw unspoken questions swimming in Elda's eyes. *She's trying to decide if I'm truly a friend or a foe*, he thought.

Amiran looked about, searching the surrounding dunes and nearby beach.

"Did you lose something, Teacher?" Ercole asked.

"My friend Tyaga was supposed to meet us at the wharf. He's the port's scholar."

"He's probably in the shade waiting on you." Ercole kicked some sand.

Amiran sopped his brow with his tunic's corner. "You're probably right. Let's go." The children followed him up the dune behind the last porter. Ahead, the temple pyramid rose high above the dunes.

***

Like living shadows, a column of vultures wheeled high above the Olmec pyramid's flat pinnacle and roosted on its stepped sides. It was a pale limestone imitation of Atlantis's great Alabaster Pyramid that Amiran judged stood only about sixty feet high. Snake-like female dragons, long and winged, were carved all the way to the pyramid's top along the zig-zag central staircase.

The pyramid stood as a sentinel against the dunes and sea. A hodgepodge of palm frond–thatched huts and longhouses fell in its western shadow. The huts formed a rectangular courtyard, which opened to a long wharf stretching into the river, where flat-bottomed barges awaited the wagons. West of that, the jungle formed a thick, impenetrable wall.

Amiran found the wagon caravan already assembled in the courtyard, waiting to be rolled onto the river barges.

Coatzacolcos existed solely to protect the Isthmus Road, the only land route connecting the Ocean Gadeirus to the

Ocean Atlas. No real threats existed against the Empire's interest on the isthmus, so only about 200 warriors manned the garrison. Fifty of them now milled around the wagon train assembled for the three-day journey across the isthmus, both by river and overland. Amiran mentally inspected the warriors.

Most reclined in the wagons' shade, listlessly smoking pipes. A few snored in the cool sand beneath the wagons. Amiran couldn't blame them — the steamy air sucked his energy away, too. The warriors' spears, shields, and chain armor rested on cloaks and blankets within arm's reach. The polish and lack of rust spoke to the garrison's discipline. Amiran had sailed in enough expeditions and fought alongside enough Atlantean warriors to know the good ones from the bad ones. *It takes a good commander to keep soldiers assigned to Imperial backwaters motivated*, he thought. Amiran looked around for Tyaga or the garrison commander, but didn't see either.

"See that wagon there?" he said to the children and pointed to the caravan's center. "The one in the middle with the veil draped over it?"

"Yes," Ercole replied.

"That's ours. Get in. I will be along soon."

The children looked back at him, and they eyed the impenetrable jungle. He sensed trepidation haunting their spirits once again, but they obediently climbed into the wagon. Amiran turned and walked up the wagons' line looking for Tyaga.

He found the pipe-smoke drifting around him intoxicating, and badly wanted a smoke himself. It came from a local plant called tobacco, this region's major export to the Empire. Amiran had grown quite fond of tobacco since his days as an upperclassman. He had several bales loaded in the wagons. He had also heard of a different type of tobacco available in Wu, one that elicited a pleasantly euphoric effect. He looked forward to studying it, and possibly sending some seeds back to the Academy.

In a few moments, he spotted the man he knew must be the garrison commander. The tall, lanky Alkebulan wore full chain and carried an Atlantean short sword. Amiran didn't see a trace of sweat on his ebony skin. Amiran noticed his hilt bore Prince Gadeirus's leaping dolphins. The man's tight, uniform cornrowed hair and beard gave him a disciplined appearance. *Whoever this man is, he likely made powerful enemies in the Atlantean army to end up here*, Amiran thought.

Amiran approached and extended his credential scroll to the officer, who snatched it without making eye contact. Amiran lowered his head, forbidden to speak until the freeman addressed him. The officer unfurled the scroll and considered it carefully for several minutes.

He finally looked up and considered Amiran with a long face, generously peppered with scars. "Grand Master of the Academy? Is that supposed to impress me?"

"No, sir. I am only a humble servant."

The warrior expertly rolled up the scroll from the center, without creasing the edges, in the manner of a literate man and returned it to Amiran. "I am Field Captain Darious, Commander of Coatzacolcos Station. Per my orders, my unit will escort these goods, including you, across the isthmus to Gadriuopolis." He looked over Amiran's shoulder at the children. "They look expensive."

"They are."

"As expensive as you, Scholar?"

Amiran met the commander squarely in the eye. "Cities have fallen to bring them here."

If that impressed the commander, he hid it well. Darious brushed past Amiran toward the caravan's front. The scholar dutifully fell in line.

"Have you travelled the Isthmus Road before?"

"No," Amiran replied. "But I've read about it. It's only a three-day journey, correct?"

Darious barked a short laugh. "Five. One on barges and four over land. And if your scrolls said it's a road, they lied.

It's a trail at best, one that continually must be hacked and rehacked. That is what we call it here, the Trail. I hope you enjoy mud, tangled roots, and quicksand. These wagons will get stuck half a dozen times a day. I will lose at least three men in the coming days if I'm lucky."

"Lose them to what?" This genuinely perplexed Amiran. This was supposed to be the Empire's backyard.

"Sometimes to accidents disembarking the barges at the upstream trailhead, especially when the river is high in the rainy season. Most are lost on the Trail. Jaguars, usually." Darious stopped at a wagon and inspected one of its wheels. He shook the rim, and apparently satisfied, resumed his brisk walk. "They lurk in the trees until someone passes beneath, and then they pounce." Like lightning, Darious spun about and gripped Amiran's throat like an iron vice, all while continuing to speak calmly. "Before the victim can scream, the cat crushes their throat and drags them into the jungle. I often don't discover they're missing until we make camp." He released Amiran's neck and looked him over with a hint of disdain. "It might take a jaguar a little longer to drag you into the bush."

Darious resumed walking. "Same with the great snakes, as big as dragons. They can crush the life out of a man and swallow him whole. Did your scrolls tell you about any of this, Scholar?"

Still rubbing his throat, Amiran shook his head.

They came to the lead wagon. Darious pointed to the jungle's green wall. In all his travels, Amiran had never seen a wilderness this thick. "I noticed your men aren't equipped with bows." Amiran pointed to the dense jungle. "Is that why?"

Darious considered Amiran. "Observant. Bows are almost worthless in there. Leviathan's warriors won't touch bows. They stick to bolos and blowguns instead. Blowguns are useless without poison, and we don't have any. We've traded the locals for it, but it's no good after a week, and we don't know how to make it. The real poison in there, Scholar, is the air itself."

He inhaled deeply. "The air is toxic to some. After a few days in the jungle, they begin to shake like they are freezing, and then their skin turns to fire. Once they start coughing, it is only a matter of time."

Darius paused and glanced back at the wagons. "Tell me, have you seen much of the world?"

"My fair share."

Darious nodded. His expression didn't soften, but it lacked malice. "I have served in expeditionary campaigns alongside scholars. I bid your kind no ill will, so I will speak to you as one who knows the true nature of the world.

"This is my sixth round trip on the Trail. There is no glory in there, only duty. Keep the children under the mesh — it masks their forms from the cats and snakes but still lets air through. It also helps repel the biting insects. Keep them in the wagon at all times, even on the barge. Have them use the pot to relieve themselves. You get out of the wagon if absolutely necessary, and only with my permission. It would look bad on me if I were to lose merchandise the likes of you. We will bring you what you need. Do you understand?"

Amiran nodded. Darious considered him the way soldiers often look upon those who dwell in civilized places, and it shamed him. Once, Amiran had been a hardened Expedition Scholar, with many lands explored and many battles to his credit. He was the last living Dragon Butcher. Amiran knew he'd become old and sodded. He judged Darious as a good soldier, and wanted his respect, or as much respect as a freeman could give a slave.

Amiran pushed the shame away and tried to focus on the job at hand. He looked about. "I was told before leaving Atlantis I would be met by the port scholar. I do not see Tyaga."

Stone-faced, Darious looked up at the temple pyramid. "He's up there."

***

High above the dunes atop the pyramid, the sea breeze blew unfettered and dried some of Amiran's sweat, but that wasn't what sent chills through his body.

Tyaga's body had almost been reduced to bones by scavengers and ants. Spread eagle over a small stone dais, Tyaga's flayed ribcage and headless corpse told Amiran all he needed to know. "They ripped out his heart." Amiran's voice, flat and lifeless, sounded as if it came from outside his body.

"I am sorry, Scholar. No man should die this way, slave or freeman," Darious said from behind. "It was the Olmecs."

Amiran turned. "I thought the Olmecs were loyal to the Emperor. I've heard no news of an uprising."

"It wasn't an uprising. These were Leviathan's own men."

Murdered. Legally, it's impossible for a freeman to murder a slave, but in Amiran's heart, it was murder just the same.

"Why?"

"It seems the princes decided to swap sides of the world. Two weeks before your arrival, I received orders to surrender Gadriuopolis to Prince Leviathan's Obsidian Guard." He held out his arms as if encompassing tiny Coatzacolcos. "In return, the Olmecs gave up all this."

Amiran turned back to the body as Darious continued, "Tyaga was the only scholar on the Isthmus, so the unfortunate duty of administering the transfer fell to him. I can tell you he performed his duty flawlessly and with the utmost honor.

"It seems the Olmec commander, a foul-tempered warrior called Quexil, didn't agree with the allocation of supplies. Two days after the transfer, they kidnapped him from a caravan on the Trail. We assumed a jaguar had taken him, and then a sentry found him up here. Quexil himself carried his head into my headquarters to brag and pay the Empire for the slave's cost."

The warrior said it all so matter-of-factly, as if it were a simple business transaction for accidentally killing a horse or cow. Amiran remembered Tyaga as a good student. Not the best student, not even close, but an enthusiastic scholar and astronomer. Like many middling students, he didn't earn an expedition, but had to settle as an administrative scholar in a backwater posting. He wanted to tell the warrior all of this, but why would a freeman care?

The Olmecs slew him in a perverted mockery of the Renewal Ceremony.

"Where is his heart?" Amiran asked, voice shaking. "I want to bury him before we depart."

"I already buried his head. His heart is…unrecoverable." Amiran turned to face Darious. The warrior stared at him impassively. "We don't have time for this. The caravan must depart. The body stays here."

Amiran looked down at Tyaga's corpse and then leveled his stare on Darious. "You fear them, don't you?"

"As I told you, *slave*, there is no glory here, only duty. If you scholars were truly as wise as they say, you'd already know this. Tyaga didn't.

"Olmecs are no better than animals. Even those that serve Leviathan's horde feast on human flesh. This is their land. They know how to fight in the jungle. Prince Gadeirus's Dolphins fly over this shore only as long as Prince Leviathan's Serpent permits it. I only have 200 men. My job is to keep as many of them alive as long as I can. If I can do that, my command here will have been a success, and I will be able to live with myself."

Amiran stared dumbfounded at the garrison commander.

"Do not judge me too harshly. The Trail teaches humility. If Tyaga had learned that, he'd still be alive. I hope you are wiser than he was, because in five days, I deliver you into Quexil's hands."

32. The Trail.

"Do not fret with mortal concerns. Eventually, the God of Death will ease their suffering." —The Sixth Lesson of the God Poseidon to his children, from the Ancient of Ancients.

- The Chronicle of Fu Xi.

***

Palm trees and sunlight surrendered to tangled vines and mirk. The jungle pressed down on them from every direction. Amiran fought the feeling of being trapped, squeezed. The towering trees shredded the sunlight, leaving the Trail in perpetual twilight. Instead of providing cool shade, it was as if the trees trapped the heat instead. The jungle kept out the breeze like a fortress wall. Each breath felt like inhaling water. Sweat poured off Amiran's brow like rain, and his light cotton tunic clung to his chest.

Amiran reclined against the chests and trunks along the wagon's forward bulkhead. The oxen's harness rattled dully behind his head. The teamster, a gangly Erubian slave with no teeth and leather for skin, hummed softly to the beasts. To Amiran, it sounded like a lullaby, and would have had the same effect had it not been so unbearably hot.

Every time he tried to close his eyes, an enormous insect buzzed near his face. The mesh kept out most of the insects, but a few made it through. Welts covered Amiran's skin, despite the pungent oil the commander gave them to rub all over their body. At his feet, Elda lay on her back, hands behind her head. She hadn't moved in hours. Ercole hung over the wagon's back gate like a wet towel, staring off into the jungle.

Progress came agonizingly slow. The Trail seemed to fight the caravan's progress at every step. Even disembarking the wagons at the way station proved harrowing. "Way station" was an exaggeration, as it consisted of nothing more than a muddy river-bar and an open shoreline hacked from the jungle. Soldiers and teamsters labored for hours to push the wagons off the muddy shore and up the steep hill where the Trail began in earnest.

Tangled roots, hard as stone, jarred Amiran's spine with every bump. Vines and branches brushed up against the wagon, occasionally snagging and tearing the mesh. The teamsters often resorted to ropes and tackle to get the wagons up and down steep grades. Rushing streams and mud bogs dogged them every few miles. Occasionally, paving stones lined the Trail. These stretches were few and far between. Darious said engineering attempts failed long ago.

"Earthquakes break them up, landslides bury them," he had said. "The Trail refuses to be tamed." Here, the Empire threaded a needle between two oceans. If the garrisons on either end ceased their unending battle to clear the Trail, the jungle would claim it in weeks.

Amiran yearned to venture from the wagon and look around, to study the soil and rocks. What if a canal, not unlike Atlantis's five circular canals, could be dug across the narrow Olmec Isthmus from Coatzacolcos to Gadriuopolis? With enough manpower it could be done, he thought. The College of Engineers had often debated the practicality of cutting a canal east of the Giza colony connecting the Azaes and Reed Seas, thereby opening major exploration into the far east. The lingering war with Attica had forestalled such endeavors. On this side of the Empire, there was no war. Occasionally, the jungle thinned enough for him to see the

Coatzacolcos River paralleling their journey to the south. Too shallow for ships, and too treacherous for anything larger than a canoe, it was unsuitable for navigation. *Maybe this river could serve as a starting point to dig a canal.*

Amiran pushed the idea from his mind and returned his attention to the warriors slogging beside the caravan. One had died from a snake bite while unloading the barges. Another had been crushed when a wagon slipped from its ropes going up a slippery hillside. Another failed to show for roll call this morning.

Almost since they entered the jungle, native women and children waddled up and down the column under the weight of huge gourds filled with water. Occasionally, a warrior beckoned one for a drink. The warriors traded colorful ceramic beads for the water. Elda had marveled at how strong the squat natives were, especially for their short stature. They drifted among the caravan, seemingly materializing and melting into the jungle like spirits.

"They never smile or speak," Elda said in Attican as the wagon rattled down a relatively flat stretch. "Who are they?"

"They are Olmecs," Amiran answered in her language. "They are native to these lands and the first peoples the Sons of Poseidon encountered on these shores. The gods named the two sister continents for them. They enjoy special favor under Prince Leviathan."

"Why?" Ercole asked.

"They are exceptionally fearsome," Amiran replied.

"Where are their men?" Ercole looked about fearfully.

"We will deal with them when we reach Gadriuopolis in two days."

Ercole suddenly gasped and pointed into the jungle. "Look!"

Elda and Amiran peered through the mesh and saw two enormous eyes staring back at them. Elda recoiled and clung to Amiran. "Giants!"

Amiran smiled and shushed her. "In a manner of speaking, yes. I hoped we'd see these. I've read about them, but wasn't sure if we'd pass them in daylight." He slid across the wagon to the side closest to the apparition. He beckoned the children closer and pointed to the enormous stone head, as big as the wagon, solemnly staring back at them from the Trail's edge. Vines crept up its sides like serpents, and shrubs and undergrowth covered its lower face. The warriors shambled by the statue without a glance.

"What is it?" Ercole whispered in awe.

"One of the Ten Sons of Cleito. The Olmecs carved them long ago to honor Poseidon and his immortal children."

"Look, there's another one!" Elda slid on her knees to the wagon's edge.

"Which is which?" Ercole asked.

"I don't know. With the exception of the Obsidian Guard, few Olmecs have seen the gods. This is more as the Olmecs imagining them."

"They're terrifying," Elda said.

"What are the gods like, Teacher? Have you met one?" Ercole asked.

"I've met them all except two, one of which we will all meet soon. Prince Leviathan will arrive in Gadriuopolis the coming weeks." Amiran grew quiet as he watched the massive heads slowly pass by on each side, staring impassively into the wagons as if examining them.

"So, what are they like?" Ercole repeated.

"Perhaps the Olmecs imagined them best," Amiran said dryly.

The children remained silent, staring into the darkness and lost in their own thoughts as the idols faded behind them.

***

Ercole's voice stirred Amiran from a restless slumber.

"What is in those chests, Teacher? The big ones you are leaning against. Is it something to eat?" Ercole asked in Attican.

"Ercole! Teacher is sleeping," Elda admonished her brother.

Amiran straightened up, slightly disoriented. "Is it sunset?"

"I don't think so," Elda said. "But I think it's soon."

"I'm sorry, Teacher," Ercole said. "I should have looked to see if you were asleep."

"That's fine, Ercole. I'd be glad to tell you."

Elda slid closer. "I was wondering about that, too."

Amiran tapped the one to his left with his outstretched arm. "This I will show you when we get to Wu." He motioned his thumb over this shoulder at the chest behind his back. "This one, my dear Ercole, does have food; the richest, most nourishing food in all the world. Would you like to see it?"

Both children slid forward, suddenly full of energy and curiosity.

"Pull the canvas over the wagon first, and light the lamp," Amiran said.

"But Teacher, it will get stifling in here!" Ercole protested.

"What is in here isn't for those beyond this wagon."

Reluctantly, the children obeyed. The air became even more oppressive, but the children didn't seem to care. The small oil lamp hanging from the center spar dribbled enough ruddy light to see.

Amiran turned around and gave his attention to the chests. Except for the symbols on their lids, both chests were identical.

"You are privileged to even see these chests. Few in the Academy have glimpsed them, let alone seen what is inside. These are the personal property of the Great God Poseidon himself."

"They are beautiful," Elda remarked.

"Indeed, and ancient." He pointed to the symbols barely discernible on the lid, painted in a slightly lighter shade of lacquer. One was Gadeirus's dolphins on an oval shield, the other Leviathan's coiled sea serpent on an identical shield. "They are called Expedition Chests, and are under my care and supervision as Expedition Scholar." He tapped the twelve keys arranged in a tight circle centered on Leviathan's chest just below the lid. "There are twelve keys on this one, each bearing special symbols. Gadeirus's chest only has ten keys. I will open Leviathan's Expedition Chest when the time is right."

"When is the time right?" Elda asked.

"When we find a dragon."

"What's in it?" Ercole leaned forward, eyes wide. All concerns about the heat seemed to be forgotten.

"Power."

"What do you mean?" Elda asked.

He smiled, pleased at their curiosity. "You will see what lies inside this one"—he patted Leviathan's Expedition Chest—"when we get safely to Wu."

"Why do we have to wait?" Ercole pressed.

"Because this power is too dangerous to expose here. It is a power you are meant to wield." He patted Ercole's head. "All in good time."

"What about the other one, the one with Gadeirus's symbol on the lid?" Elda asked. "The one with the food?"

"Food of sorts, yes, but also the most dangerous object in all the world."

"Wow!" Ercole breathed heavily and leaned forward. Elda noticeably shrank away.

Amiran caressed the smooth, oval keys just below the lid, each sealed with clear resins resistant to sun and salt. "Six keys bear unique symbols: a white horse, a red horse, a black horse, a gray horse, a white shield, and a red sword. Their ancient meanings are lost even to the scholars, though we do enjoy speculating about them. The next four are more understandable: A scroll, a horn, a lyre, and a five-pointed star. Only the Grand Masters, since even before Vulcan himself, know the combinations to these chests. They are changed after each expedition, and spoken only to Poseidon and the next Expedition Scholar. Writing it down is forbidden. Inside this one is the greatest gift ever granted to mankind."

"What is it? Please, tell us!" Ercole could not contain his excitement.

Amiran reached behind his back and quickly tapped out the proper sequence on the keys without looking. There was a satisfying click and a slight puff of air as the heavy lid cracked open. "It is Truth."

The children inched forward on their hands and knees as Amiran slid to the side and lifted the lid. It felt even heavier than he remembered. "Come and see."

A red metallic cylinder, almost as long and wide in diameter as the chest itself, rested snugly in lush purple felt lining the chest. A shimmering tide of light ebbed and flowed over its surface as the wagon rocked. It reminded Amiran of pulsing blood.

Living Truth, he thought.

An exaggerated female dragon, long and snakelike, coiled around the entire cylinder from bottom to top. Its head rested on the cap, face-up in the chest.

"Wow!" Ercole repeated, his amazed face bathed in crimson light.

"Move back." Amiran gently brushed the boy aside and reached into the chest, feeling for something just below the cylinder. He found the small lever and flipped it. Instantly, the cylinder pivoted on its base. A steel spring mechanism, connected to a lacquered wooden cradle, slowly elevated the cylinder to its full upright position and stopped with a sharp click. Now the dragon could be fully seen.

As if on cue, Ercole gasped "Wow!" once again.

"I've never seen anything so beautiful!" Elda whispered.

Amiran caressed the dragon. Its stubby hind legs gripped the cylinder's bottom, and its foreclaws gripped a quarter of the way from the top. The head rested on the cap, and two small rubies gave its eyes fierce fire. "This is called the Dragon's Egg. This type of dragon is mythical — its body is too long, and the head is a mix of carp and maybe a lion. Why Master Vulcan chose this creature to be the vessel's symbolic guardian is a mystery lost to time, as he left nothing in his writings about it. The particular orichalcum alloy has never been duplicated, even by the Academy's greatest metallurgists. It is as hard as orichalcum, and yet retains gold's luster."

"Why is it so rare?" Elda asked.

"Gold and orichalcum refuse to mix. Gold must be added to the fire-bile and iron on the first casting. Gold somehow destroys the process. The red metal always separates and floats, and will not bond. The gold turns to vapor, often killing the smithy in the process. It is just too expensive to attempt. Master Vulcan left no record of how he did it."

"Oh, for goodness sakes, what's inside?" Ercole shouted, the suspense too much for him to bear.

Amiran laughed, and caressed the dragon's head in just the right way. The jaws popped open, revealing seven needle-like teeth, two on top like fangs, and five smaller ones on the bottom jaw. Ercole reached out, but Amiran seized his wrist.

"Beware the dragon's bite, young man. Each tooth is a switch that must be flipped in the correct order. They're coated with an infinitesimally small amount of poison, recharged when the jaws are closed. The antidote for the first switch is the second switch in the sequence, and *only* the second switch. Yet, on its own, the second switch is a poison, and is only nullified by the third switch in sequence. Once started, one must flip them in exact order, and quickly, or an agonizing death comes soon after. Do this correctly, and quickly, and there are no ill effects."

Ercole slowly withdrew his hand, silently mouthing, "Wow!"

"Are you ready to see what is inside?" The children nodded emphatically. Elda slid a little farther away into the shadows, while Ercole crept closer.

"I need quiet; this is a difficult task." Amiran grimaced in concentration. "It's been a while, let me see if I can remember the combination."

"You mean you don't know?" Elda said, flabbergasted.

"I do." He shrugged. "It's just been a while. It's a rare day when I open the cylinder."

Elda slid farther across the wagon.

"Hurry up! Hurry up!" Ercole writhed as if he needed to pee. "I want to see what's inside."

"Okay, here it goes." Amiran turned and took a deep breath, and then quickly flipped the teeth.

Amiran froze, and then straightened up. "Uh oh."

"Teacher?" Elda said, her voice quaking. "Master Amiran?"

Amiran fell backwards and began shaking and convulsing.

"Teacher!" she shouted and rushed to his side.

Ercole began to shake Amiran. "Teacher!"

Amiran erupted in deep belly laughs as tears rolled down his cheeks.

"That wasn't funny!" Elda fumed. "Not the least bit!" She hit Amiran in the belly, which made him laugh even more.

"Yes, it was!" Ercole rolled onto his side, laughing.

Elda huffed and crossed her arms, biting her lips in an obvious ploy not to smile.

Amiran sat up, struggling to catch his breath. "I am sorry, my dear. I could not resist. Please forgive me." He sighed and pointed to the cylinder. "Look."

The dragon's arms were now open, as if waiting for an embrace. The cap had opened on its own, tilted back ninety degrees. The dragon's jaws were closed, and its eyes stared toward the heavens.

Elda hesitated and looked back at Amiran.

"It's safe, but do not touch what is inside."

Breathlessly, the children slid on their knees to the chest's edge and peeked into the container.

"That's it?" Ercole looked back at Amiran, clearly disappointed. "All of this, just for some old scrolls?" He huffed and slinked back and resumed his vigil at the wagon's back gate. "I thought it was going to be something amazing." He poked his head under the canvas and crossed his arms, further ignoring anything having to do with the chest.

His reaction wasn't unexpected, but it disappointed Amiran nevertheless. *He is a typical boy*, he thought. Elda, on the other hand, suddenly abandoned all fear and peered into the cylinder, eyes wide.

Seven open-ended cylinders filled the Dragon's Egg. Some were even subdivided into small compartments. Six were packed cases, but the seventh remained empty.

"What are they, Teacher?"

A student's enthusiasm is nourishment for the teacher's soul, he thought.

"These are the summation of human civilization's combined knowledge that has flourished under the gods' domain. Food for the mind and soul." Amiran took a deep breath, trying not to become overwhelmed by the power of it all. "The first major compartment holds the complete and original Song of Atlas. Each of these ten smaller scroll cases contains a chapter, from the dawn of time to the epoch where Master Vulcan sat at Poseidon's feet and recorded the saga."

"They look very old," she remarked.

"So old, I dare not take them out. When we do, we handle them with cotton gloves lest our very touch cause them harm."

"What of the others?"

Amiran pointed to the next five in a row. A mix of leather and ivory tubes. "These represent the Four Colleges of the Imperial Academy's combined knowledge. We update these every fifth year. It is a great event for the Academy. The Masters of the Four Colleges prepare diligently for the induction ceremony." He pointed to each case in turn. "There is the College of Engineers and Metallurgy, the

College of Music and Poetry, the College of Medicine and Agriculture, and the College of Geography and Astronomy. These are the colleges founded by Vulcan."

"I want to read them all!" She turned and looked up longingly to Amiran. "I beg you, please."

He didn't have the heart to tell her only the greatest of scholars were allowed to read the texts. Nor did he have the heart to tell Elda only men could be scholars. He refused to crush her thirst for knowledge. Instead, he would feed it.

"Libraries are one of the first structures built by Expedition Scholars in any colony. I heard the one in Wu is excellent. Almost everything in here, you will find there. When we arrive, you shall have full access to it. I promise."

She smiled up at him, eyes twinkling. "Thank you, Teacher!" She embraced him around the shoulders. Taken aback, he didn't quite know what to do other than stiffly pat her back.

"Why is one case empty?" Sometime while they were talking, Ercole had slipped back across the wagon, his curiosity apparently overwhelming his disappointment.

Amiran gestured to the empty cavity. "The future, of course. There must be room for future scholars to answer the questions we don't even know to ask."

"What are those scrolls?" Elda pointed to the last remaining case. "They look really old."

Six thin, cracked parchments, bundled as if hastily wrapped in common twine, leaned against the side of the large case.

Amiran thought for a moment about how to answer that question. "This cylinder was created just for those scrolls. Everything else the Academy added later. Think of the cylinder's contents this way." He pointed to the Song of Atlas. "This is Revelation, knowledge of divine origin, handed down from god to man." He waved his hand over the next four cases. "This is Discovery, information collected by the mind and hand of man." He pointed to the empty case. "This is the Future, a hole our progeny will either fill with our hopes or fears." Finally, his hand rested over the frail, gray parchment, bare in its container without a scroll case. "This is Truth, the Ancient of Ancients. Without this, Revelation, Discovery, and the Future are meaningless."

The children stared silently at the old scrolls as Amiran closed the Dragon's Egg. It sealed with a muffled click. Amiran reached under the egg, and with a click, the cylinder rotated and leaned sideways until it once again rested flush within the chest.

"Speak of nothing you've seen here. This knowledge was only meant for you."

They nodded, and Amiran closed the chest.

Outside, a man screamed.

Startled, the children jumped.

Amiran knew that kind of scream. Someone had just died.

The wagon stopped.

"Stay here!" he commanded and pushed past them to the back of the wagon. Amiran threw back the canvas and stared at the demonic face of an Olmec warrior.

***

"You will pay for my warrior's death." Commander Darious stood defiantly at the caravan's front, one of his men crumpled at his feet. Behind him, his warriors stood ready, swords drawn.

"Your *warrior* was a clumsy oaf. He walked straight into my warrior's macuahuitl." The Olmec brandished his heavy club, lined with sinister shards of obsidian glass. "My warrior thought he was a pig. It's understandable the way you all stumble about, making so much noise." The Olmec nudged the body with his bare foot. "Pig meat is good meat."

Darious's sword flashed a hair's breadth of the Olmec's long neck. "Touch his body again and you die."

The Olmec stepped closer and pressed his neck against the blade. "Quit playing games and go home. We guard the caravan now."

Darious's voice quavered. "My orders are to escort the caravan to Gadriuopolis."

"Prince Leviathan has different orders."

The thick jungle pressed close, presenting little room for Darious's men to maneuver. Amiran looked about and saw only a few Olmecs behind their leader. He scanned the jungle, spying dark eyes staring back through the undergrowth.

The Olmecs were armorless, wearing only loincloths and fearsome war paint slathered in jagged patterns to break up their outlines against the jungle. Amiran slowly approached Darious from behind and whispered, "Commander, there is nothing to gain here. 'Only duty, no glory,' isn't that what you said? You were going to hand us over to the Olmecs eventually — now is as good a time as in Gadriuopolis."

"Shut up, slave!" the Olmec commander barked. "You have no right to talk among freemen."

Amiran summoned his courage and continued to speak. "He can't harm us, but he can hurt you and your men. This isn't worth it."

Darious held his sword at the Olmec's neck for a few moments longer, and then slowly lowered it. "Scholar, have it entered in your journal that I, Commander Darious of Prince Gadeirus's Garrison, transfer responsibility of this caravan and all merchandise in it to Quexil, Commander of Prince Leviathan's Obsidian Guard."

"See how easy that was? It only took a slave's counsel and the price of one pig." Quexil laughed.

Darious turned to his second-in-command. "Gather remaining supplies from the lead wagon, then assemble behind the caravan. Double column, shields outside."

"Darious," the Olmec called out, but the commander kept walking away. "Do you miss Gadriuopolis? Your quarters are nice. I enjoy them so, just like I enjoy your former slave women, especially that little Erubian girl, the one you seemed so fond of." Darious paused, but didn't turn. She was so eager to please, so"—he bared his filed teeth—"tasty."

Around them, the jungle laughed.

Armor and weapon's rattle faded behind him, leaving Amiran alone with the Olmec. This new commander looked Amiran up and down with dripping disdain. "You are a fancy slave, yes?"

Amiran nodded once.

He gestured with a nod behind Amiran. "Back there, in that wagon, more fancy slaves?"

Amiran nodded once again, careful not to give away his thoughts to the savage. He'd had few dealings with the Olmecs, but their cruelty and bloodlust were legendary. The only attribute that eclipsed their viciousness was their fanatic loyalty to their patron god, Prince Leviathan, the one they called Paqua.

Amiran needed time to assess this new threat.

Corded muscle pulled over bone, there wasn't anything soft or subtle about Quexil. Every feature sharp and jagged, he was a flesh extension of his obsidian club.

"Why are you so fancy? Do men use you and them"—he nodded again back to the white wagon—"like women?"

Amiran had to choose his next words wisely, because they would determine how much hell this creature would inflict on him and the children for the rest of the journey. He suspected Quexil had clear orders not to kill or harm him and the children. He knew such men delighted in tormenting others, and would concoct ways to torture them without touching them. One cannot be subtle with monsters.

Amiran rolled up his right sleeve, revealing his trident brand. He spoke loud enough for the Olmec's henchmen to hear, and in clear, simple Atlantean. "I am the property of the Great God Poseidon, Prince Leviathan's father. He protects me." He pointed back to the wagon. "He protects them."

If this impressed Quexil, he didn't show it. Amiran pressed on, "Should any ill befall them, or me, those responsible will answer to the Great God himself."

Quexil began to laugh like a hyena. "Get back in the pig wagon, fancy slave."

Unsure if he had made things better or worse, Amiran returned to the children.

The caravan resumed its westward trek as Commander Darious and his warriors vanished down the Trail to the east. Unlike Darious's warriors, the Olmecs didn't stop for darkness, and yet the caravan seemed to make better progress in the jungle's pitch black than under Darious's men in daylight. The Trail began to consistently pitch downhill, and the humidity felt less intense. Somewhere in the night, Amiran thought he heard screams echoing through the trees, though he couldn't be sure if it was human or beast.

Western Territory of the Empire of Poseidon.

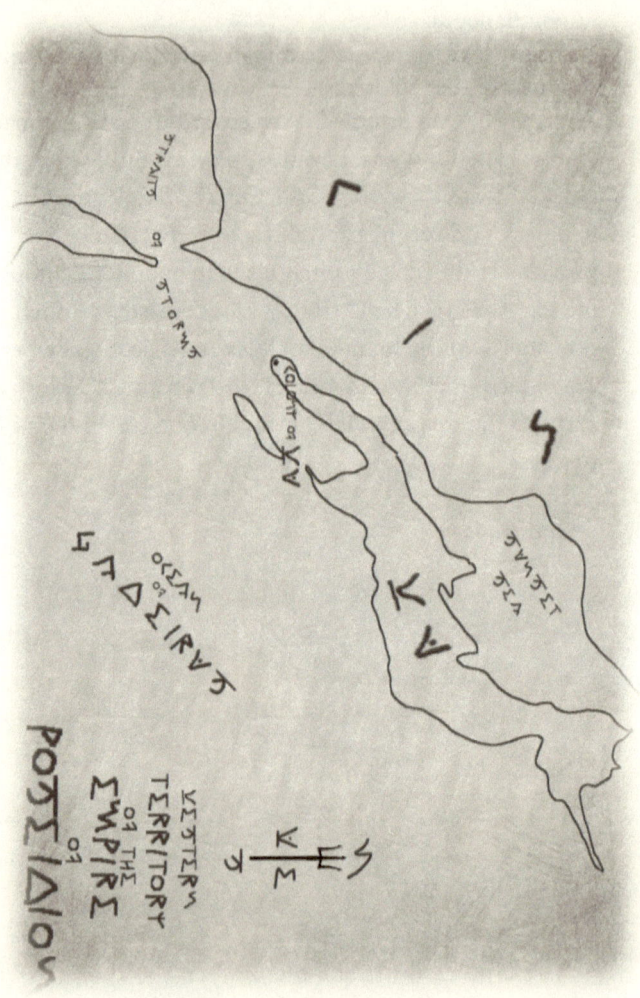

33. Wu.

"Mortals are happiest when in bondage, where they become like stupid, fattened sheep. The shepherd is most at ease when the sheep are in the pen. Let men roam free for too long, and they become as wolves." —The Seventh Lesson of the God Poseidon to his children, from the Ancient of Ancients.

- The Chronicle of Fu Xi.

***

Six months had passed between their arrival at Wu and Fu Xi's entrance into Amiran's life. The long journey across the enormous Ocean Gadeirus had been grueling, but without significant mishap. Amiran spent those long months tutoring the children in language and writing. Thankfully, Leviathan and Quexil usually left them alone. Upon their arrival at Wu, Amiran focused most of his time preparing the children to fulfill their roles as Royal Butchers.

The library in Wu, every bit as grand as Amiran had heard, served as his classroom. He relieved the previous colony scholar, who joyously caught the first available ship back to Gadriuopolis. Amiran immediately put the children on a rigid routine. Every morning Elda and Ercole studied from the volumes lining the library's shelves. Following this, Amiran tutored them in language, arts, and mathematics.

After the noon meal, they trained in butchery before reporting to the gym for physical conditioning.

Elda relished the mornings and feared the afternoon; and Ercole the opposite. It astonished Amiran how similar and different the fraternal twins were. Ercole only loathed academics, but Elda truly feared being a Royal Butcher. She desperately wanted to please her teacher, but the reality of what her title entailed terrified her.

Amiran spent the first day familiarizing the children with the dangers they'd face as Royal Butchers. He laid out exactly how a dragon was tracked, ambushed, slain, and butchered. The lesson continued as late winter sunlight traced its way across the stone floor. Elda turned white and began to tremble. Ercole merely looked perplexed.

"I don't want to burn to death," she cried softly. "Please, Teacher. I can't do this."

"Practice breeds confidence. This is the heart of training. If you can do it here, you can do it for real," he said.

"We can, sister," Ercole tried to reassure her. "If we do it right, we won't burn. You did it, didn't you, Teacher?"

"I did." Amiran smiled warmly. "My teacher trained me on this mock-up exactly how I will train you, and he had never even seen a dragon! I have. I can tell you what to expect, and how to stay alive, and when it is all over you two will be legends. Poseidon himself will sing your praises."

Amiran stepped around the mock-up to where Leviathan's Expedition Chest rested. "I promised you the time would come when we opened this chest."

He entered the secret sequence on the twelve keys, and the lid popped open just as it had on Gadeirus's chest all those months ago. Inside, the children saw three satchels, a large ceramic urn, two scroll cases, and a rolled-up velvet blanket.

Amiran knelt down and, grunting, removed the heavy urn and set it down on the floor with a dull thud. It had a wide mouth, two iron rings on the sides, and an even wider base.

"I could almost fit in that!" Ercole remarked.

Amiran pointed to the satchel and then the urn. "The harvest goes in a satchel, which in turn is placed in the urn."

"What's in the urn?" Ercole asked.

"Nothing right now. It will be filled with fresh water. Notice the wide base so it won't tip over."

Amiran picked up a satchel, and then unrolled and untied it. "This is large enough for a bile sac or two tarsal glands. Feel how soft it is." He held out the large bag, which was covered in thick, padded leather, and opened it, showing them two large cavities. The children touched the fleece-lined interior.

"If it becomes apparent there is a dragon close by, I will smear animal fat mixed with oil on the inside as lubricant. I'll do the same to the urn's mouth."

"Will that make it safe?" Elda asked in between chewing her fingernails.

"The satchel offers some protection from shock and puncture, but isn't guaranteed to be airtight. It is only the first layer of protection. The sacs and glands must be kept away from air. Once they are in the satchel, it must be submerged in the urn to be truly safe." He picked up a large cork stopper with leather straps on either side. "This plug seals the urn, and straps down to the handles to prevent leakage."

Amiran then unrolled the blanket, revealing two red knives, and a dozen tin clips. He picked up a straight blade about six inches long with a wickedly serrated edge on one side, and a thin obsidian strip on the other. "You won't have time to hack through the dragon's scales with steel — it's not sharp enough. Only orichalcum can do that. This blade is used to slice through the thick neck muscles. Remember, a dragon doesn't have bones. It has cartilage like a shark; it's softer than bone but more flexible." He put it down and picked up the hook-like blade. "This is what you'll use to sever the bile duct, as well as the tarsal scent glands."

"What about these funny clips?" Ercole picked one up and clipped it to the end of his finger.

"In the coming days I'll show you exactly how to use them. They will keep you safe while you are harvesting," Amiran said.

"What about that scroll case, the one made from glass?" Elda asked, pointing to what looked like a large vial.

"Those aren't scrolls. They are a very special kind of parchment used to find a dragon. I can't open them until I'm ready to use them."

"How?" Ercole asked.

"Dragons are like other animals that use scent to find a mate. When a bull dragon wants to breed, he emits a powerful musk from the glands on his hind legs. The scent can travel for thousands of miles and is permeated with fire-bile. When even the smallest trace of fire-bile touches this parchment, it turns the paper from green to red. I will cover more of this in future lessons."

Amiran stood and turned his attention to the full wooden and leather mock-ups. "This is a full-sized model of a bull dragon's neck. The other is a bull's hind leg. Both were brought in pieces from Atlantis. Using these, I will show you where to cut, how to pry the neck muscles apart, and where the bile sacs and musk glands are located. We will spend hours memorizing a dragon's anatomy. Ultimately, you will be able to efficiently locate the precious bile glands, even when blindfolded."

"Teacher?" Elda asked, still looking worried. "You said only twins are selected to be Butchers, and only children, right?"

"Yes."

"Why?"

"Twins, especially identical twins, have a special bond. They often know each other's thoughts, and can work quickly together. As one learns, so does the other. They compensate for each other's weaknesses. As for why they must be children, smaller hands can squeeze into places an adult's cannot, as you shall soon see."

Ercole frowned. "Where is your twin?" he blurted.

Elda gasped. "Did your twin die harvesting a dragon?"

Amiran had been expecting that question. "No," he lied. "My brother perished on the long voyage to the northlands. I harvested the dragon alone."

"I am sorry," Elda said.

Amiran smiled. "That is very kind, but it was a long time ago."

***

The days passed, and the children learned the grueling art of dragon harvesting. Ercole naturally took to the training. After much patience, Amiran finally coaxed Elda into successfully completing the drills. As she repeated the process, her performance and confidence grew.

While Amiran taught the children, Prince Leviathan's fleet explored Cin's coast, which lay across the narrow Sunset Sea from the Wu island chain.

One morning, word came from the harbor that Leviathan had returned from his latest foray. Breathless messengers returned from the port, reporting the prince had found something extraordinary. The wharf village flocked to see for themselves.

A stranger on a strange shore.
Many Olmecs had been slain!
One who battled the Prince to a stalemate!
Another god, one not of Poseidon's ilk!

That fateful morning, Amiran stood upon the balcony overlooking the palace's grand entrance, watching the procession make its way up from Wu's harbor village. He finally glimpsed the one he would come to know as Fu Xi strolling beside Leviathan not as a conquered subject, but as an equal.

"Gremis, the Ancient of Ancients is true!" Amiran whispered to the wind.

34. Amid the Ruins.

"Mortals' fear and hatred pass from generation to generation as effortlessly as water over the falls. Make them fear you and hate one another, and ye shall rule forever."- The Eighth Lesson of the God Poseidon to his children.

- The Chronicle of Fu Xi.

***

Amiran felt blood's tell-tale trickle down his distended ankles. Even though the stretched skin had grown numb, he sensed the flesh slowly beginning to split open with each itch and pop. Forbidden to look down, Amiran could only endure the agony his body had been transmitting for what felt like years. His burning hands throbbed mercilessly. If Elda had not treated them before Leviathan's return, Amiran felt certain he would have already died from infection.

Two long days had passed since Fu Xi had destroyed the Colony of Wu. For two long days, Amiran stood in one spot in what had been the palace's Gray Tower, the colonial library of Wu.

Now Leviathan sought answers.

Amiran's mind commanded him to remain standing and stare straight ahead. To disobey Leviathan invited death. What did it matter if Leviathan killed him now? He'd be dead soon, anyway. Amiran's body could not withstand much more torture. He vaguely sensed water running down his face and neck, soaking his tunic. His swollen throat begged him to lift his face to the heavens and let the rain fall into his mouth.

The rain quickly found its way to the glowing timbers, and a sizzling sound filled the chamber like the buzzing of summer cicadas. Many parts of the palace still smoldered. Acrid smoke still drifted through the ruins, further searing his throat before rising up through the roof's gaping hole. The tower had tumbled, its supports burned away in the fire. Charred ceiling beams crisscrossed overhead like the ribs in a disemboweled beast.

It wasn't his body's torture that truly wounded Amiran, but his spirit's torment. The burnt paper stench from thousands of incinerated scrolls assailed him. Amiran tried to tell himself this was a necessary sacrifice. Leviathan's invasion fleet now rested at the harbor bottom. The wharves, along with all their massive storehouses filled with invasion supplies, still burned. The quarry lay in shambles. One demigod had singlehandedly destroyed the city, but that conflagration had spread to the palace, and the beloved library.

Maps. Star charts. Poetry. Dissertations. Tide tables. Quartermaster inventories. Countless reports from Expedition Scholars. Scorched rolls lay at the scholar's feet like the battlefield dead. Ink leached from the paper and flowed in rivulets like blood. Amiran could not save them.

Three solaces comforted Amiran in his agony. First, Fu Xi had escaped. At this very moment the demigod had likely reached Cin's coast. With his two speedy horses, Fu Xi likely sped toward his mother's fortress deep in Cin, carrying a warning of Leviathan's coming. Second, only a few of these scrolls were originals. Copies existed in the libraries at Gadriuopolis and Atlantis itself. Finally, Amiran took comfort that Quexil endured equal agony beside him. As long as the Olmec stood, Amiran willed that he would die before he'd let the savage see him fall.

The downpour intensified, blinding Amiran. Thunder rolled and lightning flashed, illuminating blackened scroll shelves and collapsed tables. Amiran swam in and out of consciousness. One moment Leviathan stood before him, the next moment he did not. How long had Leviathan been gone? Did he even leave? Maybe the demigod stood behind him now, waiting for the scholar to buckle just to cut him down.

Quexil cried out something unintelligible, and then murmured feverishly the way a dog whines in its sleep.

Amiran took a chance and cracked open his mouth and tilted back slightly in a desperate bid to channel water down his throat.

A strange sound crawled through the library, burning through the rain and thunder's din like acid through wood. The rain turned icy as the hiss grew louder. Amiran closed his eyes and began to shiver uncontrollably. He suddenly found himself transported to a memory long ago along Erub's icy north coast. Here the frigid ocean and jagged black mountains clashed in a place the natives called the Norge.

***

It was Amiran's first expedition, but he wasn't a scholar, only a boy of ten years wearing the white loincloth. Prince Gadeirus and his Expedition Scholar, a young man named Gremis, had tracked a bull dragon to its lair. Footsteps stretched two miles leading to their ship anchored off the ice floe. Ahead, sharp cliffs thrust to a featureless gray sky that shed snowflakes like an afterthought. Amiran shook uncontrollably, even though both he and his brother wore white wool in layers and polar bear furs.

"Soon." Gremis patted his shoulder. "He's close. Up there, in the cliffs. Can you hear him?"

Amiran could. The hissing sound floated across the unbroken snow.

Arius shivered beside him. "A bull?"

Amiran squeezed his brother's hand.

"He knows we are here," Gremis said, his excitement palpable. "I wager he's young, unsure, and warning us to leave his territory. Now

that we know the bull is here, we will backtrack to the ship, sail up the coast, and set our trap."

"How do you know he…he…is young?" Arius asked, voice quaking.

"If he were more experienced, he wouldn't have given away his presence, and we'd be dead already."

In the distant mountains, the hiss blossomed into a terrible, screeching roar.

***

Amiran startled back to full consciousness and caught himself before falling over. Thunder retreated into the distance. Lightning flashed, illuminating a pale man leaning against a shelf. Suddenly fully aware of his surroundings and uneasy, Amiran blinked the water from his eyes.

Quexil shrieked again.

Lightning strobed, and the vision vanished. The hissing sound remained, but now Amiran recognized it as water slowly dripping on smoldering timbers. He closed his eyes again, and opened them to see Leviathan before them, red sword resting between his legs.

"I ask again, slave, what did you say to Fu Xi?" Leviathan.

"I said what you commanded me to say, my lord," Amiran gasped.

"He lies, Great Lord!" Quexil shouted.

"Silence," Leviathan commanded.

He returned his attention to Amiran. "Tell me again, what did you tell the betrayer the night he destroyed all that is mine?"

"As I have told you before, Great Lord. He inquired repeatedly about the sounds coming from the quarry. I tried to divert his attention. He would not listen."

"How did he cross the Sunset Sea? Where did he get a boat?"

"I don't know, Great Lord," Amiran gasped, trying to think clearly. "He departed the library into the storm, agitated…clad in the Traitor's Armor. I never saw him again.

He had set his mind to action. He is a god, and I am only a mortal."

"Do not patronize me." Leviathan slowly paced around the two men like a cat. "You are the master of my father's Academy, his prize. I know your powers, and I do not underestimate them. So tell me again, how did Fu Xi reach the western coast so quickly? Even a god cannot fly. How did a boat happen to be there, waiting on him? Why wasn't it in the harbor with the rest of the fleet?"

In his mind, Amiran chanted the Song of Atlas to calm his racing heart. *Gods never forget. Gods are patient.* Keep your answers simple, feign ignorance, and use silence and a shrug as a cloak.

"I do not know, Great Lord."

"I beg you to listen, Mighty Paqua!" Quexil spoke again, calling him the name only the Olmecs used for their demigod. "I saw Fu Xi emerge from the library where this slave filled his ears with lies and witchcraft. I tried to stop Fu Xi there, and I tried to stop him again at the harbor."

Leviathan turned his attention to his Olmec captain. Amiran strained to see them out of the corner of his eye.

"If this scholar has betrayed me, it is a crime of deceit. Your crime is one of incompetence. I return to see my palace and find my fleet burned, and only a handful of your warriors are dead? You faced Fu Xi with my army, and yet let him pass. Now you stand before me, quivering with weakness. I should have you skinned alive and fed to your own men."

Quexil fell to his knees at Leviathan's feet. "Let me redeem myself! Let me begin with shedding this slave's blood."

Leviathan placed the sword tip on Quexil's ribcage and slowly traced a thin red line from one side of Quexil's chest to the other. "The mark of failure will mar your tattoos forever. Rise and return to your men. By dawn, if you still live, you will be redeemed. Fail me again, and this cut will be far deeper."

Quexil groveled low before Leviathan, showing no signs of pain. "Thank you, oh Great Paqua!" With that, Quexil backed away, bowing the entire way.

Leviathan had just announced to the Obsidian Guard he sought a new commander. Amiran knew before dawn Quexil's men would kill and skin him. When Quexil returned to the garrison, his senior leaders would see the mark, and immediately challenge him. One by one, any who wanted to lead the army would fight Quexil to the death. If Quexil defeated one, then another would step forward for their chance. All comers were invited to challenge not only Quexil, but whoever finally defeated him. There would be no rest, no water, no mercy for the Obsidian Guard until sunrise. Whoever finally emerged victorious would eat Quexil's flesh and wear his skin, and thereby gain their former commander's power, as well as the power of all who challenged him.

At dawn, the victor would face the rising sun and declare his loyalty to the Great Paqua.

Leviathan stepped behind Amiran as the rain began to diminish. "I cannot see what is in your mind, but your deceitful workings are clear." Something struck Amiran's knees, and he crumpled into a heavy wooden chair, the very chair he had used in the library since their arrival. Amiran gasped as his knees screamed at the act of finally bending. "Sit, and collect your thoughts. I have other questions before I pass judgement.

"Let us talk in the way that pleases your kind, Scholar. Let us talk of facts. Mortals love facts. You think stating the obvious somehow makes you clever." He brushed away some charred scrolls from a table and sat on its edge. Leviathan poked his sword tip into the floor and began to break away stone chips as he talked. Disdain dripped from his lips. "Here are some facts, at least as I see them. The invasion is obviously on hold. There isn't enough good timber in all of Wu to rebuild the fleet. I have only three ships, not enough to launch an invasion. I have nothing to feed my army, except perhaps the people of Wu itself, but then I'll have no workers to rebuild the colony. Scholar, what do you advise?"

Amiran tried to clear his mind. "Send courier ships to Gadriuopolis for reinforcements. It will take two years to reconstitute the fleet. In that time, concentrate our labor on harvesting food and rebuilding the city. Use the remaining vessels to probe Cin's coastline and gather captives and intelligence."

Leviathan's sword tip popped free a large stone chip, which struck Amiran's swollen ankle. Blood and water spurted out. "That's a prudent course of action, but it gives Fu Xi at least two years to prepare, and perhaps even attack Wu."

Amiran chose his words cautiously. He had to blend truth and deceit in the right proportions. "True, but Cin doesn't have steel. They have no experienced armies. Whatever Fu Xi can cobble together will be no match for an Atlantean army. Fu Xi will likely leverage other strengths."

"What strengths?"

"Our Empire's forays beyond the coasts are exceptionally rare. We have no experience mounting a continental campaign, at least one without major rivers. We don't even know what Cin's rivers are, let alone if they are navigable. He needs only to retreat before our armies, stretch our supply lines, and isolate us in a strange land. Then our superiority can be neutralized. We need time to establish strong footholds along the coast, explore and map, and turn the local tribes to our side. This might take years, even decades."

"I don't have years," Leviathan said as if to himself.

The response shocked Amiran, and he struggled to contain his surprise. *There is something else at play here*, he thought. *Something critical I am missing.*

"You have spoken at length about a theory your ancient predecessor, Vulcan, held about the size and shape of the world. How certain are you that this is true, and the world is truly round?"

Amiran kept his guard up. "I am absolutely certain. Star measurements I took at different latitudes as we crossed the Demarcations of Rains into the Demarcation of Stars mathematically support Master Vulcan's ancient hypothesis. The world is round, Great Lord, and it circles the sun."

"Would you wager your life on it, and the lives of the two Royal Butchers in your care?" Leviathan let the full weight of his stare rest on Amiran. "How long would a journey from Wu to Giza take?"

Amiran took a long breath, trying to collect his thoughts. He already knew the answer, but chose each word carefully. "When Gadeirus founded this colony decades ago, he made several mapping expeditions along Cin's coastline. He sailed as far north as the Icelands. One expedition ventured south as far as the Demarcation of Winds, where the coast turned westward. That hints at the possibility of a southern passage. If the Sunset Sea continues west, and isn't blocked by an unknown land mass, an unimpeded journey to Alkebulan's eastern coast is possible. If the Reed Sea is actually is part of that greater body of water..." Amiran paused for a moment, trying to read the god's expression. "You could potentially connect the Empire both east and west, and Poseidon's power will truly encircle the world. Your Obsidian Fleet will command three-quarters of the world."

Leviathan looked down at his sword tip. Over the course of a few minutes, he had displaced enough gouges to create a continuous scar in the floor. He pointed to one pit. "Wu is here." He etched an "X" above that pit. "Icelands block the north." He pointed to the other side. "Giza is here." He dragged the tip across the stone beneath the pit, sparks popping. "A possible water passage lies to the south. Is this in accordance with Vulcan's theory?"

Amiran nodded. It was close enough.

"My remaining fleet will probe the continent's underbelly. If this is true, the Empire will invade Cin from

Wu in the east and Attica in the west. I will crush Cin and Fu Xi in between."

"My Lord, we don't know if Cin has an underbelly. It's only a theory."

"Then let us prove or disprove it. The Expedition Chests survived the fire, as well as the Dragon Chains and my…" he paused. "And *Poseidon's* Butchers. In one month, we sail in search of the Southern Passage. If in the process I can find a way to penetrate Fu Xi's lands, I will take it."

Amiran nodded and slightly bowed in the chair. "So it will be, Great Lord."

Leviathan stood and stared at the pitted floor, rain running down his face. "Your services and counsel are valued, Scholar. I'm sure you will understand why I must do what comes next." He looked past Amiran. "Bring it in," he spoke to someone unseen.

Amiran heard a scuffle, and several slaves dragged what Amiran thought might be rafters from the palace. Then his blood froze as he recognized it as a crucifix. Made from two charred heavy rafters crudely bound together with iron spikes and ropes, they dropped it at Amiran's feet. The slaves bowed to the god, and backed away. They were replaced by two Olmec warriors. They impassively flanked the god.

Amiran considered the crucifix with fatalistic calmness that surprised even himself. All the chests were saved from the fire. The children were safe. Fu Xi had escaped. The Gray-Eyed Queen still fought in the west, and Quexil would not see the dawn. Whatever Leviathan's plans, or his interest in Vulcan's theory, Amiran could go to his death knowing he had furthered human freedom. To some degree, he had bested a god.

He can kill me, but he hasn't defeated me.

Amiran looked the god in the eye. "Only I know the combination to the Expedition Chests. If you kill me, you'll never slay another dragon, even if you find one."

"We both know I cannot touch you as long as you wear my father's brand. The game you are playing, whatever it may be, is a dangerous one. I still need your services, and you still need me if you are to see a dragon again, and prove your pet theory."

There it was, the truth out in the open.

"You remain in my good graces, Master Amiran. You also remain my Expedition Scholar…for now."

Leviathan signaled again, and a moment later the two Olmecs dragged a naked and bleeding man before Amiran and cast him down beside the cross.

"Sunnah!" Amiran gasped.

On all fours, his long, tangled hair covered his face. The poor soul trembled like an animal.

"Before I let you return to the children, I wanted you to witness this execution. It seems two horses are missing and my stablemaster cannot account for them. He said they broke loose and ran off during the fire."

Sunnah looked up through swollen, black eyes. Amiran struggled to maintain control.

"It's strange no other horses broke loose that night, or that these were the very animals Fu Xi learned to ride on. Do you know what happened to the horses, Amiran? I think it was one of my black stallions, and a gray mare. If you know where they went, just tell me and I'll let the stablemaster return to his duties." Leviathan waited for a moment and signaled the Olmecs. They seized Sunnah and pinned him to the cross. From somewhere a hammer and spikes appeared. Then the pounding and screaming began.

They tied the crucifix to a charred upright beam, where, for the rest of evening, Amiran watched the gentle stablemaster slowly die. The god remained silent behind Amiran's chair like a sentinel. Shortly before dawn, Sunnah released his last breath, and Leviathan finally spoke.

"In the gardens, you will find a tent where the children are sleeping. Your belongings are there. By mid-day you will begin preparations for the expedition."

The scholar could barely walk. His ankles had stiffened horribly as he watched Sunnah die. He gripped the walls for support as he hobbled from the ruin and onto the palace grounds. The sun climbed over the ocean beyond the harbor. Even with last night's rain, smoke still rose from the wharves and painted the dawn crimson.

Alone and utterly exhausted, guilt and self-loathing crashed down over him. Sunnah had not divulged anything. If he had, Amiran would be dead now, too. Sunnah willingly made the sacrifice, he told himself. He had to believe that to find the strength to go on.

He saw tents at the garden's edge. Did the children know he was still alive?

A lone figure emerged from the rising sun. Amiran squinted at the imposing silhouette striding up the hill, gripping a club in each hand. A cape hung from his shoulders.

Horror overwhelmed Amiran as the figure materialized into an Olmec warrior drenched in blood. Quexil passed by as if in a trance. Numerous human pelts hung from his shoulders, tied by their arm skins.

35. Children of the Sea.

"Compact freemen from across the Empire, sailors wore their hair pulled into top-knots, exposing tattooed faces. Sailors commemorated each voyage with a unique tattoo. Their first tattoo, known as the temple voyage tattoo, was usually a simple drawing of their maiden ship on their forehead. Subsequent voyages' symbols varied widely and radiated downward across their face, neck, and trunk. The crustier sailors' nautical resumes disappeared under the black sash circling their waist. Some even had tattoos approaching their ankles. The black ink, which stood out even on the darkest Alkebulan, made their leathery skin even darker, and stood in marked contrast to their white trousers."- The Last Scholar

- The Chronicle of Fu Xi.

***

The theory of a great southern passage around Cin survived the expedition's first month at sea. Amiran busied himself surveying and mapping as new worlds revealed themselves with every dawn. The fleet picked its way southwest through tropical waters dotted with lush archipelagos and smoking volcanic islands. This morning they paralleled low, palm-covered shores several miles to their north. The ships stayed far enough from shore to avoid expected reefs. The seas barely rippled under a light easterly wind. So far, they'd encountered nothing worse than light monsoonal showers, which started every afternoon and died away shortly before sunset.

Amiran made sure his daily observations were completed at the exact time every morning prior to the daily rains. Elda always assisted him. The crew went about their duties, occasionally giving the scholar and his young assistants disdainful looks.

Amiran looked up at the sails, trying to get a better estimate on the wind. Elda looked up and squinted, mimicking her teacher.

Elda took intense interest in everything Amiran did. He could not have asked for a better student. He often found young men eager to prove themselves to their teacher, but Elda wanted to please her teacher. This made her an excellent listener. She was a voracious reader, flying through the scrolls he had brought on the voyage. After the evening meal, she would seek him out to discuss what she had learned that day. Amiran looked forward to their talks every bit as much as she did. Elda's intensity and attention to detail had, for the first time in his life, allowed Amiran to trust someone else with his personal navigation kit.

Each morning, she brought the kit to the deck, and, if the seas were favorable, carefully arranged all the components on a small folding table in the exacting manner Amiran had specified. He often watched her from the hatch's shadows. He noticed whenever concentration overwhelmed Elda, she bit her lip. He'd never seen Ercole exhibit the same trait.

When Elda had finished, she would patiently stand to the side as the Grand Master inspected the scientific equipment, with his journal scroll and inkwell set to the side. The scroll would be unrolled to the next available entry, and the quill charged. It only took a few days for Elda to master the procedure. When Amiran had finished taking his daily observations, Elda would dutifully dismantle, clean, and pack the equipment, even going so far as servicing the Time Sextant.

Today, as always, everything was in perfect order. Amiran began the session with a journal entry. It began with the date and exact time, and the same oath, *"In the service of Glorious God Poseidon, I, Amiran the Scholar, record my observations to the best of my knowledge and as accurately as possible."*

"You are enjoying this, aren't you, Teacher?" Elda remarked as she assisted Amiran with his morning measurements on the ship's forecastle.

He looked up from the scroll. "Why wouldn't I be enjoying this?" He pointed at the metal jar filled with quicksilver. "What's the reading?"

Wearing light leather gloves, she looked closely at the temperature and density columns. "Twenty-two thermal units, *anddd*…" Elda peered closer at the marks etched into the glass, "74.3 density units."

"Wind?"

"I took that reading first," Elda said as she looked over Amiran's shoulder. "285 degrees at four nautical miles per hour."

Amiran looked up at the stocking hanging from the mast top and grunted. "If the westerly current holds, Captain Ploarchos should only need enough sail to steer."

"Why are these measurements so important?" Ercole, bored with helping the lookouts, approached them.

"They are important because Teacher says they are!" Elda snapped.

"Because they hold the answers to riddles we don't yet know to ask," Amiran said patiently. "But they also hold answers to questions we *do* know to ask, like 'Where are the dragons?'"

Ercole's boredom transformed to excitement.

"Ercole, stay here. Elda, please clean and put away the equipment. I'm going below deck for a few minutes."

Soon, Amiran returned with the glass scroll case under his arm. Elda had everything orderly secured in his navigation kit. Amiran quickly inspected it, and then closed the lid.

Then, he sat on a crate and looked at the children. "The air above behaves much like water. In fact, we sit at the bottom of an ocean of air." He looked up. "It has currents like the sea — we call them winds. Birds 'swim' in this ocean instead of fish. The wind behaves differently depending on how warm or cold it is. Like tides, the ocean of air's behavior can be predicted, though not as reliably. Predicting its behavior is why I measure it every morning."

"I don't understand," Ercole said, intently eyeing the glass scroll case.

"Let's say this morning your sister gave me a much lower reading than 74.3 density units. That would tell me the air above us was thinning, perhaps because it had begun to churn and warm. I would therefore expect it to be accompanied by warmer readings from the thermal column, and maybe a stiff southwest wind. What do you think that would mean?"

The children looked at one another and shrugged. Then a deep voice, like gravel being ground under a boot, spoke from behind them. "It would mean a coming storm."

Amiran nodded deferentially to the ship's master. Captain Ploarchos nodded once, and then strolled toward the aft deck without another word.

Prince Leviathan may have been an immortal son of Poseidon, but at sea only the ship's captain is a god. In the Empire of Poseidon, warriors may be feared, but sailors were admired. No sailors were more admired than the Masters of the Whip, captains of the Empire's mighty fleet. Captain Ploarchos, the *Draco's* legendary master, was the most admired of all. Amiran watched him join Leviathan and Quexil on the aft deck.

Only slightly shorter than Leviathan, the captain stood boldly beside the immortal. Some said Ploarchos was himself a demigod. His stature only lent credence to this myth, and added to his mystique. A bearish man, wide and swarthy, the sea and sun had burned Ploarchos's olive complexion almost as dark as an Olmec. While he wore the traditional black cotton trousers and leather vest of an Atlantean ship's captain, he shunned the black turban fashionable among other Masters of the Whip. His frizzy hair and beard framed his square face like a mane forged from steel wool. The captain's right hand casually rested on a common Attican short sword hilt. His left hand gripped the latigo coiled on his hip.

Only Atlas himself could bestow the latigo upon an Imperial Captain. The ceremonial whip symbolized the captain's authority. After sailing halfway around the world on the *Draco*, Amiran never saw Ploarchos use it. His will and voice were the only whips he needed.

"The captain is exactly right," Amiran resumed his lesson. "And if that were the case, I would advise Captain Ploarchos to sail with haste for the nearest sheltered cove, or even the open sea — anywhere except around all these shallow reefs."

Ercole nodded thoughtfully. Amiran knew the boy appreciated this new knowledge's practical utility. Amiran stood. "Thankfully, today the air above is stable, and the winds steady and predictable, as is the current below our feet. The stars and sun tell us we are sailing the tropics, and nearing the belly of the world."

"You're talking about Master Vulcan's theory again, aren't you, Teacher?" Elda said.

"Yes. The Globe Theory, as it's formally called. So far, the measurements you've helped me take have reinforced that theory."

"How will you know for sure it's true?" Elda asked.

"When this fleet sails into the Reed Sea from the east. Only then will we have definitive proof one can sail west to reach the east." Amiran considered the scroll case. "Are you wondering why I'm holding this?"

"Yes!" Ercole almost shouted.

Amiran smiled. "The air is stable. The winds come from the west, exactly where we are heading. Sometimes, winds like these carry messages"—he lightly tapped the case on Ercole's head—"for those who know how to listen."

Amiran stood and unscrewed the airtight lid. With his finger, he quickly removed one pre-cut square, about two palms wide, and resealed the case. With several brass tacks he removed from a pocket, he attached it flat to the ship's railing. "From this point forward, whenever we encounter stable weather like this for more than three days, we shall place an emerald paper on the rail."

"What do we do if it turns red?" Ercole asked.

Amiran glanced back at the aft deck, where Leviathan considered them.

"We hunt dragons."

Ercole's excitement amused Amiran. He remembered being that age, and adventure's seductive allure.

"Canoes off the starboard bow!" the lookout shouted.

Amiran and the children rushed to the starboard bow. Four outrigger canoes had just cleared the reef's breakwater. Each held ten bare-chested men, rowing hard toward the ships.

***

The fat *Orion* and *Leo* anchored next to one another, while the slender *Draco* anchored closer to the reef. Wreaths woven from exotic red and white flowers floated in the sparkling water around the hulls.

Six longboats, all packed with Obsidian Warriors, rowed through a gap in the reef into a sparkling lagoon. The natives in the canoes surrounding them sang a joyous-sounding tune. They sang too fast for Amiran to fully understand, but their language contained familiar elements.

Quexil's warriors sat stone-faced.

Amiran grinned with delight as he let the warm water wash over his arm. The scholar had seen many beautiful beaches in his journeys, but none as perfect as this one. The shimmering white sand, only a few feet below the emerald surface, made the water look like tinted glass. Amiran could not help but return their infectious smiles, but he knew these people would never be the same after this day. Scholars had protocols for these moments. Leviathan and the Olmecs were unstable variables he had never had to deal with on an expedition. If possible, he had to steer this first contact to a peaceful resolution. If the natives remained friendly, the Olmecs might be mollified.

Amiran patted his navigation kit and eagerly anticipated the opportunity to record their language, oral history, and customs. He couldn't prevent these people's fate, but could document their existence before the Empire gobbled them up. He might also steer Leviathan's thoughts away from staying too long and spare these beautiful people the slaver's brand.

"Your Highness," Amiran addressed Leviathan as the shore neared. "The village's presence indicates fresh water must be nearby. The island appears to be formed from coral limestone, and is likely poor in minerals. The reef's gap is too narrow for an effective anchorage. I'd wager the soil is poor, too. These people likely survive solely from fishing. I doubt this place is worth our time."

Leviathan ignored him. Quexil's gaze locked on the natives like a wolf.

The hull scraped the sandy bottom, and the oarsmen steadied the boat. No one disembarked, waiting for Leviathan to take the first step onto this new shore. As Expedition Scholar, it was Amiran's duty to record the first words the god spoke in the new land. He had the stylus and scroll at the ready.

Leviathan placed his hand on Quexil's shoulder and planted a sandal in the sand. He strode halfway to the palm trees as Quexil and Amiran followed a few paces behind. Leviathan surveyed the village. Even in his gleaming armor, he seemed a dark presence in this bright world.

Amiran had been in this situation before with both King Atlas and Prince Gadeirus in Erub's far north. The immortals always wore the same haughty expression when stepping forth in a new land. All they see is theirs.

Weapons and armor rattled as the Obsidian Guard disembarked the longboats. They efficiently formed a steel wall behind Leviathan, from the palm trees to the surf. Amiran stood slightly behind the demigod's left, Quexil to the right.

The villagers beached their outriggers a few yards away and, still singing, approached the shore party. There were perhaps twenty men, all unarmed, and triple the number of women, children, and elderly.

They are all children, Amiran thought. The heavily armed war party only yards away didn't seem to alarm them in the slightest. They pointed and laughed, seemingly oblivious to the weapons' true nature. *I don't think they know what weapons are*, he thought. There were nets drying on the beach, but he didn't see so much as a fishing spear.

Innocence stood unafraid in death's presence. The Atlanteans, grim entities from the world's far side, faced the children of paradise. Naked, with lightly tanned skin and slanted eyes typical of those in this corner of the world, their men stood a head shorter than the Obsidian Guard. Only the women's small breasts and hairless genitalia distinguished them from the men. Amiran had difficulty determining relative ages, as even the elderly exuded youthful joy. A knot formed in Amiran's stomach. He wanted these people to flee.

Amiran wiped the sweat from his brow as the sun climbed higher. His armor felt absurd. He wanted to strip it off and splash naked through the surf with these beautiful savages.

A healthy-looking man with broad cheekbones and a hint of gray in his long black hair stepped forward and fell to his knees before Leviathan. *That's a good start*, Amiran thought. *Be submissive, and maybe your people will get out of this alive.*

Giggling women rushed past the kneeling man Amiran assumed was their chieftain. They carried wooden bowls filled with colorful, unfamiliar fruit, and laid them at

Leviathan's feet. Still laughing, they slipped back behind the men.

One girl stopped behind the chieftain. As far as Amiran knew, she could have been anywhere from thirteen to thirty-one. She had no stretch marks on her abdomen, but neither did the women holding babies. She caught Amiran staring at her and smiled. Even he could not mistake the invitation in her eyes. A jolt of excitement rushed through him. He averted his stare and quickly recited the Codes of Celibacy under his breath. Amiran took a deep breath and opened his eyes to find Leviathan staring down at him with a cold, mocking smile.

A warrior handed Quexil a lance bearing Leviathan's standard, which he plunged into the sand. "His Royal Highness Prince Leviathan hereby claims this land and all its inhabitants in the name of the Great God Poseidon and the majestic realm of Atlantis!"

The kneeling leader held his arms wide to Leviathan and spoke in a high tone with sharp, popping consonants. Then he bowed until his forehead touched the sand. Not surprisingly, Amiran understood much of it. These people spoke a dialect distantly related to Fu Xi's.

He's afraid, Amiran thought, *even if his people are not. He doesn't know who we are or what we want, but he senses we are powerful and he's protecting his people the only way possible.*

Amiran knew the ultimate fate awaiting these children of the sea. Eventually, they would all wear Leviathan's brand. Some would be taken aboard the ships. If Leviathan followed protocol, a small contingent would remain here to rule until a colonization fleet could be sent, which might take years. In that time, the Olmecs would break them. Their lands would be taken, and their people enslaved and scattered across the Empire.

Amiran's heart ached.

"It's a dialect akin to Cin," Amiran told Leviathan. "He welcomes you and acknowledges your divinity."

Leviathan considered the man groveling at his feet. *"Fu Xi?"*

"Fuxi?" the man looked up and smiled warmly in response.

Shut up! Amiran thought.

"Yes, *Fuxi*." Leviathan's eyes narrowed.

The chief nodded enthusiastically as the words spilled out so quickly Amiran had difficulty understanding.

"Scholar, I take it Fu Xi and Nuwa are known to these people."

"Yes, my lord," Amiran responded, trying to hide the fear growing inside. "He says Fu Xi is their great teacher and he praises the God of Names and the Goddess of the West."

"Tell him we, too, have come to honor Fu Xi."

Amiran swallowed hard, and translated Leviathan's statement. The chief nodded and smiled warmly.

Leviathan pointed to the young woman standing behind the chief. He turned his hand over and curled his finger.

The girl touched her chest as if asking, *"Me?"*

Amiran remained calm and did his best to translate. "Come forward."

The chief, still kneeling, scowled impatiently at the girl, hissed twice between his teeth, and jerked his thumb forward toward Leviathan. He turned back toward Leviathan, nodded, and laughed nervously.

The nymph timidly stepped forward, eye-level with Leviathan's abdomen.

Leviathan gently lifted her chin. "Beautiful," he said.

Amiran translated, "He says you are beautiful."

Leviathan pointed to several large, reddish-yellow oblong orbs in the fruit bowls. He brought his fingers to his lips as if to eat. She offered one to Leviathan. He wrapped his huge hands around her delicate wrists, bent down and, with teeth bared like a predator, took a large bite. Juice squirted over her fingers and down her wrists. Unsure, she glanced back over her shoulder at the chief. He nodded at her as if to say, "Please him."

Leviathan tightened his grip around her wrists and began to slowly lick the juice from her hands. Amiran glanced at Quexil, who leered the way a jackal covets the lion's kill.

Leviathan straightened to full height, took the girl firmly by the shoulders, and turned her around to face her people. Other than the surf lapping against the shore, silence settled across the beach.

Leviathan turned to Quexil. "These people worship Fu Xi. Let us honor their hospitality as the God of Names once honored ours."

Quexil and his warriors surged forward. The chief's severed head fell to the sand. A steel wave broke over the hapless children of the sea.

Amiran's papyrus and stylus fell to the sand. He looked on impotently as another tribe joined the Empire.

36. Courting the Ghost.

"Truth and power are eternal enemies. They can only coexist when one is a slave to the other." - The Ninth Lesson of the God Poseidon to his children, from the Ancient of Ancients.

- The Chronicle of Fu Xi.

***

He is here.

Her eyes flew open to a late afternoon sun. She inhaled thin air so cold it hurt. The doe dragon soaked up his musk bubbling up from below like a volcano spewing fire into the heavens. She scanned the ground miles below, unsure how long she'd been asleep. Ahead, a narrow sea stretched between two arid grasslands. To her left, the sea narrowed into a wide, muddy estuary far to the north. To the south, it widened to the horizon, where sprawling flats covered its eastern and western shores. The eastern shore's sandy flats stretched for miles inland until terminating in distant cliffs. Beyond, icy peaks jutted on the horizon. *Those distant mountains must be the heart of his territory*, she thought.

The dragon heard her mother's voice on the wind. *"A doe wanders the world, but a bull never strays far from his birth cave. His territory is sacred, and he will kill to defend it. His scent is an invitation extended only to the doe who first answers his call.*" The thought another doe may have arrived first terrified her.

"You are first!" Instinct replied. "He is close, perhaps hunting the shore below."

What large game could inhabit such a desolate flat? she thought. Urgency burned in the dragon's blood and drove her to find this bull.

The dragon knew one day the overwhelming urge to mate would seize her, but her mother's lessons didn't adequately prepare her for the primal rawness coursing through her flesh. Nothing else mattered, not even the agonizing pain she knew soon awaited. The time had come to pay the terrible price for flight upon the Mother of Winds.

The dragon shook her head to clear her mind. The resulting weight shift slowly rocked her body. With steeled resolve, she dipped her left wing and entered a large, spiraling descent. She lowered her broad head and flattened her ears against the gale. Nictating membranes snapped over her eyes with each turn west, when the Mother of Winds blasted her snout. After several spiraling turns, the strong headwind ceased, signaling the dragon had descended below the Mother of Winds. She braced herself for the coming agony.

Fresh ice crystals blossomed across her body as frigid scales encountered warmer, more humid air. The thin layer sparkled in the naked sunlight and amplified her scales' proud colors. For a brief moment, from head to tail, the dragon transformed into a crystalline rainbow, a sparkling daytime star. The ice's extra weight uncomfortably accelerated her descent. She flexed her wings and rippled her scales, shattering the layer. The ice slowly fell away, a cloud of shimmering diamond dust against midnight blue.

As she descended below the ice cloud, the sky above lightened from black to hazy blue, and the sun regained its power to warm. The frozen veins in the dragon's thin wings started to thaw. Fire-bile in high concentrations prevented frostbite and ice crystals from forming in her blood.

However, it didn't keep the blood from thickening. Now warm blood flooded her wings, from the delicate membranes to the thick wing roots where her shoulder blades extended and narrowed into spars. Corded muscles, which comprised most of her body mass, fused to the hollow spar bones by powerful tendons. This became the battleground where warm blood and frigid flesh clashed.

It started as a deep, dull ache. In seconds, the pain flared outward across her wings like a thousand tiny teeth gnawing her shoulders. She struggled to control her descent, knowing the worst pain lay ahead. The fresh blood finally reached her delicate wingtips, with their extensive network of nerve endings. White-hot agony slashed into her back and dug into her chest. The dragon fought the suicidal urge to fold her wings tightly against her body in a desperate bid to warm them.

Darkness.

The dragon opened her eyes with a groan. Sky and sea rapidly alternated in her vision. She had blacked out, and now found herself plummeting toward the sea. She snapped open her wings and gripped the thick air. The dragon pulled out of the dive only feet above the waves and banked toward the nearby shore.

Tingling replaced pain. Flush with abundant oxygen and his pungent musk, euphoria smothered her. Once-dormant glands flared to life and injected mating hormones into her blood. She needed to find him, immerse herself in his heat, and...

...surrender.

A lifetime of isolation and loneliness recklessly pushed her toward the shore seeking the odor's source. The dragon needed to be...

...dominated.

She sliced through sticky air, skimming perilously close to the waves. Drool mixed with fire-bile dripped from her snout, creating floating candles in the surf. The doe yearned to immerse in his...

...*power.*

"I'm coming!" she roared.

As if sensing her excitement, dolphins raced her shadow, leaping and darting toward the shore. Tumbling breakers flashed beneath, spraying her wings with mist that did nothing to cool her heat. The beach blurred beneath, and sea gulls darted to avoid her.

She had found the scent's origin.

The dragon slowed and circled above the ruined man-dwelling. The scorched heap sat isolated on the sandy plain, several hundred yards from the surf.

Confusion's cold finger dampened her passion. *This is where he left his mark, but why? There is nothing here.*

"Find him!" Instinct roared, pushing such thoughts aside.

After a few low passes it all became clear, or so it seemed. The hovel's remaining walls, streaked and blackened, encircled a gray ash and charred log mound that was once the roof. This bull had obviously dealt sternly with a human infestation at his territory's borders.

Massive claw scrapes, much larger than anything she could produce, surrounded the dwelling. She'd never seen a bull's scrapes before, but once again Instinct guided where Intellect failed. Those marks were the source of the scent she'd followed for days.

She looked toward the distant mountains, but couldn't see them from this low altitude.

"His territory is vast," Instinct purred, eager to satisfy her desires. "He must be powerful indeed." Another wave of pleasure rippled through the dragon, stealing her breath.

Turning into the wind, she soared upwards and hovered a few hundred feet above the beach. Wings beating rapidly, she mimicked the gulls hovering around the man dwelling. She flared her nostrils, trying to catch a fresh whiff that would lead her east to his lair. Then something else tickled her nose, something wonderful, something too good to be true.

Neither Instinct nor Intellect could believe what her nostrils proclaimed.

Another bull dwelt in the northern mountains. His scent felt far heavier in her delicate sinuses, probably representing an older, more virile male. The scent deposited in the claw scrapes below tasted lighter, younger. She'd stumbled on the territorial boundary between two bulls' kingdoms.

The cocktail of sex hormones forced a shudder. An involuntary stream of urine washed over the dragon's hind legs and musk glands, announcing her immediate readiness to mate. If the winds were favorable, her message would reach the northern bull, whether she intended to mate with him or not.

Now an agonizing choice faced the young doe, one she'd never imagined possible. Except for her mother, she'd never detected the presence of, let alone seen another of her kind. She'd begun to believe she might be the last dragon. Now, in one day, she caught scent of two rutting males.

A venerable dragon lurked perhaps a day or two's flight northeast, a pittance compared to the long journey she just suffered. If she had lived in antiquity, when a nomadic female could take her pick from a host of bulls, she might have investigated the more preferable suitor. If she were just a little older, the doe might have been able to control the urges coursing through her body.

Today, they controlled her.

"It's too far," Instinct counseled impatiently. "The young bull will do. He *must* do."

She wheeled about and glided towards the hut.

The bull had deposited his scent in the scrapes, as both a warning to other males and as a signal for potential mates. The clawed earth surrounding the ruin testified to a young bull twice her size.

The dragon made one more pass to scan for danger, flared her wings, and landed in a cloud of blowing sand beside the deepest scrape.

"Touch them!" Instinct commanded. "Know they are real and you are not alone."

The scrape's edges were crumbling and dry, signifying it had been excavated several days earlier. She lowered her snout and inhaled until her chest could expand no more. His intoxicating musk made her dizzy and drove her excitement to a fevered pitch. No longer able to resist the urge, she leapt into the scrape.

She rolled onto her back, writhing playfully like a snake on a hot rock, pushing sand piles up on either side. The dragon closed her eyes in ecstasy, as her purring rumbled across the beach like rolling thunder. Rolling and rubbing, the doe covered herself with his mark. Pheromones oozed from her haunches, blending her signature with his, and pledging both her body and soul to a male she'd never seen. Her scales rippled and flashed, changing from bright maroon to emerald green to brilliant azure. Ecstasy and hope became one, and, for the first time in her life, the long-endured emptiness receded.

The dragon opened her eyes. The largest human she'd ever seen stood only yards away, clad in glittering, blood-red metal conforming to his body. Fearsome simian eyes glared at her through the conical helmet's "T" slit. He leaned against a lance, one leg crossed in front of the other, and gripped a red sword.

Hissing, she rolled upright in a spray of sand. The dragon backed up a few steps and scanned left and right, but saw nothing else.

Her mother's voice screamed, "Run!"

"He is alone," Instinct reassured her. "Kill him and finish mating. You are strong, he is weak."

The dragon crouched into a battle posture and spread her wings wide, dwarfing the human. Swinging her long neck and tail, she further attempted to intimidate him.

The armored ape did not flinch.

Her mother's words came back to haunt her. "Men seldom travel alone. Like wolves, their confidence is always proportional to their numbers. Avoid them if you wish to live."

Instinct remained mute as the last sex hormones surrendered to adrenaline. Clear-headed, the young doe finally recognized the terrible danger, and knew she had been betrayed.

Youth and inexperience betrayed her. If the young dragon wasn't so achingly desperate for another of her own kind, she might have recognized the warning signs.

Her eyes betrayed her. She failed to notice the bull left no other tracks except for the scrapes placed equidistant around the hut. A few more minutes' deliberation and she would have concluded no dragon would have created so alien, so artificial, a pattern. Perhaps then she would have also noticed the sand had been swept smooth in other places.

Her nostrils betrayed her. She failed to investigate the burned hut, or her snout would have warned her oil and wood scorched the walls, not fire-bile. If she would have taken the time to examine the other scrapes, she would have discovered none were marked with his scent. A more experienced female would have immediately recognized dragon blood traces, urine, and adrenaline mingled with the young bull's sex pheromones. And she would have detected the faint traces of human sweat corrupting the surrounding sand.

Her ears betrayed her. She failed to recognize the muffled clink of metal beneath the surf's roar.

Now the scrapes looked wrong. Now she saw the smoothing marks. Now she smelt the wood smoke. Now she heard clinking metal, hidden somewhere only yards away. Now she detected dragon blood and piss, testimony to a dying dragon's agony. Beset with warnings on all sides, she ignored them all until doom revealed himself in blood-red armor.

Dread gripped the young dragon. *I've been courting a ghost,* she thought. *Oh, Divine Serpent Mother help me, I've fallen into a trap!*

Instinct again found her voice. "Kill him!"

Scales tightened and clicked from head to tail. Her brilliant colors instantly faded to match the dirty brown sand.

With a guttural bark, the crimson warrior suddenly came to life. She didn't understand his language, only his intent.

"Fly!" her mother's voice screamed. The dragon cocked her hind legs to leap into the air. Sand-covered flaps sprung open all around her. More armored humans scrambled from holes like angry ants. Arrows descended on her from every direction. Barbed metal tips ripped through her wings in agony far worse than the thawing she had just endured. The doe yelped like a pup, stumbled forward, and collapsed.

"Get up!" her mother's voice and Instinct shouted in unison.

Despite the ripping pain, she stumbled to her feet and flapped her wings. With each downward beat, tremendous air pressure tore and widened the gashes in her right wing's membranes. Unable to generate enough lift, she rose only a few feet before flipping over with a thud.

Bull dragons were bred for battle, not delicate females. She desperately looked for an escape.

I will run, she thought. *I'll burn the crimson warrior and have a clear escape.*

She took a deep breath and swallowed hard, summoning her fire-bile. Instantly, her belly warmed. Crouching low, shredded wings tight against her back, she prepared to charge.

The crimson warrior stepped back, crouched, and cocked back his lance. He barked again, and to the dragon's left a large flap opened and dozens of small, naked humans emerged from a trench. A heavy chain bound their ankles to one another. Upon seeing her, they shrank away. Some shook violently and released urine and feces. A few tried to crawl back into the trench, but were repelled by warriors wielding whips. Under the lash, they screamed and stumbled forward. The miserable chain gang spread out and lurched toward the dragon.

Horrified, she skittered away sideways. The black, rusty chain segments stretched about fifteen feet between each of the pitiful humans. Loose strands attached to each segment, spiked with twisted metal and jagged barbs, dragged through the sand behind them.

One of the chained humans tried to crawl back into the pit. Even through her terror, she pitied the poor creature. Like a weasel, a warrior popped up, shot an arrow into the creature's head, and then dropped into its hole. The rest of the line lurched toward the dragon, dragging the chains and the body with them.

Horrified, the dragon turned and bolted in the opposite direction, banishing all thoughts of battle. She slid to a halt as another flap exploded open directly in her path. With whips cracking against their backs, more humans emerged and fanned out, pulling their chain tightly between.

Chain gangs now closed in from all directions, cutting off any escape. Panic's chains had already ensnared her mind. Rational thought quickly slipped away and Instinct took over.

"Burn a hole through their line!" Instinct commanded. "Leap over their bodies, and flee to the mountains."

The dragon took one more breath, letting mucus mix with the fire-bile churning in her gut. The crimson warrior seemed to sense her next action, and shouted to the rest. The warrior men covered themselves with metal shields and dropped back into their holes. The miserable creatures on the chains screamed. A few held their hands over their faces, while others tore at their ankles, trying to free themselves.

She could not afford to show mercy. The dragon tightened her throat muscles, narrowing her long esophagus into a small aperture. The fire-bile emerged like a flaming rope — a long, dripping tendril of liquid flame. She shook her head back and forth, spraying as many as she could. The fire coated trench covers, sending warriors scrambling out for safety.

Blazing forms thrashed in the sand, jerking against the chains. The dragon made a dash toward freedom. Before she could leap over the chain gang, piercing agony ripped through her rear haunch. The crimson warrior's sword penetrated her heavy flank. She fell before reaching the burning bodies. As the dragon struggled to rise, he plunged the lance into her thigh wound.

To the crack of whips, the remaining chain gangs advanced.

The dragon turned and snapped as chains raked her injured hind leg. She crushed a withered old human with a sickening crunch, and tossed him away like a cat tosses a dead bird. The humans attached along the chain followed the dead man through the air. Like a malicious whip, the links became airborne, and, in a cacophony of screams, barbed sections twirled and whirled outward with whooshing sounds. Like briars, the barbed ends snagged her flank and whiplashed broken bodies across her back, entangling her in a living net. Those still alive at the chain's ends yanked away in blinding fear, further tightening the snares.

NO!

She tried to shake them off, but the more she struggled, the deeper the barbs burrowed under her scales and pinned her wings. She bucked violently, revolted by the soft, squishy humans thrashing her. A few humans untouched by fire-bile dug their heels into the sand. Her thrashing tail swept them off their feet. They flew into the air along with burning corpses, and were quickly pinned to her tail by the chain. Simultaneously bashed and burned, they died quickly. Wounds, chains, and bodies weighed her down as the archers resumed the barrage. Encumbered and entangled, she flattened against the sand and tried to shield her eyes.

"Serpent Mother, help me!" she bellowed. The warriors momentarily shrank back at her roar.

As if in answer to her prayer, a strange calm settled in her heart. *My jaws and foreclaws are still free to attack*, she thought. She focused all her attention on the crimson warrior and vengeance. In that moment, she accepted her own death.

Dragging chains and bodies, she lunged with all her strength. The crimson warrior did not yield, but instead lowered the lance and charged. She feinted left, trying to lure him to commit, and then lunged right to flank his outstretched lance and snare him in her jaws.

He planted the lance tip in the sand and vaulted over her neck, landing like a cat behind her. The dragon snapped, but tasted only air.

She struggled to halt, but weakness and her burden's crushing inertia carried her forward against her will. Her long neck now lay exposed and defenseless before the crimson warrior. She whipped her jaws right to meet his attack, but the crimson warrior struck first.

She felt no pain, only a tugging sensation as scales surrendered to the red metal, leaving muscle, cartilage, and arteries naked before the enemy's blade. The world rolled left and turned upside-down.

She tried to inhale, but no air found its way into her lungs. Her massive, blood-starved heart desperately beat. The dragon found herself a numb witness to her own death.

A few feet away, a dying human female lay facing her, eyes wide and also taking her last breaths. Charred from the waist down, legs broken and twisted, the chain squeezed the human's abdomen into an unnatural, wasp-like shape. They stared unblinking at each other as the human's mouth repeatedly opened and closed like a fish stranded on the beach.

The dragon also opened and closed her jaws, trying to utter her name to the Serpent Mother, the Naming Ceremony's final act.

"Remember," she hissed and surrendered.

37. Blue Fire.

"Dragon's flesh, permeated with fire-bile, decomposed immediately. Within minutes of death, a dragon would spontaneously combust in blue fire hot enough to melt steel. The body would burn until everything, scale, cartilage, and tooth, turned to fine ash. Water could not stifle a dragon's fire once ignited, but could neutralize unlit fire-bile." - The Last Scholar

- The Chronicle of Fu Xi.

***

Amiran approached the dragon. Its long, graceful neck and equally long tail left no doubt as to its gender. *She's small*, he thought. The beast's powerful, barrel-like midsection bulged larger than a full-grown elephant.

"It's small," Leviathan remarked, looking down his nose. Amiran detected faint irritation in the prince's voice. "The roar heralding her arrival indicated the possibility of a larger beast."

"Yes, my lord," Amiran agreed. "Her roar previewed her fighting spirit." He took off the stifling helmet. The heat and humidity were oppressive.

Leviathan removed his helmet, placed it under his arm, and continued to examine the dying beast. Two Olmecs, clad in a dull bronze version of the prince's armor, hurried forward to take Leviathan's helmet and bloody lance.

Amiran pointed at the lance and shouted at them, "Wash that weapon in the surf immediately! Every drop of blood must be removed at once. Then rinse it with fresh water and dry it thoroughly before you return it to the arms master." They hurried off, obviously eager to remove themselves from the beast's presence.

Leviathan's gray eyes betrayed nothing. In times like this, when the god became an emotional void, Amiran feared him the most. *He's thinking about something*, Amiran thought, *and it's not the trophy at his feet.*

Amiran took a deep breath and refocused at the task at hand. *One monster at a time.* He pointed to the gaping neck wound where air still gurgled from the gash. "My lord, we must harvest the beast before she draws her last breath. I beg you to step away in case things go wrong."

Leviathan's eyes suddenly came to life. "Proceed with the harvest. Join me when you're finished."

Amiran bowed low as the prince departed.

Amiran looked about impatiently. With the dragon's life quickly fading, time had become his greatest enemy. Leviathan made the kill, but the job of harvesting the body belonged to Amiran. He cupped his hands and shouted across the beach, "BUTCHERS!"

A few Olmecs, including Quexil, gathered around the beast. They tossed their helmets and breastplates on the sand, exposing their sweaty skin to the salty air. Like Leviathan, they wore war paint of ochre squares, red triangles, and white zig-zags. They whooped in their blood-curdling Olmec tongue, pounding their chests and dancing around the dragon with their obsidian clubs held high, as if those primitive weapons played some part in this victory. Quexil prodded the dragon with his sandal and jerked away, as if it would suddenly leap up.

"It's real!" To Quexil and his men, these beasts were only tales handed down by their fathers, who called them the kulkulcan, the winged serpents.

"Stick around and you will find out how real she is," Amiran said impatiently, looking about for Ercole and Elda.

"It's a girl?"

"Why do you think we used bull dragon musk? Now, if you're finished, get your men away from the dragon so I can go to work."

Quexil gave Amiran a cold stare. "I grow tired of your sharp tongue. One day you'll find yourself without the prince's protection. When that day comes, I'm going to gut you like Great Paqua did this dragon."

"You may want to remember it's not the prince's protection I enjoy, it's Poseidon's. Now, please leave and take your men and let me harvest this beast."

Quexil stood his ground. "Poseidon is halfway across the world — the prince is here."

Amiran laughed. "No, the prince is over *there*." He pointed across the beach where body slaves removed Leviathan's armor at a safe distance. "The dragon is right here and you are wasting my time. If I can't harvest this beast, I will blame it on you. However, if you remain standing next to her for much longer, you won't be around for me to blame."

Quexil sneered and turned away. He signaled his men to retreat.

Amiran called after him, "For the love of Poseidon, tell your men to pick up their damn gear. I won't be held responsible if it gets destroyed."

Amiran stepped toward the dragon and almost tripped on a severed human hand. All around him, broken bodies lay tangled in the twisted chain. Several bodies burned. Fire-bile's acrid reek mixed with burning hair and flesh. Some still lived, even a few still pinned to the dragon.

A young girl tangled to the beast's spine screamed for help. A man near the dragon's haunch worked his way loose and dropped off the beast, his shredded left arm dangling by his side. Unfortunately, an Olmec tackled him and dragged the poor soul away.

Amiran wanted to help them, but could not. He'd become adept at suppressing his horror. He had to put those thoughts to the side and focus.

Across the beach, Elda and Ercole hurried toward him from their trench far removed from the battle. With leather satchels slung over their shoulders, they wore only bleached white loincloths. Necklaces dangling with tin clips jangled as they ran. Closely behind, four warriors followed. Two carried Leviathan's Expedition Chest between them.

Amiran carefully examined the dragon. Blood pooled in the sand under the neck wound. Air whistled though the gash. He scanned the beach where the dragon's blood had splattered over a wider area. The smaller drops were already smoking.

Far across the beach, Leviathan looked on dispassionately from his black throne. Garbed in a loose linen tunic, he sipped wine from a golden cup. The warriors reclined in the sand around the prince, spectators as to what might happen next.

Panting, the twins stopped in front of him and dropped their satchels. Hands on knees, they caught their breath and warily eyed the dragon. With a soft thud, the warriors deposited the heavy chest and threw open the unlocked lid. Straining, the men removed the heavy ceramic jug filled with water, and lodged its wide base firmly in the sand. They then retreated to join their comrades at a safe distance, leaving Amiran alone with the children. Amiran looked at the chest and then to the dragon, judging the distance. *It's far enough*, he thought. *It should be safe here.*

"Take a knee," he said and stripped off his breastplate and sword. "Collect yourselves, but only for a moment." Amiran knelt before them. He smiled and tried to exude fatherly confidence.

Trepidation filled their soulful eyes. *By Poseidon*, he thought, *please don't let them notice how much smaller she is than the wooden mockup. Her throat will be significantly narrower, making their task more difficult.* Amiran, then a twelve-year-old boy, had removed the bile glands from a bull twice as large as this pitiful specimen. It was that bull's preserved musk that lured this dragon to her doom.

"Quickly, give me your hands."

He rubbed each child's delicate hands, pretending to examine them. He did this strictly to calm them, as he already knew their fingernails were properly cut and dulled. "Good hands." He tenderly patted their cheeks and smiled. "Listen and listen well. No amount of practice can prepare you for the death you are now witnessing. You must ignore those on the chain, both the dead and dying, and soon all of this will be over. Do you understand?"

Elda closed her eyes, turning slightly pale. Ercole gulped, but kept his eyes locked on Amiran's.

"Good, let's get to work. I believe in you. This moment will seal your glory."

Amiran sensed some of their worry evaporate. He took a few more seconds to mull the decision he'd been delaying until this moment. A thousand factors flurried through his mind, considerations he'd weighed countless times since the voyage began. He reached into the chest and removed the small, tightly rolled velvet blanket. He unrolled it, revealing the two orichalcum knives. He handed the longer, reverse-hooked blade to Elda. "Harvest the glands."

Relief washed over her face. She took the knife and hurried to the beast's hindquarters.

He extended the straight, serrated knife to Ercole. Amiran detected the slightest tremble as the boy took the blade.

"You can do this, Ercole. I'm right here with you."

The boy looked at the dragon. "It's so much smaller than I thought it would be."

For a moment, Amiran saw his brother Arius in Ercole's expression.

"We'll get through this together." Amiran took the knife. "I will make the first cut. Come!" They sprinted to the dragon's neck and knelt. Amiran ran his hands over the beast's interlocked crescent scales, searching for the tell-tale swelling. A chain lashed a dead slave upside down over the beast's neck. This forced Amiran to shove the tight chain aside, costing precious seconds.

More blood droplets began to smoke across the beach.

"There, Teacher, just above your hand." Ercole pointed to where the scales slightly bulged beside the corpse's head. Blood trickled out of the dark man's mouth, and dripped into the dragon's wound.

Akul, Amiran thought, *the slave's name was Akul.*

Amiran glanced at the blood pooling below her neck. It had begun to smoke, too. Now flames emerged like candles across the beach.

Amiran felt around the swelling's edge, sometimes wedging his finger beneath the scales, until he encountered what felt like a rib.

"That's it!" He grinned. Amiran shook his head, trying to shed the sweat from his brow before it trickled into his eyes. Amiran wedged the serrated side under a scale and, with two hands, plunged it in with a grunt. When he felt the tip scrape cartilage, he twisted the hilt and sliced laterally. The skin pulled away as he cut along the neck's length. Amiran handed the blade to Ercole, then, with both hands, pried the flesh apart, exposing a thick pad of fatty tissue protecting what lay below.

The fire-bile-soaked flesh's stench made his eyes water. He had forgotten how the vapor burned one's lungs.

Ercole gagged. "It stinks worse than you described, Teacher!"

"Sometimes words are inadequate."

The beast's flesh slowly warmed under Amiran's fingers as he peeled back the heavy, yellow fat to expose a white cartilage cage. Three thin, rib-like bones covered the bile sac, a delicate yellow pouch lodged tightly in the dragon's neck.

"Teacher!" Ercole gasped and pointed at Akul, whose eyes suddenly opened and stared pleadingly at Amiran.

"Rahama," he croaked in his own language. *Mercy.*

"Look away, Ercole." Amiran brought up the knife and, with one clean stroke, sliced open Akul's throat. "Mercy is yours. Sleep, brother," Amiran whispered and closed Akul's eyelids.

The slave's blood gushed over Leviathan's inflicted wound. That's when Amiran noticed air no longer gurgled through the gash.

"The beast is finally dead. Time is running out."

Ercole carefully watched as Amiran cut the two lower, thicker cartilage bones at the sac's lower end, and pulled them away. Amiran could not touch the upper bone. Any attempt to cut, or even move it, would rupture the thin sac. It could only be removed by snipping and sealing the duct at the top of the sac leading to the dragon's esophagus, and then gently sliding the pouch backwards beneath the upper bone until free. That was a job for young, small hands.

Amiran shuffled backwards, took a gulp of clean air, and coughed.

He handed Ercole the knife. "Your turn. Do it just like we practiced, my boy."

Ercole nodded and took the knife. He slid around Amiran and knelt over the embedded sac.

Amiran's hand, sticky and covered with blood and fat, began to warm. Even if his hands burst into flame, he would not leave Ercole's side.

Amiran looked back for Elda, but couldn't see her over the dragon's abdomen. Amiran almost touched his beard, but then quickly lowered his hand. He didn't need to add a scorched face to his scar collection.

Ercole tapped the clips tied around his neck to make sure they were still there. He took a deep breath, and then slowly inserted his fingers between the sac and the bone. Ercole bit his lip as he probed for the bile duct.

"Teacher, it's hot!"

"You have time, just keep going."

The flesh squished between the boy's fingers as he felt for where the duct tube joined the throat. Amiran could tell the space between the bones was almost too tight, even for Ercole's fingers.

"I feel it!" Ercole squealed with excitement.

"Good, stay calm and pinch it just like I taught you. Have the clips and knife ready."

The boy worked his finger under the duct, careful not to stretch or rip it. Behind him, Amiran bit his lip and unconsciously moved his hands, mimicking the boy's movements as if he could guide the child by sheer will.

The duct slid out and stretched precariously under his index finger.

Amiran stopped breathing.

The boy smiled, fear replaced by growing confidence. Ercole placed the knife on top of the dragon, then reached up and pulled a clip off the slipknot. He opened the clip and then placed it on the duct between the esophagus and his finger. With his other finger, he flattened the duct towards the sac, trying to squeeze all the precious bile back into the sac. Ercole snatched another clip and placed it over the duct, a hair's width from the other clip.

Amiran breathed again.

"Is this good, Teacher?" he asked.

"As good as it's going to get, my boy. Now, the blade."

The boy flipped the blade over to the obsidian side and held it a hair's width above the narrow duct between the clips. Amiran forced himself to relax and breathe. If so much as one drop of fire-bile leaked and made contact with the air, they would die. The boy steadied his hand, and then touched the tip to the duct. With only a wisp of smoke, it parted like wet paper.

One more step, Amiran thought, *and then we have to go through this again.* The dragon had two such bile sacs, each more valuable than the prince's entire fleet.

Ercole's fingers slid under the sac into the tight cavity snuggled between the cartilage cage and the neck muscles. The consequences would be instant and catastrophic if the sac scraped cartilage, or burst from being squeezed too tightly. As if delivering a baby, Ercole gently pulled the sac under the cartilage, liberating it.

The sac was about half full, which surprised Amiran considering she unleashed a full fire attack only minutes before she died. *If she had survived three or four minutes longer, the beast could have unleashed another fire attack*, he thought.

"The satchel, Teacher, the satchel!" Ercole screamed with excitement.

Amiran grabbed the heavy leather and opened it as wide as he could. Amiran had prepared it with thick animal fat lining the fleece inside. Ercole gently lifted the bile sac. The thin membrane sagged dangerously under the liquid's weight. He slid it into the satchel, letting it slowly settle to the bottom.

"We did it!" Ercole shouted.

Amiran nodded but didn't smile. He bit his lip, suppressing the pain as his hands began to blister. "Come, let's place this in the water jug. We must quickly wash our hands and then remove the other sac."

Ercole pointed to the hole in the dragon's neck. "The flesh is beginning to smoke. We haven't much time."

Amiran looked back at the gaping wound. Smoke tendrils began to curl into the sea breeze.

"Wash your hands or they'll burn before you finish removing the second bile sac."

"We don't have time!" Ercole protested.

"Do what I say! It's a chance we must take." Amiran turned and hurried to where Elda lowered her satchel into the jug. Amiran submerged Ercole's satchel into the water, and the burning subsided from his hands. A thin, oily film rose to the water's surface, then dissipated. The fluid in the membrane sac would be safe, but if it broke open, the surrounding water would prevent it from exploding.

"Teacher, I retrieved both glands!" Elda said.

"Good girl! Wash the blade and wait here until we're done." With both scent glands and one bile sac safely sealed in water, only the last bile sac remained.

There might still be time, he thought.

Amiran turned to tell Ercole to dip his hands in the jug, but saw his head poking above the dragon's neck. He already had the beast cut open and the skin and fat peeled back.

Amiran heard sizzling above the surf's roar. The dragon's flesh began to exude thick blue smoke, partially obscuring Ercole's face.

Time had run out.

"Ercole!" he shouted and sprinted toward the dragon. "Get away!"

"I can do it!" Ercole shouted without looking up, his hands working frantically. Then the boy blinked, and his grin turned to a frown. A thin golden stream, almost like urine, squirted over Ercole's chest, face, and hair. He looked up in stunned disbelief. Ercole dropped the knife and held out his hands, eyes pleading for salvation.

"Arius!" Amiran shouted.

A blue flash simultaneously consumed Ercole and the carcass. The shockwave threw Amiran and Elda backwards into the sand. The heavy urn shifted, but did not tip over.

Elda leapt up toward the inferno, screaming her brother's name. Amiran caught her arm. She kicked and screamed against his grip as her brother perished yards away. Blue flames swirled and danced over the fiery mound, instantly eradicating any trace of Ercole and the slaves pinned to the dragon's corpse.

Head buried against his chest, Elda sobbed and pounded her fists. Embracing her, Amiran squeezed his eyes shut and stifled his own tears.

The smoke carried a sickly sweet stench. Clubs held high, the Olmecs danced around the fire.

38. The Beach.

"Orichalcum metal was the ultimate symbol of Poseidon's divine rule on earth. Therefore, all dragon harvest belonged to the Emperor alone. Hence the need for the Expedition Chests.

"The first ten chests were crafted when dragons roamed the kingdom itself, one ark for each of Cleito's sons. Centuries later, Poseidon made two more for the Bastard Gods. Each chest bore a demigod's symbol, but belonged to Poseidon. The chests symbolized the earth and sea. Poseidon delegated rule, not dominion, to his offspring.

"Like Poseidon's dominion, the Expedition Chests were built to last forever. The heavy cypress does not age or rot. The mysterious lacquer, imbedded with orichalcum dust, was impenetrable to any fire except those of dragons. The orichalcum frames and lid sheaths made these arks impenetrable to air and water. The locking mechanism could not be picked.

"Poseidon placed the Expedition Chests' stewardship under the Imperial Academy. The stewardship remained unchanged even after the First Purge. The Expedition Scholar opened the chest at the prince's command when the time was right, but the scholar was forbidden by Poseidon himself from divulging the combination. This was the only commandment that carried the death sentence for a god.

"In this manner, Poseidon pitted mortal against demigod, much as he pitted his divine children against one another." - The Last Scholar

- The Chronicle of Fu Xi.

***

Amiran knelt before Elda, firmly holding her shoulders. She shook uncontrollably, and Amiran feared he wouldn't be able to reach her through the grief.

"We are not finished, Elda. We will grieve later, but we must focus now."

He turned her tear-streaked face toward the urn. "Look. Tell me what you see."

She focused on the steam rising from the vessel. Amiran saw understanding burning its way through her pain. "Tell me, what must we do next?"

"We must remove the air and seal the jar."

"Yes!" He kissed her hands. "Show me, just like we practiced."

As if in a trance, Elda stepped to the chest and removed a cork plug, seven inches in diameter, made to perfectly seal the jar. Two rubber tubes protruded from the plug's top and bottom. She pushed the plug firmly into the jar. Amiran retrieved a much smaller jar from the chest, along with a bronze hand pump and a torch. Elda unsealed the small water jar and dipped one tube into it. Amiran connected the other tube to the hand pump.

"Now what?" he asked. Elda looked at him dully and then returned to the chest. She returned holding a thick wax puck and two thumb-sized tin disks. Each disk had two tacks resting in pre-drilled holes on each end.

Amiran nodded. "Good." He knelt by the jar and proceeded to pull and push the pump's handle. In a few seconds, water spurted from a hole in the pump. Without prompting, Elda pressed a tin disk to flatten the tube emerging from the water jar against the cork plug. She used the butcher blade's hilt to press the tacks into the cork until the tube fully sealed. The hand pump wouldn't budge, indicating all air had been removed from inside the urn.

He nodded, signaling she could do the same to the tube emerging from the cork. Once she sealed that tube, Amiran disconnected the pump and examined the seals to ensure no water leaked. "Give me your blade and the wax," he instructed, and she obeyed.

Amiran inspected the blade for any lingering dragon blood. Satisfied none remained, he tucked it in his belt. "I'm sending you back to the ship. I will return as soon as I can."

"I want to stay with you." Elda began to cry again.

"Your work here is done. You did well, my child. Ercole died a hero. Even the gods will honor him. Before we can grieve and celebrate his memory, I must complete our work here. Now, go back to the ship."

Amiran pointed to one of the four Olmec warriors assigned to the harvest detail. "Honor the Great God Poseidon and escort his property back to the ship."

Without another word or looking back, Elda departed down the beach with her escort. The ship lay at anchor several miles downwind from the ambush site.

Amiran picked up the torch and returned to the blazing corpse. The wind had significantly weakened as the sun neared the horizon. The smoke settled on the beach in a low, hazy fog. It left his skin feeling oily and irritated. Amiran held the torch slightly above the blue fire, and it burst into flame. Before he turned back to the chest, something beyond the fire caught his eye.

Far down the beach, along the water, two receding figures fled toward the darkening horizon. In the haze, Amiran discerned they were a man and woman, each dragging a short chain remnant. He couldn't recognize the male slave from this distance, but the female's lithe stature marked her as the chieftain's daughter captured early in their journey. The fire-bile must have melted the chain, freeing them before they could be incinerated or crushed. Amiran looked about to see if anyone else had spotted them. Most of the Olmecs had returned to Leviathan's encampment. If any of the Olmecs had spotted them, they would already be in pursuit. The smoke and darkness soon enshrouded the fleeing slaves, and the lapping waves wiped away their footprints.

Run! Amiran, thought. *Run, and never look back. Perhaps, somewhere out there in this undiscovered land, you will find freedom.* Amiran dragged his attention away from the escapees, lest his lingering gaze betray them.

He returned to the jar and severed the tubes just outside the clamps. Amiran then placed the wax puck atop the cork plug, and held the torch slightly above it. Slowly, the wax melted and entombed the tubes, and sealed the cork to the jar. Amiran removed the hooked knife from his belt, and pushed the hilt bearing Poseidon's seal into the soft wax. He tossed away the torch and picked up the water jar, pouring the remainder over the warm wax seal.

"Honor Lord Leviathan and place the urn in the chest."

The Olmecs complied, and in a moment the harvest urn rested in its deeply padded conformal space. Amiran further secured it with a leather strap. It wouldn't budge, even if the chest was dropped. The lid had a conformal padded cavity to further protect the urn. Amiran wrapped the hooked knife in the velvet blanket. He momentarily considered the empty pocket where the straight blade should go before rolling it up and placing the blanket in its cavity. He returned the pump and jar to their conformal cavities and then closed the lid. He listened for the tell-tale clicks signifying the locking and trap mechanisms had reset. Then he stood and turned to the Olmecs. "Bring the chest and follow me to Lord Leviathan. You shall have the honor of helping me present his prize."

The scholar trudged across the sand toward Leviathan, exhaustion creeping into his limbs and thirst parching his throat. Perhaps, the god would be satisfied, and the audience would be short.

***

Flickering shadows and dancing blue light painted the beach in ghostly hues. Darkness brought little relief from the sweltering humidity. Amiran knelt head-down before

Leviathan for so long memories of the ruined library in Wu began to creep into his thoughts. Leviathan exchanged light banter with Quexil and his favored lieutenants as wine gurgled into goblets. Finally, Leviathan addressed him, "Rise, Scholar."

Amiran obeyed.

Leviathan reclined in his high-backed mahogany throne. Relaxed and nursing a cup, Quexil sat to Leviathan's right in a slightly lower chair. Leviathan gestured to another chair several feet to the god's left. Amiran hid his suspicions and bowed low before sitting.

Leviathan turned to the serving girl. "Pour the scholar wine."

Amiran slowly took a deep swig without fear. Gods have no need for poison. Amiran wished it was cool water instead, but arched his eyebrows as the succulent, full-bodied taste drenched his parched throat. "Elysian, thirteen years aged. Excellent, my lord. I am honored." He took a deeper draw, and the slave refilled the goblet.

"Both of you have done well today." Leviathan turned his attention to Amiran. "I will say, I didn't think this bay would be promising in the least. When you began tacking dragon papers to the rails, I thought you mad. Yet, they turned red almost immediately. It is a rare day when a god is surprised. Now that we have our prize, tell me what you were thinking."

Amiran looked into the goblet and collected his thoughts. "The coast has been gradually drawing us north for several weeks. We are near the Demarcation of Winds, which as you know is the same latitude as the kingdom's home island, which in ancient days teemed with dragons. Like the home islands, I believe we are nestled between larger continents."

"You are speaking of Vulcan's theories again, about the world being round," Leviathan interrupted.

"Yes, my lord. I believe the Reed Sea's southern mouth is just to our west or perhaps this bay could lead to the Reed

Sea itself. We are only a month at most from reaching Giza. We stand at the joining of two, perhaps three continents, much as Atlantis sits at the conjunction of Olma Minor and Olma Major.

"Asu is to our north and east, Erub is northwest, and Alkebulan is to our west. Like the kingdom, this place is another crossroads of the world. Here, oceans, continents, and winds converge. If there was one place we would find a dragon, it would be here."

"I can imagine my brothers' astonishment when I march into Giza from the west, bearing a chest full of fresh dragon bile!" Leviathan laughed, quickly joined by his warriors.

The serving girl filled Amiran's goblet again.

"You, Great Lord, will be the first to sail around the world and prove it is round," Amiran added when the laughter died down.

"This bay, how far do you think it stretches north?"

"The water here is shallow, and brackish. It will likely terminate in a river estuary, leading deeper into Asu."

"Where do you think this river will lead?"

The wine relaxed his tongue, and Amiran felt himself warm to the subject. "If we are truly where I believe, it may lead to the legendary freshwater sea that lies east of Attica. We've heard of this landlocked sea for over a century, but the war has prevented any exploration. The Atticans tell of golden cities and terrible horsemen around this sea."

"This river could be a back door into Attica?" Leviathan remarked casually.

Amiran's heart froze. "Potentially, my lord, but we'll never truly know until it is fully explored. It's just one of many river mouths we catalogued along Asu's southern coast, any of which could lead into the continent's heart."

Leviathan grunted noncommittally and pointed to the Expedition Chest, changing the subject. "Tell me of the harvest."

"We recovered both hind glands and one nearly-full bladder." He swallowed hard. "Unfortunately, one butcher has perished, the boy. His knife fell into the dragon fire. We will retrieve it in the morning when the blaze has died. The blade will be fine, but the hilt will have to be reconstructed. I do not yet have an accounting of how many chain slaves died in the harvest."

"You were fond of the boy, yes?"

Amiran responded cautiously, now regretting the wine. "He was an excellent slave. He died valiantly trying to glean the second bladder for you and Poseidon's greater glory."

Leviathan stood and strolled to the chest. The two Olmecs stepped back and knelt at the god's approach.

"My father will not be pleased at the loss of one of his butchers. They are so hard to find and train." Leviathan knelt before the chest. What happened next did so quickly. Amiran didn't register the moment until the chest was fully open.

Leviathan turned and grinned at Amiran. "You look shocked." He caressed the urn, and then slowly closed the lid. Leviathan took the wine bottle from the servant's tray and recharged Amiran's goblet. "My father told me many amazing things before we departed on this great expedition, including the combinations to every Expedition Chest. It seems the day came when his mistrust, dare I say fear, of his mortal subjects became greater than his fear of his sons." Leviathan leaned down close to Amiran, the mask of magnanimity evaporating. "Perhaps his missing Renewal Dagger opened Poseidon's eyes to what I have known all along."

Hands grabbed Amiran from behind and pinned him to the chair. Ropes immobilized his chest and bound his arms to the chair. Blows pummeled his face and abdomen before the world went dark.

***

Tepid salt water dribbled into Amiran's mouth and splashed his face. He managed to open a swollen eye. In the distance, the dragon fire still burned. Blackness had swallowed the sunset hues, and campfires were scattered across the beach.

"He's awake," Quexil said from beyond sight. Amiran tried to turn his head, but aching pain down his neck advised him otherwise. Before him, Gadeirus's Expedition Chest rested beside Leviathan's chest. The lid was open, revealing the Dragon's Egg resting in its cradle.

"So this is what you want to smuggle to my sister." Leviathan stepped into view and looked down at the cylinder. "I can only assume the lock is laced with the same orichalcum poison used in the Expedition Chests. I was told this contains many scrolls bearing the Imperial Academy's combined knowledge. I was also told you are part of a plot to smuggle it to my sister, as if it might be of some value." Leviathan closed the lid dismissively and considered Amiran. "There is nothing of value in here. I will toss this into the sea the way you insects discarded my father's dagger."

Leviathan looked out into the darkness where the surf broke against the shore. "The sun will rise soon. Quexil wishes to flay you alive and eat your flesh, so that your power will become his. I have considered his request, but first I wanted to speak to you one last time, Grand Master Amiran."

Wracked with pain, Amiran swam in and out of consciousness. He tried to speak, but his ribs hurt too much to do anything other than summon breath.

"Everything I said earlier, I meant. You've proven Vulcan's theories correct, and delivered the world into my hands. Your plot, however, has failed. Shortly after your departure from Atlantis, my father ordered all the 'Owls' crucified along the inner colonnade. The word went out across the Empire. Expedition Scholars, acolytes, plebes…all put to the sword, crucified, or burned alive. From Wu to Giza, every scroll and Academy document was ordered burned. The Academy was razed, stone by stone, all the way down to the deep catacombs. Your precious Academy is now a necropolis."

Amiran bowed his head so the god could not see his agony. The sobs came softly at first, each filled with physical suffering.

Leviathan tossed a small scroll wrapped in black ribbon into the sand before Amiran's chair. "This message arrived before we departed Gadriuopolis. It details how Gremis died, perhaps with the most agony. He divulged what had become of my father's Renewal Dagger, how it had been cast into the sea. You are one of two scholars left alive in the world. The other is your betrayer, the poet Olorun."

"You lie," Amiran whispered.

"I was told he is your friend. He traded your fellowship for the right to partake in carnal pleasures. Flesh for flesh. Fair, wouldn't you say?

"My father turned your friend against you the way you turned Fu Xi against me, but that is of no matter now. You've handed me so much more than Olorun ever gave my father. If what you say is true, we will be in Giza in a few weeks, and this fire-bile will be in Atlantis in six months. My father will use it to forge a new Renewal Dagger, and bequeath me the entire Empire. If my brothers were unable to destroy Athens in our absence, I will do so in short order. Then, I will turn my armies east, and conquer Asu all the way to Cin. Between Wu and Giza, my forces will trap Fu Xi, while my fleet encircles him from the south. From pole to pole, the world will be mine, thanks to you, Amiran."

Logic and rational thought melted away under despair's onslaught. Amiran had been completely broken.

"My original plan was simple. When we came within sight of Giza, I turn you over to Quexil. I did not expect to find a dragon on this voyage. This harvest has changed everything.

"We break camp in the morning. The *Orion* and *Leo* will sail west to Giza. The *Draco* will sail north, with most of the supplies and the army. And with you and our remaining butcher."

Amiran looked up. "You saw it, too?"

342

Leviathan grabbed the chair, lifting it and bringing Amiran's face within a hair's breadth of his. "Tell me what you saw!"

"She hesitated. The dragon caught scent of something else before she landed."

Leviathan dropped the chair and Amiran winced. The demigod laughed. "What, pray tell, Scholar, could draw a doe dragon in heat from lure spore so close at hand?"

"Another bull."

"I will not ask you whether or not you planned to tell me." Leviathan signaled someone beyond Amiran's sight with a slight nod. "Know that I plan to hunt this bull dragon, and I still have need of you."

"What if I don't help you?"

"I hand Elda over to Quexil's men after she harvests the bull. Help me, and she lives the rest of her days in comfort. Help me, and I kill you quickly and mercifully myself after the harvest. Either way, I get my dragon."

"It's not much of a choice."

"No, it's not. Let's quit pretending you'll choose anything else other than my terms. You'll continue to function as Expedition Scholar, only without the prestige that comes with the title. Do you agree, slave?"

"I agree only if you remit Elda to my care. She needs more training if she is expected to butcher a dragon without her brother."

"Agreed," Leviathan said quickly as two slaves stepped into view carrying a brazier, a branding iron, and a common bronze slave collar.

"What is this?" Amiran asked.

Quexil stepped into view, holding an obsidian knife. The blade sliced deeply into his right biceps. As if outside himself, Amiran dully registered his own screaming as Quexil slowly sliced off his brand.

"The Academy is dissolved. You are now mine. Your new slave name will henceforth be Twice-Burned."

Swimming in and out of consciousness, Amiran only remembered Quexil gobbling the skin flap and attached muscle bearing Poseidon's trident. The iron mutilating his flesh, and the burning stink, drove Amiran back into the darkness

39. Master of the Whip and the Serpent Lady.

"Never fall in love with a mortal. Thou wilt sire no children. Their love will not survive the grave. Thy grief will be eternal." - The Tenth Lesson of the God Poseidon to his children, from the Ancient of Ancients.

- The Chronicle of Fu Xi.

***

The sea water felt like sweat. Chained naked to the foremast like a sacrifice to the sea spirits, Amiran's legs splayed ahead of him and his wrists stretched painfully over his head.

The *Draco's* gilded dragon-head prow buried itself into another wave, only to be heaved high into the air, as if the ship wanted to take flight. Tepid water geysered over the railing, drenching Amiran and everything else on the deck. With each plunge, Amiran glimpsed the approaching coastline. The dead-fish stink and dirty brown streaks intermingling with blue water told Amiran a nearby river emptied into this shallow bay.

Sun-baked chains seared his skin. Heat and salt stoked his thirst. Deck planks dug into his buttocks, and the mast left jagged splinters in his back. Each saltwater dowsing stung his scorched biceps. The wound throbbed with each heartbeat. Amiran ignored it all. His hatred provided a soothing balm. Amiran glared at the god's back.

Prince Leviathan stood alone on the prow. He hadn't moved since they embarked with the dawn tide, and now the sun burned overhead in the hazy sky. Arms folded, the prince appeared relaxed, his legs casually absorbing the deck's pitching and rolling. His soaked cape defied the wind.

Without their usual banter and singing, the *Draco's* crew avoided the prince as they carried out their duties. A dark mood had settled across the ship.

At dawn, the crew silently watched the *Leo* and *Orion* vanish over the southern horizon. Alone, the *Draco* turned north. It wasn't just the fleet breaking up that spooked the sailors. Over a year at sea had left them exhausted, and seeing a real dragon had validated their superstitions. Rumors that the prince stalked an even more fearsome dragon terrified them.

Amiran looked up at the sails. The black canvas strained against the wind. The yards and spars were rigged to catch every wisp chasing them northward. As the ship slogged into the head sea, the opposing waves crashed over the bow. Then, an unexpected ice-cold wave left Amiran begging for the sun's warmth.

How can that be? Amiran had never encountered the sea changing temperature so drastically.

The prince looked down at his wet hand, as if also contemplating the sudden change.

Amiran heard the chains rattle behind him. His irons loosened and clunked to the deck. Sweet relief washed over his shoulders. A pair of high black leather boots, stained with salt and in bad need of polish, stepped into view around the foremast. A hammered copper bowl, corroded green, dropped beside him and threatened to topple as water sloshed over its rim. Amiran squinted up at the figure blocking the sun.

"Are you going to sit there all day, damn fool, or are you going to drink before the bowl fills with sea water?" Captain Ploarchos boomed with his usual authority.

Amiran buried his face in the bowl and drank greedily like a dog.

The black boots strolled to the prow.

"The wind blows hot at our back and the sea runs cold against us," Ploarchos called to the prince. "We approach a river mouth with a wind over tide, a poor combination in this humble sailor's opinion, to be sure."

Leviathan turned and met the captain halfway across the deck, close enough to where Amiran could hear them above the wind and waves.

Amiran dropped the empty bowl and let it roll back and forth across the deck. He turned his attention to the titans before him.

Ploarchos stood toe-to-toe with the prince. "My lord, if it is your intention to sail up this river, then I say we make anchor here and wait for the tide. I'll send a launch upstream and scout the shoals and sandbars before we commit."

"We enter the river now," Leviathan replied.

"It's an unnecessary risk. *Draco's* belly is stuffed full. She's in no shape for river raiding."

"The river goes north, and that is where my prize dwells." The prince looked out over the sea with a strange expression. Something unfamiliar danced behind Leviathan's eyes.

Doubt?

"By 'morrow's dawn I'll know the lay of the river. If we go in now, we'll face treacherous overfalls. The breakers likely hide sandbars or worse."

"The *Draco* will enter the river now." The prince took a step closer to the captain and lowered his voice. "I will retire to my cabin, confident you will bring us safely into the river."

"Aye, if that be your will, my lord." Expressionless, Ploarchos nodded slightly.

As Leviathan brushed past, Ploarchos called after him, motioning to Quexil and several warriors leaning idly on the railings. "I want them below. I can't have jungle men fouling my deck when there is serious work to do."

The prince signaled Quexil and the warriors. They obediently filed into the main hatch, but not before Quexil shot Ploarchos a poisonous look.

Ploarchos shouted once again to the prince, "Let me take this dog off his leash." He gestured to Amiran. "He's underfoot, and I may have use for him."

Prince Leviathan looked at Amiran with indifference. "If you feel so inclined." With that, Leviathan turned and vanished down the stern hatch.

"Breakers off the bow!" the lookout shouted from the rigging high on the main mast.

Another cold wave washed over the deck, catching Amiran off guard. He sputtered and spat out a mouthful of fresh water. When he opened his eyes, Ploarchos lorded over him, his meaty hands on his hips.

"I suspected you'd end up in chains or dead before this voyage was over."

Amiran held up his hand and squinted, trying to see him.

"I can't have a chunk of rotting meat lying about, tripping up my men," Ploarchos bellowed. Amiran wasn't sure if the captain was angry or amused.

The captain pointed to his first officer, a tall Olmec named Yowtel. "Unchain this fool and by Poseidon's swinging dick, get him something to wear."

In a few minutes, Amiran wore a plain tunic and sailor's trousers, but without a freeman's black sash. Ploarchos leaned against the starboard rail, studying the waves breaking against the hull. Amiran stood behind him. Captain Ploarchos turned to Amiran. "Stay here with Huecuto, my helmsman. Stay out of his way and stay out of mine." He studied the waves. "The next hour or so will be interesting."

The small, wiry sailor manning the helm nodded and smiled at Amiran, proudly displaying a solitary tooth. Huecuto, a tight ball of corded black muscle and sharp bone, always wore a sly grin as if he knew some secret joke. Amiran found it difficult to believe the sailor could turn the immense wheel which dwarfed him.

"Oh, I'll take care of 'em, Captain!" Huecuto winked at Amiran in a way that made him slightly uncomfortable. "You just sit back and listen to ol' Huecuto, scholar-man, and you'll be just fine."

"Captain!" a sailor's excited voice called from port side. "The sea, it is alive!"

Ploarchos and Amiran rushed to the railing and looked down. Under the dark swells, sea creatures flowed and parted around the hull. Gray, silver, and black forms became a single school swimming in the opposite direction.

Hundreds, perhaps thousands of different species, stretched as far as the eye could see. "Have you ever seen such a sight?" Amiran whispered, looking out toward the horizon.

"No," the captain replied. "They're so thick you can hear them striking the hull. Can you feel it?"

Amiran felt slight, rapid tremors in the railing.

The crew crowded around the rails, squeezing between the catapults and ballistae lashed to the decks. They murmured and pointed as giant sharks swam next to porpoises and sea turtles. All of them fled the river's mouth, swimming in unison toward the open sea.

Amiran looked up at the masts. The seagulls had vanished.

"They swim away from the river," Ploarchos said and then turned his attention back to his crew. "Back to your stations!"

"Breakers ho!" the lookout shouted.

In a few large strides, Ploarchos reached the main deck, driving his men back to the rigging. He shouted to Huecuto, "Hold your course!"

The *Draco* plowed forward against a living tide.

Huecuto grunted, looking confused.

"What's wrong?" Amiran asked.

"Nothing, I suppose. I just reckoned the captain would turn east or west and run broadside to the river's mouth, nice and slow-like, in the deepest water he could find."

"Why?"

Huecuto's grin returned. "You scholar-men ain't so smart, I guess. Kinda soft, too, like a woman." Huecuto leered and cackled, furthering Amiran's discomfort. "The captain and me, we've done a whole mess of river raiding. Once, we went up the Styx with no moon, caught the Klyopians napping, and sacked the city. Either the captain's going to send a scouting boat in first, or he's going to cruise nice and slow up and down the mouth, swinging the stones and feeling for bottom. He always makes sure he knows what he's getting into." Huecuto grimaced and motioned up to the sails. "This is different. He's going full sail right at the river."

Amiran studied the rapidly approaching coast and contemplated Huecuto's words.

From the main deck, the captain turned and pointed at two sailors young enough to still be called boys. Judging from their unmarked faces, this was their temple voyage. "Swing the stones and swing 'em fast. Call out each and every depth."

The boys ran to the bow and snatched two neatly coiled ropes. Each rope had a circular stone with a hole cut in the middle secured to the end. Brightly-dyed knots spaced in equidistant intervals lined each rope. The boys tied the ropes to brass cleats and heaved the stones to starboard and port bow. They let the rope drop until they felt the slightest slack formed, then referenced the first colored knot above the water line. Oncoming waves washed over the boys as they cast and recast the sounding lines. Their teeth chattered as they called out the depths.

"Three and one quarter fathoms!" shouted the port boy.

"Three fathoms true!" replied starboard boy.

"Getting shallow near the breakers," Huecuto said. "Sandbars live near rivers — they rob some spirit from the current. The current finds new spirits in the deep water to make big waves again."

Amiran listened, knowing he could learn something from this sailor.

Ahead, he saw waves pounding against the shallows. "The waves break away from the river, not towards shore," he said, unsure of what he saw.

"The wind and current a-fightin' each other." Huecuto's smile ebbed away. "The captain, he knows what he's doing."

The river current, aided by an ebbing tide, pulled across the sandy shallows, tripping the water and causing it to pile up into a violent barrier, impassable even for the *Draco*. Amiran didn't see any breaks in the whitewater. So much driftwood and timber had washed up on the sandbars, it formed a wall as high as the deck. The jagged, imposing heaps looked like fortifications. *The sandbars act like reverse reefs*, he thought, *as if the sea is trying to protect itself from the river*.

"One and a half fathoms!" Starboard Boy called.

"How shallow will she float?" Amiran asked.

Huecuto laughed. "At fightin' weight, sweat and blood is all it takes to float the Serpent Lady. But we ain't at fightin' weight."

The captain returned to the aft deck, apparently satisfied Yowtel had the crew back at their stations. He shouted to the lookout, "Find me a damn channel!"

"It's all breaker, Captain!" the lookout shouted down. "I can see the bottom. It's shallowing out fast."

"One fathom true!" shouted Port Boy.

"Three quarters!" shouted Starboard Boy.

Captain Ploarchos blew out a deep breath.

"Darker water off the starboard bow!" The lookout above pointed.

Ploarchos bounded to the starboard side, climbed a few rungs up the netted shrouds, and scanned the water. Amiran approached the rail behind him.

"Aye." The captain grinned and pointed. "Do you see it, Scholar? That stretch, where the waves break and collapse away from each other…there is no debris and the water is a shade darker."

"Yes…yes I do." Amiran's heart sank. Threading the *Draco* through that narrow gap wasn't possible.

"Those are the river's gates, and I intend to enter." Ploarchos turned and shouted to the helmsman, "Full right rudder!"

"Full right rudder, aye!" Huecuto echoed and spun the giant wheel hard.

"When the sails think about luffing up, ease back to port," the captain called out.

"Aye, Captain," Huecuto responded.

The ship heeled slightly over to port as the wind caught the sails from the side.

With the breakers as a reference, Amiran finally saw how fast they were traveling. The wind blew across the deck stronger than he first suspected. He didn't understand the captain's actions. On this course, grounding the ship became a real risk. *Why doesn't Ploarchos just back off and come at it from a straighter angle, where he can sail down the channel's middle?* Amiran thought.

Overhead, the sails flapped and popped. The captain shot Huecuto a merciless glare.

Huecuto smiled sheepishly and brought the wheel back to the left. "I'm easing it back, Cap'n. Easing it back."

"First Officer," Ploarchos shouted above the wind, "keep the sails trimmed for full speed!"

Yowtel strode the main deck, carrying a small, ornate stick. He pointed it and commanded the men in the rigging to tighten a line here or shift a spar there. The sails inflated once again. Amiran gripped the rail as the *Draco* leaned farther to port. The ship balanced precariously between wind and current. In the sandbar's current shadow, the waves were smaller, and the ship accelerated.

Exhilaration raced through Amiran as the *Draco* dashed towards its fate.

"Half rudder port. Favor this side of the channel," the captain calmly called to the helmsman.

Amiran looked back at the broadly-grinning Huecuto.

"Why isn't the captain aiming for the center?" Amiran asked. "We're about to run aground on this side."

"The cap'n, he's smart." He winked and tapped his head. "Huecuto is smart, too, like the cap'n." Huecuto shook his head with mock concern. "Tsk, tsk. You…you not so smart, scholar man. You see, the water runs one way, we go another. The sandbars squeeze the water into the channel, where it runs *real* fast. Too fast for the wind to push the Serpent Lady through. The current is still fast on the side, but not too fast. When the Serpent Lady runs fast, she runs high!"

The brilliance, and risk, in the captain's plan suddenly dawned on Amiran. The opposing current accelerated in the narrow channel, but was slower against the sandbar. The faster the *Draco* ran, the higher her shallow hull planed. The opposing current became an advantage, not a liability.

It was still a dangerous gamble. Stray too far to starboard and the powerful current would spit them out. The *Draco* would flounder dangerously into the wind amongst breakers and sandbars. Ploarchos would have to lower the sails and float with the current, losing a good deal of control. Stray too far to port and Ploarchos risked grounding or tearing her hull out on a hidden reef.

The captain is threading a dangerous needle, he thought.

The breakers and debris piles were now only fifty yards away.

"Scraping bottom to port!" Port Boy's voice carried over the crashing breakers.

"Quarter fathom to starboard!" Starboard Boy responded.

Amiran crossed over to the port rail and looked down. He could see the bottom, providing a reference for the ship's breathtaking speed.

What Amiran took for dark sand was actually tens of thousands, perhaps millions, of bottom-dwelling fish and crustaceans scuttling over the sandbar for the open sea. *Why are these creatures fleeing the river?* he thought. Amiran didn't have the time to ponder this mystery as a low, gritty sound shushed along the port side. The ship lightly bounced off the sand, each gentle impact slowing the *Draco* and making her run a few inches deeper.

Amiran looked across the deck. The sailors labored with fluid intensity, working in perfect synchronicity as the ship teetered on disaster's edge.

"Debris starboard!" someone shouted.

Amiran returned to the rail in time to see logs speed past through the bottleneck channel. A few slammed against the hull.

Without looking back, the captain raised a closed fist to Huecuto. "Steady…steady."

The roar became deafening as the ship approached the debris piles and breakers. The most violent rapids churned immediately to port. More shattered timber and brush hurtled over the mound of turbulent water only feet away. If the ship held this course much longer, it would tear them apart.

Ploarchos dropped his fist and shouted, "Hard to starboard, *now!*"

Huecuto grunted as he pushed the wheel hard right, away from the maelstrom and toward the channel's widest point between the sandbars. The *Draco* shuddered as the keel slammed into something underwater. Amiran lurched forward and almost fell.

Everyone held their breath and waited to see what would happen next.

"Back to port! Back to port!" the captain shouted and waved his arm left.

Huecuto streamlined the hull with the current and looked up at the sails. He muttered under his breath and lurched his body back and forth as if willing the ship forward. "We're hanging on the sand. Come on, sweet Lady. More wind, more wind, more wind..."

The ship hung motionless at the narrow's cusp. Like titans, the wind, tide, and sandbar battled to claim the Serpent Lady. The bow started a sluggish, sickening pivot starboard on the sandbar as the current overwhelmed the wind.

Amiran squeezed the railing, a helpless bystander to his own fate.

"No, no, no!" Huecuto struggled to bring the prow back to port.

A warm gust suddenly blew across the deck, halting the pivot. Amiran heard a soft scrape beneath the ship, and then the *Draco* slipped free. A hearty cheer erupted across the deck.

Amiran exhaled and slumped against the rail. He watched the debris piles and breakers slowly pass to either side. From this close, the shattered timber didn't look so much like a fortress as a monster's ragged teeth.

Are we escaping the beast, or willingly entering its jaws? Amiran wondered.

"Five fathoms!" Starboard Boy called as the *Draco* passed into the expansive river. Amiran expected shallow, brown water. Instead, they slipped through a flat, deep lagoon. Featureless shores lined each bank with grasslands beyond. About a mile away, two large islands covered with marsh grass occupied the river's center. A wide channel stretched between them.

"Helm, hold your course," Captain Ploarchos said, displaying no apparent satisfaction in his crew's feat, as if he expected nothing less from them. He climbed down from the netting and took his place next to the helmsman.

The southerly wind had weakened considerably and carried a new scent as they passed beyond the breakers.

"Death!" the Port Boy shrieked.

The sight and smell assaulted Amiran simultaneously. The oppressive, rotting smell permeated the humid air. Bloated, hairy carcasses floated everywhere and clumped into stinking islands. The waves rolled them up and piled the corpses against the debris field's leeward side. Most were elk, deer, antelope, and other herd animals. It was the shaggy giants, some with fearsome tusks and horns, that drew his attention. The bodies bumped against the prow with soft, sickening thuds. The men recoiled from the railing. Panic rippled among those who, moments ago, bravely faced the deadly sea.

"These waters are cursed," someone grumbled.

"We should turn around, lest the devils who slew these beasts do worse to us!" a bolder voice declared.

Yowtel stood in the men's midst on the main deck, seemingly unsure how to handle the brewing unease. Perhaps so much death frightened him, too.

From the aft deck, the captain put his hands on his hips and sternly considered his crew. "Stop your bellyaching. Back to your stations." His hand rested on the latigo.

"It must have been dragons!" a young sailor cried. "They will kill us if we sail any farther."

"Would you rather face a dragon or Prince Leviathan?" The captain laughed. "As for me, the choice is easy."

The men looked at one another, their mood suddenly subdued. One by one, they drifted to their stations.

"First Officer, proceed under quarter sail and press up the center channel between the islands. Slow and steady. Keep a fresh look out on the bow and the rigging. Stand ready to drop anchor at the first sign of trouble. Keep swinging the stones and call out anything less than a fathom."

Yowtel nodded, obviously relieved the crisis had passed. Amiran wasn't so sure.

"Scholar, walk with me." Hands clasped behind his back, the captain strolled to the far stern, Amiran in tow. "Tell me, do you know what all this means?" he whispered and nodded to the dead animals.

Amiran wasn't certain, but he had an idea. He paused, trying to shape the right words in his mind before speaking.

"Well, be quick about it, before the prince comes back on deck and you return to chains."

"The river is flooded, but I'm sure you already know this."

"Aye." The captain nodded. "This is why we're sailing between those channel islands." He pointed to the grassy islands. "I suspect that is the original river mouth and the deepest water. Everything around it was, I suspect, once dry."

"Yes, but…" Amiran wasn't sure he should speak his mind, or even if he could find the right words. Master Alec's warning about the ocean on top of the world echoed in his mind.

"Tell me what you believe."

"The river is flooded and the animals were simply caught in its path. This is truth, but not all the truth. This is no ordinary flood. Water this cold only comes from two sources: springs or glaciers. Springs don't flood like this."

Ploarchos stroked his beard and looked out over the dark water. "Yes, I would agree, but we are far from the Icelands. It can't be glaciers."

"It must be glaciers. Sometimes there are glaciers high in the mountains, but I am sure a mountain glacier didn't flood this river, nor kill all these animals."

"How can you be sure?" Ploarchos's eyes narrowed skeptically.

"The water's sheer volume speaks to a massive source. Look how much of the surrounding land is inundated; the water extends well beyond the normal floodplain. The timber piled up on the sandbars is white pine, birch, and cottonwood, none of which are alpine flora. Finally…" Amiran shook his head, trying to believe the words coming from his own mouth. "…many of these dead animals are only native to the Icelands. As impossible as it may sound, I believe they were swept to their deaths thousands of miles to the north. They were carried here by floodwaters of staggering proportions."

***

Before nightfall, Amiran found himself in irons again, though with enough slack to move his hands. Ploarchos let Amiran relieve himself before he placed him back against the mast. He allowed Amiran to keep the clothes, and gave him a blanket.

The *Draco* skimmed over smooth water as the bloated sun vanished in the west. Amiran gauged the river was well over a mile wide, almost as wide as the great Icamiaba River which sliced through Olma Major's jungles. Amiran wished he had his papyrus and stylus to record all the wonders he witnessed today. He knew Elda was safe in the hold, and hoped she had his navigation kit.

A black boot slid a bowl of salted pork where Amiran could reach it. "The prince might notice the mercy I've shown you, and toughen things up a bit. There's nothing I can do about that."

Amiran did not trust the captain's kindness. "I spent over a year on your ship and we barely exchanged words.

Now you risk Leviathan's wrath to show me kindness?" Amiran said. "I want to know why."

Ploarchos raised a bushy eyebrow. "Making demands, are you?"

"I'm certain you would ask the same if you were in my place."

Ploarchos raised himself higher and looked back at the prince, who stood on the aft deck with Quexil, and out of earshot. He knelt next to Amiran and spoke in a low voice. "I must have served on two dozen ships, mostly colonial biremes and triremes, before I landed a position as second mate on a deep-water carrack. Eventually, I became her captain. She wasn't much, but she was mine.

"Like all smart captains, I always haul personal cargo during my voyages along with contracted manifest. My personal cargo tends to run on the exotic side, things I think will fetch a high price. Well, one day I was docked along the Second Ring Wharf, coming back from a long Erubian run, the Breton coast to be exact." A ghost of mirth touched Ploarchos's face. "Have you ever been to the Second Ring Canal Wharf, Scholar?"

"No, but I know its reputation." Amiran knew it as one of the seedier quarters in Atlantis, a refuge for thieves and cut-throats.

"Reputation? It's the dirtiest, nastiest hole in the Imperial City, too run down and despicable for even a flea-bitten Erubian rat...and a perfect place to sell my wares.

"Well, I was on the dock." Ploarchos laughed, and his iron mask fell away. His eyes twinkled in a way that made Amiran feel richer for witnessing it. "And this…this gangly beanpole of a boy, dressed finer than a temple whore, comes along sticking his prominent beak in my personal cargo! How he got there without getting a knife in the back was beyond me. He strutted around like an old hen.

"I was going to pummel the brat, scholar or no scholar, and throw him in the drink. Come to find out this fearless young scholar often frequented the more dangerous quarters looking for trinkets from faraway places. I didn't want to like him, but, by Poseidon, I couldn't help it. He told me things about my cargo…well, I had no idea." He winked and wagged his finger. "He helped me fetch twice the price for goods. Scholar my ass, he should have been a trader! All he wanted in return were a few stones with some scribbles on them or some dusty scrolls I picked up along the way.

"Over the years, he always met me dockside. I brought him artifacts from across the world, and he brought me the finest wine…" Ploarchos was now somewhere else, reliving happier times. "We drank and talked of gods and women. Well, I talked about women and he listened." Ploarchos's hard face melted into a smile of shadowed regret.

Amiran stared at the captain in wonder. Ploarchos spoke as if he knew old Gremis since he was a young man, yet the captain didn't look any older than Amiran.

"I think he had something to do with me getting the *Draco*. I know scholars of his stature, and yours, have…had…sway in court. I tried to thank him by secretly arranging a liaison with a high-priced whore. I couldn't imagine a man, especially one his age, going his whole life without knowing a woman's pleasure. The bugger turned me down! He said he 'had his vows to knowledge' or something.

"He was arrogant and stubborn and brilliant…" Ploarchos paused and fought to compose himself. "…and my only friend." His voice darkened as his eyes lifted to the prince on the aft deck.

Amiran fought back the tears as he listened to Ploarchos talk so warmly of his old mentor.

"I'll send Elda up from below from time to time to bring you food and water," Ploarchos said.

Amiran fought back the tears.

"Tell me, do you truly believe we'll find a dragon up this river?"

Amiran looked him straight in the eye. "Yes."

Ploarchos stood and donned the ship captain's iron mask once again. The Master of the Whip shouted to his crew, "The sun sets in the west and sends our prayers to Father Poseidon. Lower the sails and drop anchor!"

Amiran leaned his head back against the mast and watched the stars emerge one by one. Stunned by Ploarchos's tale, fresh grief washed over him. He mourned not just for Gremis, but for all the massacred scholars.

Amiran watched the twilight heavens unfold. A shooting star streaked across the sky. Another shooting star streaked out of the north, and then another and another. The crew stopped what they were doing and looked to the heavens. Thick, sparkling sheets fell from the sky. The meteor shower emerged from the constellation surrounding the North Star for which this ship was named – *The Dragon*.

40. Aryq

"Death is an invisible collar reserved only for mortals. The only judgment ye should fear is mine." — The Eleventh Lesson of the God Poseidon to his children, from the Ancient of Ancients.

- The Chronicle of Fu Xi.

***

Amiran didn't like the look of this jagged country. He knew bull dragons preferred this kind of terrain. They stood on a narrow cliff in a deep river gorge. Below, the river tumbled in a tumult of foam and fury. The sky above the chasm walls was only a thin blue slit. They were bathed in perpetual shadow.

The river thundered so loudly Amiran found it difficult to hear the captive. The goatherd knelt before him, his hands pressed together in supplication. Quexil stood behind the old man, sword pressed to his nape. Like the canyon, deep crags etched the goatherd's face. Tears mixed with blood from the gash in his forehead.

"Totaresh!" the old man repeated again and gestured down the gorge.

"What is he saying?" Quexil spat impatiently. "Does he know the way ahead?" Quexil kicked the old man to the dirt. "Ask him if this trail will take us beyond the gorge."

Amiran fought for control and spoke in even, measured tones. "Master…" The word burned on his tongue. "Perhaps if I had a few moments alone with him, I could find a way to communicate."

Leviathan had charged Amiran with the land expedition's logistics, but Quexil antagonized him at every opportunity.

The *Draco* had sailed into a wide lake at a mountain range's feet. Like a wall, the peaks stretched east and west for as far as the eye could see. Here, a giant waterfall poured from the gorge, feeding the lake. The ship could go no further. Approximately 300 feet above the narrow beach, the expedition established a basecamp on a wide cliff at the gorge's mouth. Quexil's scouts had captured the goatherd late that morning as they ventured a few miles into the dark defile.

The Obsidian Guard had requisitioned the man's goats and gorged themselves in camp. In the meantime, Quexil had dragged Amiran into the gorge to interrogate the captive.

"You question him in my presence." Quexil pointed his sword at Amiran. "No tricks."

Amiran nodded. "As you wish." He knelt on one knee and put a hand on the old man's trembling shoulder.

The goatherd possessed a dark, leathery complexion, but his sharp facial features and straight hair were like an Attican. He had thick hair, mostly silver with just a hint of red. He dressed in a goat-hair tunic, a wide leather belt, and goatskin leggings and boots. His clothes were singed in some places and streaked with soot. He smelled strongly of wood smoke. Terrible burns, perhaps only recently healed, grotesquely scarred one side of his face. The wounds left one eye blind and milky-white.

Amiran tried greetings in several Attican and Erubian dialects, but nothing worked. And yet this man's dialect seemed oddly familiar. Amiran struggled to place it.

"Totaresh!" the old man repeated and pointed up the gorge.

Amiran grew frustrated.

Totaresh. Something about the word kept gnawing at him.

It's probably a noun, he thought, *perhaps this land's name or his people*. Amiran had a hunch, and leaned in close. "Kako ti je ime?"

The goatherd nodded rapidly and pointed to himself. "Zelko! Zelko!"

"What did you say?" Quexil demanded.

"I asked him his name. It is Zelko. I had a hunch."

Quexil sheathed his sword and smugly crossed his arms. "Hunch about what?"

"His language is not akin to those we've encountered to our east, but to our west. His speech is similar to a barbarian tribe east of Attica, a people called the Thrax."

"So what?" Quexil narrowed his gaze.

"It means I can talk to him, at least a little," Amiran said.

What Amiran didn't tell Quexil was the Thrax inhabited a mountainous land south of the fabled inland sea. Before she rebelled, Princess Athena had sent an expedition from Attica to find this sea. Instead, they found grasslands and fierce horsemen. They returned bloodied and empty handed. If Amiran found the Thrax, then this river might originate from the inland sea. If true, Attica was due west. Amiran needed to learn as much as he could from Zelko.

Zelko seemed visibly relieved Amiran understood him and immediately proceeded to beg for his life. Amiran tried to calm the old man, but Quexil repeatedly interrupted and demanded to know what was said.

"Please, just a few more moments." Amiran tried to buy some time. He handed the old man his waterskin and

pointed north. "Mira … recite mi što se nalazi ispred."
Peace...tell me what lies ahead.

The old man spoke rapidly between gulps. Amiran put up his hands, trying to slow him down. He smoothed out the moist dirt in front of Zelko. "Krtati…krtati." *Draw...draw.*

Zelko nodded and set about drawing a map in the dirt. He drew a line with a half circle to one side and then acted as if he were waking. "Sunce."

Amiran understood and nodded. It was the rising sun. "Istok…east."

"Da!" The old man beamed a toothless smile, his terror temporarily forgotten. His burns twisted his joyous expression into something unintentionally maniacal.

Zelko drew the gorge, which he called aryq, and how it emerged into a valley somewhere to their north. He continued the line representing the river, showing how it ran north from the valley. North of the river, he drew another mountain range, which looked like a fortress with three sides. The river terminated there. He drew two more rivers, each emerging from the fortress mountains' east and west flanks.

Amiran pointed to the fortress mountains, where the three rivers emerged. "Sto?" *What?*

Zelko excitedly tapped the mountains. "Totaresh!" He pointed south down the gorge from whence the expedition came. "Flek!" *Flee!*

He's warning us.

Amiran stood and wiped the dirt off his knees.

"What did he say?" Quexil demanded

"This river gorge is the only path through these mountains. It leads to an east-west running valley, and then another mountain range beyond, where two more rivers emerge."

Quexil pushed for more information. "Where are his people? How far is the valley?"

To Amiran's relief, two breathless warriors arrived from around the bend.

"Get as much information as you can out of him," Quexil said and then stepped aside with the warriors in private council.

Thankful for the respite, Amiran returned this attention to Zelko, who held a finger up as if trying to get Amiran's attention.

"Poslušajte!" the old man said intently. *Listen!*

Zelko excitedly pointed to the fortress mountains. "Totaresh!" he repeated.

This word still baffled Amiran. He shook his head.

"Totaresh," Zelko repeated and made motions with his hands like a bird flying over the map. "Totaresh pozar!" Zelko grimaced and made claws with his hands. He then motioned his fingers along the map through the gorge as if they were running. "Zeljko!"

Amiran's eyes widened. He drew flames in the dirt. "Pozar?" *Fire?*

The old man slowly nodded. "Ne." He winced and pulled back the long sleeve from his goat-hair tunic, exposing a blistered, reddish-yellow burn on his forearm. "Totaresh pozar."

Zelko scratched a new drawing. A small, crude image materialized under his stubby finger. It had a long neck, two wings, and four legs. He pointed to the drawing. "Zmaj."

"Da!" Amiran pointed north. "Zmaj!" *Dragon.*

"Je Totaresh zmaj?" Amiran asked. *Is Totaresh a dragon?*

With large, exaggerated strokes, Zelko drew another dragon, this one many times larger than the first. Zelko tapped the drawing. "Totaresh je Gospodar e Zmaj." *Totaresh is the God of Dragons.*

Amiran hastily erased the images as Quexil and his men approached. "What did he say?"

Amiran sat back on his bottom and ran his hands through his hair. "He's babbling."

"You can tell it to Lord Paqua. He summons us to immediately return to camp."

Zelko's Map.

41. Visitor.

"Gods do not panic. Gods do not fear." - The Twelfth Lesson of the God Poseidon to his children, from the Ancient of Ancients.

- The Chronicle of Fu Xi.

***

The sun started its descent into the west as they emerged from the chasm. The wide ledge overlooked the enormous lake at the mountain's feet. Zelko was immediately placed in chains and led away to join the other common slaves portering expedition supplies.

Leviathan's small field tent had been erected near the gorge's mouth. The waterfall spilled from the chasm approximately 100 feet below them, and then tumbled into the lake another 200 feet below. The army, along with all its slaves, supplies, armament, and baggage, crammed the ledge stretching almost to the beach. A narrow gap in between the two columns barely left room for people to walk. Here, the army waited for Leviathan's next orders.

Now that everything and everyone had disembarked, Amiran marveled at how much had been packed into the *Draco's* narrow hull. It was truly a testament to Ploarchos's skill that he safely brought the heavily laden vessel through the river's gauntlet.

Amiran looked down at the lake below. When they disembarked yesterday, a dozen yards of shoreline separated the cliffs from the lake. Amiran had cautioned the prince not to make camp on the shore, suspecting the enormous lake didn't exist until the recent flood. Today, the shoreline had shrunk to half its original size. By tomorrow, Amiran suspected the waves would lap against the cliff.

Then, to his shock, Amiran saw the *Draco* sailing away.

"Why is the *Draco* leaving?"

"I don't know." Quexil seemed just as perplexed as Amiran. He addressed the warrior guarding the prince's tent. "Tell His Highness we are here."

"My Captain." The guard bowed his head. The young warrior's eyes shifted left and right, as if he didn't know what to say.

Quexil sensed his unease. "Spit it out."

"The prince is inside…" The guard hesitated. "…speaking with someone. He told me he is not to be disturbed, even by you."

This clearly irritated Quexil.

"Who is it?" Quexil demanded.

"I do not know." The warrior's voice cracked.

Quexil eyed the guard suspiciously. "You do not know who enters or leaves the prince's tent?"

The guard trembled. Obsidian Guards were brutal, but Amiran knew they were never cowards. Among their kind, it was better to die than show fear. The guard cleared his throat and took a deep breath.

"No one entered the tent."

"Do not play with me, Nahuatl." Quexil struck him across the face. "Or I'll skin you."

"Captain, I speak the truth! Listen, you can hear His Highness speaking. There is another voice, do you hear?"

Quexil cocked his ear and listened. Amiran craned forward and tried to hear what transpired inside. He heard low voices. One was the prince's, and one was not, though he couldn't understand their words.

Quexil shoved Amiran toward the cliff wall and pointed to a boulder. "Sit and wait until I call you."

Amiran sat and observed.

Quexil huffed and walked around the tent, examining its bottom hem. The prince's slaves used heavy rocks placed over the oiled llama wool to augment the stakes, which worked poorly in the trail's loose shale and thin soil. If someone slipped under the tent, they wouldn't be able to replace the rocks over the tent's hem. The rocks were untouched. Quexil treaded lightly between the cliff wall and the tent, making sure he didn't slip in the shale and fall onto the prince's tent. He emerged next to Amiran and scowled. Quexil looked down the trail at the expedition camp, as if the answer to this mystery might be found there. The rest of the expedition party, slaves and warriors alike, rested in against the cliff, soaking up the sun and eating a meal of hard cornbread.

Quexil approached the guard again. "Think carefully, Nahuatl. Did anything unusual happen while I scouted the gorge?"

"Perhaps an hour after you entered the gorge, the prince emerged from his tent and gave the orders for the *Draco* to depart immediately. He commanded no one was to disturb him, and to send runners to retrieve you and the scholar."

Quexil looked to his lieutenants for confirmation. They merely nodded. Over the next few minutes, Quexil and his men tried to make sense of the strange events and ignored Amiran.

Amiran remained quiet, listened, and learned. He didn't listen to the Olmecs. He tried to hear what transpired inside the tent. The mystery was almost too much to bear.

The speech was not Atlantean — of that he was sure. Unlike Atlantean, the consonants blended together smoothly, flowing like water. Amiran was sure he'd heard this language before. He leaned in closer, trying not to appear too obvious. A familiar word drifted from the tent, and then another. A rush of sudden excitement coursed through him.

They spoke in the First Tongue, the very language written upon the Ancient of Ancients. It was a language lost to time and not suited for mortals. Amiran resisted the urge to press his ear against the tent. He needed to know who was in there with Leviathan. Could it be Poseidon? He'd heard credible stories of the god appearing and disappearing across the Empire, but there had never been definitive proof.

Amiran glanced at Quexil and his warriors, who still had their backs to him.

It's worth the chance, he thought. Amiran quietly stepped into the shadowed gap between the tent and the cliff and put his right ear against the tent.

The voices ceased.

He turned his head to listen with his left ear, and came face-to-face with a stranger dressed in black.

Startled, Amiran jumped back. The pale-skinned Erubian, almost an albino, dressed in black from head to foot. He towered almost a head above Amiran. He seized Amiran by his metal collar and lifted him off the ground. The man in black examined Amiran with ice-blue eyes, the way a raptor considers a mouse locked in its talons. Amiran felt as if a trapdoor suddenly sprung open under his feet and he had tumbled into an airless abyss.

The stranger tossed Amiran from behind the tent and into the sunlight.

Quexil and his men turned around to see Amiran tumble to the ground. He tried to sit up, rubbing his neck beneath the collar.

Quexil scowled. "By Poseidon, what the…"

The tent flap flew open and Leviathan burst forth, dressed in full armor, with red sword dangling by his side.

"Get everyone up! Pack as much as you can onto the horses. Everyone porters, and that means you too, Quexil. We leave now."

Amiran sensed something was horribly wrong, something he didn't understand, perhaps even beyond his understanding.

The prince strode along the cliff, barking orders, Quexil following closely behind. Amiran stumbled after, looking about fearfully for the man in black.

"My lord, I have great news!" Quexil said, trying to keep up. "A valley lies to the north through the canyon. The way forward is open."

"I don't care. Your scouts overlooked a trail half a mile back. Get your men, horses, and the slaves loaded and moving up that trail with the utmost haste. We must reach the mountaintop before sunrise tomorrow."

Quexil craned up at the peak thousands of feet over their heads. "My lord, if you could just tell me…"

Leviathan struck Quexil across the face, launching him against the cliff. Quexil slumped unconscious against the rock. Everyone looked on in stunned silence.

He's afraid, Amiran thought in disbelief.

The prince glared at his army. "Do not question me! Carry what you can and follow. I promise you this: those who fall behind will surely perish." The god pointed his crimson sword toward the soaring peaks. "If you wish to live, climb!"

42: Escape.

"In Atlantis, no one was born free. The baby's mark was always burned into newborn's flesh. By Poseidon's decree, freedom was earned on the battlefield or at sea. Few slaves, especially those who had already received their adult brand, ever considered freedom. Most found comfortable servitude preferable to dangerous freedom. A freeman would be debranded with steel and fire by a god or another freeman. As the scalding metal obliterated the old brand, the freeman whispered, 'Freedom waits beyond the fire.'" - The Last Scholar

- The Chronicle of Fu Xi.

***

Leviathan's unexpected edict left the camp reeling, and there was little time to organize the expedition to climb the mountain. Fear simmered, even among the Olmecs. Leviathan and several of his best warriors, taking the five horses with them, immediately began the trek to the peak, leaving organizing the ascent to Amiran and Quexil. Quexil assigned warriors and the strongest slaves to porter Leviathan's baggage train, to include the Expedition Chest, the Olmecs' military baggage, and food supplies. After that, Quexil too began the climb. In a mad dash, everyone else began grabbing whatever supplies were nearby and joined the line marching up the trail. With Elda's assistance, Amiran fell into his old role as Expedition Scholar and quickly restored order. He organized the caravan as best he could, ensuring critical supplies were not abandoned. Amiran made sure he wore his navigation kit on his back. He could not chance it getting left behind.

By dusk, Amiran, Elda, and one remaining Olmec were the last depart to the ledge. That's when he spotted Gadeirus's Expedition Chest resting on its side against the cliff like discarded trash. Amiran rushed to the chest and turned it upright.

"I thought you said Leviathan tossed it into the sea?" Elda said.

"I thought he did, too. It feels heavy. Maybe, just maybe." He entered the combination, and the lid popped open, revealing the Dragon's Egg. Amiran closed his eyes and fought back the overwhelming emotion. He closed the lid. "We must get this up the mountain."

"You two, hurry!" the warrior shouted.

"It's too heavy." Elda shook her head.

Amiran grabbed the chest by one handle and began to drag it toward the trail.

Exasperated, Elda followed. "Teacher! It's too heavy."

"I won't leave it," he replied, and then shouted at the Olmec. "Help me. This is part of Prince Leviathan's personal baggage mistakenly left behind."

The warrior took one look at the chest with Gadeirus's seal, and obediently lifted the other handle. The three of them rushed down the ledge among the few remaining discarded bags, bundles, and boxes until they reached the trail snaking its way up the mountain. To Amiran's satisfaction, most essential gear had been saved.

***

Throughout the night, the river swiftly carried the *Draco* toward the sea. With a clear sky, Ploarchos had no qualms sailing at night knowing the river had only grown deeper. Leviathan's unexpected order, with no accompanying explanation, for the *Draco* to immediately abandon the expedition and set sail for open water, left Ploarchos perplexed. Regardless of the reason, he shared his crew's relief at returning to deep water and, ultimately, Giza. They had been at sea longer, and discovered more new lands, than any expedition in Atlantis's long history. The dragon had been enough for the crew; it was time to go home. If Leviathan's intent was to strike out overland toward Attica, so be it. It was no longer Ploarchos's concern.

***

The chest grew heavier with each step. Somewhere in the night, the warrior abandoned them. Elda helped Amiran best she could, pushing the chest while Amiran pulled, but he bore the brunt hauling the treasure up the mountain. His arms burned and his hands had turned numb as ice.

Dressed only in her thin, thigh-length dress, Elda presented a pale silhouette against the hard-black sky. Her breath floated against the cold stars and seemed to merge with the Milky Way. In the darkness, they talked for comfort against the freezing misery.

"I've never been on a mountain." Elda's teeth chattered. "Are they all this big?"

Amiran yanked, Elda pushed, and the chest scraped a few more feet up the trail. Amiran took a few steps backward and they repeated the process. "In Olma Major, there are mountains far larger than this. On the east side are endless jungles, and on the west slope there are bone-dry deserts."

"I've decided I don't like mountains, Teacher."

"Me, too." He laughed.

"I'm so cold." Her voice sounded weak. Amiran knew Elda was entering a dangerous phase of what Expedition Scholars called cold sickness. "Can we stop and rest?"

"No. Sunrise is coming soon," he said. They had begun to bump into abandoned supplies along the way. Amiran saw shapes in the darkness he recognized as bodies, where the weakest slaves had simply lay down and died. The expedition possessed some cold-weather gear amongst the supplies, but none of it had been unpacked in the haste prior to their ascent. "Keep helping me, Elda."

"Yes, Teacher."

Amiran yanked, Elda pushed, the chest scraped, and the process repeated. Amiran looked up the mountain. High above, a line of torches preceded them. How high, Amiran didn't know, but he and Elda had been left far behind. Whatever danger Leviathan feared would likely find Amiran and Elda first.

"Why is it so hard to breathe, Teacher?" Elda asked.

Yank. Push. Scrape.

"The higher you go, the thinner the air."

"That's the ocean of air you spoke of?"

"Yes."

"Oh."

Yank. Push. Scrape.

"How much higher before it runs out?"

"We don't really know, but dragons fly much higher than this."

"Don't they get cold?"

"I suppose they do." Amiran chuckled. *She has a scholar's natural curiosity*, he thought.

Yank. Push. Scrape.

"Wasn't the dragon b-beautiful?" Elda said.

Amiran paused. "Yes, she was."

"Her f-fire was so hot. I could feel it in my bones. I wish I could f-feel a little of it now."

Yank. Push. Scrape. They climbed in silence for a long while before she spoke again. The cold even numbed the constant throb in his biceps. He sensed blood trickling down his arm and freezing as the scabs tore under the strain. Amiran endured. He'd been colder before.

Yank. Push. Scrape.

"Ercole wasn't afraid of fire. He always enjoyed helping P-Papa with the f-f-forge."

"Your brother possessed a man's bravery. Your father would be proud of him."

"Did Ercole suffer, Teacher?" He could see her shivering even in the darkness.

Amiran halted and slowly straightened. His spine popped as he fought to keep his balance. "No, Elda. He did not suffer."

"I understand," she whispered.

Amiran realized how truly steep the slope had grown. Elda wasn't just pushing the chest; her weight likely prevented it from backsliding. If the slope became any steeper, it would be impossible to drag the chest any higher. He glanced to the east at the false dawn.

Amiran bent over and winced as his back screamed. "Here we go, one, two three, push!"

Yank. Push. Scrape. Elda's meager shoves felt weaker with each cycle. Amiran's shoulders ached, but remembering the stranger in black, and the fear in Leviathan's eyes, drove the scholar onward like a latigo at his back.

"Teacher, can't we remove the Dragon's Egg and j-just carry it?"

"Most of the weight is the egg and not the chest. Carrying the cylinder risks accidentally triggering the poison trap. The older scrolls will crumble if we try to carry them ourselves."

Elda reluctantly leaned against the chest once again, digging her sandals into the slope.

"Teacher?"

"Yes, Elda."

"After w-we killed the dragon, when I was in the hold with the other slaves…they said Poseidon killed all your friends. Is that true?"

Amiran paused and caught his breath. "Yes. Ready? One, two, three…go!"

Yank. Push. Scrape.

After several iterations, Elda whispered, "I'm sorry."

Yank. Push. Scrape. Darkness surrendered to vague blue and black shapes.

"I must catch my-my breath. Please." Elda leaned against the chest, heaving and shaking uncontrollably.

"All right, but only for a moment." He straightened again and looked around. The pink horizon gave Amiran enough light to see streaks of last winter's snow clinging to the slopes. If this barren mountain had any trees, they would be above the tree-line. The lake, now a tiny mirror far below, reflected the rosy pre-dawn. It was an impressive summit, the largest of all the visible mountains in the surrounding chain.

He turned around and craned toward the peak. A few silhouettes carrying torches stood out against the lightening sky. A line of discarded supplies littered the way to a ledge perhaps 200 feet above their heads. Thankfully, the slope didn't steepen any further.

"We're almost there, Elda. By mid-morning you will be warm again." He stooped and pulled the handle.

Yank.

Scrape. The chest barely moved.

"Elda?"

Amiran slid down around the chest to find Elda fetal on the ground. He cradled her in his lap like an infant. The chest slipped, and Amiran placed his back against it. "Elda, wake up!' He began to furiously rub her skin, trying to rouse her.

The sky began to rapidly brighten, and Elda's condition worsened. Amiran knew what he must do. The sacrfice only took a few moments. When Amiran finished, he looked east, expecting to see the sun peeking around the mountains, but realized that wasn't where the light came from. Screams floated down from the summit above. He looked over his shoulder and realized the skyglow came from the north, behind the mountain.

A brilliant fireball erupted from behind the peak. Showering sparks and shedding smoke, it cleaved the heavens in two.

43: The Horrid God.

"A god's wrath is as cold and patient as winter. Rest assured, judgement is inevitable." – The Thirteenth Lesson of the God Poseidon to his children, from the Ancient of Ancients.

- The Chronicle of Fu Xi.

***

At dawn, the crew cheered when they realized the rising floodwaters had washed away much of the debris blocking the river's mouth, giving the *Draco* clear passage to the open sea.

Their cheers died when the fiery star plunged into the ocean beyond the southern horizon. In a brilliant flash, it gave birth to a monster like a titan of old. The beast rose into the sky on a torso of fire and smoke, and commenced devouring the world. Its head mushroomed as it gorged until it scraped the heavens and knocked the stars from the sky. They fell in sheets over their heads, accompanied by booming thunder.

Ploarchos's terrified men begged him to turn around or beach the ship.

"Where?" the captain chastised, hand resting on his latigo. "Where shall we run?"

It wasn't enough, and some crewmen began to bolt for the launches. He saw mutiny's seeds growing. Ploarchos knew some were even contemplating jumping and swimming to shore. This wasn't a storm or an enemy fleet. This wasn't even a dragon, but terror incarnate.

For the first time as a ship's captain, Ploarchos reached for the latigo. He caught himself, flexed his fingers, and dropped his hand. "We cannot turn around. The tide is stronger than the wind." He pointed back to the monster. "If we beach, how far can you run before the beast catches you? You know the sailor's code — 'To die on land is to die a slave.' Is that what you want?" He paused. "I am afraid, too." The men quieted. He took a deep breath and continued, "Yes, I am afraid. In all my long years as master of this vessel, I have never been afraid. If I fear this doom, what can I expect from you?"

He only heard the wind, and the waves breaking against the hull.

Ploarchos paused, swallowing back his emotions. "Let us sail down Death's throat together."

"What shall we do?" Huecuto asked.

"We sail for the mouth of this confounded river, beyond the bay and back to open ocean. Then we turn west and make a run for Giza. If any ship can outrun this monster, it's the *Draco*." As the stars fell, the captain tried to make himself believe his own words.

By mid-morning, they had cleared the river and raced for the open ocean. The monster had already eaten the sun, plunging the world into fiery twilight.

With a stone face, Ploarchos paced behind Huecuto, gaze fixated on the looming monster. The sky had vanished, replaced by the titan's swollen belly stretching horizon to horizon. Red and orange flares erupted from its underside.

What horrid god is this?

The *Draco* hurtled for the bay's narrow straits leading to the ocean. The shore was only a few miles off the port and starboard railings. The current ran south toward the monster, faster than any current he'd ever encountered.

Ploarchos contemplated his options as he withdrew an orange from a pocket and began to peel it. "You were wrong, Gremis, old friend." He broke away a segment and popped it in his mouth. Sweet juice squirted down his throat. "The world isn't round. It's flat and there are monsters waiting at its edge."

"The shore! The shore!" Port Boy shouted.

Ploarchos watched the shoreline rapidly extend to meet them.

"The western shore does the same!" another sailor shouted.

The *Draco* started to accelerate.

"The water recedes," Ploarchos said grimly.

The *Draco* lurched starboard as a hot gale burst from the south.

"Unfurl all available sail!" Ploarchos shouted. "Helm, keep hard to port. Keep her pointed down the channel!"

The channel vanished faster than Huecuto could turn the wheel. "It's drinking the ocean. By Poseidon, it's slurping us up!" the terrified helmsman cried.

Ploarchos shoved him out of the way and seized the helm. Before he could spin the wheel, the *Draco's* bow pitched down, accompanied by a loud scraping, like sandpaper on wood. The deck violently shuddered, spilling everyone to the planks. The masts snapped. The ship rolled hard to starboard and skidded to a halt.

Ploarchos tried to pull himself up, but water gushing over the stern swamped him. The captain and helmsman tightly gripped the wheel as the retreating current washed over the *Draco*, dragging dozens overboard and away with the tide.

After a few moments, eerie silence reigned. Ploarchos pulled himself up and looked around.

The grounded ship listed almost forty-five degrees. The sea had vanished. Around the ship, exposed reefs stood like pillars and ledges. He scanned the deck, trying to account for his crew.

"Yowtel?" he shouted, but only groans answered him. "Huecuto?"

The helmsman stood, but didn't relinquish his death grip on the helm. "That monster…it drank the ocean."

Ploarchos answered calmly. "Aye, it did."

Then the monster roared.

Again, Ploarchos came to and stumbled to his feet. No one else stirred. Huecuto slumped against the wheel, blood pouring from his ears. The masts were now completely gone, along with most of the rigging. Tattered black sails, splintered wood, and blood covered the planks. Timber and broken bodies surrounded the ship. Ploarchos called out, but only heard the ringing in his ears.

"My crew, my beloved ship," Ploarchos muttered. The ringing in his ears subsided.

The sky had grown pitch black. Only fiery streaks and tongues of flames spitting from the sulfuric clouds provided any light. The monster was almost upon them.

Ploarchos heard Huecuto groan and helped him to his feet.

"I can't hear, Captain," Huecuto shouted and pointed to his bloody ears. "I feel something, though. Do you feel it, too?"

"Yes." Ploarchos felt the rumble, a low bass concussion that shook his insides. The deck began to vibrate.

"By Poseidon!" Huecuto shouted and pointed south.

At first it was only a thick, black line. As it approached, Ploarchos fully comprehended what he saw. Black, undulating mountains loomed on the horizon.

Huecuto looked about in desperation. "We're gunna die, aren't we, Cap'n?"

Ploarchos grabbed the wiry little helmsman's hand and placed it firmly on the *Draco's* wheel. He smiled down at the shipmate he'd trusted to steer keep his beloved vessel for many years.

"Man your post. Set the course."

Huecuto smiled weakly up at his captain. "Aye, Captain. The course is set."

The Master of the Whip placed his other hand on his latigo and locked a defiant gaze on the tsunami. The wave crest vanished into the clouds. The ocean became vertical.

The earth shook. Bodies and debris on the deck danced about. Deck planks cracked and split.

Ploarchos gripped the helm. "Hold together, Lady. Hold on just a little longer until you'll feel the sea once more."

"Cap'n…"

The monster devoured the Serpent Lady, and raced north.

***

Amiran now fully appreciated Leviathan's fear.

The force that plummeted from the sky had already begun to rip the world apart.

The scene unfolding to the south defied anything in Amiran's experience or study. The Grand Master Scholar had no intellectual framework to describe the unfolding scene. A northern gale screamed around the mountain toward a boiling southern horizon. Deafening thunder shook the mountain as sooty clouds belched fireballs across the sky. Amiran instinctively understood hellish destruction would soon be unleashed upon them. Reaching the summit only a few hundred feet above was their only hope.

Amiran placed Elda behind the chest to shield her from the wind. He donned his navigation kit, and wasted no time stripping the dead of whatever rags they possessed, including a small blanket. He hastily wrapped them around Elda.

Olmecs and several slaves bounded down the slope toward them.

Amiran shouted for help. They ignored him, snatched discarded supplies, and scurried back up. Amiran tried to gauge how long it would take to carry Elda to the top and then return to retrieve the chest. That's when he spotted a small rock outcropping perhaps eighty yards above and just to the trail's right. It looked just wide enough.

Amiran looked back to see an ink-black cloud swallowing the horizon. The lake visibly shrank, as if being sucked downriver. Awestruck, Amiran watched the approaching storm in all its malignant glory as it consumed the grasslands. Unusual wisps danced across the undulating cloud tops. In that moment, Amiran's intellect finally comprehended what he beheld — a wave rivaling the mountains hurtled towards them.

Amiran threw Elda over his shoulder, grasped the chest's handle, and pulled with all his might. He dug in his heels, trying not to slide or drop Elda. The chest seemed to have grown heavier, stubbornly surrendering only inches. Then, the northern gale ceased. For a long moment, deafening silence reigned.

Then a concussion smacked Amiran from behind, sending him tumbling uphill and spilling Elda. A hot hurricane swept up the mountain, peppering Amiran with stinging dust and pebbles. He shielded his head as the mountain trembled again. Finally, he dared to look.

Far below, the tsunami broke against the mountainside. Filthy, boiling rapids clawed their way up the slopes. Geysers erupted skyward, dousing Amiran in warm, salty mist.

Knowing they had only minutes to live, Amiran struggled to stand against the howling wind. He snatched Elda and dashed up the mountain. Around him, the earth started to crumble into landslides. Boulders tumbled by. Amiran's lungs screamed for air and his thighs burned, but he dared not slow. He heard the flood close on his heels like a wolf.

Mesmerized by the destruction, Leviathan and Quexil barely gave Amiran a glance as he scurried over the summit's rim. Amiran gently set Elda down and collapsed, struggling to catch his breath. To Amiran's surprise, the summit was more of a plateau than a peak. Slaves, and even a few Olmecs, cowered in huddles away from the rim. Supplies had been hastily dumped in heaps across the expansive plateau.

Amiran's legs trembled as he struggled to stand. He stumbled to join the spectators lining the rim. He needed to see what would happen next. The scholar had to witness this cataclysmic event, even if it was his last living act. Waves churned only a few hundred feet below as the slope began to melt into the maelstrom. Then Amiran spotted the Expedition Chest. The ark containing mankind's combined knowledge since the dawn of time slipped sideways, and then tumbled into the flood's waiting jaws.

The scholar dropped to his knees and sobbed into his hands.

As if unsatisfied with the sacrifice, the waters continued to climb. The Olmecs fled from the edge, leaving only Leviathan, Quexil, and Amiran along the rim. Then, the flood halted its upward march only feet below the summit. Waves sprayed them with filthy salt water. A dark ocean stretched forever, and surged through what only moments ago was a mountain range. Now it was an island chain. Lightning flashed across the sky as fat raindrops began to fall.

"What does all this mean, Great Paqua?" Quexil, pale as any Erubian, looked up at his god.

"It means we're going to be here for a while." Leviathan turned to Amiran, his expression unreadable. "Establish camp."

**

With his betrayal, Olorun had paid his way into the Alabaster Pyramid. While a new Great Purge raged through Atlantis, he'd surrendered himself to all he had been denied. With a blue flame from his fingertip, Poseidon had burned away Olorun's brand, speaking the words, "Freedom awaits you beyond the flames." He'd beckoned the poet to enter the naos beyond the throne. Olorun had approached, but hesitated when his bare feet touched the pitted floor below

Leviathan's Pillar. "No scholar has ever set foot in that place," Olorun had whispered to himself.

"There are no more scholars." Poseidon had smiled seductively and wrapped his arm around Olorun's waist. Olorun had passed beneath the portal to claim his reward, and left behind the tortured screams of those he once called "brother."

Deep in the carnal darkness, the poet lost himself, and all sense of time. Here, nothing was denied except light. Unlimited wine, pleasure, and the White God dulled the scholar's once formidable intellect, but could not absolve his guilt. Enduring a slow spiritual death, he wandered numbly in the luxurious abyss. The deeper he went, the more horrible the pleasures. Ecstasy and suffering became indistinguishable.

Time resumed its dominion when incredible power shook the pyramid's roots. Thunder, like 10,000 hurricanes, beat against the stone mountain. The marble floor rippled under his feet. Water poured into the darkness, extinguishing lamps and lives. The underworld's denizens fled like rats from its bowels. Among the panicked, Olorun fled up the staircases, abandoning darkness and seeking the light. After what seemed an eternity, the Alabaster Pyramid vomited a handful of survivors into the throne room.

Olorun stumbled to the throne room's exterior balcony and leaned against the parapet. He shielded his eyes against the brilliant sunlight, and beheld the unimaginable.

Atlantis had vanished.

Muddy rapids stretched to the horizon. Nothing remained above the turbulent sea except the Alabaster Pyramid. No evidence remained of where once the Central Canal ran true east where the sun rose on the spring equinox. Any trace the greatest city on earth once existed had been erased. Even the soaring seven spires of the King's Palace, which rivaled the Alabaster Pyramid in height, were gone.

Master Alec's warning echoed in his mind. *If it breaks all at once, a wall of water a mile high and thousands of miles across will descend down the Hahawakpa River basin and pour into the Sea of Leviathan. Once there, it can only funnel through one place before it pours into Atlas's Ocean.*

An enormous crash beside him sent Olorun spilling to the balcony floor. He shielded his head as ripping pain tore through his back. Wincing, Olorun struggled to stand. He felt blood running down his back. Bright limestone chunks littered what was left of the balcony. Its northern third had been cleaved away. Highly polished limestone blocks that sheathed the pyramid's face, and gave it its name, shattered and tumbled into the floodwaters. The dull granite underneath almost looked black.

Small figures below caught his attention. Hundreds were scrambling up the pyramid's face, trying to flee the disaster. The waters were rapidly overtaking those that did not get crushed by the falling limestone.

The Alabaster Pyramid is a mountain almost 500 feet above the city, and 600 feet above sea level, Olorun thought. *The granite underneath is immoveable! Each stone weighs over two tons. The pyramid will survive.*

The balcony trembled again and then shook. Olorun felt the floor drop slightly. Below, the frothing waters surged, claiming all those climbing the pyramid's east face.

The waters were rising, but the pyramid sank deeper with each tremor. His only hope hinged on reaching the Celestial Platform at the pyramid's summit, where Poseidon would hold his Renewal Ceremony. The stairs were along the temple's southern face. He could reach the stairs through the throne room.

Olorun reentered the pyramid and hobbled through the throne room. His path only lit by the four ceiling slits and the balcony entrance, he stumbled over debris and bodies. Water from the central fountain and the four canals made the floor slick. With each step, the searing pain in his back intensified and shot down his legs.

Then the world shook again. Olorun slipped and fell sideways across something hard. Stabbing pain shot through his neck, and then nothing. The agonizing pain he had felt moments ago vanished. Olorun lay on his side, facing the throne. He tried to get up, but his body would not obey. He tried to call out for help, but couldn't summon enough breath.

Now he could hear the flood churning outside. Master Scholar Olorun knew his end had come.

A metallic groan echoed throughout the throne room. A thin, crimson light ray beamed down upon a man slumped on the throne, head in hands. Olorun tried to call out to Poseidon, but no sound came forth. Another metallic shrill echoed, followed by more light pouring down upon the throne. A translucent vision glided into view. She skimmed just above her shimmering reflection on the floor. Flowing white robes trailed behind her. She passed by one of the great mirrors Poseidon had turned away from the sun centuries ago. It tilted upwards as she passed. Its unlubricated hinges protested but could not resist the ghostly woman's power. She waved her hand at the final mirror, and sunset hues exploded across the throne room. Awe banished Olorun's fear.

She stood before Poseidon. The crimson light didn't illuminate her as much as it infused her. When she spoke, she became like a mirror, reflecting and directing a greater power. Olorun recognized her words. She spoke in the First Tongue, as recorded in the Ancient of Ancients.

"Uzza, judgement is upon us. Your time has come to depart the Water."

Poseidon lifted his head, his expression stoic. "I am ready, Gaia. Take me home."

She raised her arms. "Let the spirit and the flesh be parted."

The world shook, and the flood gushed into the throne room. The Alabaster Pyramid slipped below the waves, and

Atlantis, along with the world as it was before, vanished forever.

Part 4: The Canyon

"They have become like us. Nothing they dream to do will be impossible." - Poseidon to his offspring regarding mortals, from the *Ancient of Ancients.*

- The Chronicle of Fu Xi.

44: In the Belly of the Snake.

"Mercy is the sweetest form of resistance." - *Lo Proverb.*

- The Chronicle of Fu Xi.

***

"There must be another way."

"This is the only way," Zelko replied, gesturing with both hands to the inky crack descending into the earth.

Atamoda shook her head rapidly. "I will not go into the underworld."

"It is not the underworld, patesi-le." Zelko shrugged. "It is just my cave. A good place to protect goats from wolves in summer."

"Only the a-g'an dead dwell below the earth."

"We must and we will." Amiran didn't look up as he lowered the heavy leather bag from his shoulder and placed it at his feet. He opened the drawstring and removed two cloth-wrapped torches. He paused for a moment and felt the damp satchel occupying most of the bag's volume. Thankfully, it was cold. The slightest warming would signal the satchel was no longer properly sealed, and the musk glands inside would soon detonate.

Amiran retied the bag and glanced down the mountainside. Pre-dawn mist filled the gorge. "Soon Quexil's dogs will follow."

A timber pile partially obscured the cave, which overlooked the narrow trail winding through the gorge.

Zelko had to zigzag across the steep ridge several times in the darkness before finding the opening. They were so close to the camp Atamoda could hear voices carrying down the mountainside. If the cave had been only a few more yards up the gorge, or not covered with flood debris, it would have been discovered weeks ago. If it were daylight, they would be plainly visible to anyone on the trail.

"I've looked up this slope every time I've entered the gorge, and never suspected there was a cave here," Amiran said.

"Even before all of this timber, no one could see it from below." Zelko winked. "If I had been faster and not so old, I would have reached it before those red demons caught me."

Amiran thought about Zelko's statement. "True, but then you'd be dead."

Zelko frowned for a moment, and then chuckled. "For once, being old paid off."

Amiran knelt on a flat rock at the cave opening, breaking tiny twigs from the timber. He collected them in a loose pile. He furiously struck a flint stone with his knife hilt. "We will have light, Atamoda, so there is nothing to fear. Zelko says if we don't delay, two torches will be enough to get us to the other side."

Amiran's reassurance fell on deaf ears. Thinking about descending into the fissure made Atamoda breathe heavy. Even in the frigid air, Atamoda broke out in a cold sweat. A dank, fetid smell wafted up from the hole, like something long dead. She gulped, struggling to keep her voice under control. "Perhaps we can skirt the camp from above. If we are quiet and surefooted, they will not see us."

Flint gave birth to a small flame amongst the twigs. "We would leave a trail. The Olmecs would capture us before mid-morning." Amiran held the unlit torch and looked up at her sternly. "I'm going to light this, and when I do, we are committed. We must waste no time. Zelko will go first with the torch. You will follow, and I will be right behind."

Zelko gave Amiran a hard look, his scarred face almost looking sinister. "We have an agreement, yes?"

"Yes," Amiran said impatiently.

"What agreement?" Atamoda asked, looking between the two men.

"When we reach the other side, we go west, away from the northern mountains," Zelko said.

"You have my word, Zelko. We stay as far from the fortress mountains as possible. When it's safe, we head west and take the satchel to the Gray-Eyed Queen."

"Good." Zelko nodded, satisfied.

She started to ask *safe from what?* when the torch flashed to life, startling her. Amiran looked at Atamoda and held up the bag. "Leviathan cannot claim his prize without this. If we can find the Gray-Eyed Queen before Leviathan finds us, we've won a significant victory, and bought Kol-ok and Elda time."

"What about the other satchel in the urn?" Atamoda asked.

"That won't do him any good, at least not yet."

In the distance, a drum began a slow and monotonous beat. "The army is abandoning base camp. If they don't know we're gone, they will shortly."

The light made Atamoda feel naked and exposed against the ridge. She felt bile beginning to creep up her throat. Amiran handed the torch to Zelko, who quickly scurried into the hole. With some effort, Amiran hefted the leather bag over his shoulder. "I'm right behind you. Be brave, Atamoda. Just follow the light, and you will be fine."

Atamoda swallowed her fear, and descended into the earth.

***

With his army at his back, the demigod surveyed the way ahead. The column stretched deep into the slit-like chasm from whence they came. Leviathan studied where the chasm intersected a much wider canyon. Here, a shallow east-west running river meandered through deep mud. Beyond the canyon, high cliffs vanished into mist.

Slave and warrior silently looked on. Five blood-soaked pikes lined the slope overlooking the canyon. Each shaft impaled a warrior. Fifteen Olmecs formed a circle at their dangling feet, each letting their slain comrade's still-warm blood fill their mouths and cover their bodies before kneeling at Leviathan's feet. Quexil knelt before them, head bowed low before his god.

The demigod considered the impaled bodies. "What has become of my favored sons?"

"Your jaguars are here, Great Paqua!" Quexil flattened himself in the mud at Leviathan's feet.

"Does the fire of conquest still burn in your breast, or have you grown soft eating fish and lounging in camp? Or should I hand your obsidian clubs to the slaves? I am beginning to think they would serve me more faithfully." Leviathan scornfully considered the bodies. "These five let *slaves*"—he spat the word, rage threatening to slip loose again—"slip past them."

"Set your mighty jaguars loose, Great One, and we shall bring back their hearts!"

"My mighty jaguars have become lazy dogs!" Leviathan kicked Quexil, sending him tumbling down the slope.

Leviathan stretched out his arms as if to encompass the sky and shouted, "I am betrayed at every turn!" He turned to face his army. Elda stood at the caravan's head, tightly hugging herself against the cold and horror. He gently cupped her chin. "Swear again you know nothing of Twice-Burned's betrayal."

"I swear," she said, eyes downcast.

"I believe you." Leviathan turned her head to look upon the two mangled corpses that were once his body slaves. "I believed them, too." He smiled down at her. "You have served me well. Continue to care for the boy. I sense you have feelings for him, and that is good. Soon, he will fulfill a great destiny, and your loyalty will be rewarded a thousandfold." Leviathan turned his attention to the warrior standing behind her. "Send her back to the boy."

The warrior escorted Elda away, and Leviathan returned his attention to the kneeling Olmecs. Quexil had extricated himself from the mud and returned to his place at Leviathan's feet. The demigod ignored him.

Leviathan pointed the sword to the line's right. "You five will follow the gorge west." He then pointed the blade to the middle five. "You will follow the gorge east." Finally, he aimed the blade at the line's left. "You shall find safe passage across the canyon, and then scout north." He lowered the blade and addressed them all, "Those that return with Twice-Burned, the goatherd, and the harlot will drink the blood of those who do not."

They remained motionless, heads bent to the earth.

"Go."

They snapped to life and scattered into the canyon.

Leviathan addressed Quexil. "Rise." His captain dutifully obeyed. Leviathan continued, "Our progress is too slow."

"The way ahead is blocked by mud so thick it swallows everything, Great Lord."

"If Twice-Burned could find a way, then shouldn't you?"

"He left no trail," Quexil responded.

"Am I to believe they went south?" Leviathan fumed. "Have the scholars discovered a way to walk on water, or have your jaguars lost the ability to track prey?"

"No, Great Paqua."

"Follow the northern scouts. When they find passage through the mire, report back to me."

Quexil bowed and slowly backed away.

"Quexil, one more thing."

His captain looked up.

"If none of the scouts return with Twice-Burned and the harlot, you shall occupy the next pike."

Quexil bowed low again and scurried away.

***

Leviathan's army slithered like a snake down the mountainside, carrying Kol-ok along like a piece of undigested food trapped in its belly. A solitary drum sounded a dry, monotonous beat from somewhere ahead. Around his cage, half-dead slaves pressed against one another as they shambled along the narrow trail. The mountainside dropped off precipitously to the left. In the distance, a great body of water stretched to the horizon under a slate-gray sky.

Kol-ok sat cross-legged, wrapped in heavy furs. Shame filled his heart as he watched the four men struggle supporting his cage. He didn't understand how they could carry him, let alone walk, as emaciated as they were. Every time one slipped or fell, Kol-ok feared he would go tumbling down the mountainside to his death.

He desperately looked about for Elda or his mother. It continued this way all morning until they entered the dark chasm. Then the drum ceased. The porters lowered his cage and collapsed in exhaustion. Three porters lay against the slope, bony chests heaving. A few feet away, the fourth bearer had stopped moving entirely, unblinking eyes fixed skyward. In a few minutes, the Olmecs replaced him with another starving slave and dragged the corpse away.

Maybe the worst is over, Kol-ok thought. *Maybe from here the going will be easier.* The defile ahead squeezed between the mountains, as if they were marching into a monster's jaws.

A haggard old slave woman stumbled under a heavy yoke swinging two jars. She stopped by the cage, carefully set down the yoke, and dipped Kol-ok a gourd from one of the jars. He shook his head and pointed to the bearers. She looked about nervously and offered it to Kol-ok again.

"Give them a drink first," Kol-ok tried to tell her in Atlantean.

"You must drink first — it is Leviathan's command." Elda stepped into view. "They cannot drink until you do."

Kol-ok leaned his face against the bars and took a token sip. "Fine, now take care of them."

The slave nodded obediently and tended to the porters.

Elda slipped a moldy bread wedge and jerky scrap through the bars. "Eat. It's all we'll get today."

Her wet cheeks and red-rimmed eyes testified to recent tears.

"What happened?" he asked.

Elda looked around like a trapped animal. She had been his beacon of hope during the long, desolate weeks. Seeing her like this terrified him almost as much as the day they'd been captured.

"Amiran and the goatherd escaped last night," Elda whispered.

Kol-ok repositioned on his knees and gripped the bars. "Did Amiran tell you anything?"

"No, they just vanished. Leviathan flew into a rage. He tortured his body slaves. He impaled last night's sentries." She sobbed for a moment. "He questioned me…" Fresh tears welled up. "Your mother vanished with them."

Kol-ok slumped and leaned back.

"Amiran abandoned me! The slaves are dying! Ten perished this morning. The Olmecs gather the bodies for butcher." She paused and stared into the chasm. "I fear something horrible awaits us up there, Kol-ok. We are all going to die, one by one."

Kol-ok swallowed his own panic and took her hand. "My mother would not have left without good reason. I know this. They have a plan, they must! And we must have faith in them."

Elda didn't seem to hear him.

"Elda, be strong for both of us."

Elda backed away, shaking her head. "I can't…I can't anymore." She turned and fled.

Kol-ok glanced over at the porters still resting against the slope. They had begun to shiver. Fate had presented them only three choices, and each led to the grave: freeze, starve, or collapse from exhaustion. Fate had only offered Kol-ok one path, and that still remained a mystery. Leviathan was saving him for something Elda didn't know or wouldn't divulge.

His mother's escape filled Kol-ok with hope, not dread. He prayed to the Nameless God for her deliverance. Kol-ok also prayed for Elda. If she couldn't be strong for him, he would be strong for her. He could not control his fate., only how he dealt with it. That thought gave Kol-ok a strange peace.

"Hey," he called out to the nearest porter, a man perhaps as old as Kol-ok's father. He possessed those strange, narrow eyes common among many slaves. The porter looked at him dully. Kol-ok broke off some of the jerky and held it out. A spark appeared in the man's eyes. He looked about to see if any of the guards were watching, and then cautiously approached the cage for a morsel. One by one, Kol-ok did the same for each porter until his meager ration was gone.

There were five wolf skins stuffed into the cage's narrow bottom. One by one, Kol-ok gave them to the porters while the guards were not paying attention. With suspicious gratitude, they covered their heads and shoulders. The remaining wolf skin did very little except blunt the cage's sharp edges. Kol-ok's knees ached, and his legs and buttocks became noticeably colder and far more uncomfortable.

He held his breath as the guards passed by. Their eyes passed over the porters and somehow didn't notice, or care, about their new cloaks. The slaves looked at one another in relief, and then at Kol-ok in true gratitude.

In the distance, the drum resumed. Whips cracked up and down the line. The porters shouldered their burden. One of the porters gave him a fleeting smile.

Kol-ok was once more in the belly of the snake, slithering into the gorge's darkness.

45: The Crooked Spear.

"Ezra had been taught from an early age to hide his weaknesses. Lo men let our weaknesses simmer far closer to the surface than the hardened steppe dwellers did, or even the Hur-po. The a-g'an knew someone always lurked in the shadows, ready to exploit their weakness. The Lo lived in light, and knew few shadows. Trust ran in our blood.

"Ezra found it easy to give strength, but didn't know how to accept it. He could quickly trust someone with his life, but not his heart." - Conversations with the Uros.

- The Chronicle of Fu Xi.

***

The bonfire blazed as if the Lo intended to burn down all the Nameless God had not drowned. They had been without fire since their braziers were swept overboard months ago. The firelight brightly illuminated the canyon wall to the cliff tops high above them. Tall shadows danced against the yellow-clay cliffs as people passed in front of the flames. Ezra welcomed the heat, but not the light.

The Lo camped where the deep canyon opened to the mountainside. The fire's heat blanketed the sandy beach beside what, only hours earlier, had been a raging river. Now it had diminished to a creek that tumbled down the mountain in a series of small waterfalls.

The fire comforted Ezra's body, but disturbed his thoughts. *We are in a strange land, but we've posted no pickets*, he thought. That part of his mind spoke with Asul's voice, the man who was once his teacher and captain of House Azubehl. *A good leader continuously evaluates his situation and that of his forces,* Asul would say, *and always assumes the enemy is watching.*

Who else could have survived the Deluge, he thought? *'The world is wiped clean,' isn't that what Aizarg had said?* Ezra tried to enjoy the fire and relax, and be thankful for the abundance of wood and fresh water.

Shattered timber choked the canyon. The raging river that marooned them had shrunk to a shadow of its former power. The water had turned icy cold, with no trace of salt. *Water and wood are not in short supply*, he thought, *but food and shelter are another matter.*

Ezra and Su-gár reclined in the shadows just beyond the firelight. She rested her head on Ezra's chest while Bat-or slept between them. Aizarg's child had been asking for something to eat all evening, and wanted to know if Alaya had gone to the same place his mother and brother had. Fussy and crying, the child had finally fallen asleep under the fire's spell. Su-gár's intimate presence against his body and the child at his feet stirred feelings in Ezra he'd never entertained before. *Is this what a husband and a father feels like?*

Ezra had known battle, and he had killed. Yet, among these men, these *good* men, he still felt like a boy.

Aizarg, the man he admired almost as much as Asul and Okta, held council. *Almost.*

Ezra sensed a deeply buried brokenness in the Uros. Ezra didn't judge Aizarg for that, but didn't understand it either.

The men argued among themselves well into the night, each taking their turn advocating a course of action. Two camps had formed, one led by Levidi and the other by Ghalen. Behind them, the women whispered. They had no Isp to give them voice at council. When each man spoke, he held a crudely fashioned spear, nothing more than a sharpened stick. When finished, he handed it to the next man. During the voyage, Okta had explained many Lo customs to Ezra, including the Council of Boats. The spear was how the clan recognized the current speaker.

Aizarg held up his hand, and everyone fell silent. The firelight accentuated every crag and wrinkle in his face. He looked a thousand years old. "Ghalen shall hold the spear once more, and then Levidi. After that, I will decide."

Ghalen pulled the spear from the sand at Aizarg's feet. He slowly paced around the fire, the light reflecting off his shaggy blond mane and beard. *He looks like a lion*, Ezra thought. *He is Aizarg's natural successor.*

Ghalen turned to Levidi. "We've searched diligently for our lost, including my beloved Sana. We all mourn. If Sana were here, she would say the obvious — there is no food or game. Every day we delay is a day closer to our doom."

Levidi kept his eyes downcast, face like stone. The tension was palpable.

Ghalen strode around the fire, addressing the people. "We have nothing. Starvation is only days away if we do not freeze to death first." Ghalen pointed east into the darkness. "Okta showed us the way! At dawn's first light, we should follow him and the sea. Where there is water, there is hope. We must leave these cursed highlands, descend to the lowlands, and follow the sea. These mountains are death." Ghalen plunged the spear into the sand before the Uros and returned to his place.

Ezra saw many nods among the men and women.

"Do you see how several have migrated to Ghalen's side of the fire?" Su-gár whispered. "If we were in boats, they would be paddling to Ghalen's side of the Kol-lo-hely."

Ezra sensed a chasm forming between the two friends. He hated to see them in opposition.

"I will hear Levidi speak," Aizarg said.

Levidi sprung up, snatched the spear, and began speaking quickly. "I do not argue with Ghalen about where we should go, only when! All I ask for is more time. We have not exhausted our search. Alaya, Spako, and Sana are missing. It doesn't mean they're dead." He pointed to his chest emphatically. "We're not dead! They must be somewhere up that canyon. We are their brothers and sisters, their people. They need us. It is our duty to find them. Dead or alive, we cannot leave this land until we have found them." Levidi searched the Uros's face for a hint of compassion. The Lo talked excitedly among themselves. The murmurs died away as Aizarg stood. "We've searched all day and into the twilight and found no sign of our people."

"We both know that was only a scratch," Levidi responded. "The barge traveled deep into the canyon before it finally broke apart. Our people could be strung out for miles. If we abandon them now, what does that say about us?"

"Our children will starve if we stay here!" a woman shouted. "It's getting cold, and we have no skins to keep us warm!"

The council fell into chaos.

"Ghalen's plan is sensible," Ezra whispered. "The people are hungry and frightened."

"Levidi is frightened for those he loves." Su-gár looked up at Ezra. "I understand his helplessness. I felt that way when my father went to find the Narim. I knew he wasn't coming back. And I knew my mother wasn't coming back when the water demons took her. Levidi is grasping for hope."

Ezra felt lost, too. He remembered when House Azubehl of Hur-ar fell to usurpers. His sister Sarah had been sold into slavery. His beloved mother, First Wife to Prince Azubehl, had been worked to death in the kitchens. He had

401

escaped assassination, and survived in the most unimaginable place, Hur-ar's sewers. Those terrible days eventually led him to this moment.

"Hope shows up in the strangest places," he said. Su-gár pressed close to him. They were both alone in this world. Ezra wrestled with his feelings. If he should dare love Su-gár, would fate snatch her from him, too?

Ezra's attention drifted back to the council. The uproar slowly died as Levidi turned to Aizarg with a hardness and determination Ezra had never seen him display before. "If the Uros decides that we must go east, then I will go west. Aizarg, you say the way home is always forward. Wherever she is, that is my home. I will not abandon my wife." Levidi plunged the spear into the sand and returned to the shadows.

Aizarg wearily picked up the spear as if it weighed more than the enormous wedding barges that brought them to this place. He studied the shaft before finally speaking. "It is not simply by chance we find ourselves here on this beach, under the stars. Given the river's terrible gauntlet, and our raft's poor condition, we should have lost many more than we did. I sense the Nameless God's hand in our deliverance, guiding us to an unknown fate. Yes, we have lost much, but we still cling to hope and each other. The Nameless God has not forsaken us. We must also cling to the memories of our dead.

"Those I have lost still speak to me *here*." He tapped his heart. "I hear Atamoda, and Kol-ok"—Aizarg glanced at Ezra—"and Sarah speaking to my heart. I'm sure all of you hear your loved ones in the quiet moments, or when you are most frightened.

"Atamoda's spirit stays my tongue when I want to speak too quickly or harshly. Sana's spirit will stir my blood, too, perhaps during those times when I may not act forcefully enough. My daughter's voice seems the most pronounced now, perhaps because I walk once again on dry land in a strange place, surrounded by mountains." He smiled warmly. "I once climbed a mountain, and I did so with my eyes closed. I was far too terrified to open them. I would have failed had it not been for the quiet voices of those not afraid. They gave me their strength, and I trusted them.

"Sarah's voice is speaking to me now, brightly and clearly, lighting my way just as this fire lights the night." Aizarg turned to Ezra and held out the spear. "She tells me to let her brother, the son of Okta, speak."

Su-gár nudged Ezra. "Take the spear."

Ezra found himself standing uncomfortably close to the flames, holding a stick pretending to be a spear. He'd never been good at wielding a spear, and didn't feel any more comfortable holding this one. Now the voices of those he loved filled his head: Sarah, Asul, Mother, Left-Hand, Okta…which should he listen to?

Still looking at the spear, Ezra began to speak. He felt like he was outside himself. The words sprung forth without conscious thought. "The Lo's prowess upon the waters brought us here alive." He looked up at Ghalen. "You didn't leave the sea, it left you. It carried Okta away and left nothing to the east, no animals, no forest, nothing but mud. If we chase the sea, we will die before we ever catch it."

"Then where do we go?" Ghalen asked impatiently.

"The mountains," Ezra replied.

The council erupted into chaos.

Ezra caught Su-gár's eyes. She motioned as if lifting the spear. Ezra raised the spear over his head, and the voices slowly quieted down. "Beyond the canyon, we've caught glimpses of green highlands. Those are meadows untouched by the flood. I learned to hunt in high mountain pastures like those. If any animals survived, that is where we will find them." Ezra looked up beyond where the firelight cast shadows on the canyon's rim. "Those pastures aren't covered with snow. If there are still animals alive, they won't return to the lowlands as long as they have food. Up there, we might find enough game to survive. We can make a base camp just above the canyon, and send hunting teams to higher elevations. Others can scavenge in the canyon for timber and firewood."

"We cannot climb these cliffs!" Levidi shouted.

"The walls are made of clay, not stone. I have seen several places where the cliffs are crumbling. Finding a way out shouldn't prove difficult."

"Why don't we just camp here?" a woman asked.

"If it rains again in the highlands, even just a little, it could flood the canyon without warning. We should not linger here." He also wanted to say the canyon was an indefensible position, but prudence held his tongue. "There may be a way out to the west, farther up the canyon. I recommend we camp here for now, and send a small party upstream to find a way out. We could also use that opportunity to search for our missing, including Ba-lok and those from the other barge."

Aizarg looked directly at Levidi.

Levidi seemed visibly relieved.

Another spoke from beyond the firelight. "We'll need spears. Real spears. There's plenty of wood here, and even good stone for spearpoints."

Ghalen grinned at Ezra like his old self. "If you think there is game in the highlands, well, by Psatina, let's go get it!"

"We can use boiled bark strips to secure the spearpoints," someone else added. "It's not as strong, but it will work."

"Boiled with what?" a young woman shouted. "We have no pots."

"Bah," an older woman scoffed. "There's plenty of clay. Give us a day and we'll have pots for boiling."

Ezra stood dumbfounded as the Lo began to converse with one another about spear making, pottery, and dozens of other ideas feeding off his plan. Then, one by one, the people stood and repositioned behind Ezra.

Aizarg took the spear. "You have done well."

"I just know places like this, that's all." Ezra shrugged in dismay as almost all the Lo now sat on his side of the fire.

"That's enough. Before dawn, take Ghalen and Levidi and find our people, and a way out of the canyon. We will busy ourselves here preparing for the journey to the highlands."

Ezra returned to Su-gár, who gave him a warm hug. He looked down at the sleeping Bat-or, and a sudden pang stabbed him deep inside.

Everyone who has ever put their faith in me is dead, he thought.

***

No one remained awake in the deep predawn. He slithered like smoke through the sleeping mortals clumped around the bonfire's embers. To anyone bothering to open their eyes, he would appear as a smokey wisp, or be sensed as a sudden chill.

They hadn't even bothered to establish a watch, he thought with amusement. *They think they are safe*. He knew their peril had just begun.

He found Aizarg curled close to the embers, his child snuggled closely. His presence congealed into a dark dragon's head looming over them, ghostly teeth bared and ready to strike.

"You have lost your precious staff, Uros," he hissed. "How unfortunate."

Nuwa and the orichalcum staff had stood between the Black Dragon and the Lo. Without a mortal host, Nuwa grew weaker. Fate or the Enemy stripped the staff from the Uros, and abandoned the Lo to the Black Dragon's mercies.

He had no mercies.

At his earthly kingdom's doorstep, the Black Dragon possessed great power. It would only take a mere thought to slaughter them all. Yet, these mortals were now inconsequential. Staff or no staff, their part in this game was over. The Red Dagger drifted ever closer to Leviathan's clutches. This is all that mattered.

"Sleep well, Uros. Enjoy the last glowing embers of peace. In the coming days, you will know only suffering. I leave your fate to Leviathan and my son."

The Black Dragon dissolved into the night.

46: Ambush.

We entered the canyon as survivors, and emerged as combatants.

- The Chronicle of Fu Xi.

***

In some strange way, Virag almost pitied the Minnow Clan. They had survived the Cataclysm that, according to Aizarg, had been summoned by a god to destroy mankind. The Minnow Clan's elation making landfall died inside a muddy ravine. A new threat replaced the Cataclysm, one the Lo were ill-suited to handle.

The flood retreated to the hazy western horizon, leaving a wasteland in its wake. The Minnow Clan had abandoned the raft teetering on the mountainside. Following the narrow trail Kus-ge had discovered, Ba-lok led them east into the mountains. The trek proved muddy and slow. As mid-morning approached, the sun struggled to assert its dominance from behind lifeless clouds. They struggled through a ravine so narrow only two people could walk abreast. Ba-lok called a halt, and the men leading the ragged column began to squabble among themselves. The women and children huddled in the ravine's center, where the sun reached the bottom. They used this opportunity to eat, and to feed the children. Virag and Kus-ge lingered at the column's rear, where Zirev served as rear guard.

Zirev leaned against a makeshift spear. Bazee ran through the mud to her father to give him a jerky slice before scurrying back to her mother. He slowly chewed, seemingly content. Ahead, the men loudly argued whether to continue up the ravine or backtrack and look for another way. Their shouts echoed loudly.

Virag found a boulder large enough to keep him out of the mud and sat upon it. With sucking sounds, he extricated his feet from the icy mire. Virag scraped gluey mud globs from his feet and legs. Kus-ge slogged toward him. Without even glancing at Virag, she slipped into the shadows between the boulder and the ravine wall, and squatted. Virag turned and, with irritation, thought she might be using his resting place to relieve herself. She caught his eye and nodded up. Virag followed her gaze to the ravine's rim, where the remaining clouds had finally surrendered to a brilliant blue sky. A dark figure watched from above.

"Damn," Virag muttered to himself and joined Kus-ge behind the boulder. He waved his hand to get Zirev's attention.

Zirev considered them as if they were mad. "What are you two doing?" he spoke with his mouth full before a thrown dagger plunged through his neck. He slowly fell forward into the mud, still looking at them as if they were mad.

The attack struck simultaneously from columns to the front and rear. The Lo heavily outnumbered their attackers, but it didn't matter. The killing was over in mere moments. Five Lo men lay dead, including Ba-lok.

They separated the men and women and began ransacking the clan's meager belongings. Virag found himself on his knees with the rest of the Lo men. The red-skinned warriors beat several men at random, and took the younger women into the shadows to use them. The children wailed in despair.

A warrior snatched Kus-ge up by the hair. She coolly met his stare, but Virag noticed her hand instinctively brushing her thigh for her daggers.

The red warrior wrapped her hair around his fist and bent Kus-ge forward, his intent clear. The one Virag pegged as their leader by his arrogant smirk and profuse tattoos kicked the underling off Kus-ge. He snatched the dragon necklace from her neck before slapping Kus-ge to the mud. The leader held it up to his underling and barked something. He looked warily from the dragon pendant to Kus-ge, and then tucked it in a pouch tied to his loincloth.

Perhaps the leader has laid claim to her, he thought, but his behavior was puzzling.

Kus-ge didn't appear ruffled by the encounter, nor did she seem upset at Ba-lok's bloody body only a few yards away. She kept quiet.

Kus-ge is studying them, looking for an opportunity, he thought. Her eyes met his, and an unspoken understanding passed between them.

If we work together, we'll survive. To hell with the rest.

If she had slipped into madness during the long voyage, it seemed to have passed for the present time.

Shortly after, the red warriors prodded the Minnow Clan up the ravine like wolves driving sheep. Virag found it unsettling they forced the Minnow men to shoulder the dead. He found the red warriors' filed teeth equally disturbing. They penetrated deeper into the mountains as the day wore on. Virag took the opportunity to study the enemy.

Their skin appeared perpetually sunburned. They spoke in soft syllables, intermittently interrupted by harsh stops and starts. They were squat but graceful and powerfully built, with jet-black hair cut short and even around their heads. Bizarre tattoos, geometric zig-zags and blockish demonic imagery, covered their bodies. Strange, spotted furs draped their shoulders, and loose chainmail (some of the best Virag had ever seen) fell to their waist. Otherwise, they only wore loincloths and no footwear.

Virag strongly suspected these red men hailed from a tribe with a Scythian temperament. Virag had never seen weapons equal their gracefully curved blades, even surpassing the finest Hur steel. The swords and mail sharply contrasted with the primitive clubs tied to their waists. The ornate designs painted on each club matched that warrior's individual tattoos. These strange warriors' mix of primitive and extraordinary weapons and armor perplexed Virag.

As a successful trader, Virag fancied himself an expert on human nature and the steppe's different tribes. He wagered the red men didn't belong in these mountains any more than the Lo did. Mountain living begot certain crafts these people seemed to lack. The Aryans and Havilah wore heavy furs and thick boots crafted from goat, deer, and elk hides. Whatever spotted, short-haired beasts the red men killed to make their shoulder cloaks were clearly not suited for these climes. Virag deduced these men weren't horsemen, either. Their knees were straight, and they were far too nimble on their feet. The swords and chainmail didn't seem part of their nature, either. Virag wagered their clubs, needle-like teeth, and tattoos were better clues to their true origins.

47: The Stream.

"Ezra and Sana saw what we could not." - *Conversations with the Uros.*

- The Chronicle of Fu Xi.

***

Morning's cold overcast gave way to blue skies and warmth as the men trekked west. Around every bend, huge timber heaps and vast mud pits impeded every step. In some places the canyon walls had begun to collapse, but not enough to permit the men to climb out. Hunger became their constant companion. Ezra filled his belly with water from the stream trickling through the canyon's center, but it did little to dull the pain. Worst of all were the biting flies that seemed to swarm from the mud itself.

Levidi always led the way, pressing relentlessly forward. He spoke little. Now, as the sun began to slip toward the horizon, Levidi stood atop the largest timber pile they had encountered, swatting at the flies as he tried to keep his balance. "It completely dams the stream. There is a muddy pond stretching for several hundred paces upstream, and then another timber pile. I can't see any farther than that. We can probably swim it."

Ghalen leaned against his spear. He held up his hand and squinted at the sun silhouetting Levidi. "Do you see a way out of the canyon from up there?"

"No."

Ezra wasn't paying attention to either of them. The clear, cold water flowing around his feet commanded his attention. This water wasn't seeping from under the pile. It seemed to spring from the ground.

"I said I think we can swim it," Levidi shouted again.

Ghalen shouted back, "Sunset is coming. We may have to turn around."

Ezra splashed around in the water, searching for where it bubbled up. His search led him to the canyon's north wall. Here, the water deepened to his knees and grew colder. The current tugged his legs.

"Ezra?" Ghalen called after him.

"This is the fresh water's source," he said. "I think what Levidi is looking at is the remnants of the salt water flood."

Levidi called down, "Yes, the water smells briny and stale."

Ezra stepped around a small outcropping in the canyon wall, and spotted a fissure. "Ghalen! Levidi! Come here!"

In a few moments, all three men stood in the water, studying the fissure. Ezra knelt and peered in. "It's filled with water, but I can see daylight."

"So what?" Levidi said impatiently.

"The stream is cold because it either comes from underground or snowmelt." Ezra snatched a leaf floating by and held it up, grinning. "This is an aspen leaf; it grows in the mountains."

Ghalen's eyes grew wide. "Could this be a way out of the canyon?"

"Maybe," Ezra said. "The tunnel looks plenty wide for one man. I think we should explore it."

To his surprise, both Ghalen and Levidi took a step back.

"What's wrong?"

Ghalen took a deep breath. "To go underground is…evil. Taboo. The underworld is a realm for demons."

Ezra realized they were both genuinely terrified. He found it hard to believe, as these men had faced dangers far worse than this fairly harmless tunnel.

"I'll go. Wait here," Ezra said, trying not to grin. He didn't want his friends to think he was belittling them.

Levidi grabbed his arm. "No, it's too dangerous!"

"Listen to me, both of you. I've been underground before, many times."

Ghalen and Levidi considered Ezra in astonishment. Levidi slowly removed his hand.

"Stay here. It shouldn't take long." Without another word, Ezra slipped into the crack.

He found this place far more preferential to Hur-ar's sewers. The water was clean and clear, and not that confining. Ezra waded farther into the cave as the water deepened. The light came from above. Looking up, he realized this fissure stretched all the way to the surface. Soon, the walls widened, and the light ahead brightened. It wasn't long before Ezra found himself in an enormous vertical cave.

He waded into a wide, clear pool at the bottom of the circular pit. The cave stretched about a hundred paces in diameter. A thin waterfall fell opposite from the fissure. To his right, the cavern's south rim had partially collapsed, forming a wide shoreline. Several tree trunks rested atop an earthen and stone pile that had fallen in from above. The debris formed a crude ramp leading up to the rim.

Heart pounding, he waded back to Levidi and Ghalen. After explaining the fissure was open to the sky, he managed to convince them to follow. In a few moments, they stood together examining the debris pile.

"With a little work, we could fashion a path up the pile," Ghalen said and patted Ezra on the back. "Do you think it leads all the way out of the canyon?"

"There is only one way to find out," Ezra said and began to scurry up the pile.

"We need to keep going west," Levidi said.

Ezra halted and looked back.

Ghalen considered Levidi with patience. "The Uros wanted us to find a way out, too. This could be it."

"He also wanted us to find our lost," Levidi replied.

"Levidi, the way out of the canyon might be before us," Ghalen said. "We must find out before we go on."

Levidi looked back at the fissure, and then up at the deep blue sky above the cavern. "All right." He sighed, clearly exasperated. "But hurry."

Ezra resumed the climb. Soft earth crumbled under his feet, forcing him on all fours. He reached the first tree trunk and scrambled up it. Ezra stood and hopped from one fallen trunk to the next all the way to the top. Behind him, Ghalen followed, albeit at a slower pace. Black soot covered his hands and feet, and Ezra realized these tree trunks had been heavily scorched. Levidi stayed in the cavern, impatiently watching them.

Tall grass lined the rim. Cool air washed over him as Ezra clenched the grass and pulled himself up. He found himself looking over a wondrous sight.

"By the Nameless God, it's beautiful!" Ghalen huffed as he climbed out behind him.

Thick meadow grass, so lush and green it almost hurt to look upon, covered a vast slope rising to the north until it abruptly terminated at iron-gray cliffs. Just ahead, a sparkling stream, perhaps ten paces across, cut through the meadow grass and cascaded into the cavern. The grasslands paralleled the canyon west until they met the hard-blue sky. Widely spaced, blackened tree trunks and stumps dotted the grasslands. The cliffs formed an impregnable, glacier-topped wall blocking the northern horizon. To Ezra, these mountains brought back memories of the landscape surrounding Hur-ar, but on a far greater scale. The canyon twisted through the valley's center like a great serpent.

Beyond the canyon, barren mountains guarded the valley's southern flank.

"What do you see?" Levidi called up.

"Join us and see for yourself!" Ghalen shouted down.

Huffing and muttering the whole climb, Levidi reluctantly joined them. He looked about as if in a daze. "No flies up here," he muttered.

"It looks like there might have been a forest fire," Ezra said.

"Hmm," Ghalen remarked. "Judging by these trunks, this was once a mighty forest."

The landscape's parallels to Hur Valley are uncanny, Ezra thought. This place hearkened to the stump fields along the Hur River.

Ezra began to wander about. He found more trunks and stumps partially hidden in the tall grass. "I think this happened recently, perhaps not long before the Deluge."

"Well, this is all nice and good, but we need to keep going in the canyon," Levidi said.

Ezra turned to Levidi. "From up here, we can follow the canyon much easier, and see everything below."

Levidi's eyes widened. "Of course! Well, what are we waiting for, let's go!"

"We must return to camp and tell the Uros what we've found," Ghalen said.

Ghalen and Levidi began to argue again, and Ezra wanted no part of it. He turned his attention to the stream. He traced its meandering path uphill, eventually losing track of it. Ezra scanned the distant, ice-capped cliffs and spotted a misty waterfall glinting in the sun. *That must be where the stream comes from*, he thought. Ezra knew judging distances accurately in the mountains could be difficult, but he reckoned it would take an hour or more to reach the cliffs.

He turned around, shielded his eyes, and surveyed the valley. The ragged canyon crudely interrupted the valley's otherwise smooth, concave bottom. *It's as if the Deluge carved it out like a sharp knife through flesh*, he thought. Ezra shuddered when he considered the flood's power, and that he had somehow survived.

Ezra knelt beside the stream and scooped a handful of thick, black soil. He sniffed it and rubbed it between his fingers. Ezra had little education in agriculture, but this soil appeared far richer than the dirt in the stump fields that once produced enough wheat to feed Hur-ar.

"This would be a good place to settle," he said aloud. "This land is good for either crops or grazing, and it's defensible from every direction." He looked over his shoulder to see his friends still arguing, and ignoring him.

He dropped the dirt and wiped off his hands. Ezra's heart almost leapt out of his chest when something along the bank caught his eye.

"Come here!" he shouted.

Levidi and Ghalen kept squabbling.

"I said come here!"

"What?" Levidi snapped.

"Look."

They peered over his shoulder.

"Game!" Ghalen exclaimed.

"I've never seen a deer track that big," Levidi said, astonished.

"It's called an elk, and you find them in highlands like these."

"That's fresh," Ghalen said.

"We need bows," Ezra said. "We won't get close enough with spears."

"We need to keep looking for Alaya and the rest." Levidi's tone grew desperate.

"No, Aizarg must know about this place. Our people are hungry and there is game here. That comes first."

"Aren't you concerned about Sana?" Levidi snapped.

"I am concerned!" Ezra had never heard Ghalen raise his voice before. "Those enormous timber piles choking that canyon were forests once! This is testimony to the water's power. It is only by the Nameless God's hand any of us survived those rapids. We should all be dead, Levidi. Either Sana drowned, or she is fine. There is no in between with her. If Sana lives, she will likely find us before we find her. This is what I have accepted in my heart. I've also accepted the reality Spako is probably dead, too, and we'll never see the Minnow Clan again."

"I must find Alaya! She's alone out there." Desperate tears ran down Levidi's cheek. He looked lost, teetering on the hopelessness edge.

Ghalen embraced his friend as Levidi softly sobbed under an avalanche of emotions.

Ezra remembered that horrible hopelessness, watching hidden from a drainpipe in House Azubehl's palace courtyard as a usurper slaughtered those loved. He felt it watching helplessly as Virag the Slaver led Sarah in chains through Hur-ar's gates. and then watching her die in Aizarg's arms.

He hurt for Levidi, and felt powerless to ease his suffering.

Ezra interrupted, "Ghalen, the canyon is too treacherous to navigate at night. Perhaps we should all camp here and in the morning, you head back. Levidi and I will keep searching to the west. We can cover far more ground along the rim than in the canyon. We will meet you back here tomorrow at sunset."

Levidi suddenly looked concerned. "Ghalen, can you get back alone?"

Ghalen smiled and nodded. "Of course. I'll follow the rim east until I come to the camp."

The men looked at one another and nodded in silent agreement.

"Thank you, Ezra." Levidi wiped his eyes.

"We understand what you feel," Ezra said.

"I know." Levidi sounded as if he almost felt ashamed. "I can't live without her."

"I hope I feel that way about a woman one day," Ezra said.

"I hope you do, too." Ghalen grinned. He hefted his spear. "Now, tell me about these elk."

Levidi lifted his ear to the wind. "Shh! Do you hear that?"

"What?" Ghalen asked.

Then Ezra heard it, too. A faint musical note hung on the air. It seemed to emanate from the sunset, a haunting melody carried on the wind like a living spirit.

"Singing!" Levidi exclaimed.

"Not just singing, it's the ai-halah," Ghalen said.

Another voice joined the song, one stronger and closer. It echoed from the canyon, closer and stronger. It strengthened and lifted the song, transforming it from one of longing to one of hope.

"It's her!" Levidi shouted to the others. "It's Alaya! She sings the birth song, I know it." Levidi cupped his hands over his mouth to join the song, but Ezra gripped his arm.

"No."

Levidi looked hurt.

"No," Ezra said quickly. "We must listen if we wish to locate them."

This was only partially truth. Ezra didn't want to betray their location, either. A dark unease gnawed at his mind.

Then, from the east, another chorus joined the song.

"That is our people back in camp," Ghalen said.

"The canyon is acting like a funnel," Ezra said. "It's channeling the sound from far away. I've seen mountain canyons do this before."

"I count three distinct locations," Ghalen said. "The first sounds like it's coming from the south, perhaps on the opposite rim. The second from the west, upstream. Then there are our people in the east."

"Yes." Ezra nodded. "I agree."

"Listen!" Levidi hushed them and pointed west. "Do you hear it?"

Another chorus drifted on the wind and joined the others.

"Who are they?" Ezra said.
"The Minnow," Ghalen replied.

48: Mud and Blood.

Leviathan dogged my thoughts from the moment I escaped Wu. It had been my hope the Cataclysm had wiped all Poseidon's offspring from the earth. Then, one night high in mountains during the flood, I stumbled across two escaped slaves bearing his brand. The slaves had perished, but their presence served as a warning Leviathan still lived, and likely hunted me.

- The Chronicle of Fu Xi.

***

Stinking mud, thick and sticky, waited for her around every corner. It splattered Sana and coated the horse. It gritted between her teeth and streaked her hair. It often forced Sana to lead the horse. Sometimes she encountered mire so thick she feared it would swallow them both. Several times only the horse's incredible strength enabled their escape from the mud pits. Sana tried to stay on the sandy places near the canyon walls, but that had its own dangers.

Throughout the morning and afternoon, landslides rumbled throughout the canyon — one had narrowly missed them. If mud and landslides weren't enough, huge timber piles often forced Sana to double back and find a side canyon.

The river wasn't flowing anymore and had fragmented into numerous isolated ponds. Some she could avoid, others she had to wade through, like now.

Leading the horse by the reins, Sana slowly waded through the knee-deep water. It stank of brine, and flies swarmed mercilessly.

Deep in her heart, Sana knew stealing the horse had been a mistake. The steed was of little use in this maze. She thought about the stranger from last night. How did he get into this place with a horse, and why? Who was he?

"He shouldn't have been so careless," Sana said to no one in particular as she vainly attempted to swat away the insects.

The horse neighed.

"I'm glad you agree. The Scythians say a careless man is a horseless man, and a horseless man is a dead man." She reached up and wiped a glob of mud off the horse's snout. "You are much too pretty to be slogging through all of this."

He was handsome, too, Sana thought. The stranger's face stubbornly invaded her thoughts; the way he stared at her across the fire, and his warm smile as they washed the horse together. When she stood over him, rock in hand, he seemed almost too beautiful to be real. Sana felt no shame about stealing the horse, but did feel ashamed about stealing a kiss from the unconscious man. It just happened. Ghalen wasn't her husband yet, but she truly loved him, which made her impulsive act even more confusing.

Sana stumbled and fell face first into the water. She stood up and gasped. "Enough stinking mud! Enough water! *Enough, enough, enough!*"

Her voice echoed down the canyon.

The horse stared at her.

"Don't look at me like that. You're no help." She snatched the reins and continued the slog.

"What did he call you, anyway?" Sana thought about the way the stranger spoke, the way his voice lifted and fell in almost a musical way. He probably bestowed the horse a beautiful, powerful name.

"Until I can think of a good name, I'll just call you Black." Sana shrugged. "It's not very original, but I'm too tired and hungry to think of anything else."

She'd thought about the exotic red armor she saw in his saddle bags. She'd never seen such craftsmanship. The crimson metal matched her red dagger, adding to the intrigue. The old woman that night on the barge never told her how it came into Setenay's possession.

"He had a beautiful smile," she caught herself saying. "A kind smile. He pulled me out of the water, fed me, and gave me warmth. And I hit him with a rock. "

The horse neighed.

"I know!" she shouted at Black. "I made a mistake, and now you are stuck with me." Sana halted and looked up at the sky above the canyon rim. "And I am stuck here. Sunset is coming in a few hours. We have to find a dry place for the night."

It wasn't unusual for Scythians to talk to their horses, but Sana felt immediately comfortable talking to this one, as if he understood everything she said. Yet, sometimes Sana felt as if he were being too judgmental.

She saw a sandbar up ahead and led the horse out of the water. The fog and overcast that dogged her morning had evaporated by noon into a cloudless sky. The sun had warmed the sand, a welcoming sensation on her toes in contrast to the slight nip in the air.

"I hope this dry sand lasts a while," Sana said and mounted Black.

The canyon narrowed up ahead, and a bend appeared. She rounded the corner into despair. A mountainous timber heap blocked the canyon.

"No," she whispered. Sana approached the twisted heap. She tied Black's reins to a limb and began to climb. It became quickly apparent the horse would break a leg if she tried to lead him over. Sana's spirits dropped even more when she finally reached the top.

Another enormous timber pile stood about a hundred paces across a brown pond, stretching wall-to-wall across the canyon. Gnarled and jagged timber poked above the water like broken bones. The buzzing flies were almost deafening.

Sana sat down atop a thick log jutting from the pile, put her head in her hands, and began to cry.

Below, Black twitched his tail and looked up at her.

She wiped her eyes and shouted at him, "I am NOT feeling sorry for myself!"

Sana absently caressed the log she sat on, surprised how smooth it felt. Then her fingers brushed against several equally spaced bumps. She glanced down and saw thick ropes wrapped around the wood.

The barge! They came this way. Sana stood and examined the pile for more barge logs, but didn't see any. She looked over the pond. She'd swim it if she had to, but the ragged, submerged timber made it dangerous. Sana scanned the canyon walls flanking the pile.

Maybe, she thought. She might be able to use the smaller timbers to fashion a crude ladder.

There is a way out, but not for Black, she thought. *I'll have to let him go*.

"It's the only way," she whispered, and carefully climbed down.

She petted Black's snout and spoke softly. "I'm going to let you go. Go find your old master. He probably still has a headache. Be careful in the mud. I'm sorry I dragged you all this way for nothing."

Sana began to untie the saddle bags and the lance when Black skittered sideways. "Don't be sad!" She patted his flank. "I want to take you with me, but I can't."

The horse began to prance, and Sana realized he was alarmed. She looked over his side. Five figures stood in a line blocking the canyon, the sun at their backs and steel in their hands.

Sana's instincts recognized the danger, and she didn't hesitate. Drawing the lance, she swung onto Black and charged, unleashing a Scythian war cry. As if knowing exactly what to do, Black bolted at the line's center.

One man pivoted to block her. Sana glimpsed his devilish grin filled with needle-like teeth before her lance passed cleanly through his chest. The other men quickly converged. Sana flattened against Black's mane and clenched the reins tightly. She felt the steed tense up in preparation to leap.

Almost free, she thought.

Excruciating pain erupted across her head. Sana felt the horse come out from beneath her, and then the world went black.

***

A horse whinnied. Short, warm hair pressed against her cheek. Head throbbing, Sana managed to pry open her eyes. Defying her nausea, Sana forced herself to sit up. She sat atop Black, but something felt different. She wasn't bareback, but perched upon a strange seat conforming to the horse's back. Ropes tightly bound her wrists and secured them to a protrusion poking from the leather seat.

Three bloody corpses lay at the timber pile's base. They wore no armor. Fearsome geometric tattoos covered their red skin. They weren't from any tribe she recognized. Someone dragged a fourth body by the ankle from the puddle. Sana recognized the dark red armor.

Could it really be him?

The stranger slung the body with the rest. Sana looked around the canyon for more armored men. Surely, he didn't kill them all by himself.

He approached. Sana struggled to no avail against the knots.

The warrior removed the conical, T-eyed helmet. Black hair spilled over his shoulders, revealing the man from the night before. Anger simmered behind his eyes. Sana prepared herself for the worst. Sana didn't understand his words, but fully recognized the tone, as he began to scold the horse.

***

Shaking a disapproving finger, Fu Xi confronted Heise. "You just let her run off with you? Just like that, no consideration to everything we've been through together."

Heise dipped his head and timidly nuzzled Fu Xi.

Fu Xi tapped his chest. "I'm hurt."

Mystery stared down at him incredulously. She wasn't going anywhere this time, he made sure of it. All her daggers were stowed in the saddle bags, except the red blade. He had tucked that one in the belt loop beneath his armor.

"You're a mess." Fu Xi cradled Heise's head and gently petted him. "I forgive you. I'm sure it's more fun to have her thighs wrapped around you than mine. Anyway, you left a trail so easy to follow I'm surprised I didn't find you earlier."

Fu Xi looked up at Mystery and rubbed his head where the lump had almost receded. "We are going to have to learn to get along." He pointed to the dead bodies and their snapped swords. "One of them escaped. I know you don't understand me, but from this point forward we are hunted." He lifted the sword he had liberated from the Olmecs. "And in the end, steel won't be enough to save us."

Fu Xi took Heise's reins and led them back down the canyon. "Your tracks told me you didn't miss many puddles." He glanced back at her and winked playfully. Mystery turned away and grimaced.

"Thank you for leaving me the armor and dagger. They came in handy. Judging from their tracks, my guess is Leviathan to our southwest. If he has scouts, that means he has an army. I don't know how he got here, or how he survived, but we're going to climb out of this canyon and put as much distance between us as we can. First, we have to make a stop."

49: Voices on the Wind.

"Beware, my son. Gods are every bit as susceptible to self-deception as mortals. We are cursed to witness humanity pay the price for our foolishness." - The Goddess Nuwa

- The Chronicle of Fu Xi.

***

Leviathan stood alone.

High upon a rocky outcropping, he surveyed the army encamped below, and listened to the wind's dark counsel.

"Do not concern yourself with the witch. She will pay for her betrayal," the disembodied voice hissed. *"Her child shall serve a higher purpose."*

Below him, the army camped in the "T" intersection where the narrow gorge spilled into the valley's wider canyon. The column's last vestiges filed across the makeshift bridge spanning the muddy flats. Even without Amiran's engineering knowledge, the Olmecs had managed to build it. Several slaves had stumbled off the logs and sunk beneath the mud to their deaths, but most crossed safely. If Amiran had been here, the bridge would have been far sturdier.

The sun had already slipped below the southern mountains, bathing the canyon in ruddy shadows. Beyond the canyon's opposite rim, he saw bright green meadows and ragged white glaciers bathed in stark sunlight. Slaves and warriors had begun constructing crude ramps from logs and

426

earth. These would soon reach the rim, and by tomorrow the army would climb out of the canyon and begin their trek north.

"You promised me a queen," Leviathan said.

"I did not say it would be her," it rasped. *"Patience, isn't that what Poseidon taught you?"*

"My father is no more — isn't that what you told me?"

"Yessss…" it hissed. *"As are your brothers. Atlantis and her empire are buried. The world is yours alone."*

"Did my sister perish, too?" The elusive shadow danced in his peripheral vision, vanishing whenever he tried to focus on it.

"You are the last son of Poseidon," it eluded.

"My father made many promises he could not keep, too."

The frigid wind swirled around Leviathan, tugging at his cape.

"Is not your army intact because of my *timely counsel?"*

Below, the porters carried the boy's cage across the log road. Elda hovered protectively nearby.

Perhaps Leviathan didn't need the scholar to slay the beast that dwelt somewhere to the north, either. Perhaps, but he needed the dragon glands Amiran stole.

"I see your thoughts. Doubts have no place in a god's heart. What lies to the north will be yours if *you are strong enough."*

"I need what the scholar stole," Leviathan said. "Tell me where he is."

The apparition's laugh sounded like a stone being rolled over a tomb. *"This you must accomplish on your own, Son of Poseidon. If you are not strong enough to catch a runaway slave, how can you be worthy to inherit the world?"*

"What of the boy?"

Leviathan watched Kol-ok swing back and forth inside the cage, desperately holding onto the bars as the porters stumbled over the bridge. Many of the logs had already slipped below the mud under the weight of so many feet.

"Deliver the boy safely to me in the valley beyond, and I will fulfill my promises."

Leviathan grasped his sheathed sword's hilt. "And what of Fu Xi?"

"The Son of Nuwa has lost the Traitor's Sword. He is no longer of any consequence. In due time, you will crush him." The swirling gust quickly died away, and the air grew still.

Leviathan stood waiting, but the voice never returned. "Promises." Leviathan sighed. The only traits shared by gods and mortals were their inability to keep promises and the proclivity for betrayal.

Leviathan despised needing a higher power's patronage, or a mortal's services. He hated *needing*. A true god has no need for mortals. Leviathan accepted the Dark God's help, but would never trust him. For ages, he had bowed to Poseidon, only to be shunned. Leviathan was not ready to bow again. Poseidon had weaknesses; perhaps this mysterious Dark God possessed similar weaknesses. He unsheathed his sword and rested the tip between his feet on the bare rock.

The Dark God's spirit had come to him in dreams and visions since his final meeting with Poseidon. With each visit, the spirit grew stronger and more visceral. The Dark God finally appeared in flesh in his tent, as a pale Erubian bearing grim warnings only hours before the Cataclysm — *flee up the mountain or perish*. The Dark God often visited in dreams during the long months on the mountain, sometimes as the Erubian, sometimes as a terrible bull dragon sheathed in fire. The Dark God claimed to be older and even more powerful than Poseidon. He filled Leviathan's dreams with images, events known only to the gods who walked the earth in ancient days.

Poseidon and Nuwa had corrupted the world, he had said. The Cataclysm was the Dark God's plan to cleanse it. He promised Leviathan a new empire, greater than even Atlantis, and an immortal queen to rule by his side.

Leviathan would rule, and restore Creation to its intended order.

All of this could be Leviathan's, if he only accomplished two small tasks.

I need those glands, Leviathan thought as the blade twisted into the stone. A chip popped loose with a spark.

Campfires came to life as the last of the army's column finally cleared the bridge.

"Amiran will pay." He ground the sword's tip deeper into the rock. Watching Gadeirus's Expedition Chest, with Amiran's precious Dragon's Egg inside, slip below the flood had given the demigod immense pleasure. That pleasure evaporated as his thoughts turned to Atamoda.

He took her, Leviathan thought. *Amiran poisoned her mind with his lies, just as he had poisoned Fu Xi's.*

He tried to force Atamoda's face, her smell, her voice from his mind, but her memory would not be denied.

Another chip broke away from the stone. He closed his eyes and twisted the blade again and again.

A god cannot forget, and a god cannot forgive.

Leviathan could not forgive Poseidon for betraying his mother, nor could he forgive Athena betraying the Empire. These were betrayals of blood and oaths. Fu Xi's betrayal was one of friendship and patronage. These betrayals filled Leviathan with rage, but vengeance could salve these wounds.

Atamoda's betrayal left Leviathan feeling only emptiness.

Leviathan sheathed his sword, and withdrew the silver hairbrush from the small bag tied to his waist belt. He held the brush, considering it, when in the distance a long, mournful melody floated on the air.

***

"Is it…?" Su-gár asked, standing beside Aizarg.

"It is," he whispered.

"I've never heard the ai-halah sang that way," Su-gár said. "Do you think it is Alaya?"

Aizarg didn't answer. The Lo gathered behind the Uros, staring toward the dying sunset and the deepening darkness. Then, somewhere in the canyon's depths, another woman's voice intertwined with the original voice.

Excited whispers stirred among the people.

"It must be those from the other barge!" Su-gár exclaimed. "Ezra has found them!"

Aizarg turned to his people. "Our sisters call out from the wilderness. Answer them."

One after another, the Lo women joined the song. Su-gár also lifted her voice. None of the men joined the ai-halah. Aizarg's heart told him this was a time for men to listen. In a few minutes, the original voice died away like a thread snapping under too much weight, and the Lo fell quiet.

"We break camp at dawn and follow Ezra's trail, and the ai-halah," Aizarg commanded.

50: The Slave Pen.

"*Wisdom knows when to be the teacher and when to be the pupil.*" - *The Last Scholar*

- The Chronicle of Fu Xi.

***

By late afternoon, the narrow ravine spilled into a wide canyon. Stinking mudflats, perhaps what might have once been a river, occupied the canyon's center. An army bivouacked on sandbars below the northern cliffs. It was as Virag suspected — these five men were only scouts for a much larger force.

They herded the Lo over the mudflats across a log bridge, and into a makeshift corral in the encampment's center. Virag casually examined the splintered logs that formed the stockade, partially buried in the soft sand. The crude pen had gaps wide enough for a child to slip through. However, the steep canyon walls and deep mud effectively made escape impossible.

The Lo joined perhaps forty other captives already in the corral. The newcomers stared in shock at the living skeletons, who wore crude metal or leather collars. They stared back at the Minnow with dead eyes. Their condition even made Virag uneasy.

Virag found himself in familiar circumstances, surrounded by death and in a power hierarchy based on fear and violence. The world made sense again.

Hevas had the Lo huddled together and whispered empty platitudes of reassurance to one another. "It's going to be all right," and "Don't be afraid." Judging by the slaves already in the pen, Virag knew it wasn't going to be all right. They should all be afraid. They should be terrified.

Virag stood apart along the stockade perimeter. To his surprise, Kus-ge joined him.

"Who are they?" she asked, looking at the starving slaves.

"Us in about a month, unless we find a way to ingratiate ourselves with our new masters," he replied dryly.

Virag thought himself a worldly man. He'd visited Hurar many times, the place he thought of as the center of the world. Virag had seen all manner of strange people and customs in Hur-ar's Grand Market. The Hur-po were incredibly tolerant of anything and anyone that wasn't virtuous. The human diversity Virag saw in this one slave pen left him stunned. The red men must have conquered many lands.

How far did we drift all those many months? he thought. The Cataclysm had forced Virag to reevaluate what he thought he knew about the nature of power, and even the existence of gods. What he saw here forced Virag to reevaluate what he knew about humanity itself.

"What do you suggest we do?" She raised an eyebrow.

Virag nodded at Hevas. "Why don't you ask your husband's successor. Isn't he your new sco-lo-ti, and aren't you his patesi-le? Or are you still too wracked with grief?"

"Hevas is only slightly less foolish than Ba-lok was. He'll soon join my husband in the next world." Virag would have been shocked if Kus-ge had shown any grief.

She glanced over his shoulder where the red men had laid out Ba-lok and the rest of the Minnow bodies near a bonfire. "You at least have a chance in this place," she said.

"Are you patronizing me? Why not bribe me with your charms?" Virag laughed. "My help doesn't come free, you know."

432

"Neither does mine," she said.

Perhaps two-dozen red warriors gathered around the stockade and gawked at their new captives. Virag didn't need to understand their words to grasp their conversations. They leered at the Lo women and laughed, making obscene gestures with the hands, hips, and tongues. They pointed at those they desired, including Kus-ge, but made no move to enter the enclosure and take the women. In a few minutes, the leader who had led the capture party, whom Virag now called Sergeant, broke up the gawking warriors.

"What do you make of our captors?" Kus-ge asked.

"I don't know, at least not yet." He scanned the encampment. "Look how they light their campfires in orderly rows, like the Hur army once did. That shows organization and discipline. Yet…" He trailed off.

"They seem too savage for that," Kus-ge remarked. "Like…"

"Scythians?"

"Yes, and…no. Different."

Behind them, Zirev's children whimpered, asking their mother when their father would come rescue them. Virag and Kus-ge watched the activity in camp for a long spell before Virag spoke again.

"It appears this army is recently arrived," Virag said, trying to shut out the children's whining. "They're still establishing camp. This is a sizable force." He pointed to the northern canyon walls. "They're building ramps. That must be where they're going."

Kus-ge nodded. "Do you think that is where they are from?"

"No. If they go north, they go to conquer."

"What do you think that is?" Kus-ge pointed to a cage hanging from a hook. Big enough to hold a large beast, animal skins completely covered it.

"I don't know, maybe supper."

Several red men loitered around the Lo bodies, talking and laughing. The slaves stopped piling firewood on the bonfire, and began constructing a spit suitable to roast a large boar.

The sun had almost set when Sergeant followed another warrior to the corral. Sergeant pointed to Kus-ge and spoke deferentially to the older and taller warrior, whom Virag affectionally dubbed Axe Face. Virag stepped away from the bars and knelt, lowering his head. "He's their leader," he whispered to Kus-ge, who followed his lead.

Axe Face haughtily paced back and forth, examining the Minnow as they cowered against the stockade's far side along with the original captives. He slid his sword between the bars and pressed it under Virag's chin, forcing him to stand. Using the sword tip, he forced Virag's head from side to side.

Now I'm the merchandise, Virag thought. *I better look expensive.*

Axe Face did the same to Kus-ge, while Sergeant presented him the dragon pendant and spoke quickly. Axe Face stared hard at Kus-ge, and then strode off.

"Something about your pendant interests them," Virag remarked. "Where did you get it?"

"It was a gift from Bal-eeb," she said absently, watching Axe Face march off to the tents.

Both of them had business dealings with the Lion of Hur-ar before the Cataclysm.

"Where did he get it?"

"From Shellbaz, High Priest of Ba'al."

Virag grunted. *Shellbaz would have been right at home around Axe Face and his merry band*, Virag thought.

"Your pendant might be a stroke of good fortune, or it's going to make our visit here extremely complicated," Virag said, and looked over at the bonfire, and blinked. It took a moment for him to comprehend what he was witnessing.

The red men were butchering the Lo bodies. The sound of cracking bones and laughter drifted into the pen.

Virag glanced at Zirev's widow. She hugged her children tightly, and hadn't yet seen the events transpiring by the bonfire. Kus-ge gasped. A few others saw the butchery and screamed. Hevas forced them to turn away and corralled them around the widow and her children, blocking the bonfire. They all embraced one another, facing away from the unimaginable.

Virag averted his eyes, not immune to the horror transpiring at the spit. Kus-ge looked away, too, but didn't flee to her people's embrace.

"I don't think that fate awaits those who stay healthy enough to work," Virag said.

"How can you be so sure?" Her voice shook, and Virag wondered if her madness might have returned. "They're going to devour us, like the water demons!"

Virag pointed to the other slaves. "For now, they need us as labor more than food. Otherwise, there would be far fewer of them in here." Virag didn't know this, but he needed to believe it.

A long wail drifted through camp. At first, Virag thought it might have been a wounded animal, like a great cat, but the sound didn't die away. It carried and transformed in the way only a human voice can. Virag had spent enough time in the marshes to recognize the ai-halah. Somewhere in the distance, a Lo woman sang a mournful, longing song. When Virag ruled the Limita, the boundary between the marshes and steppe, he found ai-halah an irritating fact of life.

Warriors and slaves alike stopped what they were doing and lifted their faces as the other-worldly song permeated the canyon. Virag watched the uneasy warriors glance about. *Like most barbarians, they are superstitious*, he thought. The effect on the Lo, and even the other slaves, was quite different.

The starving slaves struggled to their feet. The song seemed to invigorate them. The Minnow Clan also rose to their feet. In moments, their chorus floated into the night to blend with the female voice. Virag thought he could hear other voices, too, but the canyon's echoes distorted the sound. Around the camp, the red men lifted their noses, as if sniffing the wind. *They may be superstitious, but they aren't stupid*, he thought.

"Fools," he spat. Virag knew Aizarg and the Crane Clan were out there somewhere, and now this army knew it, too. The Lo had unwittingly betrayed themselves to predators.

One Lo did not join the chorus. Kus-ge crossed her arms and looked about with an irritated, or maybe fearful, expression. Virag wasn't certain.

The song lasted only a few minutes. The Lo resumed their huddle, the slaves took their places at the paddock's far side, and Virag resumed his observations.

The encampment seemed to resume its previous activity. While Kus-ge leaned against the bars and stared off into the night, Virag sat down, placed his chin on his fist, and tried to think of a plan.

A dark-haired girl on the cusp of womanhood emerged from one of the smaller tents. She hurriedly walked across the camp, averting her eyes to the horror taking place at the bonfire. She wore leggings, a long-sleeved tunic, and high, fur-lined boots. The gray cloth was simple, but of a fine cut and material, possibly wool.

Royalty, perhaps?

She carried a small bowl and approached the cage. The girl lifted one of the furs draped over the bars and, smiling warmly, sat on her knees. She lifted the bowl, and two hands emerged from behind the furs and took it. What happened next occurred so fast, had Virag blinked he would have missed it. A familiar face briefly emerged in the firelight before slipping back into the shadows.

The girl's smile melted away as she looked over her shoulder at the butchery by the fire. She hastily closed the flap over the cage and returned to her tent.

Virag whistled softly between his teeth. "I didn't expect that."

51: The Ravine.

A child does not learn to speak by talking, but first by listening. It was around tribal campfires, carefully listening and watching, that I became known as the God of Names. I listened to the old men tell their stories to young men. I heard the wise words the old women dispensed to young mothers. The children made it easiest of all, providing a basic primer for a tribe's lexicon. Through the millennia I had honed my skills to the point that one night of listening around the campfire could unlock a new language.

Amiran's tutelage in the Library of Wu, opening the Empire's many exotic tongues, had increased that skill exponentially.

- The Chronicle of Fu Xi.

***

Sana examined the bindings securing her wrists to the saddle horn. She knew eventually the stranger would get careless again and she could escape. Yet, that voice in the back of her mind kept reminding her he had saved her not once, but twice. How did he slay all those men? Surely, he could not have taken them by surprise. Those warriors were well armed and likely skilled fighters. And how did he find her so fast?

Most of the canyon slipped into shadow. The air grew still and quiet. The stranger briskly led the horse through a maze of side canyons with sandy bottoms. There wasn't much flood debris here, and less standing water. Sana did not recognize anything from her own journey. They turned into another narrow side canyon. Judging by the tracks, he'd been this way before.

This man is quite a mystery, she thought. Sana grinned. "That's what I should call you, 'Mystery,'" she said.

He momentarily turned around, his expression unreadable, and then resumed leading the horse.

Sana caught whiff of cooking meat, and thought her mind might be playing tricks. Her stomach instantly growled. They came around a corner and she saw an enormous shape, bigger than a horse, partially blocking the ravine. A long, straight log trailing frayed ropes rested against the ravine's wall.

A hulking man squatted with his back to them, slicing chunks from the carcass. Her breath quickened as Sana recognized the demon fish the Lo had slain shortly before entering the rapids. Hearing their approach, the man stood and turned.

"Spako!" she shouted.

Holding a slab of flesh and slack-jawed, Spako considered her. Then he joyously lumbered forward. The Sammujad squeezed her midriff so tightly Sana couldn't breathe. Spako looked at her tied hands and then the stranger. "Sana," Spako beamed and pointed.

The stranger lifted an eyebrow and then untied her hands. Spako lifted her up and spun her around. Sana couldn't help but laugh.

Spako set her down and extended the fleshy slab. "Hungry?"

"Where are the rest?" Sana asked.

"Just me and…" Spako's eyes lit up above his bushy beard. He grabbed Sana's hand and pulled her around the corner.

A fire and lean-to were nestled in the ravine's dead end. Spako bent down, and beckoned Sana to look. He pulled away the stranger's horse blanket, and Alaya's smiling face beamed back up at her. A newborn suckled at her breast, and Aizarg's staff rested by her side.

∗∗∗

They rested by the fire. Sana gorged herself on steaming meat. The stranger sat apart from them in the shadows, sword on this lap.

"What's her name?" Sana adored the black-haired infant sleeping in Alaya's arms.

"I haven't chosen one yet. Levidi and I had some ideas, but…" she trailed off. "I want him here when she's named."

"I understand," Sana said. "We'll start searching for them in the morning. I found a piece of the raft to the east. How did you and Spako survive?"

"When the barge began to break up, I held on to whatever I could. It ended up being Aizarg's staff. It was lodged in its hole. Our log broke away, and we found ourselves alone and stranded here."

Sana frowned. "The staff didn't burn you?"

"No, and it never came out of its hole until we were safely beached. Then it came out with little effort," Alaya continued. "I started to go into labor almost immediately after we beached." She smiled warmly at Spako. "He built this shelter and never left my side."

"Water go down quickly. Spako find lots of sticks," Spako said around a mouthful.

"I was in labor all night. Sana, I was so scared. The baby was coming, and…" She wiped away a tear. "We didn't know where everyone was, or even if they were still alive. Then this man"—she nodded to the stranger—"walked out of the fog this morning."

"He hit Spako hard, but Spako not mad at him." Spako rubbed his eye, and that's when Sana noticed the bruise.

"Spako was only trying to protect me." Alaya looked over at the stranger, who slowly ate and kept watch on the ravine's entrance. "He defeated Spako so quickly!"

"Not quickly!" Spako seemed insulted. Alaya giggled.

"It became apparent he didn't want to hurt us." Alaya looked down at the baby. "She was coming, stranger or no stranger." She looked up at Sana, face radiant. "He delivered her." She leaned in and whispered, "I think he may be a healer. He did it effortlessly, like a midwife. I was afraid the baby would die since we are on land, but the man seemed to know exactly what to do, even tying off the cord."

Sana looked over at the stranger as Alaya kept talking. "He handed me my baby and then put on that red metal clothing, and just walked away. I think he tried to tell us to wait here, and he would be back." Alaya embraced Sana and sobbed with joy. "And here you are!"

"Do you think you can travel?"

Alaya frowned. "I think so."

Sana told her about what had transpired that day, and how she came to meet the stranger.

Alaya seemed deep in thought. "Where would we go?"

"East. We follow the flood and find our people."

The horse whinnied.

The stranger sprang up, sword at the ready, and peered down the canyon. Then, Sana heard a woman's voice, lonely and majestic, wavering in the twilight.

Alaya gasped. Spako stop chewing and perked up. The otherworldly song strengthened, and permeated the ravine as if coming from everywhere at once.

"That's one of our people!" Alaya stood, child in her arms. Before Sana could protest, Alaya lifted her voice and joined the song.

***

Across the emptiness left in the Cataclysm's wake, a solitary soul called to her own, and they answered. It wasn't only the young mother that joined the mysterious song. An almost imperceptibly faint chorus lifted through the canyon to join the woman and mother. Then, slightly closer, a second chorus joined in.

The primal song bewitched the God of Names. Never had he experienced anything so deeply visceral. Here, beyond the Cataclysm, Fu Xi experienced a new dimension to the human spirit, and his own.

The other voices, including the mother's, carried their hopes over the canyon walls and into the coming night. The solitary singer's presence lifted their spirits like a beacon, yet the original voice remained deeply primal, and not buoyed by the others' joy. It reverberated through Fu Xi, as if emanating from the earth itself.

I live, she proclaimed, *but I have paid a terrible price.*

An even greater price was coming. The song died away, and Fu Xi turned around and considered Mystery, the young mother, and the giant.

Sana, Alaya, and *Spako*, he thought. *I know your names, and now I know there are others like you.*

During his search for Sana this morning, he had not only found Spako and Alaya, he had found a way out of the canyon. He knew Leviathan was out there somewhere, and likely heard the same song. By morning, this canyon would be crawling with Obsidian Warriors looking for him, and those whose voices filled the air. Fu Xi knew he had to find the rest of these people, and try to save them.

52: The Earth's Womb.

A patesi-le knows when to speak truth to the blind, and when to simply lead them to safety. - Lo proverb.

- The Chronicle of Fu Xi.

***

Dankness steeped a chamber little bigger than a Lo hut, and Atamoda's fear did little to abate. Except for a few broken sticks flattened against the far wall, Zelko's cave held little evidence anyone had ever lived there. Zelko picked them up. "What's left of my gate. I had a few goats penned here when I was captured." He looked about the chamber, confused.

"They were probably washed out by the flood," Amiran said, as if reading his thoughts. He pointed to a large crack in the wall. "Is that the tunnel?"

Zelko nodded.

"Is that where we are going?" Atamoda's knees buckled. Amiran grabbed her under the arm before she fell.

It wasn't a tunnel; it was a slit. *I won't be able to breathe. The walls will crush me. I'll be trapped, unable to turn around or go forward. Squeezed. Immobilized. Entombed. Forever.*

"No!" She slipped from Amiran's grip and bolted for the entrance. Amiran lifted Atamoda from behind, her legs still kicking. "I feel like I'm drowning!" Atamoda sobbed. "You ask too much!" Atamoda knew she shouldn't fight Amiran, but she could not control herself.

"Close your eyes and breathe. Breathe, Atamoda. Breathe slowly." Amiran's words couldn't reach that place deep inside that panicked like a trapped animal. "Don't give the fear a foothold. Keep breathing and listen to my voice."

She tried to obey, but couldn't.

"What you are feeling is normal. Do not be ashamed of it. You are a brave woman, Atamoda. You must be braver, still."

Amiran tightly embraced her the way she would often embrace frightened children. Amiran's deep, smooth voice had a calming quality. Atamoda felt herself slowly regaining control.

"You said it feels like drowning?" he asked.

She nodded quickly, but didn't dare open her eyes.

"I'm afraid of drowning," he said.

"But you have sailed far across the world?" Atamoda asked, genuinely bewildered.

"I confront my fear every time I climb aboard a ship. It's difficult, but I know I must, or the fear will win and devour me a little nibble at a time."

He clasped her hands. "Keep your eyes closed, and hold my hand. I will lead you through the tunnels."

"Amiran," Zelko said. "The torch is burning."

"Atamoda, please be strong for me."

The fear bubbled up fresh again, but she swallowed hard and nodded.

"Good." Amiran helped her stand. "Zelko, go ahead. We'll follow."

She heard Zelko grunt. Atamoda could see the torchlight through her eyelids.

"It isn't very far, patesi-le," Zelko said. "We go down for a little, and then up for a little, and we come out on the other side."

"Down?" Amiran asked.

"Yes, just a little. Then up," Zelko said matter-of-factly.

"Is something wrong?" Atamoda asked.

"No, nothing is wrong," Amiran said, and she heard him shuffle. "Stay right behind me. Just duck a little and turn sideways. That's it, good."

Atamoda held her breath as the cavern walls brushed her stomach and back simultaneously, and then nothing. "You can straighten up," Amiran said.

"Are we in the tunnel?" Her voice trembled far more than she wanted it to.

"We are, and it's far roomier than you'd expect."

"That's good." Atamoda smiled weakly, but dared not look.

In a few moments, their footfall sounds changed, as if she were hearing them twice. Sometimes, they would walk at a normal pace, but usually only at a slow shuffle. Every so often Atamoda brushed up against stone, or Amiran would tell her to duck. Through it all, the torchlight glimmered through her eyelids, and she could smell its comforting smoke. Atamoda repeatedly asked if they were almost to the other side, and Zelko would always answer in the same way: "Soon, almost there."

The air seemed to grow clammier, like an ice fog rolling in from the steppe.

"When the snow would melt in the high pastures, I would bring my goats up here from the lowlands near the sea," Zelko said. "When the spring storms shook the mountain, I'd bring them into the cave. Sometime they grazed the north slope, sometimes the south." He chuckled. "I used to sing, and they would hear me even out on the slopes. My songs would carry all the way through the cave to the other side." He began to sing a merry tune she didn't understand, interrupted by a high-pitched melody that reverberated all around even after he'd stopped singing.

"Why does it sound like that, even after you've stopped?" she asked.

"It's called an echo; it's the sound bouncing off the cavern walls." Amiran said. "Have you never heard an echo before?"

"No," she said.

"I like how the echo makes my songs sound. The goats liked Zelko's singing!" He laughed, and then trailed off. "I miss my goats. I had names for all of them."

"That was a pretty song, Zelko," she said, trying to cheer him up. "I liked it."

"Thank you, patesi-le." She heard pleasure return to his voice. "Sing us a Lo song."

"I cannot," she stammered.

"Why not?" Amiran asked. "Come to think about it, I've never heard you sing the whole time you've been in camp."

"It is difficult to explain. Are we almost to the other side?"

"Not long now," Zelko said. "Time will go faster if you sing for us."

"Our songs aren't memorized like your songs. They are called the ai-halah. They spring to life, newly born with each rendition from the marsh and sea. Sometimes it starts with a wave lightly slapping the shore, or a birdsong. One person will pick up the melody, and soon it carries to the whole village. With each new voice the ai-halah grows and changes."

"It sounds wondrous," Amiran remarked.

"There are no sounds here to give my spirit voice. This place is like a grave."

"A grave? Bah! This was my home." Zelko scoffed. "When storms blew and lightning smashed against the mountain, me and my goats were safe here. This is the earth's womb. I lit fires to keep warm. I had many skins and furs to lay on. I had food." He remained silent for a few moments. "I was happy here. The only grave it will be is mine."

"I'm sorry, Zelko," Atamoda said. "I didn't mean to insult your home."

445

They continued on in silence as Atamoda contemplated Zelko's words. This was his home, and she was ashamed she insulted it. As they shuffled through darkness, Atamoda strained to listen beyond their breathing and footfalls, to hear this place as Zelko heard it. She relaxed, and inhaled the sounds with her heart the way she would have listened to the sounds of home. Water dripped in the distance, but nothing else.

Water. Where there is water, there is life.

Atamoda's heartbeat seemed to sync with the water's metronome. The torchlight dancing through her eyelids added to the spell. Each heartbeat, each drip, stirred a new memory. She remembered her fear the night Aizarg lifted the spear and became Uros. She saw Kol-ok's face behind iron bars, and Amiran, and then Elda. She'd abandoned her own son, and nothing Amiran said could assuage her guilt. He wouldn't understand, and neither would Elda, whom she'd grown fond of. Then her mind drifted to the night of the terrible storm that swept her and Kol-ok from the Wedding Barge. Were her people still alive somewhere out there? Did they make landfall? She ached for all that had been lost, and all that she must struggle to save. Then she remembered Aizarg. Could she ever face him again?

Leviathan invaded her thoughts, and an emptiness washed over her. The entire mountain bearing down on this tiny tunnel could not equal the guilt and shame crushing her soul. In the darkness Atamoda came face-to-face with herself, and found no place to hide.

It emerged more like a moan than a note, and Atamoda didn't consciously remember forming the sound. It materialized, low and mournful, deep inside and increased in strength. All the emotions she'd kept bottled up boiled to the surface, each with its own voice. As if outside her own body, Atamoda heard her song reverberate down the tunnel. As if the mountain approved, the womb of the earth infused her ai-halah with power, and Atamoda's voice grew stronger. Loved ones drifted through her mind, and with each face the song changed. This wasn't an ai-halah inspired by nature's sounds, but by Atamoda's own spirit.

My song.

Atamoda's foot suddenly submerged in freezing water, and her personal ai-halah abruptly ended. She felt disoriented, as if she had just woken up.

Zelko whispered, "When you sang, patesi-le, I heard spirits in the mountain sing, too. They wept."

Amiran gently squeezed her hand. "That was beautiful."

Atamoda smiled, and realized she'd been crying, though she couldn't remember why.

"Light the other torch, Zelko," Amiran said.

The light beyond her eyelids grew brighter, and Atamoda felt fresh, welcome heat. "Are we almost through?"

"Yes, just a little longer," Zelko said yet again.

"Atamoda, there is water ahead. This part of the tunnel is lower than either entrance," Amiran said.

"How much?"

"We don't know, but we're going to have to wade through it. Zelko is going first. Keep holding my hand. My bag will float, so if it gets too deep we can hold on to that."

Atamoda thought she heard Amiran's voice break a little.

"Come," Zelko said, and she heard sloshing.

Atamoda steeled herself and followed Amiran.

How can water be this cold and not turn to ice? she thought. Memories of the water demons, and how their touch transformed water to black ice, sent fresh fear through her. "Don't let go of me!"

"Don't let go of *me*!" Amiran replied.

The water rose to her hips, and then her belly. It soaked her clothes and furs. Amiran's bag bumped into her as the water came up to her chest. The light beyond her eyelids seemed brighter.

"Zelko." Amiran's teeth chattered. "Slow down."

Atamoda frowned; that made no sense to her.

"You're getting too far ahead — we can't keep up!" Amiran shouted. She didn't hear Zelko, but the flickering torchlight burned brighter behind her eyelids.

Amiran sputtered. The water came to her chin. Atamoda wanted to open her eyes, but fear kept them shut.

"Amiran, what's wrong?" she asked.

"Zelko!" he shouted. "Come back!"

Atamoda's toes barely touched the bottom, and her head bumped the tunnel ceiling. Amiran slipped and yanked her down. Before she submerged, Atamoda did what any good Lo would do — took a deep breath. Fully submerged, and no longer feeling the bottom, Atamoda opened her eyes.

Golden, glimmering rays poured into the submerged chamber and danced through clear water. Atamoda could see the tunnel around her. Her feet floated only a few inches above the tunnel floor, which sharply ascended just ahead. Amiran's cheeks puffed out, and his wide eyes wildly looked past her. He still clung to the floating bag, but it was trapped against the tunnel ceiling where no space remained.

Amiran's behavior confused her. Why did he try to tug her back into the darkness from where they came? She could tell he'd begun to panic. The water, and her friend's distress, washed away Atamoda's own fear. Still holding Amiran's hand, she swam around him toward the light. It seemed much too bright for a torch. *It must be sunlight*, she thought, *and this is the way out*.

Amiran began to resist and pulled her backward with greater force. *He's running out of air*, she thought. Atamoda exhaled a little air and let her boots touch the bottom. Using the traction, she pulled him to the light.

Amiran fought with greater desperation, eyes looking about wildly as if he couldn't see. She'd seen this kind of panic before, and did what any good Lo mother would do. She grabbed Amiran's torso, and pushed off the cave floor with just enough force to knock his head against the tunnel ceiling. Amiran, momentarily stunned, went limp. She snatched his collar with one hand, his bag with the other, and lunged for the light.

Atamoda broke the surface into almost complete darkness. Gasping for air and confused, she dragged Amiran from the water on his belly. She gave him a few good smacks on the back until he began to cough.

"Zelko?" she shouted.

Only a moment ago she'd seen the torchlight shimmering brightly through the water like a beacon. As Atamoda's eyesight adjusted, she detected dim light ahead.

"He left us," Amiran coughed as he pulled himself up on all fours.

"I see light."

In a few minutes, Atamoda and Amiran staggered around the corner and found themselves in a small chamber with a narrow opening leading outside.

"We made it," Atamoda said with great relief. Her teeth began to chatter.

"Zelko!" Amiran shouted and stepped to the entrance.

Enough light trickled through the opening for Atamoda to inspect the chamber. What might have been a fire circle occupied the cavern's center, the rocks now scattered about. Broken sticks partially woven together into a light fence lay disheveled in a corner. Mud-encrusted animal skins and blankets were plastered against the cavern wall just right of the opening.

"Wait here. I'll see if it's safe," Amiran said and stumbled outside, still rubbing his head.

Atamoda shivered harder, suddenly overwhelmed with exhaustion. She wanted to lie down and sleep. Yet, without remembering how she got there, Atamoda found herself outside the cave and sitting on a large, smooth stone.

Amiran stood a few yards downhill, gazing over the valley. They were on a barren mountain slope, blanketed in shadow. Countless broken stumps disrupted the bleak monotony. Below, a ragged canyon cut through the valley's heart. Beyond the canyon, bathed in the day's last light, gentle green slopes rose to meet bold, snowcapped peaks.

Atamoda imagined herself over there, laying on the green grass under the warm sun.

Amiran slogged back up the slope. "I told you to stay in the cave."

She was too tired to answer him.

Amiran knelt before her. He examined her face and gripped her hands. His concerned expression deepened. "I have to get you warm. Go back inside; don't sit down. Keep walking until I find some wood and build a fire. We'll spend the night in the cave." With that, he turned and trotted back down the slope. A fire sounded wonderful, though Atamoda found herself not feeling as cold anymore. She struggled to stand, feeling slightly dizzy, before turning back toward the cave.

A man stood in the cave entrance, smiling warmly down upon her. She would not have recognized him had it not been for the twinkle in his eye. His round, cherub cheeks pushed his eyes into jovial half-moons. He wore a pure white robe emblazoned with a golden snake-like beast, tied with a crimson sash.

"Pug?"

Pug's living presence, healthy and happy, did not alarm Atamoda. Nor did the faint blue light dancing in his eyes. In fact, this all seemed completely natural. A part of her said she should be afraid, but at this particular moment, she was just too tired to care.

Pug extended an unsheathed sword in both hands. The blade shimmered like metallic blood. Leviathan's sword. Atamoda reached out to touch it.

53: Zelko's Goat Cave.

"Orichalcum is a cursed substance. The blood metal symbolizes death, subjugation, and immortal greed. Dragons perished to create it. The greater gods used it to infest mortal flesh. The lesser gods wielded it to war with one another. Forbidden to mortals, men lusted for it more than gold.

"This is why Athena laid down her Traitor's Sword. As it is written in the Ancient of Ancients, 'One cannot fight sin with sin.'"- The Last Scholar

- The Chronicle of Fu Xi.

***

Amiran spent several minutes looking for anything to burn. Luckily, the flood left enough broken twigs and sticks to make a decent fire. He knew the cold had seeped dangerously deep into Atamoda's body, and would kill her if he didn't warm her soon. He'd seen it many times in his expeditions. It wasn't only Atamoda's immediate peril that weighed on his mind, as he felt the cold beginning to seep into his own core.

He pondered why Zelko had deserted them. The goatherd waded into the water and didn't heed Amiran's pleas to slow down. He took their only torch, leaving them in water and darkness. Doubt plagued the scholar.

Amiran also realized it was him, not Atamoda, that had panicked. It was her actions, not his, that had saved them both. Though how Atamoda accomplished it baffled him.

The wind cut into his drenched clothing, and Amiran's teeth began to chatter again. Other mysteries swirled in his mind as he picked up sticks. There were no tracks outside the tunnel other than the ones Amiran and Atamoda made themselves. Did Zelko slip into a hidden side tunnel? Was his intent to betray Amiran and Atamoda to Leviathan all along?

Zelko told Amiran the tunnel only stretched a few hundred paces through the mountain. By Amiran's reckoning, they should have emerged on the northern slope by mid-morning, yet it was already sundown.

Arms full, Amiran studied the canyon. They'd have to cross it to reach the green slopes on the other side. Only then could they make their way west. He looked across the valley at the distant glacier-capped cliffs. *That is the ice wall Zelko spoke of*, he thought. Even from here, the cliffs looked impenetrable. *Let them stay impenetrable*, Amiran thought and looked around, hoping to spot the goatherd.

"Dammit, Zelko! What game are you playing?"

Amiran's rational mind grasped for something, anything to explain these mysteries.

He turned around to make his way back up the hill and saw Atamoda lying in front of the cave.

***

Amiran paused to feel the satchel with the dragon glands. He had not considered it may have been damaged in the cave. Thankfully, it was still cool to the touch. He returned the satchel to the bag, and removed his flint. It only took a few minutes for Amiran to start a fire in the old stone circle.

Atamoda's lips were blue, and her skin felt like ice. He soon had the fire blazing, and placed her as close as he could. Without thought to modesty, he stripped off her wet clothes.

Atamoda's flesh had turned deathly white, and her breath came in shallow pants.

She's dying, he thought.

He needed to wrap her in something dry, and looked about desperately. That's when he spotted the old skins plastered against the cave wall. Likely, they were once Zelko's, and had somehow not been washed from the cave. Amiran peeled them off, and shook them out as best he could. They were filthy and matted, but dry. They'd have to do, but they wouldn't be enough.

A cold draft stirred the coals. Amiran looked about, and that's when he saw a large, round stone beside the entrance. He had missed it in the darkness, but realized it was made to seal the cave. He tried to roll it, but the flood had deposited dirt and debris around its base. Amiran cleared the silt with his hands. Eventually, he was able to rock the stone from its divot, and roll it across the entrance. Air whistled through cracks around the stone, but it blocked most of the wind, and ventilated most of the smoke.

He noticed more skins wadded amongst other debris that had been lodged behind the stone. Amiran pulled out a goat skin and found a corpse staring back at him. He'd have to investigate this later, and returned his attention to Atamoda.

The cave began to warm, but it wasn't enough. Stripping off his own wet clothes, he laid all their garments beside the fire and then slipped between the goat skins with her. She had stopped shivering, a bad sign. He pressed his flesh against hers as closely as he could, and began rubbing her arms and legs.

"I hope you forgive me, but this is necessary," Amiran said. He paused for a moment, and then kept talking. "You may not believe this"—he laughed—"or maybe you would, but I've never been this close to a woman before. A scholar does all in his power not even to fantasize about a moment such as this. Such thoughts can drive us mad. I'd never thought I'd be with a woman, let alone one as beautiful as you."

Amiran could feel Atamoda's flesh steal his heat, and he gladly surrendered it. He thought he'd feel sexual arousal at a moment like this, but he didn't. Amiran felt a strange peace, and didn't even think to recite the Chants of Celibacy.

"I don't blame you for being with him…" He paused. "With Leviathan. You shouldn't blame yourself, either. The gods turn us against one another. They make us hate ourselves. That's their true power." He looked at her face, and realized her lips were no longer blue. Her breath became deeper, more relaxed.

Amiran kept rubbing her arms and legs, but this time slower and with less urgency. He let her head rest on his shoulder. "I don't even blame you for falling in love with him. I know you couldn't help it. He is a god, after all.

"I have done terrible things to my fellow human beings in their service, Atamoda. I've hated myself for them. Do not hate yourself."

Atamoda moaned softly, and snuggled closer, pressing every curve against his. She draped her arm across his chest, and he felt her shivering resume. He closed his eyes and swallowed hard. "I hope you don't blame me for falling in love with you. I couldn't help it, either." He tenderly brushed Atamoda's hair away from her face, closed his eyes, and kissed her on the forehead. "Because I love you, I shall not torment you with what you cannot return.

"Sleep now, my beautiful patesi-le."

Amiran leaned back and put his other arm under his head, and stared up at the cave ceiling. In the firelight, he let his mind drift. He thought of the other girl he loved, and wondered if Elda would ever understand why he left, let alone ever forgive him.

As the firelight and growing warmth worked its magic, Amiran began to imagine patterns on the ceiling.

***

Atamoda awoke to pale light streaming around the entrance stone. Amiran's bag rested beside the small fire. She smelled mold, and realized it came from mottled animal skins covering her nude body.

"Your clothes are dry; they are beside you. I will keep my back turned." Amiran hunched over on all fours near the cave entrance, wiping away dirt and studying something intently. "What do you remember about last night?"

Atamoda tried to clear her mind. "Water and darkness. And then freezing cold." She looked about. "Where is Zelko?"

"I don't know. He vanished and hasn't returned."

"Why am I...?"

"You were freezing to death. I had to get you warm or you would die."

Nothing in Amiran's voice betrayed deceit. She arose and quickly got dressed. "What are you looking at?"

"Come here — I'll show you."

Atamoda stepped beside him and looked down. He'd cleared the soil away from the cavern floor, revealing smooth rock. "It looks strange," she said.

"Touch it," he beckoned.

She squatted and ran her hands over the surface. "It's smooth."

"It's glass. The cavern has been glazed by incredible heat."

"A fire?"

"Dragon fire."

Atamoda held her breath. "Like the creature Leviathan slew?"

"Exactly. Long ago, a dragon used this cavern as a lair. Judging by its size, a female like the one whose glands are in the bag." He stood and held pointed to the cavern's ceiling. "Notice how the whole inside is glazed. I didn't notice it until I built the fire. Our friend Zelko and his goats had made their home in a dragon cave."

"What are those squiggles?" She pointed to the ceiling.

"It's called the Dragon's Mark. You find them in most dragon lairs. Their purpose is unknown."

Atamoda looked about the cave. "They're beautiful."

He nodded. "They are. They've been a subject of debate in the Academy for centuries. Even the gods don't know their meaning."

Atamoda gasped when she saw the skull.

Amiran looked back. "Oh, him. He must have been trapped here when the flood hit. His body got jammed up behind the entrance stone."

"Poor man. Do you think he was a friend of Zelko?" Atamoda stepped closer to examine the skeleton lying in the shadows.

"He never mentioned a friend." Amiran shrugged.

Atamoda examined the skeleton. Twigs, leaves, and sticks, along with dirt, partially covered the dried flesh that still clung to the skeleton. She leaned in closer, inspecting his goatskin clothing.

Atamoda straightened and considered Amiran. "He's burned on the same side Zelko was."

Amiran grunted. "Maybe they were friends. Perhaps Zelko didn't speak of him to protect him from Leviathan." Amiran grunted. "Maybe that's why he ran off, he went looking for him in hopes he survived the flood."

Atamoda shivered and hugged herself. Then she saw something symmetric and oddly artificial protruding from the soil by the right femur. She knelt and lightly brushed some dirt away.

"What's this?" she muttered, and brushed away some more. "A sword?"

Amiran knelt beside her. "So it is." He began to help her. "This cannot be." His voice shook. Amiran pulled the sword from the soil and stood. He brushed away dirt clumps and shook his head in disbelief. He grabbed his bag and strode outside. Amiran held the blade to the early morning sky, laughing with joy.

It was a simple, yet elegantly curved blade, with a round hilt wrapped in what looked like stained crimson thread. The blade looked nearly identical to Leviathan's.

Amiran swept Atamoda off her feet in a joyous hug and twirled her around. He set her down, and she felt a little dizzy, but his joy infected her.

"He must be close by!"

"Who?" she asked.

"Fu Xi!"

"The other god you spoke of?" Atamoda considered the crimson blade. She'd had enough of the gods, and didn't want another lurking around, no matter how benevolent. "Where do you think he is?"

Amiran looked about. "I don't know, but metal doesn't float. It tells me Fu Xi made it this far before the Cataclysm struck. What a stroke of luck!"

"I doubt this was luck," Atamoda whispered. A forgotten vision tugged at the corners of her mind. "I feel invisible strings attached to that weapon. Its presence here is no accident."

Adoring the sword, Amiran didn't seem to hear her. He pointed the blade to the cliffs beyond the canyon. "That is where Leviathan is heading. We have to reach it first, and then turn west before Leviathan cuts us off."

"Didn't Zelko warn you to stay away from those cliffs? Didn't you promise him?"

"We will stay as far away as possible. If we cut west too early, we'll likely run headlong into his scouts. We have to flank him before we turn west. Without our guide, I fear our task just became far more difficult. We must hurry, my friend. Our window of opportunity is limited." He turned to Atamoda. "The most difficult part of our journey is ahead of us."

She nodded. "I know, but it's the only reason I agreed to come with you. Are you sure Leviathan will pursue us?"

"He will at least send his warriors after us. Regardless, he can't enter the valley without the dragon glands. Without the dragon glands, Elda is of no use."

"Are you sure he won't hurt Kol-ok?"

"I strongly suspect Kol-ok's destiny lies in that valley, too. We have to put as much distance between us and Leviathan before he pursues us. And he will pursue, not only for the glands, but for you."

Atamoda lowered her gaze, some of her shame returning. Amiran tenderly lifted her chin. "It isn't just how he feels about you. It's that I took you. He won't rest until he possesses you again and I am dead." Amiran shouldered his bag. "It will be as I said. We will draw Leviathan away from the valley, and with him Elda and Kol-ok. If we're lucky, the Gray-Eyed Queen and the God of Names have already joined forces to our west. If fortune truly shines on us, we reach them before Leviathan catches us. Now come, we must hurry. We have to find a way across that canyon."

Amiran turned and began walking down the slope. Atamoda followed, and then halted. "What if the dragon Zelko spoke of isn't really there? He abandoned us, so how can we truly trust what he said?"

"It's there," Amiran said without turning around.

"But how do you know?"

Amiran kept walking.

"Stop, damn you! Quit treating me like a child. You're not telling me everything, and I grow tired of it. You know what Leviathan wants with Kol-ok. I'm not taking another step until you tell me."

Amiran halted and took a deep breath. "I can't be sure. It's not in a scholar's nature to speculate."

Atamoda crossed her arms and rolled her eyes. "It's in a patesi-le's nature to know marsh dung when she hears it. Amiran, of all the men I've known, you are the worst liar I've ever seen. I thank the Nameless God Leviathan is a man and not a woman, or he would have seen through you long ago. It is in your nature to tell the truth, and you've been afraid to tell me the truth since we met. I won't cross that canyon until I hear it."

Amiran stared at Atamoda as if she had hurt his feelings. "As you wish. I'll tell you everything as we walk."

Satisfied, Atamoda followed.

Amiran began talking as if he were holding a lecture, "Let us begin with something called the Ancient of Ancients…"

Part 5: In the Land of Aryq.

"In the years before her rebellion and the First Purge, the Goddess Athena took Grand Master Vulcan as her secret lover and confidant. She taught him the First Tongue, the spoken language reserved only for the immortals. Finding Atlantean too imperfect, Master Vulcan crafted an entirely new written language to capture the First Tongue's purity.

"By day, the goddess stood watch at her pillar in Poseidon's court. By night she fomented mortal rebellion among a small group of scholars she called her Owls. Deep in the catacombs, Athena divulged the gods' deepest secrets, and revealed the lies upon which Poseidon had built his empire. Vulcan crafted the saga into the epic poem the Song of Athena.

"The Song of Athena directly repudiates the Song of Atlas, the epic poem handed down by Poseidon to recount the dawn of time and Atlantis's founding. Grand Master Vulcan soon discovered the Song of Atlas was as 'a lie hidden in the truth much as a worm hides inside an apple.'

"As the First Purge washed over Atlantis, Vulcan hid the Song of Athena, along with other great works he feared would be destroyed, deep in the catacombs beneath the Imperial Academy. Millenia later, Master Gremis would rediscover the tomes, along with other priceless works by the legendary Grand Master Vulcan.

"Master Gremis translated much of the Song of Atlas and, along with Vulcan's other lost writings, organized them into what came to be known as the Ancient of Ancients. The powerful truth contained in these scrolls reignited the Academy's long-stagnant rebellion. The Owls' insurrection drew Poseidon's wrath, and brought about the Second Purge and their own doom.

"It is my task to complete Master Gremis's work, and finish translating the Song of Athena. Tucked inside my navigation kit is all that remains of the world that came before the Cataclysm." - The Last Scholar.

- The Chronicle of Fu Xi.

54: The Army Marches.

Nephilim clothed in unblemished skin, opened eyes born again, breathe deep.
Theirs is a world set out fresh by the Maker's hand, Heaven on Earth new.
Servants Ten, hearts pounding, blood pumping, praise carried high on lips mortal,
Paradise soil sacred they stand, inhale Water and power. - The Song of Athena

- The Chronicle of Fu Xi.

***

Throughout the chilly night, the surviving slaves and Lo newcomers huddled at the enclosure's opposite ends. The paddock's side along the muddy riverbed seemed to be the commonly agreed area to relieve oneself. Virag did so, and then unable to sleep, slouched against the stockade and watched the bonfire across the camp and imagined being warm.

Shadows moved back and forth before the flames. Virag sensed urgency and purpose in their movement. Then short, shrill screams echoed in the night, followed by laughter. This repeated several times before relative silence reigned once again across the camp. Virag recognized torture's music when he heard it. Virag looked around the slave pen at horrified eyes staring into the darkness.

War drums summoned the camp before sunrise. Dawn revealed five fresh pikes erected along the north cliff's base, each topped with an impaled man. To his surprise, Virag recognized them as the five warriors who had captured the Minnow.

What was their crime? Virag wondered.

Sunlight brought bustling activity throughout the camp, but no food for the slaves. Moments before dawn, Axe Face assembled a small force, perhaps twenty warriors, in the central area near the cliffs. After Axe Face issued what sounded like orders, the warriors ran up the ramp. Silhouetted by the false dawn, they vanished over the canyon rim toward the east.

They've sent a scouting party to find those who sang last night, Virag thought.

"How long before you think they'll find the Crane?" Kus-ge had approached unnoticed.

Virag shrugged. "I'd be surprised if we don't see them led into camp before sunset."

Kus-ge shook her head. "The Crane obviously don't know this army is here, or they would have been much quieter."

Virag nodded to the huddled Minnow Clan. "And those fools answered the song. The red warriors know more slaves are out there, easy pickings." Virag pointed to various places around the camp. "They are dismantling their shelters and extinguishing the fires. The ramp is completed. My guess is we're their new pack animals."

"As long as we're not their new breakfast," Kus-ge remarked dryly.

"I've been watching those big tents over there," Virag remarked. "My guess is that one belongs to that beak-faced fellow we saw last night."

"The one who took my necklace?"

"Yes, I think he is their leader. I'm surprised he didn't take you to his tent last night."

Kus-ge scowled. "I'd rip his eyes out."

Virag laughed. "Better get used to it, my pretty little marsh flower. It would be better to be his woman than a pack animal, or breakfast." He nodded at the skeletal slaves huddled in the corner. "They will work us to death, just like them. And when we're too weak to work, they will eat us. That's how this is going to work."

"I will die first," she hissed.

"Suit yourself, or we can work together."

"What do you mean?"

"They haven't raped you, yet. The pack leader always gets the pick. Work your way into Axe Face's good graces, become his woman. Try to learn what you can about who they are, and where they are going." Virag looked over the slaves. "In the meantime, I'll stay busy out here."

Kus-ge considered him suspiciously. "You never stop playing the fox, do you?"

"As long as you can be a good snake, we might survive this little detour, and maybe come out on top." He paused and looked about. "As long as nothing else unexpected happens."

That's when the flap to the large tent flew opened. Kus-ge shrank back.

A giant emerged and surveyed the camp like a king. Taller than even Spako, he had flesh like chiseled obsidian. Unlike the red warriors, he wore sandals, and a clean white tunic hanging just above his knees. A gracefully curved sword, similar to the ones the red warriors used, dangled on his hip. The black giant stretched, tucked his thumbs into his waist belt, and let his gaze settle on Virag and Kus-ge.

"*That* is unexpected," Virag said drolly.

The warriors dragged Kus-ge from the slave pen, and threw her at the black giant's feet.

"Be a good girl," Virag whispered to himself as he watched the proceedings. "This is truly their leader. Be his friend."

There was something about this black giant's nature beyond Virag's experience, and that deeply irritated, and perhaps even frightened, him. Axe Face stood at the giant's side, handed him something, and pointed to Kus-ge. The Black Giant let the dragon necklace dangle in his fingers, studying it. He said something to Axe Face, and then the warriors took Kus-ge to the large tent.

Kus-ge shot Virag a sly smile before she entered the tent. *Was that the look of a confidant, one about to betray me, or just madness?* Virag thought.

Then the Black Giant turned his gaze to Virag. This one wasn't to be trifled with. Virag bowed low.

Shouting erupted from the camp's far side. Several warriors burst into the common area, dragging one of their own under their arms. The warrior looked winded, and to Virag, frightened. He fell prostrate before the Black Giant. Axe Face barked, and he rose to his knees, repeating two words and pointing into the canyon.

"Foo Zhee! Foo Zhee!"

The Black Giant's demeanor instantly changed. He peered into the dark gorge, and gripped his sword hilt.

Whoever this Black Giant is, Virag thought, *he has an enemy.*

55: Northward.

"Cross o'er the Rivers Four to domains hidden," their Master calls deep,
"Yonder patient be, shepherds, and lead My children who will follow nigh.
"All that before was darkness is made new by My power and lambent,
"Here, the meek linger in Earth's sacred womb, yet to dwell only for now." - The Song of Athena

- The Chronicle of Fu Xi.

***

The men decided to spend what little daylight remained gathering wood and making a fire. Maybe whoever had sung the ai-halah would see it and come their way. As twilight deepened into night, they sat around the fire in silence. Ezra didn't mind the quiet, or the hunger gnawing his belly. He felt good, better than he'd felt since the rains ceased. He was thankful for not being in the canyon, and loved the soft grass under his feet. The air smelled fresh up here, as if the world had been made new. Even Levidi seemed more upbeat. "I heard Alaya's voice, I'm sure of it. We will find them in the morning," he would occasionally remind himself and throw another stick into the fire.

At dawn, they resumed their trek west, looking down into the canyon as they went. They only found a series of large, fetid pools caught between one succession of timber

466

piles after another. It wasn't yet mid-morning when Levidi pointed below and shouted, "Tracks!"

Ezra peered down. Footprints broke up the sand and mud along a narrow stretch just west of a particularly large timber pile.

"It could have been them," Levidi said.

"I don't think so," Ezra said grimly. "Look." He pointed at several bodies piled near the timber.

"Could they still be alive?" Levidi asked.

"I doubt it, judging by the bloodstains in the sand," Ghalen said. "Those are horse tracks leading in and out."

"Scythians?" Levidi asked.

Did others survive the flood? Ezra thought. "I don't know, but a battle happened here, and whoever won got the horse. Unless they climbed that pile and waded through that cesspool, they're headed west." Ezra knelt and looked down the cliff. "The clay crumbles when you grip it. It's not safe to climb down." He stood up and peered west. "If we run into whoever won that battle, we better be ready to retreat."

"Why?" Levidi asked, hefting his spear.

"Those bodies wear metal armor. See the broken swords lying nearby?"

Ezra looked at Levidi with the utmost seriousness. "We must go back and warn the others."

"No, we keep looking for Alaya."

"If our people stumble across those that did this, it will go badly."

Levidi desperately looked past Ezra to the west, and then back into the canyon.

"They wear armor. They have steel. They are a threat." Ezra kept pressing his point. "We have to think about our people right now. Things have changed."

Ghalen stepped around Ezra and Levidi. "It may already be too late." He brought his spear to the ready. "Someone is coming, and quickly."

Ezra and Levidi followed his gaze to the west.

56: Alone.

"Nephilim, find the lost! From ice land through tangle bush to scorch desert.

"Nephilim, feed the hungry! Make it known grain, vine, arbor's sweet bounty.

"Nephilim, heal the sick! Spirit's gift Grace to all who ask, given.

"Nephilim, light the torch! Prepare a path in this world for My children." - The Song of Athena

- The Chronicle of Fu Xi.

***

During the voyage, the ocean's sounds had rocked Elda to sleep. In Wu, crickets sang her lullaby. For forty nights, the rainfall had been her sedative. As the flood slowly receded, mountain's ever-present wind had rocked her to sleep. This dismal canyon offered only sterile silence.

As she lay curled up on the hastily stacked crates in her tent, Elda could not shut out the stifling quiet. There were no crickets, or even a mosquito's whine to distract her from the camp's subdued misery.

Silence and the tent became her cage.

Elda stifled her tears. Without daytime's bustle, the night held no secrets. Elda didn't want anyone to know her fear and loneliness's depths. She didn't want to add to the camp's overwhelming misery.

Every whimper and sniffle from the slave pen across the commons invaded her tent. *There are children there*, she thought. *Lo children, begging their mother for a morsel*. The Lo men conversed in deep whispers. Though she could not and understood every word, they spoke in Lo.

Alone in his cage, she knew Kol-ok heard all of this, too. His reaction to his people's arrival mystified Elda.

She eagerly went to his cage last night brimming with questions. When she opened the flap, Kol-ok had glimpsed the body by the fire. Kol-ok's horror betrayed his familiarity with the victim, and Elda hastily covered the cage.

"Go back to your tent," Kol-ok had whispered, his voice shaking. "Avoid the newcomers."

Elda had opened her mouth to argue, but Kol-ok cut her off. "Please. We talk soon when safe."

Safe? When will it ever be safe?

Confused and hurt, Elda relented. "As you wish." She slunk back to her tent, and there she remained throughout the night. For the first time since the Atlanteans destroyed her city, Elda felt truly alone. Ercole and Amiran were gone. Now, circumstance separated her from Kol-ok, and she didn't know why.

Outside, an Olmec barked an order, shattering the pre-dawn calm. *Quexil summons his warriors*, she thought. *Leviathan goes in search of those that sang the beautiful song.*

I am alone among monsters, she thought.

She jumped as the war drums shattered the morning calm. The panic enveloped her. She sat up on the crate, trying to breathe. Hugging herself tightly, she rocked back and forth, desperately fending off the desolation threatening to consume her.

The Olmecs assembled only yards from her tent. Metal rattled aggressively. Feet shuffled in soft sand. Elda could almost feel the anticipation for battle, their bloodlust, soaking though the tent with the coming dawn. Quexil barked orders and whipped his killers into a frenzy.

Leviathan and his army were about to march, intent on destroying what beauty remained in the world.

A shadow passed outside the tent. The Olmecs grew quiet.

It's Leviathan, she thought. The god's presence alone carried power.

What is Kol-ok thinking now? she thought. *I lost a teacher — he lost a mother. His people raised their voice to the sunset last night. They are out there somewhere, defenseless. Leviathan will find them. If I am frightened, how much more frightened is he? He must feel like I did watching my city burn from the harbor.*

I am all he has. He is all I have.

Shouts resounded down the canyon. The Olmecs sounded a warning. She heard Quexil shout, "Bring him here." Then, a few heartbeats later, Quexil addressed someone in Olmec, likely one of his warriors. "Where is the rest of your patrol?"

"Fu Xi!" the warrior shouted repeatedly.

A shiver went down Elda's spine. Her thoughts drifted to the kind demigod, and the months she and Ercole had shared with him in the library in Wu. Those days spent under Amiran's tutelage, wandering among shelves stuffed with scrolls, were among the best of her life. The library was gone. Amiran was gone. Ercole was gone.

Fu Xi lurked nearby, a demigod that could challenge Leviathan. Elda stood and tilted her ear toward the tent's wall.

"Where are your men?" Quexil repeated.

"His men are dead," Leviathan declared. "What of the scholar and the harlot?" A dead pause followed, and then he spoke again. "As I thought. You may still redeem yourself and save your own life. Lead us back to where Fu Xi slew your brothers and I will consider it."

"Thank you, Great Paqua!" the warrior said.

"Your jaguars stand ready, Great Paqua!" Quexil hissed. "What is your command?"

"Take half our remaining force and assemble two war parties," Leviathan commanded. "This dog will lead fifty through the canyon to where he encountered Nuwa's spawn. You and one hundred will accompany me along the rim east. We will likely find Fu Xi among mortals, probably from the same tribe we captured yesterday," Leviathan said. "Leave Fu Xi to me, otherwise kill only as necessary. We need fresh slaves."

She heard Quexil's sword rattle as he bowed.

Soon, a hundred feet pounded up the log ramps out of the canyon before silence, and dawn, returned to the camp. Sunlight painted patterns on the tent, and warmed the interior. Elda slid between two crates and, swimming in self-doubt, hugged her knees tightly.

A sun ray penetrated the tent and fell upon a familiar leather strap protruding from behind a chest. She reached out, pulled the strap, and Amiran's navigation kit slid from behind the chest.

Elda gently lifted the heavy chest and placed it on her lap. She caressed the lid and whispered the words:

"All that is observed is worthy of measurement. All which is measured should be done so accurately. All that is measured shall be recorded."

The thought of him abandoning her was easier to accept than the scholar abandoning his navigation kit. Elda slid her fingers under the steel-lined lid and entered the combination. The lid popped opened far more forcefully than it had in the past.

Her eyes grew wide at the unexpected treasure inside.

57: The Three Fools.

Seven trek, loyal and faithful to Lord's bidding, journey the world wend,
Two lovers steal ecstasy, a moment's lust in Tree's shadow sated.
Serpent Gold clings to Black Serpent unrequited, lust's bitter travail,
One god alone savage queen weds, together kingdom's dark founding. - The Song of Athena

- The Chronicle of Fu Xi.

***

At dawn, Fu Xi placed the new mother and her child upon Heise. He'd won her trust, and that of the simpleton. He wasn't sure if he'd won Sana's trust. Now that he knew her true name, he felt some sadness abandoning the name "Mystery," which he had grown fond of.

Sana stomped and shouted, pointing back down the ravine, trying to convince him they needed to reenter the canyon. Fu Xi was rapidly picking up bits and pieces of their language. It had a similar syntax to Attican, the language Amiran often spoke to his apprentices Elda and Ercole. This further reinforced his suspicion he drew closer to the land of the Gray-Eyed Queen.

Fu Xi held up the sword he'd taken off one of the dead Olmecs, and then pointed the way they had come and spoke the Attican word for enemy. "*Echthrós.*"

Sana ignored him and pointed to the others, and then down the gorge. *There are obviously many others*, he thought. *She wants me to help search for them.*

Fu Xi knelt down and quickly drew a map of the entire canyon as he knew it. Sana knelt beside him, watching him sketch.

"We," Fu Xi said in her tongue and pointed to the thin ravine along the massive canyon's north rim.
"Fight...enemies." He held up the sword again and pointed to the bruised bump on her head.

He placed his hand out like a dam. "Enemies trap...we." He drew a line coming from the west beyond his map, toward the dead end. "*Enemy*," he said, and then smashed his fist into his open palm. Using drawing and broken speech in

her language, Fu Xi tried to explain Leviathan's warriors would easily find them.

Sana studied the map. He saw her thoughts churning, perhaps shocked he had picked up elements of her speech so quickly. Sana looked up at the open sky, just beginning to brighten up the narrow draw leading out of the canyon, and then nodded in agreement. "Yes."

In a few moments, with Spako leading the way, their small band began the climb up the narrow draw. Sana led Heise by the reins, while Fu Xi brought up the rear, keeping a wary eye behind them.

Fu Xi had briefly scouted this section above the canyon when he first found Alaya and Spako. Now Fu Xi found himself looking at the broad, sloping meadows leading up to glacier-covered cliffs. Sana said something to Alaya, and began to lead the horse east.

"No," Fu Xi shook his head and spoke in Cin. "That's where I came from. There's nothing there."

Alaya and Sana began speaking at him rapidly and passionately; too rapidly for Fu Xi to understand most of it. Spako looked on, blinking.

They think their people are east, he thought. He pointed at the cliffs and motioned with his palm. "I'm taking you north, and then west," he said in Cin.

Sana crossed her arms and shook her head.

"No," Fu Xi said in her language.

She scowled, turned her back, and led Heise east along the rim.

Spako shrugged at Fu Xi and followed Sana.

Fu Xi muttered under his breath and followed.

Alaya, baby at her breast, looked over her shoulder at Fu Xi with amusement. Then her eyes drifted past him, and mirth turned to fear.

Only a few hundred yards away, a band of Olmecs charged.

***

To her shock, Sana felt herself suddenly lifted up on the horse behind Alaya. Before she could resist, the stranger unbuckled his shield, and handed her the reins. She glanced back and saw a dozen warriors like those that attacked her yesterday, closing fast. He slapped the horse's rump, and the stallion bolted. Sana found herself holding Alaya and the baby tightly with one arm and the reins with the other.

He's giving us a chance, Sana thought.

Part of her wanted to wheel the horse about, draw the lance, and fight. Alaya and the child kept Sana galloping east.

She glanced over her shoulder to see Spako and the stranger standing shoulder-to-shoulder.

They're going to die saving us, she thought. The horse flew across the grassy plains toward the rising sun.

***

Fu Xi shouted at Spako, "Run!"

The giant pounded the orichalcum staff against his palm and didn't budge. He didn't doubt the big man was a formidable fighter, but he knew the skilled Olmecs would quickly cut him down.

Fu Xi assessed the enemy force. *It's a scouting party*, he thought. He spotted their leader in front, barking orders. A warrior immediately turned around and fled west.

He's going to report back to the main army, Fu Xi thought. The rest fanned out and slowed to a walk.

"Have it your way, big man," Fu Xi told Spako. "I know you don't understand me, but they're going to try to flank us and pursue the women. We can't let that happen. So here is the plan…fight and fall back, and then fight some more."

Spako looked down and furrowed his brow.

Fu Xi stepped backward a few paces. "Fall back!" he repeated, and motioned for Spako to do the same. Confusion gave way to understanding, and Spako nodded.

Fu Xi grinned. *He's obviously fought a battle or two.*

The Olmecs surrounded them, but held their attack.

Their leader looked at Fu Xi in shocked surprise, but still advanced. Several warriors slowly advanced to their right. Fu Xi pointed his sword the leader and issued a warning in Atlantean. "If your men take another step, they die." He considered the Olmec commander, a lean panther of a man. "You know you cannot kill me."

As if in response, the leader clicked his teeth loudly, and several men sheathed their swords. They withdrew three stone balls dangling on long chords and began whirling them over their heads.

Fu Xi quickly calculated the odds and lunged at the Olmec leader. Spako roared and followed his cue. Fu Xi swatted the first bolo away with his blade. The second bounced off his chest plate. He closed the distance, and the leader went down in a spray of blood. Before he could kill another, a bolo entangled his feet. Fu Xi dropped, rolled over, and quickly sliced the cords. As Fu Xi tried to stand, more bolos entangled his arms and legs.

Spako fell to his knees, face bright red as tight chords choked him. The Olmecs fell upon them with clubs.

Fu Xi tried to ward off the blows with his armored forearms. Even with his arms pinned together, Fu Xi's blade found another victim. A club smashed his hands, and the sword flew from his grip. The Olmecs piled on, trying to further bind his limbs. Fu Xi threw them off, only to have them pile on again. He felt ropes encircle his feet. Someone pulled off his helmet. An Olmec loomed over him, obsidian club raised high. A spear suddenly plunged through the Olmec's neck and he collapsed.

Fu Xi slipped off the bindings, grabbed his sword, and stumbled to his feet.

Spako lay motionless, while the remaining eight Olmecs faced three men in loincloths, armed only with crude spears.

One of the men, not much more than a boy, picked up an Olmec sword and smiled broadly. He momentarily judged its weight and feel, before throwing his spear at the nearest Olmec. The warrior easily swatted the spear away, but the boy followed the spear and sliced open the Olmec's abdomen. The boy pivoted to the next warrior and plunged the blade under his arm.

The two other spearmen clearly lacked the boy's martial skills. The tall man with a shaggy blond mane must have thrown his spear at Fu Xi's attacker, because now he faced two warriors with only a flint knife. He dodged and weaved, but would not last long.

The shorter, black-haired man fought bravely, but with complete ineptness. He held out his spear to block, only to have it sliced cleanly in two.

Fu Xi fell upon the remaining Olmecs. In only a few moments, the only surviving enemy lay dying in the grass.

Fu Xi knelt and slowly sank his sword into the warrior's thigh. The Olmec clenched his needle teeth but did not cry out.

"Where is Leviathan?" Fu Xi said calmly in Atlantean. The God of Names slowly, expertly, worked the sword back and forth to induce maximum pain. He spared no pity for Leviathan's cannibals. It only took a few moments for Fu Xi to extract what he wanted before ending the warrior's suffering. Fu Xi cleaned his sword on an Olmec's waist wrap and collected his helmet.

The three men knelt over Spako, working to untie the bolo around his neck. Soon, the big man coughed and sputtered, but otherwise seemed unhurt. They hugged the simpleton.

Fu Xi shook his head. *These three fools just charged almost a dozen deadly killers, armed only with wooden sticks.*

Sana and Alaya trotted toward them. Sana dismounted and helped Alaya and the baby down. The dark-haired man rushed to Alaya. With joyful tears, they fell into each other's embrace. The dark-haired man showered her face with kisses. She pulled back the blanket, revealing the baby. The dark-haired man, whom Alaya kept calling "Levidi," took the infant and cradled her. Fu Xi could feel the man's overwhelming relief, and rejoiced for him.

"A good thing has happened here today," Fu Xi whispered. He turned to look for Sana, and felt his heart drop. The tall blond man embraced Sana, and they shared a deep kiss. Sana caught Fu Xi staring, and turned away, suddenly self-conscious.

Spako picked up the strange orichalcum staff and offered it to Levidi, who considered it in amazement. They exchanged words, and Levidi took it.

The horse grazed, seeming intent on enjoying the valley's lush grasses as Fu Xi stroked his flank and took the reins. Sana approached, her demeanor subdued, almost apologetic. She pointed to the newcomers and named each of them.

Ghalen, he thought. *That must be her husband.* Ghalen smiled and held out his hand to Fu Xi. The demigod accepted it. Levidi elected to hug him instead. Fu Xi awkwardly patted Levidi on the back. Before Fu Xi could pull away, Alaya and Spako joined the hug.

He glanced over Levidi's shoulder and spotted the young man they called Ezra collecting swords and pilfering the dead for whatever he could find, including several sets of the light chain shirts. Ezra handed the swords and chain shirts to the other men and Sana. Sana eyed her sword appreciatively, while Ghalen and Levidi held theirs awkwardly.

Only Ezra donned the armor.

The young man eyed Fu Xi suspiciously. *He's different*, Fu Xi thought, *as is Sana*. Ghalen, Levidi, and Alaya had similar mannerisms and speech, but Sana and Ezra were more wary.

Well, Fu Xi thought, *Spako is just Spako.*

Fu Xi suspected these were survivors from different tribes.

Ezra approached and pointed to his own chest. "Ezra." Then he pointed to Fu Xi.

"Fu Xi," the demigod said.

"Foozhee," Ezra repeated slowly, and nodded.

Introductions are over, Fu Xi thought. The Olmec had confirmed his fears. Leviathan and his army were bearing down from the west.

***

"Who is he?" Levidi asked.

"He saved our lives," Alaya said.

"He knows who these men are," Sana said. "They must be his enemies."

"How do you know?" Ghalen asked, looking over at Fu Xi.

"These are hardened fighting men," Ezra said. "I've never seen weapons and armor like theirs. The quality exceeds Hur-ar's finest blacksmiths." He glanced at Fu Xi. "His armor isn't steel or bronze."

"It's like the Uros's staff and my blood dagger," Sana said, and added dryly, "which he took from me and hasn't returned."

Ezra had never seen a warrior fight like Fu Xi. "He looks like one of the Silk People." Ezra pointed his sword at the dead men. "As for them, I've never seen their like."

Ghalen shook his head. "What does he want?"

"He wants us to go north with him," Sana said. "I think he's warning us more are coming."

Ezra caught Fu Xi watching her intently. "These men are lightly provisioned, a waterskin and some food. They must be scouts for a larger army. If so, we are in serious trouble." Ezra opened one of their food pouches. "Dried meat." He sniffed it and prepared to take a bite when Fu Xi slapped it from his hand. Fu Xi sternly shook his head. He touched Ezra's arm and shoulder, gently pinching his flesh, and then pointed to the food pouch.

Alaya gasped. "It's human flesh, Ezra. Those monsters eat people!"

Ezra considered the dead men and their needle teeth with grim understanding. He cast away the other food pouches.

"Sana, do you trust him?" Ghalen asked.

"Of course we trust him!" Alaya interrupted.

Sana smiled at Alaya. "I don't think we have a choice."

Ezra agreed. They didn't have a choice. "We can't fight them. Our only hope is to flee."

"Flee, yes," Fu Xi said. "Army coming."

58: Kombetha.

Forbidden, they tarry from Divine Decree in flesh man and woman.

"Love me as you did in days ancient," purrs Seduction. "Clad in Power!"

Skin to scale, finger to claw, serpent winged unify in the Garden,

Dragon Gold, Dragon Black, souls amar'thine seduced with Water's sweet sin. - The Song of Athena

- The Chronicle of Fu Xi.

***

It wasn't long before they came to the stream above the waterfall where Ezra first discovered the way out of the canyon.

"This is the way." Ezra pointed down. "I'll go first." He gestured to the horse. "I'm not sure he can make it down there."

Fu Xi seemed to understand. Then Ezra saw someone climbing up from the shadowed recesses. Beyond the figure, many others waited below.

Ghalen and Levidi stepped alongside Ezra and looked down. "Aizarg!" Levidi shouted gleefully.

Aizarg stopped only a dozen feet below them and smiled. "It's good to see you! We followed your tracks."

"Quickly, Uros! Come up and see!" Ghalen called down. The tone in Ghalen's and Levidi's voices seemed to ignite something in the Uros, and he quickened his pace.

"Spako, help me down," Alaya said, and in a few moments, she was off the horse. She wrapped her arm around Sana's waist. "Come, let's greet him together."

To Ezra, Sana seemed unsure, but she allowed Alaya to drag her forward beside the men. Fu Xi and Ezra had drifted from the canyon's edge beside the horse. Fu Xi kept looking over his shoulder at where they had come. Ezra knew they shared the same concern. Time was running out.

The Uros emerged from the canyon and gazed, mesmerized, at those surrounding him.

Spako broke the spell first, and lifted Aizarg in an enormous bear hug. Aizarg laughed heartily in a way Ezra had never seen before. Alaya approached next, kissed Aizarg on the cheek and presented the Uros her baby. "Levidi and I have named her Kombetha."

Ezra smiled as the Uros openly wept. "Joyful Reunion. A beautiful name for a beautiful child."

Sana stepped forward. "My Uros."

Aizarg considered her as if he could not believe his eyes. He reached out and touched her hair, "Praise to the Nameless God, for today is a day of miracles." He closed his eyes, put her head in his hands, and kissed Sana tenderly on the forehead. A lone tear rolled down Sana's cheek, and she returned Aizarg's embrace.

Ezra didn't see the blur rushing him until Su-gár threw herself into his arms, wrapping her legs around his waist and covering him with kisses. "You found them! Thank you, thank you!" Ezra didn't know what else to do except return her kisses. Bat-or hugged Ezra's leg, and stared at the horse with wonder and fright.

The Lo emerged from the darkness below and rejoiced under a blue sky. They surrounded the Uros and those who had once been lost. Then a hush settled over the crowd. Fu Xi stared intensely at Aizarg and took a step forward. Ezra handed Bat-or to Su-gár, and placed himself between the stranger and his Uros. Fu Xi tore his eyes from Aizarg and focused on Ezra, and, as if waking from a dream, smiled warmly. Ezra felt some apprehension melt away, but didn't move. Fu Xi spoke in halting Lo. "Be…at peace, Ezra. I mean…no harm."

Fu Xi stepped around Ezra and approached Aizarg.

Fu Xi addressed the Uros, "I am Fu Xi, son of Nuwa. Your people are in great danger."

59: Power and Purpose.

Shame grips her heart, to fortress peak recluse Gaia flees enceinte labor,
Sheltered deep, thousand-year slumber she waits 'till birthed a son stalwart.
Born unto her, Totaresh! Rebellion's Child and Guardian Regent,
Steward of Paradise, Terror Incarnate, God of Dragons noble. - The Song of Athena

- The Chronicle of Fu Xi.

***

"I am Aizarg, Uros of the Lo. How do you know my language?"

"I have a…gift with…spoken words," the man called Fu Xi said.

Clad in exquisite, unadorned red metal armor, the same color as his staff, the magnificent stranger stood taller than even Ghalen. He appeared well-fed, and exuded vibrance and confidence.

Sana left Ghalen's side and stepped around to confront Fu Xi. "How long have you understood me?" she said suspiciously.

He smiled and rubbed the top of his head. "Not long…enough." Fu Xi removed the wrapped leather thong holding Sana's daggers from below his armor and extended them.

Sana snatched the daggers, eyes smoldering dangerously. "What of my red blade?" she demanded.

"I may need that a little longer. I am...curious...how you came by it?"

"It belonged to my grandmother. It's mine and I want it back."

"It was my mother's first."

His response left Sana slack-jawed.

"Who sent you?" Aizarg asked, unsure of the stranger's intentions. "How did you survive the flood?"

"Uros, this man fights like no other," Ezra interrupted. "The danger he speaks of is an army coming this way. We stand no chance without him. We should listen to him."

Aizarg turned to Sana. "My Isp, what is your counsel?"

Sana didn't take her eyes off Fu Xi. "He twice saved my life. Ezra is right."

"Trust him, Uros!" Alaya shouted.

"No time." Fu Xi seemed to momentarily struggle to find the words. "This army is led by one..." He paused again and tapped his armor. "...like me. They come here now. Kill and enslave. No mercy." Astonished, Aizarg noticed how the stranger's command of their language improved with each sentence.

Ezra stared at Aizarg forcefully. "Trust him, Uros. There is no time." Ghalen, Levidi, and even Sana seemed to defer to Ezra.

Aizarg addressed Fu Xi, "What must we do?"

Fu Xi turned to Ezra. "You know battle, yes?"

Ezra nodded. "I know how to fight."

"Can you ride?"

Ezra looked at the horse and grinned broadly. "Yes!"

"Take my horse. He called Heise. Ride to tall place." He pointed to the cliffs. "Go west. Find way through tall place."

"I am a better rider!" Sana interrupted. "And I already know Black."

"You named my horse Black?" Fu Xi acted surprised, and then laughed.

"I didn't have time to think of a better name," Sana rebuffed him, as if Fu Xi's question offended her.

Fu Xi resumed talking to Ezra. "If you cannot find escape or hiding place, find place where many count for little."

"You mean a choke point," Ezra said. "Where superior numbers can't help them."

"Yes, yes." Fu Xi smiled and nodded.

In two bounds, Ezra swung himself on the horse's back. To Aizarg's untrained eyes, it only seemed to take a moment before horse and rider accustomed themselves to one another, and then they raced across the grasslands.

"Uros." Levidi stepped forward with the red staff. "Alaya had this. She hung on to it when the barge broke up. It saved her life." Levidi extended it. "It allowed both her and Spako to hold it without pain."

The staff warmed in Aizarg's hands, shimmering with the faint blue glow just as it had done those many months ago on the Wedding Barge.

Fu Xi solemnly considered the staff, and then raised his gaze to Aizarg. "Aizarg, your people must follow Ezra north, *now*. If you flee east, they catch you," Fu Xi said urgently. For a fleeting second, Aizarg thought he saw the blue glow mirrored in the stranger's eyes. Like the staff, something about Fu Xi resonated with Aizarg. He sensed a deep power and purpose burning in the stranger's soul, a power he'd only encountered once before in Noah.

Aizarg felt like they were walking the a-g'an again in the ice mists, following Sarah and Setenay into a terrifying unknown.

Aizarg looked around at those he once feared forever lost. They were all here, looking upon him expectantly. His staff was here, and so was this strange man they called Fu Xi.

Aizarg considered the man's red armor, and the tingling warmth in his hands. Then he saw Kombetha contentedly suckling at Alaya's breast.

Aizarg nodded. "So be it. We will do as you ask, Fu Xi."

Fu Xi drew his sword. "I try to slow them down, but if they get around me, they will be on you quickly."

"What do we do, then?" one of the Lo men asked.

Fu Xi addressed them all, "Follow Ezra — he will find a way. Go quickly. Carry the children if you must. Do not look back. When come to the cliffs, turn west, keep running. The cliffs will keep you from being surrounded."

***

Sana, Spako, and Ghalen lingered as the rest of the Lo ventured across the grasslands, led by Levidi and Alaya. Aizarg had decided to stay and help fight, but everyone, including Fu Xi, begged him to reconsider.

Fu Xi pointed to Aizarg's staff and then his own armor. "It is called orichalcum metal. It can only be…wrought…by dragon fire. How did you come by it?"

"That story must wait for another time," Aizarg replied.

Fu Xi nodded. He sensed his mother's power at play here. "It is a torch, to light your people's way. If the torchbearer falls, the people fall. You must go."

Fu Xi saw reluctant acceptance settle upon the man they called Uros. Aizarg turned and joined his people, the little one called Bat-or and Ezra's woman following closely.

Sana hefted her sword, swinging it crisply a few times to get comfortable with it.

"What are you doing?" Fu Xi asked Sana.

"Staying here with you."

"You cannot help me," Fu Xi said.

"Another sword always helps," she said dismissively.

Fu Xi nodded at the weapon in her hands. "You know how to use that?"

Her glare was sharper than the sword.

"I take that as a yes," he said.

Spako gripped a heavy Olmec war club in each hand like twigs. "Spako like these," he said with childish glee.

Sana turned to Ghalen. "You must go with your people."

Ghalen looked confused, and perhaps hurt. "Don't you mean *our* people?"

Sana shook her head, flustered. "Yes, I meant *our* people. You can't stay here. Your spear is useless against swords."

Ghalen hefted the shaft. "I've already killed one with this."

Sana growled and pushed him back. "Stop being foolish!"

"I'm not leaving you." Ghalen crossed his arms. "I'll use the sword Ezra gave me."

Ghalen looked like a man who had made up his mind, and Fu Xi respected his determination.

"You don't know how to use a sword!" Sana snapped. "Quit playing games. Aizarg needs you."

"I need you," Ghalen shot back. "I'm not going to lose you again."

"Please." Sana looked as if on the edge of tears. Fu Xi truly hoped Sana would relent and go with her people. Fu Xi recognized her warrior's spirit. Ghalen had proved himself adept with a spear, but Sana was correct — if Ghalen stayed, the Olmecs would quickly cut him down. Fu Xi couldn't protect either of them.

Ghalen wouldn't budge.

Sana drew a long, black dagger from her thigh strap and turned her back on Ghalen. "Then you've chosen a fool's death." She froze.

Fu Xi turned to see a pack of Olmecs running toward them, perhaps only half a mile away.

"You are both stuck here now." Fu Xi found these people's language easier to speak with each sentence. "Ghalen, stay on my left side. I will use my shield to protect you best I can. Sana, take the right side. Spako, crush any that slip past us. Remember, our purpose is to stall their advance. When I say fall back, fall back. When I say run, obey. Do you understand?" They nodded and took their places.

Guilt tore through Fu Xi's heart. These three were fully aware they were about to die for their people. Fu Xi knew victory or no victory, he'd be the only survivor.

If Leviathan made an appearance, even that wasn't a guarantee.

***

Before mid-morning, Amiran had found a way down the steep canyon walls into the gorge that didn't involve too much climbing. Crossing the river itself had been easy. What had once been a raging torrent was now little more than a series of mud-pits and stagnant ponds. They'd spent the rest of the morning trying to find a way up the canyon's north rim. That opportunity came in the form of a partially collapsed cliff. With great effort, Amiran and Atamoda picked their way up the landslide to the rim and the lush green fields beyond.

Exhausted, Atamoda quietly endured. He, too, wanted to lie down in the tall, soft grass and let the sun soak into his bones. He addressed her unspoken wish, "We rest at nightfall. There is only a narrow window of time before Leviathan's army cuts us off."

Snow-capped cliffs loomed ahead as the slope gradually steepened. Glancing behind, Amiran could clearly see the entire valley. The valley's opposite side, from where they had come, looked ashen. It was as if they had crossed from the land of the dead to the land of the living.

"Please, Amiran, slow down," Atamoda said breathlessly from behind.

"We'll rest, but only for a few moments." Amiran's bag seemed to grow heavier as they climbed. He looked up at the looming cliffs.

Atamoda sat down on a scorched log. "Look at all of these burned trees," Atamoda said.

"A great fire swept this valley, perhaps not long before the flood. The grasses here are recent, feeding off the ashes."

"This place has great spiritual power," Atamoda said. "I can feel it."

Amiran squinted and shielded his eyes as he surveyed the valley. "I'll have to take your word on that."

"The beast Leviathan is hunting, does it really dwell beyond those cliffs?"

Amiran put down the bag but didn't sit. He studied the cliffs. "I believe so."

Atamoda shivered. "Do you think we're in danger?"

Amiran shook his head. "If it had smelled us, we'd already be dead."

"You look perplexed."

"I think Zelko's story was true. This forest burned quickly and ferociously, and at incredible temperatures. It was incinerated. Only dragon's fire could do something like that."

Atamoda's eyes grew wide. "A monster did all this?"

"Dragons aren't monsters, Atamoda. They're just animals. Incredible animals, yes, but still only flesh and blood. They live far longer than humans, but eventually die. A bull dragon eats, and to eat he must hunt. He lives in balance with his surroundings. He only hunts what he needs, and guards his territory jealously."

"Guards against what?"

"Other bulls…or humans. I've seen sign of elk and deer as we've walked through these fields. There is game here. If a bull dragon lurks nearby, this place is his hunting grounds."

"You still look confused," she said.

"I am." He shook his head. "If a dragon did this, that means he despoiled his own hunting grounds. Such behavior is odd. He likely destroyed it in the process of defending it." He held out his arms as if to encompass the burnt stumps and logs surrounding them. "Such destruction as this couldn't be wrought by a single dragon, so it must have been two. That means this was a battleground."

Atamoda looked around. "It must have been terrible beyond imagining."

"Yes." He nodded appreciatively. "It must have been something to behold. When bulls battle, it's to the death. If that's what truly happened, it means the age of dragons has not passed, and the doe we slew during our voyage wasn't the last of her kind. She might have even been seeking one of these bulls."

"Didn't Zelko say he only saw one dragon?"

"Yes."

Atamoda stood. "Where do we go from here?"

Amiran turned and pointed to the cliffs. "We're almost to the mountains. Up there, we'll have an even better view and should be able to see Leviathan's army before they see us. Once there, we'll skirt west until we are clear of the valley. After that, I think we'll be safe from either Leviathan or the beast." Amiran turned to look downhill.

He yanked Atamoda down into a crouch. He pointed to a large band skirting the canyon rim at a quick jog. "Leviathan's scouts, about twenty of them."

"How can you tell from here? They are so far away," Atamoda said, voice trembling.

"They run in single file. They are Olmecs."

Amiran scanned intently back to the west, where the scout force had come. "There!" he exclaimed. "Do you see them?"

Atamoda looked where he pointed. A large host marched east.

"It looks like the main force is still emerging from the canyon, and that works in our favor. The scouts are about two miles ahead of that main force. It won't be long before they find our trail." He looked back up toward the cliff. "They could be on us before nightfall. Stay low, follow me."

"Wait," she said. "Look there."

A large group strung out in a ragged line halfway to the canyon's rim, ascending the slope toward them from the opposite direction.

"Who are they?" Atamoda whispered.

"I don't know, but they aren't Leviathan's."

"How can you be so sure?"

"Far too disorganized."

The Olmec scouts made a straight line toward the ragged band at a full run.

"The Olmecs aren't scouting; they are pursuing. They are hunting those people. That means we have a chance to slip away. Let's go. Stay low." Amiran took Atamoda's hand and pulled her uphill.

They didn't get far when Atamoda yanked him down. "Over there!"

Dread overcame Amiran. Two Olmecs ran uphill, perhaps 200 yards away. He dropped on his stomach behind a log and pulled Atamoda next to him.

"They don't see us yet," he whispered. The scouts drew closer until they stopped only about a hundred yards away. The warriors talked for several minutes as they surveyed the valley.

Amiran dared not move.

***

Atamoda shrank as low as she could behind the log. If they so much as moved, the Olmecs would be upon them in moments.

Amiran removed the red sword from his back and whispered, "Stay here."

"No!" She clenched his arm tightly.

He peeled off her hand and crawled over the log on his hands and knees until he vanished in the tall grass. The next several minutes seemed to pass like an eternity. The Olmecs laughed as if one told a joke. One of them let their gaze drift east, toward her. Atamoda slunk down.

He nudged his accomplice and pointed to where the strangers approached. The Olmecs knelt lower and began murmuring excitedly. Like predatory cats, the Olmecs crept through the grass toward Atamoda. Her hiding place lay directly between the Olmecs and their intended prey.

Atamoda flattened herself against the ground. She dared not even breathe. She couldn't hear them. Were they closer? Could they see her? She wanted to peek, but fear immobilized her.

A shadow fell across her. She looked up into obsidian eyes leering down at her. Then his head slid off and into Atamoda's lap. The warrior's body crumpled beside her in a spray of blood. Amiran stepped over Atamoda to meet the second warrior's attack. Atamoda tossed the head and rolled out of the way.

The second Olmec leapt like a cat. Amiran couldn't react fast enough before the warrior drove his club into Amiran's gut. Atamoda heard a wet crack, then the scholar stumbled backward and doubled over, breathless. The Olmec raised his sword over Amiran's head.

Atamoda leapt up and swung Amiran's bag at the Olmec's face with all her might. He crumpled.

She dropped the bag and rushed to Amiran's side. He clutched his chest, eyes wide, trying to catch his breath. When he did, it came in short, raspy bursts.

Pain erupted across Atamoda's cheek, knocking her to the ground. She rolled onto her side in time to see the Olmec, blood dripping from his forehead, looming over her, sword poised to strike. Her hand clumsily found the red sword's hilt and weakly swung it. To her shock, it passed cleanly through his thigh, cutting his leg in half as if the flesh were soft as sea foam. The Olmec fell. Without hesitation, Atamoda plunged the sword into the Olmec's throat.

She crawled to Amiran and forced his arms away. Atamoda opened his shirt, searching for a wound. "I think you have some broken ribs."

"I think you're right," he wheezed.

She laid her head gently on his chest. "Breathe in all the way."

He obeyed, and winced at the top of his breath.

"I think your lungs are okay, but we have to get these wrapped."

"You can wrap them when we are safely away from this place. Help me." He tried to pull himself up, but slumped again, wincing.

Atamoda wasn't going to be swayed. "Your ribs need to be protected or they might puncture your lungs if you take another fall." She removed her cloak, and with his knife cut a long strip off the bottom. Then she wrapped the cloak tightly around his midriff. Atamoda found a stick nearby and, with his knife, cut two holes in the material. She put the stick through the holes and began to twist. She tightened the cloak until he winced, and then backed it off half a turn. Finally, she secured the stick to his chest with the strip. The entire time, Atamoda fought not to look at the dead bodies.

Amiran examined the makeshift brace appreciatively. "That's good, Atamoda. Thank you. Now, help me up."

Atamoda stood and reached to help Amiran when cold metal pressed against her throat.

"Don't move or you'll die," someone said from behind. Atamoda held her breath, waiting for the sword to slice her throat. It was then she realized the voice spoke her own language.

60: The Battle Begins.

"If the gods were truly benevolent, and deserved our love, they would offer forgiveness, not pleasure nor power. Only through forgiveness can we wipe away the hatred that poisons our short existence. Not even my Beloved Athena can offer such a treasure. I fear if such a god existed, the price for this perfect gift would be too high to bear." - Grand Master Vulcan, from the Ancient of Ancients.

- The Chronicle of Fu Xi.

***

Atamoda closed her eyes and embraced his neck. Ezra could only mutter, "How?"

She caressed his cheek, as if making sure he was real. "Our people?"

"They are coming this way." He pointed downslope.

"Aizarg? Bat-or?"

"Yes!" Ezra laughed, unable to believe this moment could be real. He looked over Atamoda, wondering how she survived, and what manner of strange clothing she wore. "Where is Kol-ok?"

"Alive, but in terrible danger," she replied.

"We are *all* in danger," said the odd man sitting on the ground. He tried to stand but winced in pain and held his chest.

"Ezra, help me get him to his feet. He is a friend."

Ezra and Atamoda lifted the man with skin like soot to his feet. With some effort, Atamoda slung a large, dark leather bag over her shoulder.

The stranger looked at Ezra and spoke clearly in Lo, "Hello, Ezra. My name is Amiran. Are those your people coming up the hill from the east?"

"Yes." Ezra considered the bodies and turned to Atamoda. "These same men are pursuing us. I have been sent to find an escape route, or at least a defendable position."

"You cannot fight them," Amiran said. "Escape is the only option."

"Did you come from the west?" Ezra asked. "Is there a way through these mountains?"

"No, we came from the south," Amiran said. "We escaped their camp. We are looking for a westward passage, too."

"Aizarg must hear what Amiran has to say," Atamoda said. "He knows this enemy. He can help us."

Ezra saw Amiran's wounds. "Can you walk?"

Amiran nodded.

"Good." Ezra gestured to the dead Olmecs. "Where did they come from?"

"Advance scouts," Amiran said. "The army marches along the canyon. Leviathan sent them to the high ground for a better look."

Leviathan? Ezra thought and glanced south. He spotted the main force in the distance and felt sick. "Stay low," he told them. "If they see us, they'll block our escape." He said a prayer to the Nameless God that the main army didn't spot the fleeing Lo. "I must ride west."

Ezra mounted the horse. He glanced at the army far below and slouched in the saddle, trying to lower his profile. *The ground is moist, so the horse shouldn't kick up any dust*, he thought.

"You are leaving?" Atamoda looked bewildered.

"I must find a way through before the enemy catches us."

Amiran hobbled to the horse. He caressed the saddle and stroked the horse's neck, speaking to the beast softly in a strange tongue. "Where did you get this horse?" he addressed Ezra.

"From he who sent me on my mission."

Amiran closed his eyes and hugged the horse's neck. His shoulders sagged as if an invisible weight had been lifted. "Does he still wear the red armor?"

"He does," Ezra said, surprised. "You know of Fu Xi?"

Amiran opened his eyes. "Where is he?"

"He stands alone below, at the canyon's edge. He's trying to buy us time."

"Go, Ezra, do as Lord Fu Xi has commanded."

"Atamoda, our people are coming this way. They are not far behind me. Go to them. When they see you, they will have hope!" Ezra wheeled the horse around and galloped west up the ridge.

***

As Ezra galloped west, Amiran knelt and opened the black bag, and with some effort removed its primary contents, the fat leather satchel. He retied the bag and gave it to Atamoda. "You'll find it much lighter now. There's food and other supplies in there you'll need."

"What are you doing?" Amiran saw confusion wash over Atamoda.

"Our plans have changed. I'm going down there to help my old friend, and give your people a fighting chance. I hope I am not too late. Leviathan is too strong, even for Fu Xi. Whatever time he can buy your people isn't enough. By nightfall your people will be dead or slaves."

"Shouldn't you flee west, with us? What of the Gray-Eyed Queen? What of Kol-ok and Elda?"

"Unless we stop Leviathan now, we'll never reach her." Amiran untied the satchel, but didn't open it. "Your place is with your people. What I am about to do cannot be undone. Once it happens, this will become the valley of death."

Amiran saw turbulent, conflicting emotions swirling through her. She kept glancing east like a child who has become lost.

Amiran lightly placed his hands on her shoulders. "What are you truly afraid of?"

"I can't face my people. Not after what I've done."

"You've done nothing wrong," Amiran said.

"I betrayed him!"

Amiran caressed her cheek and ran his fingers through her hair, letting the sensation of her touch and her beauty sear itself into his memory. "That's what the gods do. They turn us against each other, and against ourselves. He used you, and your love for Kol-ok, against you. Don't give Leviathan that victory."

"I am afraid," Atamoda began to cry.

"I know, but you are strong." Amiran's fingers touched her sleeve over her brand. "This will fade." Then he put his finger over her heart. "Self-loathing is a far heavier collar than iron."

She tightly shut her eyes and lowered her head, unable to speak.

He lifted her chin. "In some way, you loved Leviathan. I know."

Atamoda looked up at him with astonishment. "You see more than I would have ever thought."

Amiran smiled weakly. "I admit, I am often blind when it comes to the ways of the heart."

Atamoda wiped her eyes. "It fills me with shame."

Amiran placed the red sword in her hand and gently closed her fingers around the hilt. He knelt to one knee before Atamoda, and carefully slid the blade between his collar and neck, blade facing outward. "Then let us leave our shame and guilt here. All that came before is no more."

Atamoda merely flicked her wrist and the iron collar fell away, its glowing edges sliced clean. For the first time in Amiran's life, he touched his bare neck.

He picked up the satchel. "Lead your people west and do not look back. Find the Gray-Eyed Queen. She will be able to save Kol-ok and Elda." Amiran kissed her lightly on the forehead, and then hefted the satchel. He turned to go, and then hesitated and turned around. "As a slave, the gods have compelled me to do horrible acts in their name. Over the years, those memories have almost driven me mad. I've had to forgive myself, Atamoda. Forgiveness is the only true path to peace."

"Don't leave me."

Amiran smiled like one who finally knew true peace. "All my life, I've let freedom's spark simmer in my heart. Remember, patesi-le, freedom awaits beyond the fire." With that, the scholar limped down the hill and never looked back.

***

Fu Xi chanced a glance up the slope. Aizarg's people were specks along the cliff's base, slowly vanishing over a small ridge. *They aren't moving fast enough*, he thought.

"Remember, delay them only," Fu Xi spoke calmly to his companions. "Keep falling back, stay away from the ones swinging bolos. Let me absorb the brunt of their attack."

Ghalen crouched, spear in his right hand, sword in his left. "You are but one man."

"Let me worry about that. If I get in trouble, do not try to save me." Fu Xi glanced over his shoulder at the retreating Lo. The first Olmec runners had already seen them and began to skirt diagonally up the hill to intercept.

"Follow me!" Fu Xi shouted and bolted to cut them off.

The main Olmec force shifted its advance to follow Fu Xi. He caught up to the runners as the first bolo whizzed by. The Olmecs' skirmishers repeatedly tried to flank Fu Xi, only to have Sana slow their progress until the demigod could engage.

It only took moments for them to coalesce into an effective fighting team. Fu Xi quickly began to appreciate Sana's prowess and fighting style. Sana didn't fight as much as she engaged the enemy in a death dance. She employed her sword like a shield to deflect initial attacks. Instead of counter-striking, Sana approached intimately close to her foe, making it impossible for him to engage with sword or club. Once inside his attack, she struck swiftly with her dagger, before whirling to dance with the next attacker. She announced each fresh kill with a high-pitched, wavering war cry. Her aggressiveness and unexpected lethality quickly threw the Obsidian Guard off balance.

Spako waded into the Olmecs, relentlessly pounding his clubs down on skulls and spines, and leaving crushed bodies in his wake. The enemy backed off, and Fu Xi saw several warriors preparing bolos against the giant. Sana spotted them first. She cut down the first two while they were still spinning their missiles. She slew the next two while they fumbled for their swords.

The man called Ghalen, however, fared far worse. Spear already shredded, he fought with the broken half in one hand, sword in the other. The fact he had survived this long testified to his speed and bravery, but he'd already suffered several minor wounds.

Sana, sensing her man's peril, fell back and switched from Fu Xi's left flank.

"Fall back!" Fu Xi commanded. They fled up the hill several dozen yards before reestablishing the skirmish line. This provided Fu Xi further opportunity to disrupt fresh bolo attacks. Fight, run, and fight again; the four of them repeated the pattern several times. Fu Xi always shifted right, to the west, as the enemy continually tried to flank them.

Ghalen screamed and crumpled to the grass. Fu Xi dispatched his latest attacker and then spun to engage the warrior about to cleave Ghalen's skull. Sana struck first, and the Olmec's head tumbled into the grass.

Ghalen writhed in agony, a bright red gash straight down his ribcage.

Fu Xi readied for the next attack, but it never came. The depleted Olmec scout force faltered, and slowly fell back. Fu Xi surveyed the battlefield, and knew why they retreated.

The main Obsidian Guard force had arrived, with perhaps a hundred additional warriors. They efficiently formed a battle line. They would quickly roll over Fu Xi and his companions, and easily overtake the retreating Lo.

Sana tried to staunch Ghalen's bleeding with her hands.

"Spako, help him up," Fu Xi commanded.

Spako gulped for air. He was bleeding from a dozen wounds, and bolos dangled from his arms like broken bracelets. He dropped a bloodied club, and lifted Ghalen to his feet. Sana draped Ghalen's arm over her shoulder.

"What is he?" Sana pointed her sword at the battle line. Resplendent in crimson armor, Leviathan emerged from behind his war dogs.

"Run. Your deaths here will serve no purpose. This is my fight." Fu Xi turned away and strode down the hill to meet his enemy.

61: The Waterfall.

Morn's sun confronts Golden Dragon, cold shame abandons child for east wind,
Throne o' rock, Paradise prison, he reigns Cherubim eternal.
Mother's sin, Father's sin, offspring to bear horrid price in valley pen,
Serpent Black slithers beneath sacred Tree, awaits Master's children tempt. - The Song of Athena

- The Chronicle of Fu Xi.

***

Exhilaration momentarily banished Ezra's fear about his friends' fate. The wind rushed by as the stallion thundered recklessly across the slopes. The steed seemed unconcerned about the boulders, loose shale, and shattered ice littering the rough terrain underneath the cliffs. Ezra had learned to ride from Leonus, his father's stablemaster and the finest horseman in all Hur-ar. Yet, no steed in House Azubehl's stables approached this one for speed or grace. Nor had he ever sat upon a seat crafted for a horse's back. Ezra thought the stirrups clumsy at first, but soon found them indispensable.

His elation quickly faded as, without prompting, the horse slowed to a trot.

"What's wrong, boy?" Ezra patted Heise's neck. The cliffs towered over him, conjuring memories of Hur-ar's

Cliff Wall. These peaks were higher than the Adyghe Mountains, and no Cliff Road zig-zagged up their sheer face. The cliffs weren't on a straight line running east to west, but subtly curved outward like a fortress wall. Ezra urgently had to find a way into, or around that fortress before it was too late.

The Lo were following close behind with the enemy on their heels. Yet, there wasn't so much as a ledge to hide under. He nudged the reluctant horse to a light gallop and pressed west.

Ezra heard rushing water as he rounded a small bulge along the cliff face, and found a waterfall tumbling into a clear pool. The pool in turn spilled into a series of small rapids that tumbled downhill into a meandering stream. Ezra suspected this was the same stream that spilled into the defile he discovered yesterday. The waterfall's mist partially obscured his view beyond the pool.

"Stay here, boy." He patted the horse. "That stream looks too rocky to take you across. I'm going to have a quick look on the other side." He dismounted and drew his sword. Ezra barely managed to avoid slipping as he crossed the rushing stream.

Once on the opposite bank, he could see the valley's far western reaches. The cliffs seemed to merge with the distant mountains that dropped off into far-distant plains. *That is where we came from*, he thought. *Only a few days ago, that was a sea.*

Despair overcame Ezra as he realized this land offered no escape and no protection from the pursuing army. These lush slopes would soon become killing fields. It was likely the slaughter had already begun, and the Lo wouldn't even make it this far.

Ezra considered his sword. "I will fight and die this day," he whispered. He would gallop down the hill and join the fight. *Perhaps my sword and skill might make a difference*, he thought as silent teardrops fell. *I owe it to Aizarg, and especially to Okta.* "Father, I'm sorry. You asked me to lead them to safety, but I have failed."

"You have not failed, Ezra."

Ezra looked up and froze. Across the pool, a young woman gently stroked the horse's neck. Her pure white silk dress shimmered brightly in the late afternoon sun. Golden silk veiled her face. Before Ezra could issue a challenge, she lowered her veil.

"Sarah?" Disbelief paralyzed him. His sister stood across the pool, wearing the same festival dress she wore the day before House Azubehl fell.

"This is a lie!" he shouted with trembling voice. "A Scythian arrow took your life."

The apparition strolled along the opposite bank towards the waterfall. Her shadow fell across the mossy rocks. Her muddy hem dragged the ground. Her reflection shimmered like molten silver and gold in the pool.

Ezra paralleled her along his shore. "Am I dead, too?"

Sarah smiled with sweet sadness, her gray eyes so much like his.

"Answer me, I beg!" Ezra sobbed. The two shores began to converge as they neared the waterfall. Sarah considered her brother one last time before she merged with the mist and stepped into the waterfall. Ezra leapt in after her. Water pummeled his shoulders and head, almost buckling his knees. The frigid slaps stole his breath and scoured his skin. Struggling not to slip on the slimy rocks and blinded by the torrent, Ezra felt for the cliff.

A hand pulled him through.

Ezra sputtered and opened his eyes, expecting to see Sarah. Instead, he looked upon otherworldly beauty. Ghostly blue light glimmered through a cathedral-like cavern. Luminous ice formed an arched ceiling far overhead. A long, rocky tunnel extended straight ahead, with a shallow stream running down its center, exiting beneath the waterfall. Wide, sandy banks lined the stream, which extended down the tunnel as far as he could see. Warm air carrying a hint of spring flowers wafted from the cavern's depths.

To Ezra, this place conjured memories of "The Wide," the sacred cavern below Hur-ar's streets where Slug and his thieves once reined. It was said the Wide was sacred, built by the Narim god-men ages ago. This place felt sacred, too. The sunlight filtering through the glacial ceiling gave the tunnel an otherworldly shimmer, and made the water glow.

"Mother was right," Sarah's voice drifted from behind. He turned.

Sarah stood in the ankle-deep water before the glowing waterfall that cloaked the cavern's entrance. "One moment we live in suffering, and the next we step across a boundary into perfect happiness. The gods that do battle below do not understand this, Ezra." Sarah's voice faded as she glided backwards and melted into the waterfall. "Their time is swiftly passing."

Ezra leapt after her, only to find himself spilling into sunlight and the frigid pool. He dragged himself onto the muddy bank and cried, pounding the soft earth and calling his sister's name.

The horse gently nuzzled him.

Shivering, Ezra stood and stroked the steed's neck. "You saw her, too, right?"

The horse continued to nudge Ezra, all the while whinnying and prancing nervously. Ezra held its reins and looked about, sensing the animal's unease. Then a thunder clap, more powerful than any Ezra had ever heard, erupted from the clear blue sky.

62: The Bastard Gods.

Basin obscure, mountain bowl fortress strong, demon stalks Master's children,
Twins innocent beside Four Rivers frolic beneath holy Tree wise.
Master's back turned but a moment, betrayal taints Perfect Happiness,
Father's dark shadow in slips, Totaresh cannot see evil corrupt. -
The Song of Athena

- The Chronicle of Fu Xi.

***

On a field of green, two gods in crimson faced one another. One wielded a white sword, one a red sword. Behind Fu Xi, Sana and the men fled up the mountainside. Behind Leviathan, the Olmec horde waited for their master to unleash them. Quexil stepped from behind his jackals. It took Fu Xi a moment to realize Leviathan's second-in-command wore a cape made from human skin.

"Take your dogs and go," Fu Xi said. "These lands and these people are not yours."

Leviathan laughed. "All lands, all peoples, all mine. Forever."

"Not these. Not now."

"You no longer wield the Traitor's Sword. Once again you face me with an inferior weapon," Leviathan said. "This time, I will not show mercy when it fails."

Fu Xi remembered that morning on the beach, when he battled Leviathan with a crude, bronze blade. Leviathan's blade had only nipped Fu Xi, and he knew instantly it was forged to slay gods. The steel weapon he carried now, taken from a dead Olmec, could not slay Leviathan, nor would it last long against Leviathan's orichalcum blade and armor.

"Atlantean steel will do," Fu Xi lied. He thought of Sana's red dagger, concealed in his belt. Could that orichalcum, a Renewal Blade, have the same effect on immortal flesh? This battle might answer that question. When Fu Xi's steel failed, it would be his only option.

"Today, your long immortality comes to an end…" Leviathan nodded to Sana, Spako, and Ghalen fleeing in the distance. "…and the people you have chosen to help will be my captives."

Fu Xi felt as if his long years counted only for a single breath when compared to this moment. The cool breeze swirled between his armor's joints and crannies and blew the grass in green waves. The Olmecs stirred like an evil tide behind Leviathan's dam, waiting to burst forth. Leviathan's red blade held a certainty even Fu Xi's arduous journey through the Cataclysm didn't expressly promise — mortality. Fu Xi felt something he hadn't truly experienced in his long life, death's true prospect. What would Fu Xi's life purchase this day? He knew it couldn't stop the Olmecs from swarming after the Lo, but it might buy time for a miracle.

"Perhaps I can't stop you, but I travelled halfway across the world to try."

Rage flashed across Leviathan's face. "You betrayed me."

"You deceived me."

"I called you brother!"

"I called you friend."

Fu Xi watched Leviathan struggle for self-control. To his surprise, his enemy sheathed the sword and removed his helmet. "Then let us be brothers and friends again."

Behind Leviathan, several of the Olmecs looked confused and disappointed, as if their afternoon amusements had been cancelled.

"You intended to enslave Cin. You hid that truth from me."

"My *father* intended to enslave Cin, not I. I was a dutiful and obedient son. Did you not also confess your loyalty to the Goddess of Tortoise Mountain? Tell me, Fu Xi, what has become of your mother?"

Fu Xi didn't answer, but Leviathan's words cut. He remembered his last night upon Tortoise Mountain and knew his mother, at least in flesh, was forever gone.

Leviathan took a step closer. "Should you and I do battle to pay for the sins of vanished gods? Or maybe we should battle for the bloodlust of mortals? Just blink, Fu Xi, and those people fleeing up the hillside will turn to dust. God of Names, are you ready to become dust alongside them?"

Fu Xi remained silent.

Leviathan touched Fu Xi's chest. "We are divine bastards, you and I; both cursed to neither rule nor serve. The Cataclysm was meant for mortals and the gods that bore us. Not for us. We live. We have been chosen to inherit the world, and you stand ready to throw it all away?"

Fu Xi felt his will weakening. The same hope that stirred his soul in Wu reawakened. In Wu, he had come to think of Leviathan as an older brother, the companion he had never known in the long, lonely millennia in Tortoise Mountain. Fu Xi's happiness in Wu could have gone on forever, but another voice whispered in his ear, a mortal's voice. Amiran's voice. The scholar's reason had come between the two demigods.

Leviathan took a step closer. "Remember what I taught you when we walked together in the gardens?"

Fu Xi nodded as if in a trance. He had sheathed his sword, though he did not remember doing it. Fu Xi reached up and removed his helmet, letting his long, black hair spill over his shoulders. "You said they cannot truly love us."

Leviathan's eyes searched his, almost beseechingly. "Search your heart, and tell me I was wrong."

Fu Xi remembered returning to Nushen again and again after his quests, only to have another generation pass with no memories of him. People he loved died without him, and the Stone Garden grew larger. Even Nuwa's love wasn't like that of a mortal mother; she viewed him as a tool to be molded for her divine purposes.

Leviathan provided Fu Xi the closest thing he'd ever known to a true relationship.

"If only one of us leaves this field today, the other must face eternity alone. Which fate is worse?"

Leviathan's words shook Fu Xi to his soul's ancient foundations. He looked up to see Leviathan, hand outstretched. "Only we can save each other, *brother*."

Something landed on the ground with a wet thump in between Leviathan and Fu Xi. An overpowering, pungent reek burned his nostrils. The demigods stepped back and looked down at a smoking, sizzling slab of animal flesh.

It exploded in a blinding blue flash, and Fu Xi felt himself lifted into the air.

***

Fu Xi came to, and sat up. Small burning blue globs were scattered about the ground. The fire burned with an odor Fu Xi hadn't smelled in millennia, a scent he thought he would never experience again.

Dragon spore.

Oily smoke rose high into the sky, corrupting the virgin blue before the wind smeared it toward the cliffs. It enveloped Fu Xi and obscured the Olmec line, or anything else. A spreading grass fire consumed many of the dead stumps and logs scattered nearby. Fu Xi picked up his helmet, put it on, and stood. Then he saw the Traitor's Sword stuck into the burning stump beside him.

"I am sorry, Lord Fu Xi." Like a ghost, a gaunt, black man limped through the smoke, speaking in Cin. "It was the only way."

Fu Xi drew the sword from the stump, staring at this stranger in astonishment. "Amiran?"

"Flee before it's too late," the scholar called out. "He is coming."

A sword erupted through Amiran's abdomen. Quexil slid from behind the scholar, needle teeth bared in a nightmare sneer. Amiran's eyes rolled back, and he fell into Quexil's arms like a lover.

"Amiran!" Fu Xi screamed as the smoke swallowed the scholar and the warrior.

A war cry shattered the stillness. Leviathan leapt through the fire. In an explosion of sparks, crimson blades clashed. The God of Atlantis rained relentless sword blows upon the God of Cin. Off-balance, Fu Xi parried and blocked but couldn't position for a counterattack. Fu Xi had to break Leviathan's momentum before he found a gap in his defense.

Fu Xi anticipated Leviathan's next attack, and instead of blocking, he rolled below Leviathan's stroke. He rammed his shield into Leviathan's shins, and kept rolling. Caught in mid-lunge, Leviathan's momentum sent him spilling forward.

The Olmecs stepped through the smoke and formed a ring around the warring gods.

Tables turned, Fu Xi beat Leviathan with shield and sword in merciless one-two combinations. Under the onslaught, the Atlantean shrank behind his shield. The God of Names relentlessly hammered Leviathan's defenses. Leviathan dropped to one knee, and then fell backwards, catching himself with his sword arm. The Atlantean's weakness renewed Fu Xi's ferocity. The Olmecs stood stone-faced as their god withered under Fu Xi's attack.

Leviathan collapsed onto his back and locked swords with Fu Xi. He grabbed Fu Xi's helmet and, grinning, pulled him close. "That was a good move, but it will only work once." Leviathan delivered an explosive kick to Fu Xi's chest, sending him hurtling across the circle onto his back.

The Olmecs howled.

Leviathan laughed as he approached. "I almost expected to hear you shout 'Yield!'"

Fu Xi snapped onto his feet and rushed. Leviathan feinted, and Fu Xi crumpled under a heavy and unexpected shield strike. Fu Xi struggled to his feet, again with sword at the ready.

Leviathan shrugged. "How do you expect this to end?"

Fu Xi ignored him, and attacked again. Again, Leviathan easily deflected the charge with lightning strokes and counter-strokes Fu Xi never anticipated. Off-balance, he stumbled by, and Leviathan delivered a swift kick to Fu Xi's rump. The God of Cin tumbled to the ground yet again to gales of Olmec laughter. Fu Xi lurched to his feet, his mouth dry.

"My war masters trained you for months. Didn't you learn anything?"

Fu Xi and Leviathan circled one another inside the ring. Fu Xi understood Leviathan was toying with him, trying to goad him into making mistakes.

Leviathan removed his shield and rammed it into the ground. He tossed his sword lightly from hand to hand. "That's better. Shields are for those who fear losing, for mortals."

For a moment, Fu Xi's pride entertained the thought of ditching his shield, but thought better of it.

Leviathan attacked with slashes and jabs interspersed with crushing fist strikes and kicks. The God of Names retreated behind his shield, unable to deliver a single counter-attack. Leviathan's fists and feet proved as dangerous as his blade. Sharp, deep pain shot up Fu Xi's left arm as the shield strap gave way, sending the shield flying into the grass. Leviathan delivered a spinning kick across his helmet. Fu Xi crumpled to the grass.

Fu Xi held out his sword in a feeble attempt to block the killing blow that never came. He clutched his left arm tightly against his chest. Blood spurted from the narrow gap between his gauntlet and vambrace and hissed on the ground.

Leviathan held out his arms and addressed his warriors, "Did Lord Fu Xi think orichalcum would make him a god-killer?" Laughing, the Olmecs beat their shields with club and sword.

He addressed Fu Xi with contempt. "They called you the God of Names. You spent the ages teaching mortals planting, sowing, and"—he laughed—"*weaving*." Leviathan held up his sword. "This is how I spent the ages. For millennia my half-brothers, *gods all*, tried to kill me. They were far more capable than you, my friend. My sister, whose sword and armor you pretend to know how to use, threw them down and fled before she'd face me. Even Atlas came to fear me."

Fu Xi shook with rage as his gauntlet filled with blood. The Olmecs leered in anticipation at the prospect of divine slaughter.

"My father once told me, 'My other children were born to rule men. You, my son, were born to slay gods.' My spirit was forged on a crucible of orichalcum. As for you"—Leviathan shook his head—"you'd never seen one of your kind until I found you on that shore, with your toy sword. I offered you friendship not once, but twice. Both times you spat in my face. Never again." Leviathan raised his weapon to slay the God of Names. "Everything you've ever done, every quest, has been for naught. Your long existence has been a waste."

Fu Xi raised his sword in defense.

A shadow fell across the battlefield. The wind died, and the world grew silent.

Leviathan stopped in mid-stroke and looked up.

Fu Xi saw it first. He flattened himself against the earth, pulled his shield over him like a turtle shell, and shrank as deeply into his armor as he could before the world erupted in fire.

63: Awakened from the Icy Womb.

Then we quietly descended into old Aryq, that black gorge.
We went far until we reached its evil end,
Beset with mist and cloud.
Something black I saw in front of me.
His eyes shone like the morning star.
He roared to me and I heard him.
A great curse he hurled at us,
Like a fiery sword hurled against us.
He pursued me and caught me. - Origin unknown, from the
*Ancient of Ancients. ***

- The Chronicle of Fu Xi.

***

Scents speak in exotic languages civilized ears cannot
fathom.

The stale reek of blood and sex roused the ancient
guardian from his slumber. The barely perceptible scents
corrupted his sanctuary's icy depths, and stirred his mighty
heart from its long slumber. From deep below a blanket of
ice and snow, he woke and whispered a single word with a
flaming tongue.

"Vengeance."

Slitted eyes flew open to a white blur. He tried to
stretch, but his limbs wouldn't obey. With each renewed
heartbeat, the obscene smell trickled into his nostrils and
rekindled embers of smoldering rage.

The dragon snorted and swallowed, ingesting fresh fire-bile to mix with his blood. Tingling, followed shortly by agonizingly sharp pain, invaded his frozen muscles as fresh blood flooded his tissues. He repeatedly flexed his muscles, further trying to warm them until his body properly obeyed his will.

As he shifted, cracks began to open in the ice and snow covering his hibernation pile. The stench invaded the fissures, further violating his senses. The hibernation pile began to shudder as the dragon found his strength. He never remembered the snow and ice being this heavy. A crack opened over his nostril, and the beast inhaled the coolness and filled his lungs and belly with oxygen-rich air. Deep in his gullet, the fire-bile simmered for only a moment before he belched. In a spray of flames, steam, and shattered tree limbs, the explosion blew away half the hibernation pile. The thunder echoed through his valley.

To the snap and pop of breaking ice and sticks, the dragon slowly stood. Glazed snow cracked and split on top of the pile. Steam rose from the cracks, and wet branches and logs poked out like old bones through rotted flesh. Soon, he stood erect on all fours and shrugged off the hibernation pile with a crash. Snow, ice, and rotted vegetation tumbled off his ledge and into the forest far below.

The dragon arched like a cat, joints popping in quick succession down his long neck and spine. He turned to consider what remained of the pile he had built last autumn. He'd never seen so much snow accumulation on his ledge. The drift almost covered his cave's entrance. With a sweep of his tail, he sent snow and debris tumbling into the forest thousands of feet below. With a few more sweeps, he cleared off the ledge to his satisfaction, sat down on his haunches, and surveyed his kingdom.

Still disoriented from his slumber, the dragon continued to test the air. This scent certainly came from the same doe he'd detected last autumn. This time, however, her scent originated much closer. As before, the doe's sex pheromones were jumbled in a perverse mix of adrenaline, fire-bile, and blood. The beast's breathing quickened with rekindled rage. Something killed this doe, and dragged her slaughtered flesh to his kingdom. Only one creature in all of Creation could be capable of such abomination.

He began to pace back and forth. *There!* he thought. Just below the slaughtered doe's overpowering scent lurked human sweat's salty tang. He'd never detected so much sweat so close to his kingdom. There must be hundreds of filthy humans somewhere to the south just beyond his valley. Mixed with the sweat he also detected leather, campfires, horses, and human blood. *An army*, he thought. *They dare bring an army to my kingdom's doorstep!*

Another scent mingled with men's scent, something instinct cautioned was both ancient and dangerous. A low growl rumbled deep in the dragon's belly. He lowered his head and flattened his ears. Sticking his maw over the ledge, he tested the air rising up from the bowl-shaped valley. New buds and lush, fresh leaves sprouted in the highlands surrounding his basin. He'd never seen the late spring snowpack so thick. The world the dragon had woken to made little sense, and he needed answers.

Trying to clear hibernation's grogginess, the dragon shook his body like a wet dog. Stretching his limbs and wings, he welcomed the warm blood's tingling sensation seeping into his flesh and reawakening his power. The dragon fully spread his wings, testing them and exposing the thin membranes and cartilage to the sun.

The mid-day air currents bubbled up from the valley like an invisible spring. Epoch's experience told him the wind was adequate. The dragon had not eaten since last autumn, making him an easy burden for the wind. The dragon spread his wings and leapt. The mountain thermals dutifully caught him, and the beast rose high above his basin.

His enormous shadow slipped over the lush forest canopy. From tranquil meadows and high treetops, the basin's creatures looked up without fear at their regent and guardian. It didn't take long before the dragon crossed the basin's breadth and approached the mountain wall that protected his kingdom. He gauged the height of the heavy snowpack resting atop what had been a nude ridge only the season before. The dragon folded his wings and dove. The air screamed by as the forest's deep greens rushed up to meet him. Then, only seconds before impact, the dragon snapped open his wings, and skimmed over the trees and then up the basin's rim. He left the forest behind and soared up bare, warm slopes until the thermals caught him. They lifted the dragon higher and higher until earth and rock surrendered to snow and ice. His climb slowed and then died away just as he cleared the glacier's pinnacle. A sudden, frigid headwind jetted over the mountaintop and slowed the dragon to a halt. He lightly settled onto the ice, folded his wings, and surveyed the world beyond his basin. Slowly, his ash-gray scales turned white, blending with the snow.

The changes across the southern valley astonished him. While the dragon had been responsible for destroying the forest the previous autumn, he found himself looking upon a landscape that had suffered far greater destruction than he wrought in his fit of madness. What had been a saddle-shaped, forested valley with a gentle stream in its center now lay desolated. A ragged gorge cut deeply through the valley's heart like a wound. While green meadow grass had returned to this side of the valley, the southern landscape appeared as if swept clean by the Dragon Mother's own tail. Everywhere, deep rivulets in the earth spoke to water's destructive passage.

He glanced down and saw the vermin crawling up the mountainside toward the cliffs. The edict laid down from Heaven, as taught to him long ago by his mother, echoed in his mind. *Neither man nor god may enter this valley.*

The dragon crouched low. Instinct and Intellect harmonized as he coolly studied his intended prey. The slain doe dragon's pheromones drifted up the cliff and washed over him. Through her pheromones, the doe spoke to him from the dead, and told the story of her demise. Her passion's ghost still tried to seduce him, and the bull found himself fighting off his mating instincts. *Turn it to rage and fire*, he thought and focused on the bright, terrifying scents of iron and adrenaline. She spent her last moments fighting for life. She'd been tricked, lured to her death.

She would have been mine, he thought. Several drops of fire-bile oozed from his eyes, ignited, and fell to the snow.

The dragon cocked his head sideways like a hawk. Slitted eyes darted from potential target to potential target.

Two groups.

He peeked over the edge and looked straight down at a band of humans almost immediately below, strung out along the cliff's base heading west. There were females among them, and children, too. A few males carried sharpened sticks. *They are easy kills and can wait*, he thought. The second group, much larger, gathered in the valley's heart along the gorge's north rim. Warrior males bubbled up out of the gash in the earth and raced along the rim to a place where many concentrated together. Metal glinted in the sun. *They're battling one another*, he thought.

In their midst, blue fire burned. *Flesh of my flesh! Her scent originates there*. He could suffer no more. The time had come to end this abomination.

A time for justice.

The dragon stretched his wings and let the powerful updraft lift him without so much as a flap. In order to attack with the sun at his back, he needed to cross the entire valley undetected. He carefully circled east, staying just below the cliffs to avoid detection. He cleared the highlands and dropped low until he came to the mountains' edge, and the valley opened to the east. The scene to the east greatly disturbed the old dragon. What were once fertile plains stretching far beyond his hunting grounds had been transformed to desolate mudflats. This mystery would have to wait. Other matters needed his attention first.

Dropping his wing, the dragon banked west and slipped into the growing shadows along the valley's southern slopes. His scales darkened. Here, too, all vegetation had been stripped, and the mountains lay naked. The dragon turned north and skimmed down the mountainside, picking up speed as he approached the canyon. The men came into view on the canyon's opposite side. They still battled one another, oblivious to their approaching doom.

Gliding just above the ground, the dragon opened his jaws and let air ram down his throat. It mixed with fire-bile secreting from his neck glands. The volatile brew simmered deep in his stomach, where warmth turned to boiling heat, but not yet fire. For that, more air was needed. His body reacted to the heat and rapidly produced more fire-bile.

The world rushed by until he emerged from the mountain's shadow and back into sunlight. Passing over the chasm, he pointed his snout skyward and rocketed straight up, gradually slowing until his shadow fell just short of the human mob fighting below.

A thousand feet above the battle, the dragon flicked his tail, folded his wings, and dove. The dragon's slitted eyes darted from one target to the next as he made slight adjustments to his flight path. He pulled his legs tightly against his body for maximum speed. His skin tightened, flattening his scales flush, further reducing drag and protecting him from what was to come. The scales turned bright crimson, almost perfectly matching the armor worn by the two largest humans fighting below.

Five hundred feet above the battle, the dragon closed his jaws and held his breath. Deep inside, the searing mixture simmered for a few more seconds. He stretched his neck and opened his nostrils, activating mucus glands in his throat. The slipstream rammed gallons of thick mucus into his stomach to mix with the fire-bile. Seconds before impact, the dragon snapped open his wings, snagged the air, and leveled out only a few feet above the ground. Hollow cartilage, muscle, ligaments, and leathery membranes stretched to the breaking point. The ancient beast strained to keep his neck straight against the acceleration forces. Nictating membranes slid over the dragon's eyes as his head tilted down a few degrees.

Now.

The beast vomited the thick, mucus-like fluid. Most of it formed an aerosol enveloping the humans. Larger droplets formed a fireball that clung to cloth, flesh, and steel.

The fireball enveloped all below, and sent shockwaves rippling across the valley. The blast pushed some fire-bile over the dragon, transforming him into a flaming demon.

The dragon pointed his beak skyward as the heat vaulted him through the hellish pillar of smoke and fire. The beast erupted from the mushroom cloud, outstretched wings covering the sun. Old, molted scales burned away and fell as sparks. He arched back his neck and hovered, suspended above the inferno. He drank in their screams and tasted the burning reek of man-flesh carried on the smoke like a sacrifice.

In a tongue no man could understand, the ancient one screamed, "This is my valley. HERE, I AM GOD!"

The dragon descended into the furnace, prepared to finish off any who might have survived.

64: The Two Dragons.

Perfect land Death infects with regret's choice, deceit's suffering blighted,
Timeless sorrow's mandate, Deceiver's triumph assures exile cruel.
Dragon Black holds battlefield victorious, banishment's children cast out,
Neither god nor mortal shall ever pass Paradise portal's threshold.
- The Song of Athena

- The Chronicle of Fu Xi.

***

Zelko sat on a rock along the pool's edge, fingers steepled in deep thought. He stared into the water where his reflection should have been. Broken in two, his slave collar lay at his feet. He absently fingered Leviathan's brand on his triceps, the scar fading under his touch. He could not bring himself to look at the pitch-black smoke billowing into the southeast sky.

Sarah stepped from the waterfall and lightly onto the shore. She stopped and, with mild curiosity, considered the black smoke piling high into the late afternoon sky. "I see Fu Xi finally made his half-brother's introduction."

Zelko put his head in his hands and began to weep.

Sarah glanced back at him and cocked her head as if perplexed. "Did you truly believe it would end any other way?"

"I grow weary of your lies," he said, not looking up.

Sarah laughed. "My lies? You were the one who manipulated the Lo from the very beginning. You set the wheels in motion when gave your Renewal Blade to Setenay all those years ago, as if you could truly hide it from me." Sarah considered the goatherd, as if expecting a reaction. "That's truly what you do, isn't it? You hide things, like the truth. You hid from your Master for millennia in Tortoise Mountain, taking lovers and sending Fu Xi to do your dirty work." She smiled darkly. "Well, *most* of your dirty work. At least Poseidon had the courage to confront his sins. You buried your sins in the Stone Garden, little unmarked mounds tucked away in the graveyard's dark corners."

Zelko trembled with rage. "Be silent."

Sarah ignored him. "What would Fu Xi do if he learned the truth? Would your son remain such a devoted servant?" Sarah glanced at the smoke and shrugged. "That may be a moot point now."

Sarah turned east. "In only moments, Ezra will emerge over that ridge with the Lo, and enter the portal. Your feeble attempt to draw Amiran and Atamoda west and lure Leviathan away from the Place of Perfect Sorrows has failed. The Lo are my bait, and your dagger and Kol-ok will eventually follow. You are powerless to stop it."

Zelko stood and defiantly faced Sarah. "They haven't passed through the portal yet. There is still time."

"Believe that if you wish, but our game is quickly coming to an end. It was here I tasted my first victory against your Master. My next victory will extend my power across the world, and your Master will finally lose this war."

The weight of her words crushed Zelko, because they were truth. He slumped back down upon the rock. He failed to lure the Lo away from this valley, and the portal to the Place of Perfect Sorrows.

Sarah looked Zelko up and down with an incredulous look. "I'm curious. Why do you pick the most disgusting disguises with which to clothe yourself? Old men, old women, filthy slaves, and goatherds…tsk, tsk. No wonder you're losing."

"Your presence in her form is an abomination."

Sarah smiled and laughed sweetly. "Yes, my love. Perhaps you're finally understanding what this is all about." She began to dance along the shore to music only she could hear, twirling and watching her dress swirl. She stopped dancing and looked down at her body. "I should wear women's skin more often." Sarah ran her hands over her body, cupping her breasts and exploring every curve and forbidden place.

In a flash of golden fire, Zelko's illusion burned away. Nuwa faced Sarah, eyes blazing with blue fire. "Stop it!"

Sarah ignored her. "There is something delicious about the female form. What it lacks in physical power, it makes up for in…" Sarah tapped her chin, as if searching for the right words, and then her eyes lit up with epiphany. "…*magic!*" Sarah approached the water's edge and considered Nuwa. "I think I understand why you originally chose a woman's form. The power to seduce is simply intoxicating."

"A woman's power is lost to you. You cannot fathom that love is the first act of creation."

Sarah's visage slowly transformed into the man in black. "You once loved me."

"You threw away our love when you rebelled. The Two Dragons are no longer in balance, and Creation is at war with itself."

He sighed, as if exhausted. "I don't want to get drawn into that old argument, my love. Instead, let me ask you one final question: Will your Master still forgive you should He lose this war? Is your salvation dependent on His victory?"

Fresh doubt swirled through Nuwa's mind. "My Master knows the Water's temptations are powerful. He has forgiven me."

"What price will that forgiveness extract?" The Black Dragon held out his arms as if to encompass all of Creation. "The Water's temptations are powerful because this place *is* powerful. You have chosen to reject them. I have embraced them!"

"We were never meant to remain here. This is not our home. I've come to accept this." She held out her hand. "You should, too. It's not too late."

"It is too late, Nuwa. For you and your Master." The Black Dragon strolled to the waterfall, casting a reflection in the pool. "The endgame has begun. The Tree of Life will burn, and in its place I shall erect a new Mountain of Bones." He slipped through the waterfall and vanished.

She gazed up above the towering cliffs, and remembered the paradise that lay beyond.

Whatever would eventually transpire behind the waterfall was beyond her power to affect. By divine mandate, Nuwa could not enter the cave and return to the Place of Perfect Sorrows. It was here, at the dawn of time, that the Black Dragon won his first victory against the Emperor of Heaven. In response, the Emperor of Heaven banished the Narim from Paradise and commanded Nuwa to surrender her firstborn. Totaresh guarded the Place of Perfect Sorrows with a flaming sword.

The smoke died in the east. She sensed Totaresh, but could not yet fathom Fu Xi or Leviathan's fate. Nuwa had prayed Fu Xi and Totaresh would have recognized their shared spirit before it was too late. She prayed Fu Xi's heart would not twist to bitterness for something he could not possess, just as Totaresh and Leviathan's hearts had done so long ago. A tear fell from her cheek and dropped into the pool without so much as a ripple.

Nuwa popped open her fan and covered her face. "There are many things I've still hidden from you, my love."

The goddess evaporated into a cloud of fireflies that scattered into the sunset.

The sun slipped below the western mountains as the moon emerged in the east. Silhouetted against the rising orb, the bedraggled Lo made their way to the waterfall. Above the cliffs, the constellation Draco continued its eternal flight around the North Star.

Epilogue: The Last Scholar.

(Journal Entry, Third Hour, Forty-second Minute. 26th Day of Gadeirus's Moon. 5,524 A.F., Mountain Base Camp, Prince Leviathan's Grand Expedition. It is in the service of Humanity that I, Amiran the Expedition Scholar, record my last observations to the best of my knowledge and as accurately as possible.)

My Beloved Elda,

I need no instruments to record these observations, I need only glance inward to my heart, and speak honestly as to what I find there. If you're reading this, that means Zelko and I have already fled. I hope Atamoda has fled with us. If she did, do not curse her, but praise her sacrifice. Know her anguish is every bit as great as mine. We fled to save you, Kol-ok, and what remains of humanity.

I've hurt him, Elda. A slave bested a god, and I'm counting on Leviathan's arrogance and rage to cloud his judgement. It is my hope Leviathan pursues us west. I carry both dragon glands. He needs those to secure his prize in the north. If Atamoda accompanies me, Leviathan will surely give chase. Zelko is our guide, and with his help we may elude Leviathan long enough to reach Attica (if it still exists). If, by the time you read this, the army marches northeast, then Zelko and I are likely dead. If this is the case, Atamoda is likely back in Leviathan's clutches, and we have failed.

Know that I did all I could, and died a free man.

My failure or success notwithstanding, dark days lie ahead for you and Kol-ok. You must be strong. If I could have taken you with me, I would. I could not, and for that I beg your forgiveness. You must stay and care for Kol-ok.

Leviathan will not harm either of you as long as he harbors hope his plans will succeed. Be cautious! Do not antagonize Leviathan or his war dogs. The god will grow more unpredictable as rage consumes him, and Quexil's evil knows no bounds.

Leviathan's time is running out. Every day he pursues me delays him from his true goal. The army's food is almost gone. The Olmecs cannot slaughter many more slaves, or no one will remain to walk the dragon chain. Soon, he will have to dispatch foraging and hunting parties in hopes game survived the Cataclysm. Every delay is a victory.

From this point forward, you must fully understand Leviathan's true ambitions, and what lies ahead for you and Kol-ok. What follows can be found in the Ancient of Ancients. It, and Master Gremis's primer for the First Tongue, lies here in the navigation kit. Study these works and commit them to memory! Its secrets will prepare you for what is to come, and may save your life.

Leviathan leads the army into a land called Aryq, a place forbidden to men and gods since darkest antiquity. When Zelko first described the valley beyond the gorge, I wondered if this could be the legendary Birthplace of the Gods detailed in the Ancient of Ancients. Here, a Nameless God sent ten divine servants to earth as mankind's shepherds. They rebelled against the Nameless God and were banished from Aryq. They divided the world among themselves. and some, like Nuwa and Poseidon, produced offspring with mortals.

It is my belief the Cataclysm we barely survived may have been part of a greater theomachy, a god war, stretching back to the Banishment. It is possible Atlantis and her empire, along with Poseidon and the Sons of Cleito, may have been eradicated in this theomachy. I greatly fear Athena, Fu Xi, Nuwa, and even Attica may have also been destroyed.

Leviathan was spared by a mysterious dark god, one I briefly encountered only hours before the Cataclysm. He is not unlike Poseidon, though perhaps more powerful and sinister. It is likely he is what the Ancient of Ancients calls the Black Dragon, or the Lost God of Aryq. I believe Leviathan is in league with him, and means to reestablish a new Empire of the Gods with the Black Dragon as its godhead.

Be strong, for what I am about to tell you may frighten you.

The Black Dragon requires a mortal shell, much as Poseidon and Nuwa did. Without a mortal shell, the spirit, no matter how powerful, will eventually lose its foothold in our world. To fully exert earthly power, the Black Dragon needs an earthly body. He has chosen Kol-ok. Therefore, under no circumstance can the boy enter the valley to the north. If he does, mankind will be cast into eternal darkness.

Something else stands in Leviathan's way, and thwarts the Black Dragon's plans.

A powerful bull dragon lurks in the northern valley. You, too, already know this, and understand why Leviathan needs you. Leviathan believes he can slaughter the beast with chain and steel, and expects you to harvest it. In this assumption Leviathan is greatly mistaken, for this is no ordinary dragon. The Ancient of Ancients describes this beast as Totaresh, the God of Dragons. He protects Aryq's central valley, an earthly paradise, from god and mortal alike. Totaresh stands between Leviathan and all he desires.

If I have failed, then you must find a way to free Kol-ok and escape before Leviathan leads you into Totaresh's kingdom. That is the path to death.

As you've already discovered, I saved many of the Dragon Egg's treasures that morning the world ended, but much was still lost. On that day, I saved what is most precious of all, you.

I want to say you are the daughter I never had, but that would be a lie. You, dear child, are the apprentice I always wished for.

Should you accept it, my navigation kit is now yours. I also lay my burden at your feet. It is a terrible and heavy burden, too. I would not ask you to shoulder it were you not worthy. Knowledge and freedom's candle flicker precariously in the wind against the ancient darkness. You stand as the lone guardian of humankind's future. This is your destiny, my beloved Elda.

Never accept a collar around your mind, or a brand on your soul. Let freedom's spark simmer in your thoughts and heart until the moment is right to set the world on fire.

Be the path that ushers in a world without the gods, until all men and women are free.

You are the last scholar.

- Amiran. Teacher, Owl, Friend.

- The Chronicle of Fu Xi.

***

Elda marched from the tent, navigation kit under one arm, the folding table under the other. Shadows covered the canyon's eastern floor except the sandy strip between the slave pens and where the remaining Olmecs bivouacked. Only the little bald man seemed to take an interest in Elda's activities, but she paid him no attention.

Elda halted in the common's center and, with one hand, jerked open the small table just as she had all those months aboard the *Draco*. The legs snapped out and locked with a sharp crack that echoed off the canyon's walls. It only took a few minutes for her to erect the required instruments to measure the basics: wind, temperature, and air pressure. Glass and steel gently tinkled as she assembled the components. Biting her lip in concentration, Elda handled Vulcan's Box like a holy relic, servicing and winding it just as she had watched Master Amiran do countless times. Finally, Elda laid the journal scroll, quill, and inkwell on the table's corner. She stepped back and carefully examined everything, wondering if her work would pass Master Amiran's inspection.

Satisfied, Elda dipped the quill and held it above the scroll. Elda hesitated. She looked up at the sun just cresting the rim. She closed her eyes and let the warmth caress her face. Finally, the last scholar opened her eyes and placed quill to papyrus.

"In the service of Humanity, I, Elda the Scholar, record my observations to the best of my knowledge and as accurately as possible..."

The saga concludes in the Chronicle of Fu Xi, Book IV.

Please support indie literature. If you enjoyed this novel, please rate or review this book on Amazon or Goodreads.

A NOTE ABOUT THIS BOOK

The asterisked (*) poem in Chapter 63 is an excerpt from the poem *Sosruquo and Sotrash* from John Colarusso's book *Nart Sagas From the Caucasus* (2002, Princeton University Press). I stumbled upon this ancient body of mythology during my early research for *Black Sea Gods*. This particular poem's beauty and power profoundly influenced me. My work is heavily influenced by these myths, along with other legends, myths and faiths, which echo back to the remarkable events humanity might have experienced at the last ice age's twilight.

ABOUT THE AUTHOR

BRIAN L. BRADEN is an award-winning author and photographer. His articles have been featured in a variety of print and online publications such as the Military Times, Air Power Journal and Oxford University Press. He has published several books and is the recipient of the Alabama Penman and the Darron L Wright awards for fiction.

Glossary of Terms and Characters

Adyghe (ad-YAH-gay) Mountains: To the Lo, the eastern edge of the known world, home of the Hur-po and the Narim

ai-halah (eye-HAL-ah): "The reed and the wood." Traditional Lo vocal music. Ai is female vocals, halah is male vocals.

a-g`an (AYE-ghahn): Lo word meaning 'of the steppe' or 'enemy'.

Aizarg (AYE-zarg): Sco-lo-ti of the Crane Clan and Uros of the Lo Nation, husband of Atamoda, father to Bat-tor and Kol-ok. Lo name means I give him the east, or He leads the east.

Alad (AH-lad): Young man sentenced by Aizarg to exile in a small boat during the Cataclysm when the Lo were afloat on the barges.

Alaya (ah-LAH-ya): Wife to Levidi, mother to Kombetha.

Alkebulan (Ahl-KEY-byoo-lan): Continent east of Atlantis and south of Erubia, where Poseidon first encountered humanity and where Queen Cleito hailed from.

Amiran (ah-MEER-ahn): Grand Master Scholar of the Imperial Academy, slave of the God Poseidon.

Ancient of Ancients: A collection of forbidden scrolls detailing the true origins of the gods and humanity, revealed to Grand Master Vulcan by the Goddess Athena before Atlantis's First Purge. They are stored in the Dragon's Egg.

Ayrq (EYE-rack): Birthplace of the Gods.

arun-ki: (ah-ROON-ki) Lo word meaning "village upon the womb," a stilted village built off-shore in shallow lagoons. During the Cataclysm, the Lo survive afloat in a flotilla they called the Arun-ki. The heart of this floating Arun-ki were two massive barges. While both were originally ceremonial wedding barges, one was called the Supply Barge

Aryans:(air-EE-ans) One of the three nomadic tribes of the g'an.

Ashtoreth (ASH-tore-ehth) Called "The Snake of Hur Ar", a ruthless member of Hur-ar's nobility bent on placing her son, Bal-eeb, on the throne at any price.

Asu: (AS-SOO) The largely unexplored continent east of
Attica and the Sea of Azaes . It has been theorized it
stretches east to Cin.

Alec: (AL-ek) Master of the College of Mathematics of the
Imperial Academy. Amiran's co-conspirator in the
Rebellion of Owl.

Atamoda: (At-uh-MOWH-dah) Patesi-li of the Crane Clan,
wife of Aizarg, mother to Ba-tor and Kol-ok.

Athena:(Ath-EE-nah)Demigod and twin sister to
Leviathan. Daughter of the god Poseidon and his mistress
Metis, she if often called The Gray-Eyed Queen.

Atlantis: Empire founded by the God Poseidon. The
Kingdom of Atlas lies at its core, a long archipelago with
the capital on the largest island at its far east end. The
seafaring Empire stretches along the coasts and rivers of
four continents: Olma Major, Olma Minor, and Alkebulan.
The Empire stretches across the Oceanus Gadeirus to far
flung islands, terminating on the island of Wu. While
Poseidon retains his godhead, he has relegated rule to his
eleven sons. Ten, five sets of twins, are born of his mortal
queen Cleito. Of these, Atlas is king of all. Another set of
twins was born later of the concubine Metis became
known as the Bastard Gods.

Atlas: (AT-lass) Demigod and King of Atlantis. One of five
sets of twins born to the god Poseidon and his mortal

queen Cleito. The most favored of Poseidon's sons, he rules the empire in his father's name.

Atta: (AT-uh) Levidi's grandfather, oldest man in the Crane Clan.

Attica: (att-EH-kha) Erubian region along the northern coast of the Sea ofAzaes at war with Atlantis. Led by the Goddess Athena, their capital city is named in her honor.

Ba'al: (BAH-awl) A sinister deity called The Black Dragon, worshipped by cult in Hur-ar.

Bal-eeb: (BAHL-eeb) Second Prince of Hur-ar, Captain of the City Gate. Son of Ashtoreth.

Ba-lok: (BAY-lok) Sco-lo-ti of the Minnow Clan, Second to Aizarg, husband to Kus-ge, son of Aie-lok, grandson of Setenay.

Bat-or: (BAHT-or) Toddler and youngest son of Aizarg and Atamoda, brother to Kol-ok.

Bazee:(bay-ZEE) Minnow child, son of Zirev, brother of Rev.

Black Dragon: Sworn enemy of the Emperor of Heaven, Nuwa's former lover.

Bla-la-te: (blah-LAH-tay) Xva's uncle and sco-lo-ti of the Gar Clan.

Carp Clan: Lo village of which Okta rules as the sco-lo-ti, the chieftain.

Cin: (Sin) "The Right Wall of Heaven". The lands east of Tortoise Mountain to the Sunrise Sea.

Cleito: (klee-EE-tow) Poseidon's mortal queen, who bore him five sets of twin sons to rule his empire. Her children where, in sets of twins: Atlas & Gadeirus, Ampheres & Evaemon, Mnesus & Autochthon, Elasippus & Mestor, and Azaes & Diaprepes.

Coatzacolcos: (kote-ZAH-kohl-kohse) "The Place of the Serpent", the Empire of Atlantis's primary trading port on the eastern Isthmus of Olma.

Crane Clan: Lo village of which Aizarg rules as the sco-lo-ti, the chieftain.

Council of Boats: A gathering of the more than one Lo village or perhaps the entire Lo nation, usually a festive event.

Darious: (DAR-ee-us) Field Captain in the service of the God Gadeirus, Commander of Coatzacolcos Station.

Doinna: (DOH-ee-nah) Young Minnow Clan woman.

Dragon's Egg: A orichalcum vessel fashioned by Grand Master Vulcan and the Goddess Athena in Atlantis's antiquity. Kept in secret by the rebel movement called "The Owls, it houses the Ancient of Ancients, as well as a summary of all of the Imperial Academy's knowledge.

Elda: (ELL-duh) Attican child and slave. Captured to become a Dragon Butcher. Trained by Amiran. She is Ercole's twin.

Elder Mothers: Former acolytes not chosen to serve as a shell for Nuwa who select and raise the next generation of acolytes.

Emperor of Heaven: Supreme deity over the Nephilim, lord over Nuwa. Enemy of the Black Dragon.

Ercole: (Err-KOLE) Attican child and slave. Captured to become a Dragon Butcher. Trained by Amiran. He is Elda's twin.

Erub or Erubia: (eh-ROOB-ee-ah) Pronunciations differ depending on where one is on the continent. Continent across the Oceanus Atlas from the King of Atlantis. It stretches from the warm north shores of the Sea of Azaeus to the dark forests along the Icelands. Much of its northern and eastern frontiers are unexplored.

Expedition Chests: Property of the God Poseidon himself, they contain the critical materials needed to harvest fire bile to create orichalcum. Only Poseidon or the expedition scholar can open an expedition chest, even though each Son of Atlas has one in his possession.

Ezra: (ezz-RAH) Sarah's brother, deposed Prince of the House Azubehl of Hur-ar. He became a thief known as Blade and led a gang of feral children called the Untouchables in Hur-ar's slums.

Fu Xi: (foo-HI or foo-ZI) Immortal demi-god, son of Goddess Nuwa, often called the God of Names, or the Wanderer.

Gadriuopolis: (gad-ree-oh-POH-lis) "City of Gadeirus," the Empire of Atlantis's primary trading port on the western Isthmus of Olma.

Gar Clan: Also known as the Lost Arun-ki. Kus-ge, wife of Ba-lok, hailed from arun-ki, once the farthest east of all Lo villages. Shortly after Kus-ge departed as Ba-lok's new bride, the villagers vanished without a trace, the arun-ki burned to the water line.

Gathering of Boats: A council which calls all clans of the Lo Nation.

Gremis: (GREM-is) Grand Master Emeritus of the Imperial Academy. Leader of the Rebellion of Owls.

g`an: (gh-AHN) Lo word for the open steppe bordering the marshes north of the Great Sea.

Ghalen: (GAY-lehn) Lo phrase for iron spirit. Younger brother of Masok, sco-lo-ti of the Turtle Clan.

Great Sea: Immense body of fresh water and home to the Lo people. Its northern shore is lined with vast expanses of reed beds, marshes and narrow coastal forests which give way to open steppe.

Havas: (HAHVE-as) Minnow Clan's second-in-command.

heli-dar: (hell-EYE-dar)   Lo word for the afterlife. The Lo believe it is far out to sea beyond the reach of any boat.

Heise: (HAY-suh) Fu Xi's black stallion, his name simply means "black".

Huecuto: (Who-KWU-tow) Helmsman of the Draco.

Huise: (Hh-way-suh) Fu Xi's gray mare, her name simply means "gray".

Hur-ar: (her-AR) "City of the Yellow Metal," located at the base of the Adyghe Mountains in a deep canyon overlooking the Hur River; also called Ghund-Ghund, The Place of Mazes, by the Scythians.

Hur-Po: (her-POE) "People of the Yellow Metal, those who inhabit Hur-Ar.

Hur River: River running north to south separating the Adyghe Mountains from the open g'an; spanned by the Kupar Bridge.

Ice Men: A squat, human-like race that dwells in the far north lands, largely thought to be incapable of speech.

Isp: Patesi-le selected to serve the Uros.

Kalisto: (kal-IST-oh) Master of the College of Astrology of the Imperial Academy. Amiran's co-conspirator in the Rebellion of Owl.

Kombetha (kom-BETH-ah): Levidi and Alaya's daughter.

Kedkar (KED-kar): A Minnow woman who survived landfall on the Supply Barge.

Kol-ok: (kohl-AWK) Aizarg's and Atamoda's oldest boy, brother to Bat-or.

köy-lo-hely: (coy-ee-LOW-hell-eye) Lo word meaning "the sacred place where the people gather"; a large wooden platform without a hut at the heart of the Lo community, usually in the middle of a lagoon encircled by huts.

Kus-ge: (kuss-GEE) Ba-lok's wife, hails from the mysterious Lost Arun-ki, the farthest Lo settlement to the east that vanished years earlier.

Leviathan: (lev-EYE-ah-than) Demigod and twin brother to Athena. Son of the God Poseidon and his mistress Metis, he is often called Lord Paqua by his Olmec horde.

Levidi: (lev-EE-dee) Aizarg's best friend, husband of Alaya.

li-ge: (lie-GHEE) Lo symbol meaning "balance" or "joining of flesh and spirit."

Lo: (LOW) "The people" or "the family." Nation of fishing tribes divided into different clans. They live along the Great Sea's northern shore in stilted villages over the water.

Lower Lands: In Lo religion, the part of the afterlife (heli-dar) that is a paradise.

Marebi (mare-EB-ee): Minnow man who survived landfall on the Supply Barge. He is the Minnow blacksmith.

Masok: (MAY-sock) Sco-lo-ti of the Turtle Clan and Ghalen's older brother.

Nameless God: The deity of the Narim.

Navigation kit: Basic supply kit carried by all Imperial Scholars. Contained basic navigation and record keeping tools, including timekeeping and scientific tools.

Nephilim: (Nef-FIL-um) Fallen servants of the Emperor of Heaven.

Narim: (nah-RHEEM) Also called the "god-men", they lived in the Black Fortress in the mountains above Hur-ar.

New Sun: The first sunrise after the rains ceased at the Cataclysm's waning days. The Lo believe this is when the world was born anew.

Night of the Forgotten: During Nushen's Autumn Festival's full moon, the matriarchs set about cleaning their family plots.

Nushen: (NEW-shen) Village of Goddess, an ancient village that has served the goddess Nuwa for ages. Nushen rests at Tortoise Mountain's base, protected by Nuwa's power and the Encircling River from the world beyond. The Honey Lotus bridge crosses the river and leads to the forest, and world, beyond.

Nuwa:(NEW-ah) She is also called the Queen of the West and the Celestial Queen. A goddess who sired Fu Xi with a human. She dwelt in seclusion in her temple on Tortoise Mountain above the village of Nushen.

Minnow Clan: Lo village ruled by Ba-lok as sco-lo-ti.

Metis: (MEH-tis)Lover of the God Poseidon, she bore him twins. He scorned her, and banished her and her children to the Kingdom of Atlas's swamps. The children, Leviathan

541

and Athena, survived and were later raised by Poseidon to counter the power of his other ten children.

Offering Blade: The oricalcum dagger with which Nuwa possesses new human shells during the Offering Ceremony to further her immortal presence on earth.

Offering Festival: The celebration in Nushen following the Goddess Nuwa's taking of a new mortal shell.

Oeto-sy: (oy-TOW-see) the sky god or "father above" of the Lo pantheon. Husband of Psatina, father of Sethagasi.

Olorun: (OH-lore-uhn) Master of the College of Poetry of the Imperial Academy. Amiran's co-conspirator in the Rebellion of Owls.

Ood-i: (OO-die) Member of the Crane Clan, husband of Ula, father to Su-gár.

Okta: (AWK-tah) Leader of the Carp Arun-ki. His clan shuns all contact with land. During the Cataclysm, Aizarg gave him the title "Master of Boats"

Olma Minor: Continent northwest of Kingdom of Atlas.

Olma Major: Continent south of Kingdom of Atlas.

Olmecs: Warrior tribe inhabiting the Olmec Isthmus. Both continents were names in their honor. They have sworn themselves in service to their patron god, Leviathan.

Orichalcum: (or-eye-KAL-cum) A nearly indestructible red metal alloy made from iron and dragon's fire bile. It is the only known substance that can slay a god, or be the instrument of their mortal renewal.

patesi-le: (pah-TEH-see-lee) A lo shaman, always a woman and the wife of the sco-lo-ti.

Place of Perfect Happiness: The legendary land where the Nephilim first came to earth in mortal form.

Place of Perfect Sorrows: The courtyard in Nuwa's palace on Tortoise Mountain, also called Nuwa's Inner Realm. It consists of the Altar Rock and the Eternal Tree (a replica of which grows in Nushen and is used in the Offering Ceremony) growing from a fountain that separates into four streams. Here, she performs the Offering Ceremony to possess human bodies to further her human immortality.

Pluarchos: (plu-ARCK-ohs) Captain of the Draco, flagship of Leviathan's expedition.

Psatina: (sat-EEN-a) The Earth Mother, prime goddess of the Lo pantheon.

Pug: Common slave in Leviathan's expedition.

Quexil: (Kek-zil) Commander of the Obsidian Guard, warrior and Lord Leviathan's closest servant.

Renewal Blade: The oricalcum dagger with which Poseidon possesses new human shells to further his immortal presence on earth.

Rev:(REV) Minnow child, daughter of Zirev, brother of Bazee.

Ro-xandra: (Row-ZAN-drah) Old Minnow Clan woman.

sco-lo-ti: (skoh-LOW-tee) "leader of the people", village chieftain

sagar: (SAY-garr) Sammujad spears, heavier and longer, made to defend against Scythian horse warriors.

Sahti: (sah-TEE) Wife of Xva.

Sammujad: (sam-MOO-jahd) one of the three nomadic tribes inhabiting the g'an. They occupy the fringes of the steppe and rely mostly on trading to survive. They have been pushed back in recent years by the Scythians.

Sana: (SAH-nah) Scythian princess, sister of Prince Tuma, daughter of King Sawseruquo, granddaughter of King Sosa and his captive bride, Setenay. Once pledged to marry Ghalen once she was adopted by the Lo.

Sarah: Ezra's sister and deposed Princess of the House Azubehl of Hur-ar. Sold into slavery by her father, she became a pleasure slave in Virag's camp and became Ood-i's lover. Freed by Aizarg, she led the Lo to the Narim, but perished in the Cataclysm's opening moments.

Scythians: (sith-EE-ans) Horse warriors who've come to dominate the g'an over the course of several generations, they were the most savage and feared of the three steppe tribes.

Setenay: (set-EN-aye) Patesi-li of the Minnow Clan, grandmother to Ba-lok, oldest living member of the Lo people. Called "The Grandmother of the Lo." She helped Aizarg find the Narim, but perished at the Cataclysm's opening moments.

Sethagasi: (seth-ah-GOS-ee) The sea goddess of the Lo pantheon, daughter of Psatina and Oeto-sy. Synonymous with Great Sea. Also means "womb."

Shinglay: (SHING-lay)Daughter of Xigong the Weaver. She was Fu Xi's first love.

Spako: (SPAY-koh) Sammujad mercenary once in the employ of Virag. Enormous and imposing, but dimwitted and, if left to his own devices, gentle.

Silt Flats: Place near Crane Clan village with the shallows meet the deep sea and large waves form and the village boys wave ride atop their small reed boats.

Silver Stairs: The 12,324 stairs and 19 switchbacks that connect the village of Nushen to Nuwa's Realm high atop Tortoise Mountain.

Summoning of Spears: Ceremony where the Lo choose an Uros to lead them in time of war.

Sunalei Ostu: (Sue-NAH-lay OH-stooh) Called "Sunnah," he was Lord Leviathan's master of horses in Wu. He taught Fu Xi to ride.

Su-gár: (sue-GARR) daughter of Ood-i and Ula.

Tall Men: Race of humanity most favored by the Emperor of Heaven.

Ten-ye': (TEN-yee) Crane woman, along with her three daughters, trapped on the Supply barge with the Minnow Clan after the Arun-ki broke up.

Tiejiang: (Teh-ZHANG) Blacksmith of Nushen, raised by Fu Xi.

Time of the Spear: Lo term for a time of war when an Uros leads all the Lo nation, superseding the power of individual sco-lo-ti.

Tranquil Valley: The place Fu Xi took shelter and recovered during the Cataclysm. It was an enormous basin with a freshwater sea at its center.

Thrax (Thr-ACKS): Tribe rumored to exists east of Attica, dwelling south of an inland freshwater sea.

Threshold Dragon: Stone carving over the entrance to Nuwa's Inner Temple.

Tortoise Mountain: Home of the Goddess Nuwa.

Totaresh: (tow-TA-resh)God of Dragons.

Turtle Clan: Lo village ruled by Masok as sco-lo-ti, also home to his younger brother, Ghalen.

Twice-Burned: Derogatory name given to Amiran by Leviathan.

Ula: (OOW-lah) Wife of Leedi, mother of Su-gár.

Upper Land: In Lo religion, the part of the afterlife (heli-dar) that is a where the wicked are tormented for eternity.

Uros: (UR-ouws) War Chieftain of the Lo.

Valley of the Beasts: A valley discovered by Aizarg and Levidi in the days preceding the Cataclysm. filled with a milling multitude of animals of every sort.

Virag: (veye-RAG) Sammujad Slaver, former owner of Sarah.

Vulcan's Box: Also called the Time Sextant, it's the standard chronometer for the Imperial Scholars.

Wu:(WOO) A mysterious land far to the east of Cin. Fu Xi thought of this land as the end of the earth. It is the Empire of Atlantis's farthest outpost.

Xigong: (ZHI-gong) Taught Fu Xi the art of weaving. Mother of Fu Xi's lover, Shinglay.

Xva: (ZEE-vah) Aizarg's cousin and youngest man in the Crane Clan Nation. Husband of Sahti.

Zelko: (zel-koh) Old goatherder captured by Leviathan's expedition shortly after making landfall in the land of Aryq.

Zirev: (ZII-rev) Minnow man who survived landfall on the Supply Barge.

Zuŏ: (zho-AH) "The Left Wall of Heaven". The forbidden lands west of Tortoise Mountain to the Roof of the World.